THE BITTER PILL SOCIAL CLUB

The Bitter Pill Social Club

Rohan Dahiya

B L O O M S B U R Y
NEW DELHI • LONDON • OXFORD • NEW YORK • SYDNEY

First published in India 2018
This export edition published 2020

ISBN 978-93-87457-89-8

Bloomsbury Publishing India Pvt. Ltd
Second Floor, LSC Building No.4
DDA Complex, Pocket C – 6 & 7, Vasant Kunj
New Delhi 110070
www.bloomsbury.com

Typeset by Manipal Digital Systems

Contents

Opening Act

"I have aids."

It was a typically atypical Delhi restaurant. Everything had the dull aura of contrived eclecticism. It dripped down everything from the walls to the wagging tongues as a dinnertime symphony filled the room. Sana Kochhar stared at her boyfriend and knew three things for certain; that she had to measure her words, that nobody else may hear them, and Daksh Dhiman would not leave without a marriage proposal.

"Is this your idea of role play?" she tossed her hair back.

Daksh felt the blood leave his face. "Are you fucking stupid? How does that sound like role play to you?"

"What else am I supposed to assume from it?"

"I'm trying to tell you that I'm in serious trouble, Sana. I have AIDS."

She leaned in, her voice dangerously low. "AIDS isn't even a real thing anymore, what the hell is wrong with you? It's just like a thing in Africa with babies dying and stuff."

He looked at her through narrowed eyes. A waiter walked toward their table but Daksh waved him away.

"Where do you even get such information?"

"We had a poster in school somewhere about it ya, what's the big deal."

"That was for HIV, not AIDS."

"Okay now I know you're talking crap because they're the same fucking thing."

A chill shimmied across her bare shoulders but she didn't shudder. It was as though the steady hum of everyone's voices had suddenly escalated and at the same time her hearing had closed off but for only that very specific, very annoying static sound.

"Is this like the time that you came up to me and said you have an infection?"

Daksh rolled his eyes. "It was an STD, and I got it from you."

"Well how am I supposed to know you can catch crabs literally without having sex?" She groaned with the grace of a starlet, and then, "Oh my god, is *that why we're here*?"

For the first time that evening, he looked confused. "Were you expecting something else?"

"The hell I was! I thought super-fancy-date-night was a lead up to one big ass diamond ring." She dismissed the waiter, prying the wine bottle from his hands. "I fucking wore Chanel for this."

"You thought I was going to *propose* to you? We're seeing each other for the first time in weeks."

She flung her hands in the air and reached into her purse for a cigarette.

"You can't smoke in here."

She flipped him off and fished for a lighter in the too-small beaded clutch.

The server drifted over once more. "Ma'am you can't smoke here."

"Do you have any manners? What fucking village are you from?"

Flabbergasted, he muttered. "Uhmm ... Jharsa. But that doesn't matter madam–"

Daksh sniggered and waved him away. "You can't smoke here Sana."

She narrowed her eyes at him. "I'll buy the stupid restaurant if I have to, I'm smoking!"

"Ma'am I'll have to call my manager."

Daksh leaned over, "You really can't smoke here."

She lit her cigarette and arced it away from her face. "Wait so what does this mean for us?"

He clocked an eyebrow, once again at a loss for words.

"We can still be together right? I mean we're 'Sana and Daksh' for god's sake. People have us saved together on their phones." He tried not to flinch at the invisible marquee she drew with her hands.

"I don't think you understand the situation Sana–"

"Oh I know you're not breaking up with me. I didn't spend the last five years with you for this new circle-jerk."

As much as he hated it, Daksh shivered under her gaze. His thoughts increasingly disconnecting from his consciousness.

She smashed a fist on the table. "NO!"

Now people were looking.

"Look we need to get some things cleared up here, okay? You told me you loved me, I fucking fell in love with you even though we both know that I don't need it, I don't need you. But I fell for you and then you told me you don't know who you are, I said 'babe I'm here for you, go find yourself'."

She was leaning so far in he was sure the front of her dress would slip off.

"You said, 'listen, I love you but I think I might be bi' and I said 'I'm here by your side so you can go out and find yourself so long as you come back to me; because I, Sana Kochhar, will always come back to you, because I love you till the freaking end of time'. So now *what the fuck more* do you want from me that you feel the need to come up with this AIDS stuff, D?"

All diners within a three-table radius had fallen silent as she stood towering over him like a majestic goddess-bird ready to swoop down on her prey. The unwitting waiter drifted back towards their table but Daksh shook his head in warning.

"So you really have been cheating on me." She now fully ignored him. "I don't know I guess a part of me just always hoped that you wouldn't actually do it."

"Do what?" The table on their right called for the cheque.

"You know, fuck a dude."

One defiant eyebrow rose. "What makes you think I did the fucking?"

She turned to stone.

"Are you serious right now?" now her tone was low. Now, she didn't want anyone else to hear. Not now.

"You're telling me that my boyfriend likes it up the ass and didn't even have the half-wit to use protection? Well, there's some real irony right there. I do hope you have insurance."

"I'm glad you're able to find the humour in this situation." He bitterly replied.

He signaled to the waiter. "I'll have a Jameson."

"Oh my god, is that why you ordered seafood for dinner, because you know I'm allergic to it and, what, you hoped I'd just leave? That's a low blow, even for you."

He took the cigarette from her hands and stubbed it in the salad plate with a twisted grin.

"Why don't you just let me know when your dick falls off?"

"Why the hell would my dick fall off?"

"Well isn't that what happens when you get AIDS? What's wrong with you?"

"Uhh I'm pretty sure –"

"And really, how did you not think to use a damn condom. It's like you've learnt nothing in life, I mean for fuck's sake they even use it in porn now!"

They resolved themselves to silence.

"Do you think, I mean, shall *I* get tested as well?"

"If you're asking because your birthday's coming up then no, you have nothing to worry about. I think you should still get tested though."

“Will it do me any good?”

He drained his drink and called for another.

“It can’t be of any harm. Enjoy turning 24.”

The urge to throw her drink on his face hadn’t gone, but she chose to raise it as a toast instead. “Well, that’s that then. Enjoy dying Daksh.”

“Enjoy living Sunaina.”

Chapter ONE

Running With Scissors

By the time Sana made it to the front door of the restaurant a rash had crawled up her arms. She could feel the heat prickle her scalp and a scream bubbling its way up her chest like the undigested lunch of a rickshaw driver. Nothing, not the satisfaction of the chilly interiors of her car nor the flood of likes on their #datenightselfie could get her mind off it. She sat there in the backseat and screamed into the leather.

Back at the restaurant, Daksh finished his meal in peace and paid the bill before officially going off the grid. No one would get to know of his passing until much later.

Sana didn't realize at what point she'd passed out, but when the car rolled to a stop her head lolled at an angle jolting her out of it. She sat there for two minutes wondering if the night had really happened the way she remembered it or if she'd just been tripping.

The driver was staring at her through the rear view mirror.

"Ma'am is everything okay?"

"Ugh shut up." She straightened the hem of her dress and checked her chin for any drool, already dreading the moment she'd have to relive the night for her mother.

Right on cue, Tina Kochhar spotted her from her perch in the living room with *him*.

"Sana," she tittered, "beta how come you're back so soon? How was dinner?"

She bit the inside of her cheek to stop from screaming.

"Mumma, please."

Laksh left his cup of tea and rose, towering over both of them with a half smile.

"Sup Sunny!"

She opened her mouth to fire back at him but he swooped down and grabbed her hand. Laksh had the kind of eyebrows you could only grow into, as a kid they were so big she wondered how he kept his head upright. Now when they swept up in feigned surprise he looked more handsome than stupid.

"Oh my god, what happened? Are you okay?"

Her eyes widened and she tried to get her hand back.

"Why? No, I'm fine."

"Listen", he clutched her hand, "tell me what happened. Are you feeling alright? What is the meaning of all this? Where's the ring?"

Before she knew it, she was raveling under the ferocity of his dark gaze. His smile was cruel and the tears she'd been holding back were threatening to come out. No amount of internal screaming could ease the way her breath hitched in her chest.

Lakshman Dewan and Sunaina Kochhar had been the best of friends since before most kids learnt their first words, right until they were eleven. Then his parents started fighting, as it often happens when egos are injured, sleeping in separate rooms, going through the motions of a slowly crumbling marriage, and he became someone else altogether. They tried to resuscitate their friendship once more some time towards the end of high school because it was the time to let go of the past but then his older brother forced himself on her at a party and Lakshman once again withdrew completely. Now he would drop in from time to time mostly to make small talk with her mother, raid their fridge, or share a cigarette on her balcony.

Tina literally came running over, incoherently squealing.

She could feel her mother's hands rise to cup her cheeks and she knew it would end badly.

"Aunty look, her hand! There's no ring on her finger!"

The two of them theatrically deflated like clowns but Sana was exhausted. Her chest hurt too much, she wondered if perhaps her dress was too tight and whether bread-and-butter-baskets were a good idea to make up for small talk. The room didn't have enough air, and the air conditioner was too cold. An itch crawled all the way up her body and the tears came in a hot bumbling mess.

"Fuck you," she snatched herself away. "Really, just fuck the both of you."

Tina Kochhar hadn't raised the cuss-monster her daughter had become though truthfully she hadn't really 'raised her up' at all. *Who even had the time for that stuff these days?* With her bi-weekly card games, the monthly potluck parties, and the nights out with her girlfriends, Tina had decided that no one could expect her to be a full time housewife *and* a mother, while still maintaining perfect shape with a body fat percentage of twenty-five to thirty.

She was about to tell her to calm down but Sana was already out of the room, heels hitting on every hard step up to her room.

"What was that?"

She looked at him. *They really don't make them like him anymore*, she half smiled at the thought.

"It's nothing really, she's probably having an off day sweetie, you don't think too much about it."

"No was it something I said? Should I not have ..." there was the briefest flash of hurt in his eyes.

"Listen, nothing like that at all but I think it's just that she probably didn't have a good time you know, or they must've had a fight or something. And we all know na how much she's looking forward to getting engaged. Like, I'm practically holding her back from proposing to him!" she tittered.

It wasn't the truth and the both of them knew it; Tina just had a lifelong habit for making herself the centre of attention.

She rubbed his arm to comfort him, tossing her freshly shampooed hair to one side.

"Don't get depressed about it ya now. Go up and talk to her. I'm sure she's expecting you to be there already."

Laksh was still staring at the trail her daughter had left behind, the air vibrating with her energy. He wasn't listening to her and she wondered what was wrong with her. Why couldn't he look at her even if it was just long enough to validate what she'd said? Was it not enough? Was it not enough that she cared about her Sana so much?

She rubbed his arm again without needing to and gave him a gentle push. Laksh didn't look back as he left and Tina fell back onto the couch.

It's hard to tell the exact age when women start looking old. She stared at the soft fine fabric of her dressing gown, wondering if her skin wrinkled as easily. She grabbed a furious fistful of the fabric and crushed it till her eyes burned with tears.

One staggered breath came in and out. One more – deeply in and then out. And just like that she didn't feel like crying anymore. She looked at the half drunk cup of tea that was now cold and lamented – she may not have made it herself but she had taken special care to direct Vikram on how he liked it. The cookies were the special ones that no one else in the house was allowed to touch because they were honey-sweetened and she'd picked them up on her last trip to Italy. It had been the perfect summer. Well, sort of. It was a relatively good trip if it really came down to it because she'd spent a majority of it obsessing over

Hassan. Tina firmly believed that it marked the beginning of her husband's affairs, a fact she reminded herself of every time she met with her boy-toy. As for Hassan, the bitterness that followed had set the tone for the rest of their married life and soon they'd just be a showpiece family.

Family.

"What even is a family?" she muttered. "We're a joke."

Tina promised herself to bring it up at her next Buddhism meeting, a recent addition to her social calendar by one of her friends that had at once given her life a positive makeover and solidified her dislike for Geetu. Buddhism meetings were an exercise in self validation for Tina, a source of swelling vanity. Then there was her sister-in-law.

Geetika Shroff had that specific deep voice that was cultivated over many years of cigarette smoke and taking herself too seriously. She'd never been tall, definitely not with her sister in the same room whenever the odd occasion called for it, and had thus at some point, though by no premeditation, taken to chunky antiquarian jewelry that always seemed to announce her presence in the room. The tinkle of her bangle and that low throaty hum of prayer had been more than enough to leave a bad taste in Tina's mouth. It was the same gossip in a different social circle and all things considered she had lost the ability to keep up.

Sadly there was nothing, neither appreciation of her running a successful boutique in Meherchand market nor even the death of her husband, that could've warmed Tina up to Geetu.

She picked up her phone and texted Sana.

-Beta listen, I hope everything is ok?

Delivered. Unread.

-I wanted to know if you'll have some time tomorrow

Delivered. Unread.

Last Seen: 7 minutes ago.

-I need u to give Vikram directions for that Khao Suey everyone loved so much at papa's birthday last year.
Not Delivered.

-Or can we do kimchi finger sandwiches?
Not delivered.
Connecting ...

She locked the phone and tossed it.

Vikram entered the room and asked if she needed anything else, she dismissed him for the day once he cleared the tea tray.

Tina had recently developed a habit for staying up late, not too late, though two thirty wasn't an ideal bedtime for someone who hated dark circles.

She walked to the bar and poured herself three fingers of Jack. The crackle of ice as the amber liquid hit it was music to her ears. She poured her drink and went back to the couch.

"How about some jazz ..." she spoke .

Her phone vibrated and she quickly unlocked it.

Don't miss out! Pre-approved home loans...

"Uff ... bastards don't stop at night also!" she deleted it.

All messages read. No response.
Last Seen: A few seconds ago.

Tina was sorry she'd skipped that visit to the abortion clinic. She really was, and it wasn't the first time she'd felt that way. She told herself that it was totally possible that some women just weren't cut out to be mothers, and she said it enough till she believed it.

She nodded to herself.

The playlist loaded and a soft French horn swelled around her.

The glass felt so good against the skin of her forehead, she almost didn't want to drink from it. The constant change in weather had only just left its mark on their house, all of them recovering from a light flu, the afternoon heat was unbearable and the evening wind unsavoury in comparison. Sometimes she wondered why they still lived in Delhi – there was nothing redeemable about the city, not its weather, not the people, not the constant political unrest. Someone at lunch had said the Jaat rioters had raped women in open fields and left them there, someone else mentioned dirty slurs heard from politicos at some JNU protest, she wondered what was worse. So much shit and filth in the city it was no wonder that everybody who lived here was miserable; the constant dust, the fucking pollution, it was disgusting. She wanted to go back to her mother's home, back to the Worli penthouse where she'd wasted her youth watching the city lights. Of course the Delhi bungalow was bigger and most of the family lived here but that wasn't the reason they were rooted; it was Sana and her social circle. She'd once almost managed to convince her about how the move would ensure instant celebrity for her daughter. All the important page 3 parties were in Bombay, all major magazine publications were there. It would be so easy to make a few calls and book modeling jobs for her. But once her follower count went past seven thousand, the last ray of hope had vanished and Tina had felt their roots dig deeper.

Stupid cow.

That's what she'd called her mother when Tina offered to buy her new followers. Tens of thousands of followers and all genuine accounts – because that's what she'd seen on one of those pop up ads before the office assistant had offered to install ad-block for her.

Stupid cow ... you can't just buy your way into being a somebody!

She stared at the unrelenting edges of the crystal cut glass and wondered how hard she would have to squeeze to feel it crack under pressure. She scoffed at her own melodramatic overtures and took it back to her forehead. It was an oddly comforting realization: how much she hated the city.

Her phone buzzed.

Chicas (9 members)

-Hey girls.. anybody up still?
-Hi *shona*, just sitting in bed thought I'd read today for a bit before sleeping...
-Lol where's the hubby tonight?
-Arey ya he's out na, he's travelling to Bbay for that stupid conference all week

She winced

-Where's Tina
-Right here babes... What's happening?
-Can't sleep. Let's go out na?
-Abhi it's so late darling, let's do something tomorrow night. There's an awesome happy hour place I've found we should def go there only!

She switched her phone off, only grateful for the full day of distractions that awaited her – shopping, aquaerobics and pilates, and then cocktails at night. She decided that she might try some clove cigarettes as well, live on the edge a little. The only problem left to deal with was Sana.

At that exact time, Sana's cousin Surya found herself with a strange problem of her own. She was inexplicably focused on the spider crawling over the ceiling and she'd almost forgotten about her boyfriend. They were sort of still in the middle of sex. He was also sort of married with a sort of kid. She'd never asked him about his wife or child. But the sex was always good, no it was beautiful – part of the reason they were still on that bed in a Karol Bagh guest house seventeen months later. She shut her eyes and tried to stop thinking, it was still good but she couldn't understand why she was so distracted.

Surya had always been fascinated by spiders and had often spent her time following their dance across ceilings and gardens and the corners where walls met the roof.

They climaxed and he didn't go down on her immediately, in fact she found herself counting seconds before he did. Somewhere after five hundred she got bored and opened a can of coke, which he took as his cue.

The man owned a chain of artisanal products, food items that were perfected by hand and true craft rather than mass produced. Business had never been great until a Facebook group of millenials declared them to be the best thing ever. With every heavily filtered photo, the demand went higher and his business expanded beyond honey. His artisanal honey, jams, cheeses, and breads became products that stood at the apex of the hipster food chain. Surya had often wondered at the possibilities if they had met when he was younger and single – would she have stuck around through the bad times or perhaps taken a more active role to help him – but there was always only one answer: it didn't matter. So she emptied her can and tried to find the daddy long legs spider she'd seen before while he got her off.

She lit a cigarette and gave him a kiss of approval when they were done. They stayed in bed a while longer, checking messages, calls, or any other updates they'd missed out on. Her fingers itched to open the other app, Tinder. More than scrolling through the endless barrage of memes with subtly nihilistic undertones she enjoyed the absolute absurdity of Tinder profiles. That they had first spoken through Tinder was a completely different matter – Surya had learnt to be more prudent online. It was all for a laugh really, if you'd ask her about it now she'd tell you how much fun swiping left was because they were all 'ugly losers'.

"Oh, I almost forgot," he jumped out of bed. "I got you something."

"Were we doing gifts or something?" she asked warily.

"No not at all. It was just a new batch they'd finished before I left the factory so I thought I'd get you one," he made a grand gesture of handing her the jar. "I realized I've never made you try anything we produce."

She was desperate to have as little of her skin touching that murky honey jar but it seemed impossible. It looked harmless enough but there was a general icky-quality about it that set her teeth on edge and suddenly she couldn't understand why she was with a man with a soft belly and a wife. She could feel the sickly sweet honey gurgling down her throat, glooping down her skin in a sticky trail. Suddenly she wished she were in a different country and they'd never met and she was someone else.

His eyes were expectant when she looked back at him.

"Oh-oh hey thank you," she hugged his shoulders, "it's really ... I can't wait to taste it."

She giggled then he sort of giggled as well.

"You love it then? Good." He kissed her wetly. "I got it because we met for the first time on this date, so I don't know I just wanted to do something special for you baby."

She was hyper aware of his growing excitement and fondling hands and decided to put him on a time-out soon. Her fingers where they'd touched the jar felt grimy but she wasn't sure if it was real – he didn't mind her fingers wiping against his back.

Laksh knocked softly on the door, so soft that at first Sana didn't even hear it. The second one was firmer and he entered without waiting for her permission. She was in her balcony smoking, he took it from her and gave her a slight shove.

"You know when I was a little girl I was obsessed with the world of Disney. I used to come home from school and watch *The Little Mermaid* every afternoon. Literally every afternoon. The summer bled into winter and I had every line memorized and I'd sing along even if I were only mumbling through the words. I swear it was the most amazing movie, still is if you're very drunk." She giggled.

"I was so so fascinated by how in the end the water turns into that glittering dress and she steps out of the sea and she's a transformed woman who doesn't need help walking on two legs."

The silence did something to them it hadn't done before. It got awkward.

He handed her the cigarette.

"You know what happens in the original story? The prince falls for the wrong girl and marries her and no one gets to know it's the evil witch. So she kills herself. She becomes a mermaid again and kills herself. Now that I know it I just watch the movie and laugh because that's exactly what life's like now, isn't it? You can see it happening and you can't stop it ... this ... Oh I don't know this big car crash. You know it's happening in slow-mo and you know it'll make a mess of everything but you can't do anything to stop it. So my point is, why bother really?"

Her shell was cracking right in front of him, like she was finally speaking in words than sighs. And then she snapped out of it.

"It comes down to the most basic level of Darwinism really, I'm hot and stinking rich, and I totally have like a really high threshold for douche behaviour – I mean we live in Delhi for god's sake, right. Right! So my point is why should I be the one at the receiving end of this pedestrian level fuckboy-ism?"

"So what do you wanna do about it?"

"I think I should be the fuckboy here – the concept itself transcends genders ya know! I should be the one ghosting guys after three hot dates or just straight up breaking their hearts. Why am I not totally Netflix-and-chill-ing like it's 2017 and women are on top. Here's what – I should join Tinder. Yes. And then I should just revolutionize the theory of fuckboyhood – literally for the sake of women everywhere."

Just like that she was lost.

"Wow," she put a hand to her chest, "I think I finally get the whole women-empowerment thing. If I didn't have so much money I could almost be like one of those unwashed, lesbian *mahila krantikaris* from LSR you know? Like imagine my face on the cover of a book that literally says The Theory of Fuckboyhood, like oh my god Lilly Singh eat your heart out! Wow I'm a genius Laksh."

"I think we both know none of that is happening any time soon."

She shrugged. "You never know who's willing to ghostwrite your first Pulitzer winner."

"Oh Pulitzer-winner it seems!" he shook his head. "So, *The Little Mermaid* eh?"

She blushed uncharacteristically and dipped her head away from him.

"That's adorable."

"Shut up!"

"No, really it is."

"You're sick. I hate you."

"You still remember everything about it?"

"Everything."

He made a funny sort of noise. Somewhere between surprise and awe, and walked away without explanation. She followed him, glad to be out of the gathering dust storm.

He scrubbed the back of his neck. "I can't believe how hot it is outside."

"It's terrible. I hate summers in Delhi."

"It's weird but I just I have this fear that one day I'll be driving and because of the heat I'd just pass out behind the wheel and crash and die – literally just because of the heat. It's ridiculous!" he pulled out a bottle from the mini fridge.

"No. What's ridiculous is your fiancé-to-be calls it off in the same breath as 'I have AIDS'."

"Wait, AIDS? Like ..."

"The poor-African-people thing."

Understanding dawned on his face. "Wow."

"Got it from a married guy. Like, they sort of gave it to each other I guess."

"WOW!" Laksh was impressed at his own inability to think clearly. What more could he have said?

"How long does he have till … umm."

Well that.

"I didn't ask. I just … Well I left. I don't know. Maybe my mom's right and I'm just a plain old bitch."

"Sunaina, don't be silly. You're not a bitch."

"Don't call me Sunaina," she flopped onto her bed. "And I must be if my own mother calls me a bitch!"

"I've heard you say it to her more often than she has."

"I see your point but *does* that mean I am a bitch?"

"Maybe not. More of an asshole. But that's not the point."

"It's not?"

"No," he shook his head. "The point is, are you okay with it?"

"With what?"

"With being a bitch?"

"No. But I think I'm okay with being an asshole."

"Then none of it matters anyway because you love yourself for who you are."

"Well … Someone should."

She was suddenly aware of how close they were and that tightness in her chest returned. Sana remembered how she'd pined for him silently, while Lakshman had grown up and cut her from his life. She was aware of every breath he exhaled, of how the skin of her shin was millimetres away from his. As she looked the distance lessened till only a hair's breadth. Her heart hammered in her ears.

He stood up to charge his phone but her mind was still on the distance between them. She couldn't make sense of his words anymore and he insisted on saying a lot of them. She was an island and he was lost at sea.

"Anyway, how come your friends aren't here already with a care package or something?"

"A care package?"

"Yeah dude like a thing which has a whole bunch of wine and chocolate and tissues. Like a 'hey you got dumped but it's okay he's an asshole anyway' thing."

"Wait, I thought I was the asshole."

He shook his head and Sana wanted to slap and kiss him at the same time. "Different situation. My point is – where the minions at?"

"Firstly, they're not my minions-"

"-Your posse."

"I don't even know what that is okay ..."

"Your girlies, your dolls, hoes, or whatever they call it these days."

"They're my *friends*."

"So you say."

"Shut up."

"I'm only saying-"

"Really you shouldn't even be talking anymore."

"Dude no come on. What do you even have to gain by hanging out with those girls?"

"They're nice. Also excuse you, I did not get dumped."

He raised an eyebrow, fighting back a laugh.

"Why is it so hard for you to believe? I dumped him Laksh. God you're so mean."

"Wait so you want me to believe that he told you he has AIDS. He's dying. He's also practically in love with a married man who for all intents and purposes is dying too. And he still wanted to stay in a relationship with you? At what point is that not him ending things with you?"

"Listen you're so mean, just leave please."

"Are you serious right now, S?"

"You're ruining the energy of my room."

"Oh your *energy* is it? Your energy can go fuck itself."

She threw the first thing within reach and missed his head. His whole body. Her phone went flying above and hit the wall behind him. Laksh doubled over laughing and she could do nothing but hide her face. By the looks of it she'd need a new phone even if to update her follower stats.

The door opened and they came in, dressed down in shorts and oversized tshirts – every bit the girl gang he'd predicted.

"I will take that as my cue to head home."

She picked her phone off the floor and tossed it onto her bed, she wasn't ready to see the full extent of the damage. Sana walked out with him, trying to block out the smirks and stares from her friends, shutting the door behind them.

"Listen I'm sorry if like before I was rude. I just ..."

"I know."

"I've had a very long night."

"I can imagine. Just hang in there okay?"

She smiled and nodded

"I'm here for you, yeah. Anything you need just let me know."

"I will, I promise."

"Good. Don't let this get you down." He had his hands shoved deep into the jean pockets. "You've got to just, I don't know, acknowledge how shitty the situation is, take a day or two but then get over it. Don't let this take over you."

She nodded.

"The way I see it, you're not the one who got the shorter end of the stick."

A first look of genuine hurt crossed her face. "How can you say that?"

"Because he's the one who's dying."

"Oh right. Yeah. Of course."

The tension released from her shoulders and he pulled her into a perfect hug. They fit together in a way that the air shied away from passing between them. And then he didn't let go. So she didn't let go. Her head shifted, he felt her nose brush the skin of his neck. His hand slid down her back gently and he pulled her closer, like they couldn't get close enough, wouldn't till their bodies became one. It was weird. It wasn't the right time. But it felt good.

Like waking up from a dream too soon, he backed up and their arms dropped to their sides. The awkwardness returned. In that moment she realized they shouldn't be alone together, even though she didn't mind sharing oxygen with him that way. All he could think of was how everything had been screwed over the night his older brother had groped her like she was just another girl.

Laksh left without saying goodbye, the photos lining the staircase stared hauntingly back at him as if they were meant to seem happy but everything looked too manipulated.

He passed Tina on the way out, light aura of whiskey around her. *Like mother like daughter,* he humoured. But when she kissed his cheek goodnight she licked his skin and her lips lingered far too long. It made his stomach churn but this wasn't the first time, so he ran out as fast as he could.

Chapter | TWO

The Theory Of Comfort Food

The next morning dawned without a sound as though still winded from the night before. It crept up through the cracks between the heavy curtains and the floor.

Stranger things had happened before and although she didn't know it yet, there were many more to come. When Sana woke up it wasn't to the usual buzz of notifications but to the dirge of her dying popularity. Her phone lay cold and dead on its back, the cracks so deep she could almost see through them. Her head had the feeling of suspension, like she'd left it soaking in ethanol and now it had died out on her, preserved in everlasting glory. The rest of her body registered a hangover much faster.

The knock on her door pierced through her soul, dully knocking her further into nausea but when Tina entered, in an uncharacteristically hushed way, she felt better at once. On her tiptoes even though the room was dominated by a plush slate grey carpet, her mother gently eased herself beside Sana and hugged her. There was none of the awkwardness she had anticipated, hugging her mother felt more natural than anything else she had experienced in the last 24 hours, or the last 24 years for that matter. The smell of lavender filled the room as she nuzzled into the soft fabric of her caftan, that smell made her teeth grind. Lavender macarons, candles, even towels in the guest bathroom – like little ultraviolet stamps of Sana littering her life. Tina combed through her messy hair with gentle fingers. The light of the sun filtered in, rendering the room in a soft warm glow as though she was a fetus back in the womb again, flowing down a river of milk and honey toward the center of an Eden garden.

She was talking before her lips parted. The story of Daksh and his neighbor who was married to a beautiful girl from Hyderabad who owned a stunning collection of hijabs and worked with a shelter for old people who'd been abandoned by their families. Her husband had just lost his job and had locked eyes with her boyfriend who at the time had been smoking in the backyard and while they shared a silent smirked exchange, the lives of Sana and the other girl had somehow been bound irrevocably together.

Sana cried her eyes out. Tina cooed at her, lulling her into a drowsy stance even as she hiccupped the tears away. Her mother caressed the full dome of her skull gathering her damp hair into a thick rope, which she began expertly braiding. It was then that Sana realized there are fewer than none things in life more comforting than the weight of a mother's hand across your head. She reached out and wrapped her arms around her like armor.

The theory of comfort food is perhaps more personal than the clothes one uses to cover themselves from nakedness. It can be anything from a warm bowl of rajma-chawal to beluga topped sushi, maybe not a food item at all but a cocktail of cinnamon and whiskey stirred through hot chocolate. The concept at its basest level is a concoction that can not only bring peace to a stressed soul but also evoke the feeling of home, one that's usually lost in memories as time passes and you lose yourself in the routines of a.m. to p.m. Comfort food is what reminds you of running so fast you might trip over your own feet as your mother called out to you from the porch. It is what takes you back to summers spent vacationing in the hills, of lazing under the sun, of bedtime stories even though it was the middle of the afternoon. For Sana, it was the very specific *bhel puri* her mother made with warm boiled potatoes mixed in to the chaos of peanuts, crisp mix, and freshly chopped onion and tomato, all bound together by the lightest tangy chutney. They sat in the balcony with a giant bowl of *bhel puri* between them talking of things that didn't really matter. Sana knew it was too good to be true before the sun had fully set.

That's the thing about sweet dreams, they're all the more bitter when they end. Sana woke up to the same view of her broken phone that had plagued her in her dream and even as it lit up to signal her snapchat notifications she had it in a vice grip, halfway hoping the glass of the screen would slice through her palm. She pulled herself from the warm bed and out into the clear air. The phone went over the edge of her balcony spinning like a frisbee. She traced the thick ledge where just hours ago she had leant next to Laksh.

The balcony door closed with a bang. In the time it had taken her to rid herself of the vibrating cellphone she had broken into a furious sweat. The back of her t-shirt clung to her skin. The sweat on her forehead was already drying, leaving behind clogged pores and a layer of grime. She could feel her hair matting and drying around her face. Without another thought she stripped off her clothes and pulled back her hair into a bun. Every nerve ending in her body fired up at the possibility of being seen. She could feel goose bumps raise from under her skin, trickling down her back and along the curve of her buttock. Her heart hammed so fast she was surprised her chest didn't show it's beating rhythm. Naked and alone with the hum and chill of her air conditioner, Sana could sense the rest of her day would be without repose. She drew the curtains and felt her way back to bed. Her body trilled as her body slithered into the sheets, she couldn't hold herself back from sliding her hands over the planes of her own body drawn taut from pilates and aggressive cardio. She felt the spot in her chest where her heart played the black hole blues in an endless loop, the corners of her body that were chilly and those that were warm. She ground herself so hard against the bed it should've been illegal. Her hair fell around her in an inky waterfall, shielding her from the rest of the world and drew herself deeper into the pinnacle of an orgasm that rippled from the outer tips of her toes to the crown of her head from where burst a golden light she was sure would blind the whole world.

"Oh ... my god," she exhaled into the dark room. Bowl of bhel puri this was not but she was sure nothing could come close to the caress of her bed against naked skin.

Stars from above had fallen around her, serving as a reminder that even though the sun was out they were always around. And then Chanda entered the room with a brazen half knock, carrying Sana's sickly green pre-breakfast smoothie. The broom from her other hand was tossed lazily into a corner away from the carpet, the sound snapping off the last wave of the spell. Sana scrambled to tuck herself down under the covers till only her chin was visible.

"Courier for you. Should I bring them up?" She smelled of sandalwood and sweat.

Sana nodded vaguely, eyes still glassy. "Where's Mumma?"

"She left just now, she said she'll be late." The broom lay in its corner as the maid went to retrieve the packages.

Sana waited till the door clicked shut and slid past the sheets to the bathroom. Something had changed, maybe in the air itself. Even the way the satin robe draped across her skin felt different.

Chanda returned with two boxes: one for a store launch – Kabir Baruacha's invite along with a personalized gift – the other an invite to another pop-up exhibition hosted by Gemaima Khandwala. Sana set them on the bed and fished out her backup phone. It took her an hour to prep the Instagram posts. Kabir's would go up the following morning – prime hour was from 9 to 11– and the other was for Saturday. Chanda muttered something about the low temperature, cringing under Sana and the AC's icy glare. She offered the smoothie glass and waited while Sana chugged it down.

"What do you want for breakfast didi?"

"I don't mind an omelet."

"Eggs are there but no kale for the omelet."

Sana looked at her as though she were the scum of the earth, suggesting a kale-less breakfast omelet. "Is Vikram here? Ask him to make some cereal mix like last time, but nothing too heavy ya please."

Chanda grimaced. Oats, in her opinion, were not a meal and Sana was not a horse. "Why can't you have a nice cheese omelet?"

Sana was over it. Chanda's idea of a cheese omelet was nothing more than a slice of cheese singles thrown over half cooked eggs, like they were too poor to afford a block of Gouda. *The nerve of some people.*

"Toast and avocado, sliced not mashed. And take this stupid broom away, I just want to be alone today. Clean up later."

That was the last time she spoke for the rest of the day.

She sipped the vile smoothie and pulled the peach robe off her shoulders, even though the AC was freezing her room up. The bay windows were fogging up in the corners where she could see behind the drapes. She sat and combed her hair acutely aware of the dream where her mother had been the one doing it for her. Just the memory of it hollowed her out from the inside. As much as it hurt her, Sana continued to comb her hair, staring into space. She took the sharp toothed comb and dragged it across her wrist watching the skin of her arm crack and wither under pressure. Conversations from the night before drifted in and out of her mind as she relived the night.

Once their tinder games were over and they couldn't trash talk about Daksh any longer, her friends had run out of things to talk about. Gayatri told them about an experiment where she gave up shampooing for a few months and only used hot water and baking soda instead. She knew her best friend would've expected a better response but Sana had just been a little asshole to her instead. It was truly disgusting, she'd told Gayatri, to let her scalp oils stew and rot not just her own head but also the chi of Sana's room. The way they looked at her made her question whether her friends had a sense of humour at all.

Sana looked at her own wide-eyed face and wondered if irrelevance was one of those inevitable things in life and she was on the fast train, fueled by her ego, to the bottomless pits of social insignificance. Is the demise of a beautiful girl a gentle progression where people slowly tire of you, or do they just wake up one day and realize they're simply over it. Over you.

Her shoulders slumped from the exhaustion of thinking so much. She let her head fall downward onto the dresser, hoping she could cry it out. There was something of a different nature hurting inside like, well unlike anything she'd experienced before. It felt like hunger. A hunger to feel something. Something beyond the clothes she wore and the jägerbombs she knocked back. She envisioned running face first into the large fogged up bay windows. Whether she'd bounce backward or break through. She yearned for the hurt it would bring either way. She sat down in the tub, thick lavender scented steam rising around her. She thought of the weight of water on her bare chest. She pressed a finger in the space between her breasts and pushed in so that she may be able to plug the hole in there. All it left was an angry bruise.

A fresh out-of-bed selfie later, the silence settled down around her in a way that left the room without any air at all. The white noise was all-consuming, it brought back the ratchet rash from the night before and Sana had to soak her hands in water to cool her skin. Every trace of her no-makeup-makeup was scrubbed off and she slathered her face slick with moisturizer.

"He's just a boy," she told her quivering lip, "a stupid boy. Get your shit together."

The tired reflection wasn't convinced though, so she decided to lie down for sometime.

It's just exhaustion, she thought, *I haven't had enough sleep.*

It's either exhaustion or a hangover.

Chanda dusted her room and left, only mildly protesting the untouched breakfast.

Even though it was over forty six degrees outside and the city was probably on the verge of catching fire, she couldn't find a warm spot on her bed. No matter how she cocooned herself in the down comforter that gooey warmth she wanted was just out of reach. So she just lay there, hair splayed out like an animal, thinking of how the tar in the patched up roads bubbled up in the afternoons, melting away under the hot Delhi sun. She could've gone out for lunch but no one was free. Or perhaps they didn't want to meet her – *they can all just fucking die*, she decided. Sana switched off the phone and drifted away.

It was a summer of firsts.

It was the first time Sana and her friends went shopping to Janpath. Blistering heat nothwithstanding, it was the seventh circle of hell where bad fashion and pushy locals thronged. It was the last time they went to Janpath.

It was their first unchaperoned holiday, destination: Laksh's father's new beachside villa in Colombo, because it was the first time they felt like Goa was better suited to dirty West Delhi tourists and honeymooning couples.

It was the first time she smoked pot, got so high that she never touched a joint again. They drank until the sun came up and she strolled through the wooden deck fumbling on occasion and he was there to catch her every time.

It was the first time she'd colored her hair, an ombre that would stay with her for the next few years.

It was the first time she suspected she might love him.

It was the summer of their first kiss.

-There's only going to be seven planets in the sky tonight… cuz I'm gonna destroy Uranus.
-HAHA OMG that's hilar
-☺
-whatchu up to?
-Getting some coffee w the sis.. u?

"Surya?"

He was looking at her with the strangest expression on her face.

There were things Surya had learnt from observing her family, her mother in the kitchen, the relationships her older brother Vir would find himself often in and out of, the subtle ways in which the family elders fought and shot each other down. They were the secrets she kept closely guarded. The secret to making the best chicken curry: a handful of ground cashews. The secret to curing a hangover: a spiced gin with raw egg white. The secret to getting rid of a man: abject humiliation.

"Are you … are you seriously on Tinder again?"

"No" she dipped her head "I was just checking my phone dude, chill out."

"Why can't you keep your phone aside for five minutes when I'm talking to you?"

She huffed and threw it on her lap.

There were times when plans worked out to such perfection you could wonder if the universe had arranged them that way. Placed the right accouterments at the right place at the right time without any hints so you'd miss them if you weren't aware. When Surya had met him at their usual hotel that day, she had done so without knowing how easy it would be for them to break up. It wasn't a real relationship and that she had realized only when she'd made a habit of staring at walls for spiders when they fucked. The room was exactly the same as the one they walked into every time. A simple runner by the foot of the bed, two towels arranged into disfigured swans, and two sets of pillows with *hard* and *soft* tags. She saw him slow down when the tag slid around his wrist and an overdue confusion blossomed. He stared at it and made a joke because he loved talking about how hard she made him, sadly he was completely oblivious to her fit of giggles. She thumped his belly, the soft flesh bounced thrice before he jerked himself off the bed. Surya was only vaguely aware of the cruel words that came out of her mouth, the lissome curve of her body, her cold eyes. She saw him shrink faster than a dying butterfly and with a last chuckle severed all ties between them.

"How you're that obsessed with your phone is beyond me. Listen can you please explain what happened up there? I've never seen you behave that way."

They were sitting in the cheap chain café downstairs. Surya hated the coffee there, she hated the slow service and the stale food, he knew it but he was buying and he was a cheap man. She was his cheap mistress.

"Okay whatever man geez can you get over it already? I'm so over this sissy attitude of yours."

"What kind of a person talks like that baby?"

"Okay firstly, I'm not your baby. You have a baby, with your wife", she didn't bother lowering her voice. "I don't understand what your deal is. If you're gonna be such a pussyboy over a stupid joke then you can really fuck off from here because I'm done. I can't deal."

She ended the conversation by putting her sunglasses on.

-Where at?

"Did you meet someone else?"

He looked down at her phone.

"You're seriously on Tinder *again*? Have you seen the kind of creeps there are?"

Surya laughed "Duh! I'm sitting with one prime example."

Her messages didn't go through, network was always unreliable in this corner of the city. The man didn't follow her out although he had hoped she'd split the bill, but she was also his ride back to the factory. Surya glared at her phone and the dusty street around when a curious voice broke through the din.

"Surya Singh Shroff?"

She looked back, mildly amused at hearing her full name like some royal title.

It was the first time they'd seen each other in the flesh, both of them realizing in that moment that no amount of messaging could've prepared them for it. Seeing someone in person activates a different part of the brain altogether. He was dressed in a comfortable suit with a morning paper tucked under one arm, and the brightest smile she'd ever seen. She tried to remember if he'd ever mentioned how tall he was, immediately standing straighter to avoid dwarfing in front of him but could only recall the Uranus joke. With that she remembered the rest of their mostly-sexted conversations.

Surya knew she should've been aware of the man sitting on the other side of that dirty glass wall but Dhiraj was too close to look away from.

"Well this is a surprise!"

"Are you seriously here?" she giggled. "It's so funny to bump into you this way."

"Yeah, I just finished up a meeting with potential investors."

"For your startup, right?"

His eyebrows shot up, "I'm impressed you remember. I think this means I'll have to take you out for dinner sometime."

"Oh I won't force you."

"I didn't mean it that way," she lost her breath when he touched her arm. "I really want to take you out."

"I'm yours whenever."

Now it was his turn to blush. That was impressive enough for Surya, how easily his shy smile let her in. The reality of sharing something real was upon them, nothing like the hazy nude selfies they'd shared previously. There was something familiar about him, the ease at which he put her just by talking about the everyday things. It made her wonder how he'd feel wrapped up in her arms at night.

"Don't take this the wrong way Surya, I'll let you get back to whatever you were doing, but I seriously wish I could kidnap you right now." He flashed her a dimpled smile.

"Ugh do it already!" She cringed at the sound of her own giggle.

"Don't tell anyone I'm a random creep you met online." He moved in for a quick hug. "And I really do wanna see you again, and soon."

She threw out the coffee and dialed Sana not because she expected perspective but because talking had a way of settling her nerves. True to form her sister was only half-listening.

"So what, you two are dating now?"

"No don't be stupid. He lives in Gurgaon it's practically a different country, plus when you think about it I don't even know anything about him. He's just like this convenience you know what I mean? Like yeah I mean if I'm like feeling lonely or down I can text him and he usually replies also so that's nice. And like he's actually so good with dirty talk I can't even tell you ..."

"Then don't. I beg you."

Surya knew they were honking at her, she was holding up traffic because trying to assemble her thoughts was more important. She pretended to fumble with the ignition whilst berating herself for downplaying her attraction toward Dhiraj. The truth was something she wasn't ready to accept.

"Oh wait, I was gonna ask about like this whole Daksh thing ... what do we think? Is it even a real problem?"

The truth was Surya was fucking smitten.

"What the hell kinda question is that Surya? I don't know. I wasn't born from my mother's vagina with the answers to everything in life! I didn't even know there was a difference between HIV and AIDS till he told me about it. And then I was up for a whole hour last night researching it and now I'm convinced that he must've been fucking a) without a condom and b) probably in some shady corner of Lodhi Garden or something."

"Why Lodhi Garden of all places ..." she pulled out her lipstick even as the honking grew violent. "Wait, that actually makes sense."

The midday commuters boiled over and flipped her off, snaking past the tiny squeeze of road beside her car. The guard who had until then been clearing way for her stared with murder in his eyes.

"You can get infected from peeing in the open for god's sake. What is AIDS over a UTI know what I mean?"

Sana's answer was less than satisfactory so she disconnected the call and returned to her mental soap opera starring Dhiraj, married men, and spiders.

It was around sunset from the way light slanted through the dark room. Chanda spoke into the dim corner of the bed, asking if Sana was sick. It was time for her pilates class but the day wasn't right.

"I just can't ya today."

"You must eat something, didi." She reached out with a tray of milkshake and little hearts cookies.

"That's fine, just get me some cold water." Her mouth was dry and dank from the nap. She saw a text from Tina, some half-made excuse and dinner promises she didn't intend to keep. Her mother had now been out 'shopping' for over eight hours, solidifying her belief that Tina was just a selfish old bitch. Between that and unanswered texts on the group chat, Sana was glad she'd spent the day nesting in bed.

"I'm Here I'm Here I'm Here!"

Her mother wasn't a bad person, Sana just had little patience for those who couldn't knock before entering. There were days when she woke up and found Tina sitting on the edge of her bed mid-sentence and hurt that she wasn't keeping up with the conversation. She'd protest some days by groaning 'Ma!' at her, and if life were a movie or a sanitary pad commercial they'd break into giggles and hug it out. But it wasn't and they'd always only fight.

"Hi hi sorry I've been out all day bacche. I just had a sudden load of things to do and then I toh just decided to get all the errands done today only."

"Oh okay ... That's cool." Sana balked at her nakedness under the sheets.

"No ya I'm so upset. You're going through a break up and I wasn't here only."

"Mmmhmm it's okay."

"And then Chanda told me you didn't eat anything today?"

"No ma I'm not hungry."

"Eh, but you should eat something no?"

"I said I'm not hungry what the fuck is your problem?"

"Don't shout at me, Sunaina!"

"Don't call me that!"

"Shut up. That's your name no matter what you say, you stupid girl."

"I'm not hungry."

"You have to eat you fool, you'll grow fat this way!"

"You want me to eat when I'm not hungry for what, your peace of mind or to settle your conscience? What if I get sick ya?"

She hoped her mother couldn't notice her fumbling under the covers to put her robe back on.

"Fine, don't eat anything. Starve for all I care." A part of Sana was dying with every second that passed and her mother didn't offer to make bhel puri. "Oh come come, you wanna see all my shopping?"

"You were gone for hours. What happened ...?" Her mother's chirpy demeanour was foreboding, like she was gearing her up for some terrible news.

"Ohh god long story. Also, what happened to your phone? Are you mad or what, Vikram told me you threw it off the balcony."

Sana shrugged simply.

"Do you want something to drink? Wait I'll tell Vikram to make something. He made this mojito for me the other day with some fresh cinnamon it was like the best ya. And it is so hot outside my god. I was worried I'd faint on the walk from the car to the mall and then you know how hot Minal's house also gets na sometimes!"

She went off barking orders further fueling Sana's suspicion that she was hiding something.

Her parent's bedroom was bigger than the café down the road, largely dominated by a four poster bed that had been lifted in through the balcony because they couldn't bring it up the stairs. It faced the dark grey wall that housed the enormous TV screen that no one ever used. Dark warm wood ran from one corner to the other, polished to match the mahogany dresser that housed lazer cut crystal bottles of every perfume imaginable – it always reminded her of the illustrated Ali Baba story. This was where once she'd watch her parents play an old Fred Astaire record and sway, where she'd snuggle on Sunday mornings while Hassan read the morning paper and Tina practiced her crossword. She'd watch Cartoon Network as they passed a plate of fresh cut fruits above her. Now it was a room that looked like no one used it, where her mother slept on one side of the too big bed and the other was covered in aesthetically placed monochromatic shopping bags.

Sana paused, staring at them with trepidation. Unless half her wardrobe was going to charity, she couldn't find a reason why her mother would purchase so many clothes. For a second, she wondered if any of it might be for her – as a consolation for the break up, but Tina had no clue of what had actually transpired.

Her mother was still barking instructions for dinner when she came upstairs. One knock on the door – she could knock on her own bedroom door but not her daughter's, Sana noted – and Tina found herself with some explaining to do.

"You've done a lot of shopping ... Told papa?"

"Beta there is something I didn't get to tell you last night," her guarded tone turned Sana's gut to lead, "because you were so upset and all."

Sana's silence made things worse.

"I feel really bad ... And then you and I got into a fight also. But anyway, I know how upset you were ... how upset you are. So I just wanted to do something nice for you."

"By buying out the whole mall?"

"Actually ... Well, not really. I'll show you everything and you can actually keep whatever you like." She tittered, waving a heavily ringed hand.

"Mumma just tell me what this is about na? Did something happen?"

"No no no, of course not. Your dad called yesterday. He's ... err ... sort of extending his trip because there are things he needs to take care of before the Milan office space can be set up. We ... um ... we spoke for a very long time you know, because honestly it doesn't make sense ya he keeps living in a hotel or some random B&B like this."

"So what are we doing now?"

"Papa's looking at a studio apartment there."

"Oh. In Milan?"

"Yeah and actually if you think about it, it's like kind of amazing. Because you can go and like stay there anytime –"

"But what about the apartment in New York he purchased like literally a month ago?"

"We aren't sure yet. We'll probably put it up on rent."

"On rent?"

"On rent yeah. That makes more sense doesn't it?"

Sana stared blankly.

"Do you want to go see it?"

"See what?"

"The apartment. I mean I haven't asked him about it but I'm sure it'll be cool if you go see it once before we lease it out. Maybe you can even set it up a little so we can actually charge more for a semi furnished –"

"But what about the place in Milan?" Sana wasn't sure what the actual fuck was going on.

Her mother shrugged.

"Let me get this straight, papa is going to live out of there *permanently*?"

"Yes my baby," her gooey voice grated against Sana's ears. "We think it's like for the best and all. However that does like bring me back to the shopping spree." She pointed to the bloated paper bags.

"I met Priya for brunch today and she, you know what she's like na stupid woman. She's always coming up with all these crazy ideas. But actually I kind of loved this one. She suggested we go on a little getaway, just us girls! So Parmeet, Minal, Fari, and me we're doing a super quick trip to Paris. Then I thought if I'm going there might as well go see your papa. You know make sure he's eating properly and taking care of himself. You know how he gets na!"

"And you're leaving me here." Sana laughed once, unsure of what to say.

"I'm sure you want some time to yourself also bubba. You need to be at peace I understand that. Plus this way you'll like have your friends and all around and you can have them stay over, you know what I mean? Just turn it into a little bachelor pad. The guest rooms are free – in fact I'll have them cleaned once as well."

Sana felt her knees give way as she landed on the side of the bed. Tina on the other hand was oblivious and dancing over to her bags.

"Oh oh oh and you'll never believe what I got for you my baby."

The box was hard to balance so Sana moved and placed it on the bed in front of her, splaying her fingers on the matte surface.

"I know it's not going to fix whatever happened beta. But I just wanted to see your face when you opened it."

It was the dress. The dress she'd been eyeing for her pre-wedding party. Sequinned all over with sheer panels and the faux ruffles. Her heart was still in her mouth but it didn't taste good.

"I think someone already wore this dress ma."

She realized the blood throbbing in her ears had nothing to do with the strain of holding the dress up.

"But thanks."

Tina had caught herself before her daughter saw the eye roll. She gasped at the small paper cut on Sana's thumb, from where a drop of blood had bubbled up.

"Oh god. How did this happen? My bedside drawer has a bandaid and there's some dettol in the bathroom. Quickly get it."

She flung the goddess Gucci dress, still in its box, and stood up.

"Don't worry I'm not going to stain your stupid bedsheets."

"Wash it with cold water first!"

"'Kay!" She washed her thumb and rubbed a cotton ball dyed amber from the sanitizing liquid, sniffing deeply from the bottle. It was one of her favourite smells in the world.

Her hair looked like shit and it broke her heart. She'd been lovingly growing it out because she wanted it long and fresh and perfect for wedding photos. The ombré was still there but the darker roots had grown out; she flipped it over her shoulder and went back out.

"Is it still bleeding?"

"Of course not."

She packed up the Gucci box and tucked it under her arm. "Thanks for the dress ma."

"You wanna come down for dinner?"

"No thanks I'll be in my room."

"But I'm leaving tomorrow ya, come eat with me? If nothing else just give me company."

"Tomorrow? What about a visa? Isn't that supposed to take time."

"My last one is still valid, obvi."

"Cool."

"Wait! Don't you at least wanna see what all I bought?"

"Have fun on your trip mother."

"Aye don't be such a spoilt brat –"

The door slammed shut as if right to her face. Tina stood there hands and jaw clenched tighter than a sphincter forcing herself not to cry. She wouldn't allow her daughter to ruin the beginning of her vacation. Maybe things were happening for a reason, that's the kind of stuff they wrote about in inspirational books. The ones she skimmed over standing in the classical fiction section so it could count for something. *She* had to count for something – no she did, she definitely did. She counted for something. She mattered.

Changing into her own nightgown, she pulled out a bottle of wine and started packing.

"So what's the deal with Sam," Gayatri opened a bottle of premixed rum and handed it to Sana.

"What do you mean?" she flipped the parking lights off so they were now in darkness.

"I'm really starting to worry about her, I mean those third grade NGO type clothes that she's started wearing lately and those tacky henna tattoos on her arm which seem to keep overlapping in a horrendous cycle of middle class-ness. It's just getting out of hand, no? She actually wore a Sarojini dress with her Miu Miu shoes to Paparazzi last week and I had half a mind of tipping security off to not let her enter – I swear it was so embarrassing I didn't know whether to rip it off of her and use the dress to hang myself or give my own to her. It's not like anyone there would mind seeing me in my underwear anyway!"

"Literally no one wants to see you in your underwear, Gayatri." Karishma snorted from the back seat.

"And I hate hate hate the way her hands always smell of the henna. It's sick. It makes me sick."

"Okay I literally don't even know what you're talking about I *love* the henna smell."

"Yes, at a wedding maybe. It's not like we were out for drinks at Tivoli gardens for god's sake it was fuckin Paparazzi ya!"

"Anyway, we went to Kitty Su afterwards," Gayatri paused, wide eyed, for effect "and she still had it on."

"Oh. My. God. I can't even right now." Lara lit a cigarette and motioned as if to cleanse herself with the smoke. "Like I'm unable to even, I have lost the ability to even!"

"Yeah, can you literally even imagine how bad it was?"

"If you think that's bad news I have something worse to tell you." A sigh.

Sana finished her drink and looked back with narrowed eyes. "Spill."

"She's leaving Delhi you guys, Sam is leaving Delhi." Karishma exhaled loudly. Sana saw her chest heaving under pressure through the rear view mirror.

"Wait, that makes no sense. Where is she going?"

"I thought her visa was rejected?"

"Yeah, she's moving to Pune instead."

"Ew," Sana laughed at the idea of her oldest friend living in a city like Pune, "what the hell is wrong with her?"

"I need a stiffer drink, Sana pass it here." Gayatri threw her head back with a deep swig. "I swear if she's actually joined an NGO I will kill myself."

"No no it's for Teach for India."

Gayatri swiveled in her seat as though to punch her. "Okay bitch, that's like the literal *definition* of an NGO. You know what this is exactly what starts to happen when fucking rich girls like us with hot bodies and an actual taste in fashion start mingling with that middle class West Delhi type crowd."

"Actually I think Karam is from Janakpuri." Lara giggled.

"Good god, his name is probably Karamdeep or Karamjeet or whatev."

“But what does she want to join Teach for India for ya? Her life here is beyond blessed. That girl I swear has never been in want of something – she’s said it and she’s had it, like without any room for asking, it’s just given. Her parents are fucking raking in money like no man’s business and okay, logically speaking she doesn’t, hasn’t ever in the past, or ever will have to – even if she decides to get hitched – work a day in her life.”

“Yeah, why would she wanna leave all that behind? Leave us behind?”

“Exactly! Look at what Sana is going through, I mean now more than ever the four of us just have to be there for each other don’t we?”

Sana and Gayatri shared a look.

“Five of us.” Lara muttered.

“Huh?”

“You said four of us, like she’s already gone. We’re still the Famous Five, babe.”

A fog-like silence descended in the car.

Samaira ‘Sam’ Manchanda had developed a penchant for cotton dresses from the anokhi sale bin and silver half-moon earrings. Lately every time they met she’d jingle with the ring of a thousand bells. It was the sound of crossing to the other side, passing the outer edges of Sana’s dominion. Samaira was no longer concerned with the same things, she had aligned herself with a different path. But that wasn’t what was on Sana’s mind as she reached home that night, walked up the driveway and pressed her finger into the scanner at the door. No, she was thinking about a matching pair of white shoes with the pink lights on the underside, which they wore on every special occasion for the first three years of knowing each other. Sana’s pair broke so Samaira stopped wearing hers. She rubbed the numb fingertips together and tried the thumbprint scanner ignoring the pinch of moisture in her eyes.

Fred Astaire. It wasn't that Sana considered herself a connoisseur of classical music, she just recognized Let's Face The Music And Dance too well. It was her happy place. It was the land where father met mother and danced in a tipsy blur, shifting from bare foot to bare foot, cheek to cheek. She walked down the foyer to find Tina wrapped up in the arms of someone who wasn't quite Hassan Kochhar.

Tina had first been introduced to Prateik over cocktails at a private event, they'd bonded over elderflower spritzers at PCO and shared a penchant for diamond dust quickies in the bathroom. She didn't think of him as her dealer but somehow her wandering hands always found his stash of coke. It was honestly as harmless as new friendships could be, tragic as it was funny. Tina was just desperate for a change of company, even though they kept things platonic for the most part. She didn't mind paying for his drinks – of which he could put away many – so long as they made a show of each other. That Sana had walked in on them making out like hot blooded teens in a bad slasher movie was a separate matter altogether. However, the sight of her mother in a dominatrix style bodysuit was too much to bear. As the silk satin robe Hassan had bought her on their last holiday slipped off her shoulders, her daughter slipped into the shadows and ran up to her room.

Over the course of the week Chanda tried her best to get Sana out of bed, but with a bank of posts saved in advance there was no reason for her to make any efforts. She feigned a bout of severe fever brought on by the hit of the afternoon sun – if it was hot enough to melt the tar on the roads, it was enough to make her sick – and spent her life in the pale pink robe surrounded by ridiculously soft pillows.

They reached a moot point where Chanda cleaned the room while Sana showered and in exchange she didn't badger her to eat. As if to further her torture the only program worth watching on TV was F.R.I.E.N.D.S – Sana had once declared that she'd rather be an 'autistic vegetable' than watch that show. She sniggered to herself as the memory came back to her, unaware of how the same words would come back to her just then. And so, she made a home of her bed and shut out the rest of the world, allowing Tina a bittersweet exit after nights of dining alone. Samaira called and called, having found out that Karishma had broken the news to the others, and Sana was so angry she thought she might individually pull out every hair on her head just to simmer down. Then Friday dawned and Sana Kochhar rose like an angered phoenix from amidst sushi takeaway boxes and starbucks cups to declare that she was throwing a farewell party for Samaira Manchanda.

Chapter THREE

Lonely For You Only (*Interlude*)

There were standards to uphold while hosting a party in Sana's books, you couldn't call people over without an unlimited supply of libations, there had to be one central wow-factor for which Vikram had been assigned to bring over the karaoke machine from Kama bua's house. Lastly, she knew that this was the perfect opportunity to have the neon installation set up in the main living room. At forty five past three p.m. the workers had finished and Chanda was sweeping up behind them. Sana gave the driver cash and sent him off to the godowns at Gurgaon for the crates of alcohol.

With plus-ones chiming in by the dozen, she left the backup phone unattended and soaked herself in an ice cold bath. Sana sat there, white as a ghost and violently shivering for as long as she could. The ends of her fingers, the edges of her breasts, both her feet had numbed. She was still shivering, watching her skin turn pink as soon as she'd drop her palms underwater. Nothing, not the sickly scent of vanilla nor Laksh's playlist could penetrate her skin. She always liked a drink within reach while getting ready for a party, the glass of cabernet sauvignon lay unattended as she sunk deeper into her black hole set to the sound of tenderly synthesized music. Like an island surrounded by the deep blue sea she sat in silence, even the chattering of her teeth had stopped now. Outside the city had been covered by grey skies, its residents both hopeful and lamenting the threat of rain.

By the last drop of wine, which was when she finally staggered out of the tub, the sun was setting and Sana was swooning.

"Coffee? Are you mad?" Chanda shrieked.

"Why do I have to be mad to want coffee?"

"Because you never have coffee." She huffed. "Fine, what coffee do you want?"

"I don't know ya, what kind of a question is that? Just give me the normal coffee that we have in our house."

"Hmm, do you wanna maybe try the one papa drinks? It's really really tasty."

"Yeah sure whatever ..."

"What about milk?"

There were few things Sana hated more than having a conversation through the door when she was in the bathroom, her sanctum sanctorum ruined by this unnecessary gamut of questions.

"No."

"Ok no milk."

"Just have it made the way papa drinks it."

"You want sugar in it?"

"Ugh yes sugar is fine."

"Brown or white?"

"CHANDA! I don't fucking care!"

"Should I mix it in or should I put it on the side like –"

Chanda giggled as the slipper banged against the other side of the door.

"At least tell me what do I do with this smoothie now?"

"Chanda, take it up your ass!!" She replied in hindi.

She guffawed and took it back to the kitchen.

Sana looked at her reflection and realized why she probably hated her mother, to some level at least. The one thing that woman could have passed on to her, she hadn't. Tina had these beautiful hazel coloured eyes that were immediately striking against her light complexion, they held everyone's attention in the room. Sana on the other hand seemed to have become a carbon copy of her dad, dark brewed coffee colouring her hair and eyes. In her own form of rebellion, she insisted on keeping her hair lightened even though it grew out nearly to her waist. She sat and set it in soft curls, cigarette dangling from between her lips. Sana hated sitting for too long because she feared the skin of her stomach would sag and she'd develop fat rolls. She lived in a world where people put themselves down in a show of humility (or boredom), although it was a clear show of asking for attention. Anything for some validation.

At Lara's party last month she'd complimented someone on her dress and was met with a grimace and a declaration that it was all an illusion. The girl stood and moaned about how fat she was – even though everyone followed her on instagram and had seen her in a bikini. Gayatri had leaned in and bluntly asked her, "Dude why would you call yourself fat like that?"

Visibly shaken, the girl shrugged. "I don't know. If I just say 'thanks', I kinda look like a narcissistic bitch, don't I?"

"So you tell people you think you're fat from lack of better things to say?" The irony was not lost on any of them.

How many times had Sana snatched a phone away because she looked *hideous* in a picture. Thrown away brand new clothes because they made her feel fat. Ripped and shredded her jeans, have the crotch altered so her butt would look like Kylie Jenner's in them.

"Jesus fuck," she whispered to herself, vowing to lay off coffee.

She shook off the unsavory thoughts and her robe, stepping into the soft skirt. She slid it up her legs and let it sit high on her waist, channeling a lolita vibe. The inky blue skirt hugged her waist and billowed outward, almost like a uniform. She pulled on a white crocheted top with gold hoops to finish the outfit by way of Havana in old movies.

It is a truth acknowledged statewide that nobody in Delhi ever shows up for a party on time. Ankit Kalra was not one of those people. In a city where plans were built upon 'I'll let you know's' he was the kind of guy who showed up no matter what time it was or how tiring his day had been.

Nobody really knew when he'd made it to the inner circle, it had just happened some time on a trip to Mallorca the last year. Another thing nobody knew about him was where the accent came from, he'd never lived overseas nor read much beyond bar menus or maps. Yet he dropped his jaw at certain points and subtly rolled his R's and that with the girth of his forearms had afforded him a comfortable life so far. His fatal flaw was reserved for the locker room at the gym when he reverted to the Punjabi accent and could be heard talking about partying and 'poussey'.

Among the first to reach her house, he'd taken it upon himself to fix up Sana's music and the sound was reassuring as she came down the stairs.

Another of Ankit's oddities were his warm bear hugs – though Gayatri at one point had made a joke about how the heat must be from all his chest hair. No one had noticed that he now waxed. Sana launched herself into him, grateful that he was helping out without being asked to when he could've just parked himself on the couch in his sad work shirt and khakis.

He followed her to the bar, fetching an icy beer while she flipped on the lights of the new wall sign, bathing the room in a brilliant blue glow.

"*Lonely for you only*", he let out a whistle. "I fuckin love it!"

She giggled. "Cost me a fuckin' bomb, you'd better love it."

"Why's it so sad though?"

She stared at it for a moment. "It isn't supposed to be sad actually. My grandfather, he was in the army you know full like infantry scenes and all, anyway he used to write to my grandma a lot of these like beautiful, poetic letters. And he'd always sign them with this, so I really wanted that idea to kind of just be represented here in like a permanent form you know."

Ankit swooned at the story, then drank deeply from his bottle to hide his blush. "That's crazy man!"

The silence stretched out between them. "Oh and I'm sorry about Daksh. I err I heard that you guys aren't together anymore."

She smiled and waved a dismissive hand as if it was all past her, like it didn't kill her just a little. She asked him about his day and only half heard his response.

"Oh my god, listen I could totally do with a pick-me-up, you wanna join?" she brought out another beer and led him to her parents' room.

With no roughage in their nasal passage, the face numbing coke hit them immediately. Unfortunately the beer didn't sit well in a stomach riled up with hunger juices – Sana didn't remember eating a thing since the avocado toast that morning. In minutes she was crying into a toilet bowl full of frothy vomit and life seemed to be coming full circle.

Chapter FOUR

Wasted On The Young

Ankit knocked on the door and asked if she was okay.

"Yeah, I just need to wash up in here ya."

"Can I come in, I heard crying ..." He walked in anyway.

"I said I'm fine!"

He flushed the bowl and pulled her into a signature Ankit Kalra hug because that was just his coping mechanism in a fucked up world. Sana repeated that she was fine and he silently patted her back. His jaw worked against her head when he spoke.

"Your hair smells like puke."

She laughed. "Oh crap, dude your shirt is ruined. Shit I'm so sorry."

"Sick! Your puke is on me man ... what the fuck." he laughed on his way out.

"Wait, I'll get you a clean shirt. Get rid of that, I'll tell Chanda to clean it meanwhile."

"That Chanda is going to slap me if she ever has to be around me and vomit anymore." He announced from the other side.

She covered her face and let loose a torrent of sanitizer spray all around her, flushing once more for posterity. Ankit was in the middle of unbuttoning when she walked out and they had to avert eyes to keep the moment from turning awkward. Definitively nerdy though he might've been – with his tortoise shell glasses and omnipresent kindle – Ankit also happened to be built like a brickhouse. She fished a dark shirt from her father's closet and tossed it over to him. The beer still tumbled through her gut and she wondered how it could possibly take him that long to put on a shirt. Before they knew it their eyes were locked in a stare-down that left her just a little out of breath.

"I uh can't get these buttons right."

"I can see that" she swatted his hands away and started pushing the black buttons in place. She had to keep the sides together lest her face met his chest. It was worse than algebra, her fingers that close to his skin but not quite touching. She made her way up to his chest and stopped.

"You missed a few there," he gave a single chuckle.

"Leave it, I like it that way."

He let out a full blown laugh "With my hair growing out, I'll look like a beast in front of your other guests. Do you know Jai's been waxing his chest since he was seventeen?"

"No. Way. Jaikaran waxes his chest!"

"YES! How can you not tell?"

They were still standing close enough to feel each other's breath.

"You should show it off."

"Why?" he made a move to button up but she pushed his hand away.

"I don't know," she looked up at him through her lashes, "it's kinda hot."

They kissed once, a quick kiss that was like tapping the surface of a swimming pool. Then they parted and looked at everywhere except directly at each other. She sort of cleared her throat and he sort of made an awkward remark and they sort of kissed once more but he was out the door before it was even over.

Gayatri was on her way up the stairs and he actually felt his pupils dilate.

"Hey, where's –"

"She's in there, I think she's changing." Heart in his throat he dashed past her.

Everywhere she looked, Sana saw a story either streaming live or recorded in smooth rotation. The children who once played dress up together now lived out the grown up, caricatured version of the game with their stiff collar shirts and short dresses. They passed around polaroid cameras between drinks and air kisses, every frame printed on monochromatic film. Among the cooed compliments you'd never know which was genuine, while others struck up a conversation simply to steer it to talk about themselves. Sana saw by the wide eyed nods they were all just waiting for an in – it was all about who had the longer work week, who sat through the worst of traffic, who spent the most on food and couldn't stop feeling fat.

She turned to Lara, a welcome distraction. "How was it?"

Lara ran her tongue over numb gums. "Fine as fuck, is this your mom's stuff?"

"She got it from this boy ... don't ask." Lara handed her the remainder of the gram with a sniffle.

"So ohmygod I have to tell you all about this project I've started it's so cool it's like an open community forum sitch, and it's like anyone who's feeling low and depressed can reach out and just talk you know ... you know how we just don't talk anymore? Anyway it's totally free and the person on the other side listens it out without judgment and shit and like that's, sometimes just that much is enough. You know what I mean?"

Sana handed her friend a paper towel to dab at the leaking nose. "What do you get out of it?"

"Umm scuse you, I get the satisfaction of helping someone. Like really helping, not just putting up a message on social media that like my door's always open."

Sana rolled her eyes. Lara's door could definitely benefit from closing sometimes, but, "I'm sorry I just don't see how that's helpful. To be honest it sounds a little perverted. To sit on the other side as an anonymous person listening to these people vent out about how they're dealing with something."

"Okay you're just being a dick for no reason."

"Are you even licensed to help people?!"

Beside them Ankit had been dragged into a conversation about stock prices and the inadvertent effect of property rates in Bali on the standard of living in South Delhi. Sana grabbed her friend's elbow and manoeuvered to the bar where Gayatri was swatting at the bartender.

"The fuck kinda bartender are you?" she shoved him aside, unaware of the stares. "That's not how you make a cocktail, I didn't come to sip this bougie shit 'kay?"

Sana threw back her vodka soda to avoid the disaster that usually began with Gayatri stepping behind a bar. Lara did not follow suit.

"Gigi oh my god, make me a 'skinny bitch' please."

Gayatri threw her head back and cackled. "Bitch, even god can't make you a skinny bitch. But if you want a vodka tonic then gimme two."

Sana moved away to avoid burning in a pyre of shame. She scanned the party, avoiding eye contact from anyone who'd ask her where her drink was or whether she'd show up for all days of fashion week, no she was looking for him to save her from having to make giggled small talk. She didn't see him anywhere.

"—Try the wasabi poppers, I know I hate wasabi too but these are to *die* for babe—"

"—You guys are literally the cutest! Oh my god where's your drink, get another one na—"

"—Oh my god listen don't even worry I'll have the driver drop you home—"

"—Yaas gurl try it with the dip ... so good right? Oh my god feed me too—"

"—Okay babe, seriously, if you're not wasted in the next half an hour we literally cannot be friends anymore—"

"—Oh oh I love this Berlin ArtParasites quote too! Omg they like totally get me! —"

More giggling.

"*OMG like are you totally serious right now*!"

She turned around at his voice. "Laksh, there you are!"

His hug was like a winter morning sun.

"Thank god you're here, I thought I would die," she whispered into his ear.

Her lips brushed against his neck when she spoke and he made no move to back off. Instead, he leaned closer and turned his lips to her cheek.

"I'd die without me too." He smirked.

Their second hug didn't go as unnoticed but no one around them said anything, mostly out of fear. No one survived a Sana Kochhar takedown, no one. She didn't want to leave his side but Sana knew how people let their thoughts run, she knew because she was no different.

"Hi, I'm Swati!"

They turned and introduced themselves to the girl with legs for days wrapped in cigarette pants, and eyes only for Lakshman.

"Hi, I'm Laksh. It's nice to meet you." Just like that she was forgotten.

The girl with the spidery long legs threw her a smile over Laksh's shoulder and Sana did her best to return it with grace. Karishma, while helping herself to a third cheese cigar pulled her back to the bar where the others stood.

Gayatri slapped her butt. "Hey sexy!"

She threw back a tequila and instantly regretted it. "Who the hell are all these people?"

Karishma looked around and shrugged.

"I don't know, maybe a lot of them just brought friends along, like your invite said."

"Yes for plus ones not their whole neighbourhood."

"Maybe some of them are Sam's friends?" Gayatri ordered herself another drink.

"Umm what friends? We know everyone who's friends with her. They're our friends."

"Whatever I'm over it."

"Haha Gayatri that's so rude."

"No really, I'm so done. We throw her this awesome party even though she's dropping bombs on us and leaving to work in some trash place and yeah like I get it's super nice, it's volunteer work or charity or something but what-the-fuck-ever man. She's just behaving like we're not good enough already."

"Sana, who's that girl talking to Laksh?"

She sighed. "Swati something."

"She looks like a model."

"Who's she here with?" she took another shot of tequila.

"I think she's Ankit's sister." Surya had made her way over to them, appropriately apologetic for being late.

"Ankit Kalra? No, he has two kid brothers." Gayatri ignored the way they looked at her. It was just dark enough to hide her violent blush.

"Whatever, she's a stupid slut who can go fuck herself."

Gayatri raised an eyebrow.

"Oh we don't like her." Sana took her glass and took a large swig. She raised both her eyebrows meaningfully.

"Stop it."

"You stop. It's your party man at least try and have some fun."

Somewhere Samaira had entered the party, which had swollen to the point that the air conditioning had been rendered ineffective. Sana opened the double doors to the front lawn where the party was met with fairy lights and mist fans. Lara took her for another hit and she returned feeling invincible.

Sam made her rounds, politely meeting everyone. In her mind she was sure they'd never be relatable again, they who clutched their drinks and cigarettes and laughed sloppily so she never knew if they laughed with her or at her. They who debated Modi and his henchmen as if they knew beyond their slight inconveniences, who spoke of their vacation plans with so much seriousness you'd think they were curing cancer. Social pretenses forced her to hold on to a drink, even though she'd quit since the last party where someone had spiked her cocktail and she'd woken up at a friend's house in only her underwear. They didn't really look at her, even when they spoke to her, so Samaira dipped her head and wove her way outside. She passed the bright sign that they all took pictures of, she'd seen their incessant updates on social media. The house felt like a skeletal structure, no better than a rented warehouse really. She felt three feet small remembering the days when they laughed and ran through those halls and played with a silly pink skipping rope. Of white light up shoes and picnics under a tent in the backyard.

Two people were staring at her and a third made some comment she couldn't hear, but their laughter was loud enough. She'd never been laughed at to her face before, though she'd done it to other people. Samaira had stood proudly in formation with Sana and the others and done the same. She had said such mean things that were so funny then and they couldn't stop laughing and then that meanness had become a habit and she'd become a twisted harpy who said things for the benefit of a joke even when no one was around to hear it.

What am I even doing here?

She looked at her friends, the girls she'd spent every waking moment with. They sipped on jägerbombs and danced in tandem. Outside the boys they once sought attention from hid softening guts, or worse spoke of premature wedding plans. As the pool lights came on, she set her ginger gin down and vanished with a final jingle of those half moon earrings.

"You're welcome!" Swati handed Laksh a glass of upturned jäger, a subtle hair flip ensued.

"Ugh don't you just hate everyone here."

He knocked back the shot and set his glass aside with a polite smile. "No actually. These people are my friends and you shouldn't be talking about them this way."

Visibly stunned at his reply, Swati chalked it up to ill-timed humor and laughed it off. In a city where everyone delighted in calling strangers hateful and ugly, and vehemently denied it, this boy had shut her up with unsettling ease. Sana was within earshot and she knew it, Swati had chosen her moment well albeit unaware of the outcome. It really was a room full of silly ugly men, she decided, not one she'd deign to go out with and even Laksh, well he wasn't the best but he'd. No, Laksh was something different altogether. Sana raised her eyebrows meaningfully and Swati took it as her cue to leave them.

"Dude, thank god you're here. I thought I wouldn't be able to get her off me." Laksh exhaled as Sana walked over, pulling out a cigarette.

"Why d'you wanna get rid of her?" she looked at him through droopy lids. The smoke curled out from her blushing lips.

"For the sake of it, really. She's too much, man."

"She's one of the most beautiful girls here, Laksh." She hoped her voice wouldn't crack.

"Are we feeling extra crazy today?" he pressed the back of his hand to her forehead.

She swatted him away. "I said 'one of –' shut up."

"She's a pain in the ass to talk to though."

"I don't think she wants to do much talking." She noted bitterly.

He drew his eyebrows close and stared. "Why'd you say that?"

She ignored the hollow in her chest. "She looks like she's ready for it."

His eyes didn't leave her face.

"That's irrelevant. You're the one I've been meaning to talk to all night."

"Why?" She thawed out. "Is everything ok?"

"Yeah, no it's nothing serious. I was just wondering if you wanna join me for a quick road trip. I was supposed–"

"Of course! Oh I think I'll die in this house, let's go please."

"Alright alright, but I was going with mom and dad earlie but they canned, so I got a single room instead."

"No one else is going?"

"I haven't asked anyone else yet."

"Don't." she ignored the turbulent thumping of her heart. "Wait does this mean I can drive your car?"

"Exactly, I figured you could use the time away from all of this", he waved a hand around them, "and no you cannot drive my car."

She crossed her arms in defiance.

"Super. Pack light, there's nothing to do at the fort except chilling and we can probs pack some beer along."

Her heart might've flown off if it wasn't in her ribcage. Unable to contain herself, she launched into a hug.

"At least now I'll have some company for the drive."

"Uh obvi! Why'd you wanna pass up on such awesome company."

"Don't pretend to be more annoying than you are."

"No Laksh that'd be my mother" she rolled her eyes.

The memory of an unconsented kiss echoed through his mind and so he decided it was time to go home.

"So I hear you have some interesting tattoos." Swati was back.

Laksh pinched the bridge of his nose and laughed loudly. "Yeah I do."

She snaked her hand around his arm. "Tell me everything."

"Better yet, why don't I just show you", he lifted the edge of his t-shirt to show her the line of dots and dashes that made up what was famously called the 'Lakshman Rekha'. It sat low on his hips, Sana had to avert her eyes.

The rest of their conversation was whispers and giggles, rooting her to her spot in disgust.

Swati thanked her for the fabulous party with a cheek-to-cheek kiss and left with Laksh in tow, his hand running down her back.

He looked back at her with shadowed eyes, all signs of humor gone, and gave her a mock salute. Sana still couldn't move from there. It was like a punch in the gut. No, deeper. It was like a fist slowly pushed past her flesh and bones and plucked one of her organs out, leaving her slowly sinking.

Gayatri wasn't too comfortable keeping her head underwater for too long, in fact she avoided it whenever she could. Standing at five feet nine inches did have its own benefits though, she stood upright in most pools. The stone edge was too warm for that hour but she was leaning against it all the same, head lolling so heavily you'd think it might snap right off. She stared up at the sky that never seemed to darken, perpetually burning orange with the toxic glow of streetlights and the dust of a dying city.

It really had been one of the hottest summers that Delhi had seen, she thought about how homeless people having nowhere to hide could just catch fire. The constant hum of conversation blurred to white noise when she tilted her head a little to the left, a little more and static rang through her ear. A heavy breeze lifted up the sweet scent of those very specific white flowers that only bloomed at night. She sifted it through her open fingers, standing straighter to move the joint away from her face. Her lungs filled with the half-formed memory of the scent that came from those seemingly invisible flowers, how it'd catch her unawares at the oddest spots in the city. Nights like that often remained a blur.

She righted her head and turned around so that she could stare at the motley crew of drunks, swaying in their own tableaux of douchebaggery, pushing prime snow up their sharp noses. She sniggered at the thought of it, these people who were on the wrong side of peaking in life, of their hearts forever stopped in these times as their bodies aged and sagged. She saw them softening around the middle, greying and grappling to hold on to this version of their life.

"Hey where's Sana?"

She shifted her head, looking at Ankit from the corner of her eyes.

"I..." she sniggered, "dude I don't fuckin care."

She pushed herself away from him. "Wait, why do you care all of a sudden?"

"It's not like I want to take *advantage* of her, Gayatri."

"Okay buddy, but like she'll probably be ready to hit some rebound rides right now. So I'd suggest you stay away from her and all."

He laughed and plucked the joint from her fingers. "Aren't you a smart cookie."

She turned again and leaned her back against the stone.

"No I'm actually horribly stupid."

The sky was an amber wasteland above them and Gayatri wondered at how her life was going to change. She dreamt of casting calls and the panoramic view from her house in Bombay. She took in another lungful of the sweet incense and whispered an I Love You to the moon.

"What?"

Her heart stopped beating. "What 'what'? Why are you still here?!"

"What did you say just now..."

"I thought you went looking for Sana." She dipped underwater.

"I wasn't planning on leaving you alone, Gayatri."

She ignored him.

"What did you say?" A smile played on his lips.

"Nothing." He widened his eyes at her. "Stop it Anki, I didn't say anything."

Her nervous laugh gave it away.

"Why're you so embarrassed about it?" His laugh was possibly the worst reaction in that moment.

"I said 'I love you', okay. I'm stoned as fuck. Besides I say it to people all the time."

"All the time?" he deadpanned.

"Yeah"

"All the time, Gayatri?" he sprawled on the grass in front of her.

"YES." She crossed her arms, fully aware of her childishness.

"I love you too."

The smile was gone.

"I've had a thing for you since we first met." He shrugged as if it was common knowledge.

And it had been. Everyone knew Ankit Kalra had a true-blue crush on Gayatri, including Sana who had told him to keep his distance from her. Who had told Gayatri that she just enjoyed the attention from Ankit because he was the new addition in their social circle. This was the same Sana who had started a rumour that Gayatri was a lesbian in high school when Karan Jaiswal had told her that he wanted to ask Gayatri out on a date. Worse still, everyone had believed it. The thing is, Sana had a penchant for fabricating details – not unlike her mother – and she had made up rather steamy scissoring scenarios between Gayatri and Nikita – who was actually a lesbian but wouldn't come out of the closet for nearly a decade because of being bullied. However the worst of it all was the dean calling Gayatri's parents to school to address the issue of homosexuality even though there was no school policy on it. They'd put her in therapy for a month until convinced it was all a big lie.

Ankit took a deep breath. "That's horrible."

"Yup."

"So then?"

She giggled softly and wiped her eyes. "Then what? Nothing. Karan dated Sana for like six months then moved to the States and Nitika just faded to nothingness. As for me I figured I'd be better off as Sana Kochhar's cool lezzie friend than a sad lez reject no one wanted to talk to."

She couldn't stand to see him look at her that way.

"I'm a cliché aren't I?"

"Yeah", he smiled, "but that's irrelevant."

His hands wove through her hair and when their eyes met, Gayatri leaned in and kissed him. It didn't matter. None of it mattered anymore, not the blistering heatwave nor the high banter, not even the smell of nocturnal flowers. It didn't matter that the first drop of rain had hit the parched earth. With their first kiss the spell was broken.

One finger.

Another finger.

Two fingers more.

She nudged her hand higher.

Sana's head rang with the sweet smell of cocaine. The ash from her cigarette lay scattered all over the basin, flaking over the bottles of shampoo, her make up box. James Blake crooned of his willing heart and she couldn't stop thinking of Swati's legs wrapped around Laksh's bare back.

Looking back at the cock-up of a night, Sana had no idea at what point she'd made the decision but it had come to her in a moment of absolute clarity. A plug pulled inside and all the alcohol drained out. Her hair fell unbound down to her navel, hair that she'd spent months growing out patiently snipping away split ends with surgical precision. She wanted to have a picture perfect wedding, who knew when a media house would buy the rights to her wedding photos?

Smoke from a freshly lit cigarette stung her eyes and she told herself that that was the reason she was crying. There was nothing else to it.

Her party in full swing below, Sana smoked away to oblivion fingering her hair till the smell had seeped in. Then she picked up the scissors – fingered measurements be damned – and chopped it all off from above her chest. They lied, they all lied. The movies, the TV shows, it was all fake. There was no grace in the movement of scissors against hair; it didn't fall down in singular gossamer strands. Instead the converging blades were met with resistance and none of the falling clumps of hair was in slow motion. It clung to her top, poking her through the fabric. She felt her earrings rattle as she ducked out of it. The hair went everywhere, pinching her skin from under her bra.

With blood turning vitriolic in her veins, Sunaina cut her hair at perfect level even though it took her the better part of an hour to do one side. She didn't realize she was shivering till the scissors slipped from her white knuckled grip. The handle left welts on her hands and she welcomed the pain.

The water was freezing. She shivered and peeled her wet clothes off, piling them on top of the mess of hair. Sana stayed in the shower till the shivers stopped, then she shampooed her hair. Then she exfoliated. When she got out of the shower there was nothing familiar about her besides the robe. Her room was dark and dead silent, she walked through and felt her way to the bed. Outside a loud thunderclap announced the first rain of the season, the last thing she heard before falling asleep.

Chapter FIVE

At Your Place Or Up In Space

It was still drizzling when dawn hit the city and every street corner was flooding with muddy water. Every few kilometers you could see cars abandoned on the road overnight – some cars weren't meant to withstand the downpour. Sana's front lawn glistened with puddled water and a singular flower had bloomed radiant pink in the perimeter bush. She packed her bags and took a steaming coffee to the balcony while Vikram and the others cleaned up the mess of the night before.

The weak sun was climbing higher when Laksh finally pulled up the driveway. The sight of her railroaded him so unexpectedly he didn't know if he'd have words to fill up the day. This wasn't Sana. Not the way he knew her. She just assumed he was hungover, or worse hung up on Swati. Her sunglasses couldn't hide the grimace as she fought the image of long legs crawling up a bare back. She approached his grey chariot without ceremony, threw her bags in the back and grunted a greeting. He grumbled in response, and she broke into a smile.

Somewhere on the road between Haryana and Alwar the sun finally broke through and cast its rays on the open road. Sana insisted on leaving the windows open and stopping for a bag of java plums from the roadside cart. She had a leg folded under her and looked right at home, Laksh cast her furtive looks of jealousy – his knees already stiffening.

The city withered away to bright fields that stretched as far as the eye could see, split only by the open road. The rain hadn't yet reached there but the sky had moments of overcast that threatened the darkened sort of day that looks beautiful in photographs but can never really be captured.

With her lilting voice humming along to a song of blue moon girls from once upon a Shangri-la, Laksh had sweaty palms. He no longer knew how to breathe around her because this wasn't Sana, this was not Sana Kochhar. They rolled to a stop at what looked like the last shop of the ride. He released a breath he didn't know he'd been holding back, wiping hands on his linen shorts.

She looked at him through her movie star RayBans and asked if he wanted anything.

"I wanna get some uncle chips for the room, I don't think they'd have a store after this."

He told her to get a whole bunch, the fort was in the middle of nowhere. "It shouldn't be too long now, traffic from here onwards seems pretty okay."

"We're out of the city so there'd be no more assholes driving on the road," he knew where she was going, "let me drive for a while?"

He pretended to think even though they both knew he'd concede. The only trouble was that she drove really fast but Lakshman didn't mind anymore. Every time she had leaned towards him, whether to fetch something from the backseat or make a point about how the endless summer was a direct implication of global warming, his heart stuttered. He wondered if her insides were all over the place too or perhaps he was the only one who was in freefall. On the outside she remained in a perpetual state of chill, even when his face was inches from hers because his cigarette pack had fallen off the seat and he had to strain to retrieve it. He couldn't see the thunderstorm in her.

They wound through the gentle hillocks that led them onto the final stretch with brilliant fields of wheat and mustard on either side. The flowers fanned out on till the horizon and he half whispered to her.

"Nothing happened by the way."

"Hmm?"

"Last night, nothing happened. I dropped her home and then I went home."

"Oh" she kept her thoughts to herself, "then you should've come back to the party."

The music filled up the silence and the drifting clouds returned. Sana sped up to match the tempo of the song. Thunder drawled above as the fort loomed nearer and Laksh offered to take the wheel.

They were completely soaked through by the time they made it up the ramp and into the cosy reception. The ceiling fan turned lazily sending shivers down their soaked backs. Holding hands for support they dashed to their room, his grip tight around the tinkling key. True to its name the interiors had parrot motifs all over but the room itself was beautiful, cozy with a queen bed – which went unacknowledged – and warm ivory stone walls. She immediately took to the bathroom to peel off her wet clothes and dry up, losing herself in the bathroom tiles. He was still putting on a t-shirt when she came out and Sana made to look away from his bare skin, the soft fabric of his t-shirt as it cascaded down his abdomen. His morse code tattoo taunted her with a lasting peek.

"I don't know about you but I'm getting into this bed, it's freezing." She tossed her wet clothes into a spare plastic bag.

"It's not so bad", he walked over to the tiny alcove window.

Laksh smiled as the cool air rolled in, making it a point to stay above and out of the blanket while she remained inside. The mounting tension in the air was made worse by the silence and the rain. They drifted off to sleep because the bed was soft and warming their weary bodies. Sana was the first to wake up and she found her body close enough to feel his breath on her face. She wondered if he might wake up to the sound of her booming heart. She felt each beat vibrate down to her toes and without thinking placed a hand on his chest. Her lungs might've collapsed from the stress but sleep took over and she lost sight of the sun hanging low in the hills beyond their bed. When he turned to his side, Lakshman held her hand and took her with him. She was awake but only for a moment, then she found herself nestled into his warm back. Their bodies were melting into each other, nestled in that bed made of clouds and dreams.

It was his phone that broke the spell. She immediately took her hand away and climbed out of bed, his back chilly where she'd left him. He didn't move, didn't see who was calling even though the phone was in his hand and he was looking at it. His mind was light-years away.

Back pressed to the bathroom wall, Sana waited for her turbulent heart to calm down. His muffled voice filtered in from the gap between the door and the floor, she couldn't help her thoughts running to his brother – who'd hit on everything that moved – and Swati – the way her arm had snaked around his. And then she remembered the touch of his hand on hers, pulling her closer to him.

"I'm keeping the wine in the fridge", he called out. "Also, that was Gayatri, your phone's off."

She heaved a sigh of relief.

"Do you want me to put it on charge?"

"Oh yeah, sorry. There's a charger in the front pocket of my bag."

"I have mine out, chill. What're you doing in there?"

"Nothing I was thinking I'd take a quick shower."

She heard him snicker. "Hurry up it's going to be tea time I don't wanna miss the *pakodas*!"

Kindle for company, Laksh waited for his turn at the shower while the rain gave way to a lavender blue afternoon. The sun hung paper white between the sheaves of clouds, watching over them seated in one of the fort's many courtyards.

He couldn't help but notice how the staff was extra courteous to her, hanging by her silence as she pondered over the limited coffee options. Her every 'thank you' brought out a thousand-watt smile and they would rush over with *pakodas* and cake slices at her request. He wondered if she was just used to other people being that way around her. It made complete sense that they would.

He stared at the cup of inky coffee with trepidation. "When did this happen?"

"What, coffee?" she smiled indulgently, "I don't know, I just had the worst week of my life and thought if I anyway post pictures of coffee cups on my social media I may as well give it a shot."

"Just like that?"

"The first sip changed my life."

He slapped the table. "I knew all those posts from Blue Tokai were fake. I can't believe they didn't excommunicate you."

"Why would they? I'm like one of their best customers," she grimaced at the bitter coffee. "This coffee though is absolute trash, I can't even right now."

He watched her features brighten as they walked the passage leading to their room. It opened up to a wall with bougainvillea vines creeping up one side and he'd never seen a smile that wide.

"Can you take a picture of me? I love these flowers."

It wasn't a demand.

"Wait, why don't you join in?" She pulled him close to her side and turned the phone in his hands to take the photo.

She was glowing in the shade of those violently pink flowers. He asked her if she wanted one and she pointed to the special one, in full bloom with white pips. He gently took it off the vine and she speared it straight through her hair.

They walked around the fort, which wasn't that big but it had winding narrow passages that led to different corners. At one point they found themselves facing the swimming pool, with a view of the hills sprawling on one side and a row of white chairs to the other. The sun was setting and the air was pleasantly cool now. While walking back to their room they discovered another winding passage that led them to a private turret with a stone bench running around the boundary. Both declared in unison that they should drink there.

"Why'd you keep the wine in the fridge?"

He regarded her as if she were a monkey.

She rolled her eyes. "I thought you're not supposed to have red wine from the fridge or whatever."

"It has to be at a proper temperature."

"I thought it ruins the flavor to have it cold though, no? Most restaurants they give it at like room temperature."

He gave her an indulgent chuckle. "Trust me on this. I'm going to change everything you know about wine."

She held in a cough. Laksh was right of course, red wine and pot tasted like chocolate on her tongue. Either that or she was horribly high and had no idea of what was happening. She was dizzy in the way of reading a book in a moving car, as if her soul was moving in circles beyond the limitation of her body. Her limbs felt heavy but her fingers were nimble. More than once, unintentionally, in passing the joint and between sips from the bottle – plastic glasses abandoned on the grass below – their touch lingered. Electricity crackled when skin met skin and they were floating on a bed of dreams. She followed him down the precarious stone steps, hands on his shoulders for support, bubbled giggles aplenty.

Aside from them, there were two separate groups at dinner. Occupancy was low due to the time of year and by the following day they would have the fort to themselves. They shared a small plate of spicy *biryani* and pineapple *raita*, and it was the best meal Sana had ever eaten.

They took a walk around the pool to settle down, laughing uncontrollably when either one had to stop for a burp. She lit a cigarette and they shared it, leaning close against the low wall overlooking the dark hills. They walked back to the room in silence. Lakshman brought out his iPad and they laughed till their stomachs hurt watching old episodes of Rick and Morty. He ran around the room dramatically re-enacting their favourite bits. They took more wine and a pack of cards back to their private mezzanine. The clouds above had cleared away and a bright moon hung high in the night sky. Somewhere in the distant fields they heard a dog barking over and over again and they wondered if he barked at the moon. The empty bottle was on its side and the last game lay abandoned. Sana and Lakshman had fallen into silence.

"Don't you think everyone's really desperate to fill up silences these days?"

She looked at him and smiled.

"I think it's because people are afraid of their own thoughts when there's nothing to talk about."

"I think everyone is so insecure they start wondering what the other person is thinking when they're not saying anything. And if they're thinking about them, and *what* they're thinking about them. Or if they're not thinking about them, why are they *not* thinking about them."

She giggled. "You think too much."

He scooted closer to her and draped an arm around her.

"No really, have you ever shared a moment like this with anyone else? Where you're sitting in absolute silence and there's no need to talk and it's okay not to and ... I don't know you just look at the moon or the stars or whatever."

"To be fair you can't see much of the night sky these days, especially from my place."

He shot her a look.

"But I know what you mean, and no. I haven't."

She leaned her head back to rest on his arm. He pulled out his phone from the side pocket, trying very hard not to disturb her head with the other arm. The softest song floated around them.

She rolled her head toward him. "Should I get some more wine?"

He turned to look at her and once more their faces were too close. She took in the perfect slope of his nose, long and steady. His jaw where a light stubble bloomed, the perfect cupid's bow descending into lips that were parted slightly. And the full force of him was locked in his eyes, warm and brown with a ring of fire around the pupil so kingly it avoided the whole wolfish trope entirely.

"I'll get some more wine", she unfurled from the bench.

Back in the bathroom she tied up her hair and splashed water on her burning face. Why she'd thought it was okay to not carry any makeup was beyond her understanding, she could've used a touch right then. Pinching and patting her cheeks, she grabbed the wine and headed back.

Lakshman was waiting as she'd left him, song playing in the softest volume. She walked right up to him, grandly showing off the wine and he pulled her close, holding her by the waist. He pressed his cheek against her stomach and she had nowhere left to look or run. Her fingers were tender through his thicket of soft brown hair. Neither backed down even as the song drawled to an end. This wasn't the first time they were hugging or that she was playing with his hair. Yet this was the first time it felt so intimate.

"Tell me two truths and a lie."

She set the wine bottle down beside him and he held her close again.

"Is this a new game we're playing?"

"Come on."

She hummed aloud in thought.

"I'm scared I'll die alone, without anyone whom I love and who loves me. And I'll be obsolete, gone without leaving behind something meaningful."

"How will your Instagram followers survive," he tittered softly.

Laksh twitched as she flicked his ear hard, his hold on her waist still firm.

"I would be *devastated* if mom doesn't come back from her trip soon."

"I love my name, but everyone just calls me Sana now and I think it's too late to go back to it."

He turned his head up to look at her.

"The second one is a lie. You loose."

They laughed and opened the wine for her to serve the punishment.

"So does this mean I can call you Sunaina now?"

She considered it.

"Yeah, I don't see how it changed anything though."

"Okay, wait so one round of Stone-Paper-Scissors and if you lose you have to change your Instagram name. Better yet, you have to let *me* change it for you!"

"Wow, what the fuck. Firstly, what are these games even, and *you* mister still have your turn to go with two truths and a lie!"

"First you go then I go."

"And if you lose?"

"If I lose", he paused for effect, "you can drive my car around for the next week!"

Her new Instagram handle was @dumplingKochhar.

"You make me sick."

He laughed as he updated her name on his phone to Sunaina.

"No dumpling there?"

"No, I'll add that in as your place of work. But now I can see you calling and not your social media alter ego."

"Shut up. It's your turn now."

"Fine fine, Stone-Paper-Scissor let's go."

She took a deep swig. "If you lose, you have to stop being a fuckboy."

"Okay hold up, why do you think I'm a fuckboy?"

"Because you are."

"You've got me confused with my brother."

She shot him a look.

"I'm really sorry about that by the way", he took her hand in both of his. "If there was anything I could do to make up for it I would."

Her expression softened. "It's okay Lakshman, it happened too long ago to keep thinking about it."

He pulled her into a hug.

"Fine, if you lose, I get your car for a whole week."

He laughed, "and what if you lose?"

"I think I've lost enough dignity for a night! I'm not losing."

She lost again but they didn't do anything about it. She imagined their voices reaching far into the dark fields, how they'd look on their little balcony.

The fort lights were switched off, they looked at the time and it was hours past midnight. The air grew cooler, as though the bulbs had kept them toasty all the while. They resumed their position beside each other, her head resting on his arm.

She could feel his voice reverberate in his chest when he spoke.

"So my turn again, is it?"

"Yeah, two truths one lie."

"Are you sure? I think it's your turn."

She handed him the bottle and nodded.

He drained the last of it and set it aside.

"Okay here goes."

Sana turned her head up to him, the moon cast a perfect silhouette on his face as he spoke.

"We are floating in space. No one knows what's going on. And I love you."

Gayatri peeked her head in.

Surya looked up from her laptop. "What's up?"

"I was heading out, just came to change my shoes. I'm going to Murthal with Jimmy and Karishma for paranthas do you want to me to get you anything?"

"It'll be cold by the time you get back I think."

"Oh right," Gayatri chewed her lip, "do you maybe want to come along?"

"No it's fine I'm pretty sleepy actually."

The door started to close.

"Gayatri, wait! Isn't Murthal like halfway to Chandigarh or something?"

"I don't know it's not that far."

"Who's driving?"

"I'll drive there, Jimmy on the way back."

"Be careful okay? It looks like it's going to rain again."

She beamed at her stepsister and left.

Surya plugged in her earphones, "Sorry about that. Where were we?"

"How cute were you just now" Dhiraj chuckled. "Was that your cousin or the new sister?"

She squeezed her thighs together and blushed.

"Shut up, where were we?"

"Okay so Thai or Italian?"

"Italian, I hate the taste of coconut."

"Really? What do you do with South Indian food?"

"It's not my favorite honestly."

"ARE YOU SERIOUS? How can you not like South Indian food?"

She laughed. "Why is that such a big deal? I just prefer like normal people food."

"But it is normal people food! Not liking that is like hating ice cream. You can't hate ice cream, okay?"

"I don't. I can have a full meal just of ice cream."

"Mmm I could have some ice cream off of you for a full meal."

She shivered with excitement.

"Wait, so you'll meet me midway or something?"

"Don't be stupid babe I'll pick you up. Be ready by 7."

"Wow is any restaurant even open that early for dinner?"

"It'll take us an hour easily with traffic and then we can get a drink before dinner no?"

Surya wondered when might be the right time to tell him about her low tolerance for alcohol. She was the designated driver every weekend, roaming around parties with a barely touched glass of whiskey sour, taking sips and wincing behind her hand. One time she'd puked because there was only beer and her burp was so rancid it had burnt her from the inside. It didn't help that she happened to be at dinner with her mum, Gayatri and her brilliant chief of surgery dad-of-the-year, Dev. They'd put forth the idea of living in the same house and Surya had spluttered into her napkin. Dev and Geetika were terribly upset, though Gayatri didn't seem to care. Then there was the time in Bangkok when she almost took her top off during karaoke night, but it wasn't half as bad.

She looked back at Dhiraj and fantasized tracing his razor sharp cheekbones with her fingers. The wiry oversize frames and thick curly hair made him absolutely irresistible. Although she wouldn't admit to it, Surya wondered what was wrong with him, where he was hiding his flaws. The most probable one was that he was a sexual deviant, they'd both been very open about the fact that it wasn't an exclusive thing between them. Dhiraj even mentioned that if she ever wanted to experiment he was open to most things, which could literally open a black hole of messed up shit. Threesomes were too racy for most erotica, and she wasn't too keen on the idea of sharing. Worse still, he could very probably have a wife on the side, with a kid or two. Not that it had stopped her in the past, but how could she start the next chapter of her life by repeating old mistakes? Surya reasoned with herself – having seen the outcome of girls demanding a definition to relationships, might it be so bad to go with the flow? Her perspective was her own, she decided.

From the corner of her eye she saw it descend, slowly at first with its legs gracefully looped together and then faster as it drooped to the floor. Just as it was scuttling away to her bathroom, Surya leapt up and smashed the daddy long legs with her slipper. Dhiraj laughed on the other end of the call.

"Woah, did you see that too?"

She turned back. "No what happened?"

Thunder crackled through the sky.

Surya walked over to her window and saw the bolts of lightning wreaking havoc in the purple sky.

"Be ready, I'm picking you up."

"Where are we going?" she asked already undressing.

"My favourite spot to watch lightning." He sniggered.

"Oh my," she sighed, "if you keep saying these things I swear I'll *have* to fall in love with you."

"Why don't you then?"

They were driving past Mahipalpur to the tunes of old Bally Sagoo songs, down the flyover where neon signs and tall billboards pierced the sky. Everyone had a habit of laughing at those low budget hotels, saying that they rented rooms out on an hourly basis for lonely couples with nowhere else to go, but really that somehow made them more charming. It was one of Surya's favourite things about the drive to Gurgaon, the reds and yellows and blinking whites. She always wondered what clandestine affairs went on behind those glass windows, what tired souls slumped on those beds by themselves; who else, if anyone, was there.

"You know this stretch always kinda reminds me of the Vegas strip."

"Really?"

"Yeah. I don't know what it is though." She pulled her hair to one side, "It's not the lights. It's something else"

"The lights get very silent you know. Some nights if you drive past them and there's hardly anyone on the road ..."

She looked at him.

"It's beautiful."

"Yeah. I bet it is."

"I've never been to Vegas myself so I'll have to take your word for it" he switched off the air conditioner as she lit a cigarette.

"When I went I couldn't drink or go to a lot of places, so most of my trip was just super touristy stuff and all."

"Why?"

"I was only eighteen ya, and fake IDs don't work everywhere."

He nodded sagely. Light sprays of rain smattered across the windshield.

"I'll take you sometime."

"To Vegas?"

"Yeah"

She regretted it immediately. That was such a weird thing to say, more so on a first date with someone she'd spent all of five hours in her life on a random Pokémon Go date-thing. She looked back out the window and crumpled into herself. To at once shine a light so far into the future where they might still be together, or hint that she would *want* them to be together, it was enough to drive her to suicide. When she looked back to him, he had a weird cocked eyebrow and she blushed, turning back to the comfort of the lights.

"That was stupid ..." she muttered.

He laughed as if he'd been holding it in. "Stop, it's fine. No judgments here."

"No I'm sorry I just made everything so awkward."

"For whom?"

She struggled to find an answer that wasn't narcissistic because Dhiraj was unfazed as ever.

"Anyway, where are we going tonight?"

"We're getting sushi from a food truck, there's wine in the back seat, and we're going to park at this particular spot where you can see the whole sky."

She shuddered a sigh. "Is there anything else or can we just get married already?"

The sound of his unbridled laugh set her on fire from within.

The look on his face when the basket of wasabi fries came in told her everything she needed to know, it told her she was already falling for him. He saw the difference in her, as if someone had whispered a permission to let go halfway through her second glass of wine. She threw her head back when she laughed, she didn't care about the grease on her fingers or spilling soy sauce on her tshirt. Surya Shroff was completely at ease in the illusion that they were the only two people who existed in that moment.

When he reached out and plucked the cigarette from her mouth to take a drag, when he put a hand through her hair, when he smiled at her three seconds too long, it wasn't cheap. She looked at his face and wondered when the entitlement would come through, the one that made him believe she had to sleep with him for making her have such a good time. She told herself to give it one hour, the last hour of the night before, and then she would think no more of it. And it never came; his face had that boyish vulnerability successfully disarming her with every crack of thunder.

She wasn't aware of her fidgeting hands till he had them wrapped in his. Surya looked down and saw the dent in her little finger – the strangest deformity caused by years of typing with one hand. She wove her fingers through his and found a similar though not as deep indentation on his right hand. They kissed as the streetlights dimmed unaware that lightning had struck ground close by.

He unhooked his chin from the space where her neck curved into a shoulder. The world was upside down and his guts churned. His mouth felt like someone had stuffed it with cotton balls, and the tiny slivers of dawn peeking in from the window were like death rays. Sunaina was snuggled deep into his chest, hands curled up in tiny fists under her chin. He tentatively reached out for water and drank the whole bottle, drifting back to sleep almost immediately.

Lakshman woke up again when she turned to her side, so they were spooning, but sleep took over again.

The bed was possibly the most comfortable one she'd ever slept on. The way the blanket cocooned her feet it was like being in a cloud burrito, except it was possible that the actual bed had nothing to do with it. The arm around her was strong, the chest breathing against her back a solid wall of warmth. She couldn't not take his hand and bring it to her lips.

They woke up and parted with sleepy smiles and a good morning. While she brushed her teeth he stood outside and smoked, filling his lungs with the cool mid-morning air. She came out and looped an arm around his neck, reaching out for the cigarette. Sharing his cigarette, holding him, it was as easy as breathing.

They went for a breakfast of toast and eggs with extra strong coffee and it was back to the room. The temperature was rising again and the fort didn't offer much shade. An hour's nap later, they walked down to the pool armed with their Raybans and sunblock.

Lakshman held onto her things as she walked right into the pool, smoothly swimming to the other side. Unsurprisingly he had another playlist humming up from the little speaker as the poolside chair was set up. He took the lotion and rubbed it all over, giving her incentive to come up for air.

He looked glorious in that sunlight, just beginning to sweat; she wiped her hands and took a photo. He didn't even look and she trailed circles around him like a hawk, taking photos. He cocked a smile and grabbed the phone from her. His own jump into the pool wasn't as graceful because he was too focused on taking her down with him. They called for beer that came with glasses so cold they had icicles on the surface. The sky above them was the bluest blue they'd ever seen.

He wiped her brow with a thumb. "You look so beautiful right now."

She blushed behind her sunglasses.

"What about every other day?"

“Every other day you’re like a five or whatever. Right now you’re something else.”

He grazed the skin of her neck.

“Why’d you cut your hair, Sunaina?”

The sound of her name on his lips set loose a thousand and one butterflies in her.

“You don’t like it like this?”

“I love it like this.” He moved closer to her.

She pushed herself up to sit by the edge and he positioned himself so her leg was draped over one of his shoulders, barely inches away from his cheek. She realized if he in that moment were to kiss her leg she might die.

“I love this, thanks for bringing me with you.”

He tilted his head and grazed her leg with the side of his head.

“It reminds me of the pool we have at my granddad’s house. The one in the hills.”

“Wow I haven’t been there since ... do you remember the last time we went there?”

“I think it was the summer vacation of ‘02, no?”

They smiled at the memory of running through the tomato garden, a large house with beige walls surrounded by mountains on all sides. The entire length of the back of the house was covered with bougainvillea, which her granddad primed himself, trimming and replanting whenever necessary. It was the real pride of his life, aside from his children because Hassan was ignorant, because Geetu couldn’t keep her shit together, and because Kama, well with her the proverbial shit had hit the fan a long time ago.

Sunaina remembered endless days spent with fresh juice and pancakes under the wall of flowers. The table was somewhat of a family union, a place where everyone had a proper seat with proper plate settings. It was where Commander Kochhar had seen his grandchildren grow up, growing taller every year till their end of the table didn’t look as empty. She and Surya had run their summers around the garden picking wildflowers for the table to surprise him.

"Sorry I'm just getting carried away" she laughed.

He kissed her leg, handing the cigarette back to her.

"Don't be. I'm glad this place made you think of him." And then, "I've missed you".

She wrapped a lock of his hair around her finger. "I've missed you too."

They drank their beer with the warm sun beating down on them, fiddling in and out of the pool, and everything was good. There was no talk of the people they'd left behind or things that didn't matter anymore. He made her turn off all notifications so her phone wouldn't constantly be buzzing where they'd abandoned it. She fought the now familiar urge to fling it like a discus over the ledge. She walked out of the pool and draped one of the enormous blue and white striped towels around her, parading with the grace of a pageant queen. He took a photo that was more blur than her but saved it anyway. It was Sunaina as no one looked at her, hair curling as it dried, all signs of stress gone from her forehead. He pulled two chairs together so they could sit close together while he rolled a joint. She stared at him humming softly whenever a song sounded familiar.

Lakshman lit the joint and blew the smoke straight into her face. She inhaled deeply and smiled. The wind itself grew cooler as bulbous clouds gathered above them. They lay back and he showed her silver linings that stretched almost all the way across the sky. She leaned over him and taught him blowbacks and they just lazed there giggling with hands cupping their mouths. Soon it was too cool to get back into the pool or maybe they were just too high, so they sat with their feet dipped in for a while. The sun vanished behind concrete clouds. In the sudden threat of a storm, the colours around them bloomed vibrantly. She loved when that happened, looking back at the fort walls she could see where the foliage was veining up in bursts of green against manila.

Flip flops and all in hand, they ran back to the room just as the rain began pelting at them. Taking a hot shower didn't help much, it possibly made the high worse. The room was freezing and Lakshman was sitting cross legged on the floor with the doors open and he looked at her, his profile brilliantly illuminated, and she knew she was falling. She knelt behind him and wrapped him in her arms. His nose skimmed her neck and planted a soft kiss.

"Do you want some uncle chips?"

He beamed at her, "That's the best thing anyone's ever said to me in my life."

The ride home had been torture. She was sure they'd left a piece of them back at the fort, wrapped up in that stupidly soft blanket. She'd kept pace with conversation, he'd made jokes throughout, but their hearts weren't in it. As the sun had set behind them they drove in silence. Her hand was perched between them so he could hold it whenever his was free. Sometimes he'd take their entwined fingers and press them to his lips, not in an obvious kiss but something more reverent.

In no time at all she found herself staring down her front door with a hand raised to the doorbell, fighting it for as long as she could. He watched her in silence from the car. They heaved a sigh in unison, she unaware of his watchful gaze. Chanda opened the door and dramatically welcomed her home. As if on instinct she looked back right before entering and waved at him, a final fleeting moment of that stolen happiness returned. The door closed with a loud bang but it fell on deaf ears. Sunaina felt the blood drain from her face as a shadow moved through the living room, her father's inimitable form walking to the bar.

"Dad" she spoke tentatively, peeking through the door.

"Sana! My Darling! How are you?" he swooped her up in a grand embrace.

Hassan Kochhar only loved two things in life, his beautiful daughter and making obscene amounts of money. He had a penchant for single malts, Cuban cigars, and casual flirting he liked to refer to as 'healthy'. It wasn't clear, nor may it ever be, whether he actually enjoyed these things or whether they were borrowed ideals of the finer things in life inherited from his own father.

In growing up Sunaina had felt him drift further and further away. Somewhere between chartered work trips and private parties of the social club, she'd lost her dad. The days when he used to make her sit on his shoulders, run around after her, be her best friend, they were now only memories that were so sweet they tasted bitter. She held on to them like she held on to old photographs in which she didn't look nice, tucked into the last page of the photo album.

"I'm good papa, this is quite a surprise though ..."

She watched him pour a drink, telling herself it wasn't a dream.

"I hope it's a good one," he laughed aloud. It wasn't his real laugh though, it was the kinds he saved for parties or when he was hosting a formal dinner. It was the laugh that sounded wholehearted but lacked any real emotion, one that she'd heard far too many times.

"Of course papa. I'm just ... I can't believe you're actually here. I haven't seen you in so long."

Eleven months, she reminded herself.

"I know my love I know, but now I'm here Sana. Papa's home and he's not leaving you."

"But what–"

"Sit down I need to have a word with you Sana." She gawked at him. "I'm serious, please sit with me for a bit. I have something I want to share with you."

The last time they'd had a conversation was when he had entered her room late in the evening to explain the situation between Surya's mom and Gayatri's dad.

Something didn't feel right.

"Where's mumma, isn't she with you?"

"Sana, could you please have a seat and let me explain. I've had a very long flight and I'm fucking exhausted right now."

She pushed down that slow burn of dread churning her gut and sat next to him.

“Look Sana, you’re grown up now and I honestly don’t see any point in beating around the bush about this. I just want you to know that your mother and I love you very much beta, we do. We love you till the end of the earth” she closed her eyes and wished he would stop there, “but honestly this whole situation between me and that woman isn’t working out anymore.”

“PAPA!?”

“I can’t do it anymore. I just cannot see a way of making things work. She’s just on her own bloody trip in life and I am … I’m just done.”

“What do you mean you’re done?” Her eyes stung with tears she’d held back all day.

“We’re filing for a divorce. I can’t fucking be married to that woman anymore.”

“But what about me?” she couldn’t fight the tears anymore.

“What about *me*, Sana?” his voice echoed off the walls. “What. About. Me.”

She couldn’t breathe.

“You know she’s off frolicking in Europe with her *boyfriend* right now?”

She left the couch, the room, hand to heaving chest.

“He used to work in my fucking office. MY FUCKING OFFICE, SANA! She’s gone. The bitch is fucking gone. I’ve sent her the papers and told her never to show her face here again.”

It was more than she could swallow.

Sunaina ran blindly out of the room, out the house, out of the gate. The smell of those sweet nocturnal flowers made the air heavy, so heavy she couldn’t breathe. It was as if when night had fallen it brought out a feverish heat and that heat rose up from the earth in waves. Tears diagonally streaking down her face, she didn’t stop running.

She didn’t stop till she heard his voice calling out to her. Lakshman was standing under one of the streetlights with a wistful cigarette, the purple-amber sky blazing behind him. The sight of him filled up her heart. That hole she didn't know he'd left behind fixed itself. And she ran into him with a kiss that nearly knocked him off his feet.

He held on to her for dear life, even as he staggered backwards. It was a single kiss that broke into a thousand smaller kisses, and they were gasping for breath.

"I love you," she looked into his eyes. "I think I've always loved you."

"I love you Sunaina," he gasped back at her.

"My parents split up," she could taste the salt of her tears.

He grabbed her and kissed her again, his lips more gentle this time. There wasn't an urgency in his kiss, it was an affirmation.

"Let's get out of here."

He grabbed her hand and ran towards his house, Rover yipping at their feet with shared excitement. Lakshman's dog was the only one she knew of who went for walks without his leash. The retriever hurried past them through the kitchen door and she could hear him lapping at his bowl through the garage in excitement.

"Where are we going Laksh?"

He fished out a faded helmet that looked like it could fit her.

"Anywhere!"

It was her first time on a bike. Sunaina had her heart in her throat but with her arms around his waist she could've made it to the moon without flinching. Even with all the pollution and the humidity, when the wind whipped around them it was magic. They tore down the highway, the streetlights watching over them like sentinels. The cityscape started to disperse and the buildings grew smaller, the spaces between them expanded, and at one point from the road they could only see vast open land that was bathed in that same amber glow. They turned back around just after the sprawling grounds of the Buddh Circuit. She smiled into the back of his shirt, breathing in the shadows and the pale light of the moon.

There was barely a whisper beyond the occasional car or truck, even they didn't honk on that wide open road. She held on to Lakshman and allowed the wind to wipe away the inherited bullshit of her selfish family.

He took her for a drive through the circles of Connaught Place, the gamut of brightly lit bars staring back at them in stupefied silence. The massive Indian flag that made up the central roundabout oddly unremarkable at night with no one to look at it. They wondered why no one had wrapped it up.

It was way past midnight by the time they made it to India Gate. He bought her cotton candy and soft ice cream because there was nothing much left to look at once they'd looped around the monument.

"So," she licked the melting ice cream off the side of the cone, "when can I ask you out on a proper date?"

He smirked "You want to go out on a date?"

"Yeah I think that'd be nice. We should dress up, go out and get dinner somewhere."

"Friday. I'll pick you up."

He held up the ice cream cone and dramatically finished it in one bite.

"I thought this *was* our first date" she smiled ruefully.

He melted into a smile. "That's irrelevant."

She bought him a red rose even though it had wilted from being carried around all day, weary from being thrust into car windows and other couples. The young girl grinned at them and wished for their happy future before running over to another couple. They shared a cigarette and had warm popcorn straight off the heat. She kissed him before he put his helmet on and they wove themselves back into the night.

Chapter SIX

CANDY CIGARETTES

At the age of seventy eight, Commander Asim Kochhar considered his daily walk of seven and a half kilometres an exemplary display of fitness. He would walk past the small shops selling maggi and hot tea, through the village with its dozen or so houses. It was one of the most charming hamlets around, with every house an eclectic personality on its own; yet they all came together in one harmonious picture. The mountain air was clean and pure and his walks mostly meditative. He'd walk all the way to the small café near the bridge so he could sit with Leela and talk books over butter cookies and rhododendron tea.

"You're crazy," he'd always say, "you put too much syrup in the tea."

"I do it so that all your teeth fall out and then I won't have to hear you talk so much."

Asim wasn't just a customer at the Himalayan Tea Stall, over the years it had grown on him in more ways than one. He had taken it upon himself to teach Leela how to read and write in English, how to manage her accounts, he taught her what it meant to yearn for more in life. In the terrible snowstorm two years ago, the back wall had completely caved in and Leela had

had no money to fix it. Her father had started the teashop as a means for her husband to make his daily bread but Sachin was born an idiot. He drank at night and slept through the day and in a fateful moment the river took him away.

She did her part in mourning the loss of a husband but taking over all of the work had been a greater joy. It was the happiness of finally fulfilling her life's purpose. When the snow fell that year it took a toll not just on her father's health but also the backbone of the little stall. The choice was clear but not an easy one; she needed the money for his treatment. Asim had personally funded and overlooked the entire repairs while she took care of her dying father.

At a young age Leela had understood the importance of accepting help when she needed it, precocious even as a teenager she held pride in her ability to gauge both sides of a problem. In return for his patronage, although she always told herself it would never repay her debt, Asim had free tea and cookies for life – regardless of how irksome he found the biscuit crumbs on his polo shirts. She'd often tell him the biscuits were made crumblier just to ruin his precious t-shirts. He was also the guinea pig for any new recipe that she wanted to try out. The cookbooks he offered to bring her had everything under the sun but she'd always point to the fruit and veg sellers.

"But why would I want to make those", she reasoned, "wouldn't it be better to make my own recipes? It's not like we're lacking any ingredients here in the village."

It was then that he decided to expand his backyard garden into a slightly larger farm, one that Leela could help tend to. He found her a book on gardening and curing that kept her busy for most of the month – and their lessons continued. In exchange for her help on the farm, Leela could use the produce at her tea stall, where she then started serving instant noodles with spiced veggies and omelettes with yak cheese on toast.

However none of these had cemented their bond as strong as the games of chess, Asim having found a formidable opponent after many years. So on days when her head hurt and she didn't want to read her lessons or talk of things here and there, she and the Commander played chess in silent rapture. If the weather was particularly pleasant, they'd walk down to the riverside to one of the cafés where tourists smoked joints and the coffee was actually good, and one could hear the water gushing past. On those days he'd only make it back by nightfall, always declining her offer to walk him home.

The house was too big for him. Even with the housekeeper, the cook, the servants, gardener and driver, it was too big for Asim. The rooms had grown weary of gathering cobwebs and being cleaned out. The walls flinched from their yearly paint jobs because every year he hoped the family would come by for Diwali, or a summertime vacation. It had been eight years since they'd all been under the same roof. Now their holidays involved ten hour flights and yachts, or at least that's what he could tell from Facebook updates.

The last time was when his son had driven up to propose selling the house and putting the money into opening up a nightclub. He wasn't sure what had angered him more, the fact that his son had an ulterior motive to come see him or the fact that he wanted to sell off a house Asim had literally built with his own hands. He chose to believe the latter. If he'd had a drink that night Asim would've thrashed him for the sheer idiocy. Of course since his outright refusal, Hassan hadn't called, or texted, or emailed. However that conversation had sown the seeds for a different idea – one that excited the very ends of his moustache – but true to form, the Commander had planned to sit down and properly plan out the whole idea. Decisions such as these needed an unburdened mind and a list of pros and cons, of possible investments and expenditures required. He knew all of what had to be written down, he just never did it. Instead he went about his day per usual waking up and overlooking the household chores while tea and breakfast was made, then yoga, then a walk to the village.

He harboured an immense pride toward the house, there were no exaggerations when he said he had built it himself. Of course the percentage of involvement was but a minute detail, no one needed to know what had gone down in the planning or the hiring of a contractor whom he'd strong-armed till the four walls went up. Sometimes at night he'd find himself thinking about those early years, right after he'd retired and the house still had its first coat of paint and the whole family was there. The weekend brunches, cricket matches in the untamed backyard, slow-dancing with his wife at the regiment's bittersweet reunion. Those were the days he missed the most, of bridge at the social club, formal dinners with preplanned course meals, the look of pride in his wife's eyes under the glittering chandelier. These things Asim kept safe in the corner of his mind, memories echoing with the faded glamour of old photographs – some nights he'd open the heavyset photo albums. Those mustard walls were still up but they felt cavernous with just him and a lone lightbulb to look through those pages.

"Why don't you just ask them to come see you sometime?" She placed a hot cup of tea in front of him.

"Why don't they ask to come themselves?"

Leela reprimanded him with raised eyebrows.

"Oh come on, Leela! It's not that hard ..."

"That's exactly my point. Why are you so afraid to tell them you want to see them?"

"I will have you know madam that I'm not *afraid* –"

"That's not what I meant." She sighed and folded away the plastic chessboard. "Look what I'm trying to say is that family's important, you should see each other and spend time as often as you can because before you know it it'll be too late."

He stared at her impassively, fingers smoothening his crisp moustache.

"You're practically by yourself in that stupidly big house except for one servant and a caretaker."

"Dipali is not a *caretaker*, I'm still able to take care of myself thank you very much."

"I'm just saying I think it'll be good if you just have some company there from time to time. Someone who's your family, who knows you. You spend most of your time here and –"

"I spend my time here because I like it. And because I'm hoping that one day this sweet tea of yours really does poison me and relieve me of this burden."

She clicked her tongue at him. "Your life is anything but a burden Commander-*saab*!"

"Oh please Leela, have you seen your handwriting? It could drive anyone blind. Besides, if anyone from my family wants to see me they should, I've even learnt how to make Skype calls now. I should've just raised you instead; you at least wouldn't have been as ungrateful as that lot. Possibly you would've turned out to be a better daughter, helped me run the Bed & Breakfast."

She shot him a quizzical look.

"Do you remember when he came last and proposed selling off the house?"

"I can't afford you breaking any more glasses here." She deadpanned.

He waved a hand dismissively. "Your glasses can go right to hell with my son. Anyway, it got me thinking that since no one is living in those rooms I could rent them out during the tourist season. Fix anything that needs fixing and host maybe a couple or two, peaceful travelers you know, the kinds that won't meddle around or hassle me too much. We could serve them breakfast and stuff, make a whole package out of it."

She took a seat by the window.

"Granted it would increase the traffic a little bit, but if you think about it having some more tourists drive by the village and actually staying here is perfect for everyone. Can you imagine how much Abhinandan can sell his chips and popcorn for? And how many more people would stop by here for tea?"

Leela pulled herself out of the dream where she was the Commander's daughter and looked around her little shop.

"More people coming here for tea would be good." Her voice was small but hopeful. "But you can't just start a business like this out of nowhere. You'll have to go and speak to *sarpanch*-ji and take his permission, speak to some people around and get them to support you. I remember how much work *baba* had to do just to start this little stall."

"Well I have your support don't I?"

"Of course you do." She scratched at a spot on the glass table.

"Good. So next time we're down by the river, we can speak to Anil and see how he feels about it. The more local business owners supporting me the better it'll be."

She gathered her things and made to leave the table. "Don't be so quick to bet on Anil's support."

"Let's hope for the best my dear, let us hope for the best." He winced and finished the remainder of his tea.

Hi Daddy

Hope you're doing well!

I'm sorry it's been some time since I wrote you a proper letter, things here have been running on full steam and I just haven't been able to take time out to put everything down on paper for you. The book is set to come out in a month, but hopefully I will have a few copies beforehand and I can send one to you. I don't know exactly when this letter also will reach you.

I was actually thinking I'll send Ria for a few days to stay with you and she can bring you a copy of the book. Your feedback means so much to me and I hope I get to hear it soon. Just a quick trip before her summer vacations get over you know maybe she and Surya can take a train or something – but trains have so many people I don't know how I feel about letting two girls travel alone like that.

Maybe it would be a better idea to hire a car and they can just travel safely. I made some mixed pickle also I'll send a jar for you! I swear daddy it tastes just like the pickle that mom used to make – I had the first bite and almost cried.

I think it's so good that you're helping that girl learn English, really when I read your last letter my heart was just bursting with joy. I'm thinking I too should start some home lessons, maybe for the maid's daughter or something. Although I think it's better if Ria takes them I don't know how comfortable I would be in teaching a random person like that na?

I was looking at some old photographs of the house – sending one of them with the letter – it's from that day, if I remember correctly, when you had bought the first batch of bougainvillea and how we had such a fuss over who will plant the first pod. You should see how happy mom looks in the photo I can't even tell you it's so beautiful papa. I wish sometimes that she could've seen how our children are growing up. Do you remember how she used to make us all dress up so nicely for those family photos? I was thinking about the old house in Cochin the one where all five of us are in white, Geetu had such a bad fight with me because I wore one of her frocks and Hassan had those silly sunglasses which he refused to take off even though it wasn't sunny. I guess I just want you to know how much I love you and miss you papa. I think about you every day, although with the shameless amount of phone calls I make to you I think you know that already.

I'm also sending a small pack of candy cigarettes, I didn't want to tell you over the phone when I found them online – there's like only one place that still makes them now. I remember when all of us would go for walks in the market and oh we used to eat so much junk and then have ice cream and you'd always get us the Phantom cigarettes. Do you remember how much mumma used to say no and she would get so annoyed but you did it anyway and she'd smile anyway.

All that aside, I do need to discuss something which has developed recently, and I don't know maybe it's a habit I have picked up from you I don't even know if it's a good one or bad. Hassan and Tina got divorced. I don't know all the details till now but she's left the house papa and Hassan you know I'm sure he's happy but he's just become a teenager again. It's actually like he's going through the younger years all over again, that man has not changed one bit! I think you need to talk to him about it because he's not talking to me or Geetu, and I'm sure he's not talking to Sunaina about it because honestly I don't think that girl would understand anything if it doesn't have to do with her. I don't know why you don't see it but that girl just didn't have the right upbringing because of Tina. That woman by the way has left the house; did I already write that? I don't know it's just a big mess right now over there and were I able you know I would've gone there to personally slap some sense into him. But the book actually has kept me really busy and then I've been writing some essays also for my online lectures and all. I think it's good to be busy, otherwise I would just go mental in my own house. As far as I know with Geetu everything is going very very well, touchwood! I know you haven't met Devendra for a while now but I'll try and get them both to come see you soon. Maybe they can go with Ria and Surya!! I'll plan it out don't worry, you please take care of yourself and take it easy – I was a little worried when you mentioned how much tea you're having these days. Don't drink too much if you are by yourself it's not healthy. Be happy, papa.

See you soon

With all my love,
Kama.

The house was silent as a grave except the clink of ice and the sniff of a tear. In the two weeks since Kama's letter had arrived Asim had reread it a few times, rolling it around his mind like a slowly dissolving pill. As always there were things in her letter unnecessarily written, Kama had always had a flair for saying more than required but perhaps it wasn't so much to remind him of those memories as it was for herself. She also never realized he didn't like the candy cigarettes any more than their mother had, but the smile it brought on their face was what he really lived for. He swallowed hard but that chokehold of memories didn't let go. He traced the box with his fingers, almost amused by how small it seemed after all the years and the smiles came back to him. He realized he didn't mind the taste that much really and would make it a point to tell Kama how much he missed her.

Life had dealt his older daughter one of the worst hands and he had watched her pull back from the lowest low. He had watched her suffer more than a deserved share and died a thousand deaths at his helplessness to take her pain away. For the first few weeks she hadn't left her bed, forcing them to hire a nurse to look after her. She refused to walk the five steps to the bathroom door no matter what he said, nor how he said it. How many times Geetika sat by her and held her hand and wept with her, it was a blur.

A full month had passed before Kama had braved a walk around in her own room. The nurse would have to return every alternate day to check in on her although he suspected that was more obligatory than mandated. By the time they had discovered her pregnancy it was too late, and Kama would not leave the house to get an abortion and Asim wasn't sure if he could live with that. He wasn't sure if he could take much more of it at all, really. The gang rape of his daughter was hard enough but to have a grandchild serving as a constant reminder of it was too much for him to cope with. Surely no one deserved such suffering in a single lifetime. It wasn't possible.

However it was the alternate that he couldn't wrap his head around. The concept of an abortion was alien to him, having spent most of his formative years in a village where life was uncomplicated and lacked situations as grave. It was a living thing inside her, it had a conscience. If they had it removed they would be killing a living thing. A half formed person. And then, through motherhood, Kama came back. He could see a glimmer of her older self – though it was clear she'd never really be the same. She simply told him it wasn't his choice to make. The decision was hers and she'd made it and she didn't need help, she didn't need someone to discuss the possible consequences.

"We have enough young children around –"

"I'm not doing this because you may or may not need another grandchild. I'm telling you that this might be my only chance at being a mother. A mother who can see her child from birth, raise him or her from the moment they open their eyes."

"You can very well do that with a surrogate or a thousand different ways! What is the matter with you?"

Geetu had spoken up for the first time, "It will never be the same as giving birth, papa. You'll never understand that feeling, only a woman, only a *mother* can understand."

And thus, Ria Kochhar had been born under the watchful gaze of her mother and her aunt. Asim could count on one hand the number of times he'd met the girl, their interactions mostly perfunctory though not for her lack of trying. There was something just different about her. Different in the way she stood when next to the other girls, different when she spoke, ate her food, dressed herself, everything. The family traits Asim loved seeing bloom in his other grandchildren, Kama was proud to find missing in her daughter.

Against her better judgment, Kama had pushed for open dialogue. Her father had every opportunity to get to know his granddaughter, the door was always open, that and every other clichéd line in the book – her book to be precise. She had decided that she could no longer be miserable in life at the hand of another person, family included. On his part, Asim watched from the sidelines the sensation his daughter became right from her first essay published online. From going viral to spearheading a feminist renaissance, she turned into an overnight bestseller with *The Woman on Trial in Modern Delhi*, making her a celebrity in her own right.

The publishers worked at her behest, arranging all sorts of lectures and PR events via video call. Ria was her full time social media manager, pitching in for signed copy giveaways, personalized letters, moderating group discussions – she'd even made it to a few news debates from her home office. Kama would always share her thoughts and essay drafts with her father, even when he sometimes wished she wouldn't – given their subject matter. However none of the recognition, none of the confidence in her writing, not even her daughter's pleading had helped simmer down her agoraphobia. Over the years it had become her crutch, and when the time was right she hired a contractor on her sister's recommendation to build additions on the far end of the farmhouse. A new room set up for the legal and control team – rape and death threats had become a weekly affair – a room for Ria's work and private tutors; Kama even had her online grocery schedule down to a fine art.

One.

Two.

Three.

Breathe but don't stop.

One.

Two.

Three.

Close your eyes for two seconds.

One.

You are in control.

Two.

You are the creator and destroyer of your own world.

Three.

Wipe the blood from your forehead.

One.

Two.

Three.

Push the knife deeper in his chest.

One. Two. Three.

Ruin him like he ruined you.

One. Two. Three.

One. Two. Three.

One. Two. Three.

One two three. One two three. One two three one two three one two three one two three one two three.

Kama woke up with a deep gasp, frightened more by the sight of her therapist grabbing her shoulders than the almost-memory of straddling the thing. The both of them had sweaty foreheads and shallow breaths.

"What happened?" she clutched her wheezing chest, "I don't remember much but ..."

"It ... I think it might be too much too soon." She massaged her temples. "I sort of lost control of you in the subconscious state. I don't know why it happened but you just stopped responding for a while. I couldn't understand why so I panicked and I tried so hard ... I really tried to bring you out of it but then you started just screaming and thrashing."

"Did I ... Did you know what was going on at all?"

"It wasn't hard to imagine but I'm not going to make any guesses here. If, and only if, you're feeling secure enough to talk about it we can approach the topic in our next session. In the meantime I suggest you avoid anything that can induce stress, and continue writing in your journal."

Kama let her head fall back onto the cushioned arm of the couch. Her heart was pounding and when she held up her hands she could see the violence still vibrating under her skin. She waited for it to ebb away while her therapist scratched notes, the room silent but for a ticking clock.

"It was dark but I could still see his face", she sat up straighter, "but it wasn't his face really. He looked like all of them, like one face spliced seven ways."

The note-taking was broken with a silent look.

"I was on top of him but it was weird, like they show it in the movies you know? And all of it was the same as always but also nothing like it because it felt too real, I swear I can still feel the moisture in my hands."

"And was there anyone else around?"

"I don't know."

"Hmm" she scribbled into her notes.

"It was the energy, I can't explain it. There was this thing in the air like the molecules were all buzzing in tandem with me stabbing him."

She nodded encouragingly.

"And I was sitting on his arms so he couldn't move and I could feel that manic sense of power in my hands." She pinched the bridge of her nose. "I just kept stabbing him over and over and over again."

"Kama, we can stop our session any time you want ..."

"No it's okay. I don't have a problem talking about it –"

"I hope you understand I have certain obligations as your therapist."

Her blood turned cold.

She turned around, no longer bothered by the acid spewing inside her. "What? You're going to report me – is that it? You'll go and tell the court I'm a threat to what – every man out there? That's bloody ridiculous just listen to yourself."

"Listen to me –"

"No you listen to me. I need you to help me, you're on my team you bitch! You're supposed to be helping me get better and not fucking threatening me with this random highbrow bullshit."

"I didn't –"

"No you absolutely didn't", she spat, "because you're a bloody fucking idiot." She threw the first thing within reach. A copy of her own book, the lopsided jacket now staring morosely from the other corner of the room. "You're only giving me clichés like 'you won't get better till you agree to be better' and shit. Well I do agree, I agree veryfuckingmuch right now."

She sat there and watched in silence as Kama simmered down.

"I could feel his warm body under me. I could hear the squish of every slice, the crunch of every bone. I could feel the power, the burning energy of asserting myself and acknowledging my conscious in that moment. I could feel it all, and I'm not bothered by it. It was beautiful. It was like a dream. And I'd do it all over again."

"Okay", she could sense the 'therapist voice' as she'd come to think of it had come back, "before we finish today's session I want you to think over everything one more time. Actually perhaps it's best you do it after a few hours, there isn't any rush. There are chances further details come back to you. I want you to write them down. I want you to think about how you feel about the feelings you just described to me, what is your reaction to feeling that way being in the position you were. Write them down and we will start from there next time."

Kama massaged her temples and waved dismally. Both ladies stood and huffed at each other. Dr. Ritika resigned herself to packing her notebook and folder while Kama straightened out the creases of her loose kurta. It skimmed the edges of her bare ankles as she walked down the wooded hallway to the reinforced window that ran the length of the side of her bungalow. The other woman brushed past her on the way down a spiraling staircase but her eyes were fixed on the flat dusty expanse of the sky. It was an ugly thing, the Delhi sky, especially on late afternoons such as that when the clouds lay swollen with rain. As the front door shut with a heavy thud, locks sliding into place, the corners of her house expanded outward. She turned back to face the now cavernous foyer that in its silence had become the staying place of all her fears. The silence made her teeth grind, the big empty rooms made her skin crawl. She walked through them with eyes lowered, scratching at her drying aging skin. She avoided the mirror, too scared of what might stare back at her. Perhaps it was just her mind playing tricks on her but Kama was almost certain the billowing kurta shuddered with her. She avoided the comfort of her bedroom, there was nothing as horrifying as waking up to nightfall. She avoided Ria's room because last week, when leaving her laundered clothes by the foot of her bed, Kama had found her daughter's journal. She knew the importance of privacy, or at least keeping up the illusion of privacy – after all that's the best a parent can manage sometimes. It was her poetry, she'd unsuccessfully resisted the urge to read the whole lot.

Ria was turning out to be exactly the way she had been as a little girl herself, taking life way too seriously – it showed in her every word. The two verses that she read, though severely disjointed and angst-riddled, were good. It was possibly better than anything Kama had ever written. Every word was attached to the other with the kind of brutal honesty that made her wonder if she even knew who her daughter was. Now, with the ink of her pen drying a little more with each day passing, she found herself thinking about that moleskin pocketbook a little too often.

She sat down at her writing desk feeling the ache of every brittle bone of her body, the daydreams of her ideal novel abandoned by the last empty corner. The back of her tunic clung to her skin, dampened by a cold sweat. Her fingers, even with the comforting cool of a pen between them, hovered stiffly over the empty page. She stared at her useless arthritic hands and waited for the nib to touch the dry surface of her paper but there was nothing left to dream about. Every hour of the past nine months weighed itself down on her narrow shoulders.

'*Something, anything you know what I mean? Just give em something to show that you're at least working on a new project...*' the slick voice of her publicist rang in her ear from memory. '*How was it you put it, you just have to find a better method of pretending to know what you're doing?*'

The skies darkened above her and Kama found herself wondering if a lone afternoon had turned her into a nervous wreck, how would she ever survive two whole weeks without Ria around?

Chapter SEVEN

The Axiom of Icarus

Another Saturday night saw the city come alive. At another typically atypical restaurant, Sunaina sat in her favorite slip dress. There was none of the pressure of a regular date, except an hour had passed and the boy never showed.

Tell Me Lies, Tell Me You Love Me.

The bright sign stared back at her.

She ordered another gin and tonic and threw it back faster than the two before. She ignored the way her heart beat so loud it seemed to jump around in her chest. It was a heady sort of nervousness, like standing at a precipice, an edge, the point of no return.

She shook her head at the burning red glow. "Just call him" she muttered under her breath. "Just call him ... just call him ... just call him" over and over again like a charm to ward of the growing pit inside.

The underside of her knee stuck to the spot where it met her thigh. Every breath grew shorter as she dialed Lakshman's number once more, and as it had been since the night began, the automated voice told her he wasn't in service range. She burrowed with her eyes at everyone crossing her table, nobody wanted to be in her way when she stood up.

Blows to the self-esteem that rank higher than being stood up on a date are few and far between. If a blind date stands you up, there are chances they never made it – or that they came, they saw, they ran. What happens when you know the person whom you're meeting for a date? You know who they are out there in the world and who they are not without another pair of eyes to watch. What about being stood up by someone who's already occupied your mind and refuses to leave? Sana stood in the humid street fighting the chokehold of shame, sorrow, and hunger. She hadn't eaten just so she could fit perfectly into the dress. The two lines she did in the bathroom now worked against her. And so, unsteady on her feet from the top shelf liquor, she had nothing to do but fish for a lighter.

She screamed incoherently at her phone, knocking her leg into the open door as she climbed into the backseat of her car. The tears fell bitterly, in short pained hiccups. If the time was right and Lakshman had voicemail she could've left him a message, she might've been able to vent out her screaming heart. Though perhaps he might've left her a message too, he could've told her that she might never see him again. She called Gayatri, who was at dinner with Geetu and Dev, and then she called Surya, who at the time was headed to meet her family with Dhiraj.

Unfortunately their lack of response to her crisis was the final nail in the coffin. And so, with nothing but the driveway foliage for company Sunaina hobbled to her house with broken heart and wounded knee.

She raised her hand to the fingerprint scanner but the door opened on its own. She blinked away her tears and stepped out of the way as the servant girl rushed outside, nearly tripping on her own feet.

"Chanda? What are you doing here so late –"

"Oh didi you're back so early... uh I-I was well I was, obviously, I mean there was a lot to do today you know because well Vikram wasn't there so I had to – um – take care of everything mostly on my own."

It was the middle of summer but her skin was icy cold when Sunaina touched her, Chanda hadn't been in the kitchen after all.

She looked her all over taking in the slipshod appearance.

"Why are you still wearing the suit from yesterday?" she asked slowly.

Chanda protested with her eyes in a way that told Sunaina she shouldn't be asking questions she didn't want answers to. The stretching silence sent shivers down her spine. The next words that came out of Chanda's mouth were rushed and barely registered, thrown halfway over her shoulder as she hurried into the night.

Sunaina stood there, stupefied and utterly beaten down. There were certain things she was hyperaware of in that moment; that it was night, the humidity had her hair sticking to the nape of her neck, and that she wanted to kill herself. She sensed her heart softly thumping somewhere underwater, her brain trying to move her but she walked disjointedly. Fingers went through her hair to tie it up. Lock the main door. Press the glass door into the kitchen. All movements carried out in simple perfunctory steps. She walked in and reached for a glass, the glass was made of glass and it was cool against her skin. The superficial image of her father standing only in pajamas was in front of her trying for nonchalant conversation. He was shirtless. He was rummaging through the fridge for something, half swallowed up by the double doors. When he poked his head up to stare at her it was obvious that she was supposed to respond.

"What?"

"How was your night?"

"Oh fine... I had a date."

"Oh *oh that's good*!" she'd never heard his voice that high. "Yeah in fact I remember you saying something about a date ... with Laksh right? How'd it go – um – because you're back *really* early for a date I mean it's only, what, eleven o clock right?"

Hassan grew uncomfortable under her prolonged stare. In her mind she knew there was an answer to the problem; it was simple arithmetic but her brain wasn't ready to put two and two together.

"Well, how was it?"

She straightened her spine and set the glass down.

"It was fine" she exhaled "I ordered myself a drink, waited for about like two hours and then decided he wasn't coming because I called him and I texted, his phone's dead, no one's heard from him so there's a chance he's, well, dead too. And then I came home, papa." She held the glass aloft, hoping for armour. "Now why don't you tell me how your night was?"

He surveyed her closely.

"Fine, nothing special at all really –"

"Oh oh really? I assumed Chanda had to stay late for some work because –"

"Sana" his voice boomed, "Chanda stayed this late because she had to help me –"

" –With what exactly… because I have a feeling she spent last night here too."

"What the fuck are you talking about!?" he crossed his arms defensively.

Sana cringed, finally aware of how low his pajamas hung. "Why was she in the same fucking suit as yesterday papa?"

"HOW the fuck would I know? She's poor so obviously –"

"*For fuck's sake are you sleeping with her?*"

A shower of magnets fell to the floor when he slammed the doors shut. For the first time in a long time Sunaina felt like she was talking to her father and not just a random man because Hassan physically grew taller in his rage.

"What the fuck do you want from me? That bitch up and left like this is some fucking joke, and we obviously don't mean shit. Now she's fucking her way through Europe and you", he thrust an accusatory finger at her, "you expect what?"

The glass went flying into a wall. She winced, a static rang through her ears.

"Don't I deserve to find love once more, to begin again, make things okay or whatever you call it ... How long am I expected to suffer?"

Another glass shattered against the wall. Sana swayed where she stood.

"How long?"

Another glass.

"How long!"

"Papa" she leaned against the marble island, "are you in *love* with the maid?"

Her vision faded to black.

Sometime during the final overture of Ariel's song, Gayatri entered. The bed was a mess and Sunaina lay entangled in the sheets, the last dregs of diamond dust scattered across an iPad screen. In the corner was a barrage of her last hangover-fueled shopping spree. On her phone she swiped at her shopping cart and blinked away the confirmation message. Gayatri approached with caution.

"Hey is your mom back?" Her lateness was made worse by the casual tone.

"What shit? Also where were you?" Sunaina pulled up the covers to hide her nakedness

"Tina aunty, I can smell her perfume."

She looked at Gayatri completely at a loss.

"The whole house smells of Chanel no. 5 ya, is she back or what?"

"No. It was probably the maid," she burrowed deeper into the fortress of pillows.

"Chanda?" she set her purse by the table and pulled off her heels.

"Yeah I think she stayed the night."

"Why would she do that? It's ridiculous ..."

"Because I think papa's having an affair with her."

The silence stretched between them reaffirming what Sunaina already knew. That she was out of coke, out of luck, and soon short of one best friend. Gayatri climbed onto the bed next to her without another word. It was then that she really took in the change a simple haircut had rendered on Sana's appearance. Gayatri told herself that this would be the pivotal point in her friend's life, the start of something that'd change her life forever.

They stayed that way as the little mermaid saved her prince from drowning.

"I'm leaving." Gayatri whispered.

She didn't say anything back.

"I'm going to live in Bombay for a while."

Sunaina stared into space, coiled like a viper.

"It was really random actually I like just walked in for a casting call one day and they shortlisted me and I couldn't believe they actually did and then I auditioned in front of a camera like a test shoot or whatev and I ended up meeting the director and literally dad had to fly in that very evening because they like wanted to sign me and ... Ugh I don't know why I didn't tell you sooner." She sat up straighter. "Are you even going to say anything or not?"

"You should go."

"I'm going."

"And so you should," she reached over and lit a cigarette. "When are you leaving?"

"End of this week I guess."

"Good for you."

"What is that supposed to mean?"

Sunaina tucked the sheet under her arms and sat upright, no longer worried about her exposed back.

"I mean literally that's good for you Gayatri. Because to be completely honest I like didn't see much happening for you here anyway. Except maybe a job that you'd get fired from in a few months because even though they'd say it has flexible hours you'd always be late and leave early by giving some dumb bimbo excuse," she blew a puff of smoke between them, "and truthfully that is if you don't end up in an early marriage to some beefed up

Punjabi retard from Chandigarh *or worse Canada* who would be super eager to marry you just so he can make a trophy wife out of you. And then his fat mother who'd seem nice at first would literally start demanding babies ASAP and you'd either divorce him or make him move to a different but only slightly less shady part of Canada. Or like Ludhiana. Take your pick."

Gayatri sat there, flushed as if she'd actually been slapped. "You're such a bitch."

"Oh I'm not done Gayatri. Because you know why this is really a good opportunity for you, it's because you hate everything around you. Like you even hate your dad who's quite possibly the most level headed adult I've met in my life, like I would trade for him any day but *you* can't forgive him for marrying Geetu bua. That's why you're so miserable in life and you're such a slut because of it. Yeah, I heard all about the shit you and Ankit Kalra were up to at my party and really congratulations, because I think even Anki is fucking aspirational for you, you fat fucking whore."

Gayatri eased off the bed but she wasn't done yet.

"In fact, I think you should take him with you. Get him a job in Bombay and ease him from his fucking misery. I'd tell you to stay safe because, even for a B-movie career an untimed pregnancy can be fatal, but Ankit seems like he'd have a weak sperm count to begin with."

Gayatri swallowed the bile and slapped her. Even as Sunaina's face flew away from her, she was vibrating with the anger and the hurt.

"I cannot believe how many years I've wasted in being your friend when I should've just known better."

Sunaina clapped.

"Well you can go off now, you cunt. Go and claim your future. At least this way you'll stay off my ass and maybe learn the value of some actual work, if for nothing else but to at least pay for your own coke. Good luck with having to fuck fat old men in hotels,

I'm sure Ankit would totally get off on whoring you out like that anyway. Go forth into the gaudy light of mediocrity, Gayatri."

"Fuck this. I'm done with you."

"Close the door behind you", Gayatri stormed off without touching the door, "bitch."

Naked and alone in her room, Sunaina waited for something to push past the numbness. Till it did, she stood there glassy eyed, smiling, and truly alone in the world.

Chapter EIGHT

LOVE IS A LASERQUEST

Gayatri sat scrubbing her clammy palms together hoping no one would look her way. The room was so empty it was hard to look anywhere else, even the chipped paint had blurred behind her. She was on a simple stool, tan unpolished and three legged. She scolded herself for losing focus, the stool was irrelevant. A lit cigarette slowly burned between her fingers.

Her eyes shot up at the sound of a clearing throat. The room was a reticent cave. She could feel the millions of eyes on her, she felt them on her skin.

"I guess it started, as most problems do, in school. It's not surprising when you think about it actually, kids can be so horrible to each other it's shocking. I mean sure now we're more aware of it because bullying can actually have life-lasting effects and people are trying to put a stop to it. I don't know, maybe it's just an American problem and we're still ignoring it."

No one answered. She pulled a long drag.

"There was this girl, I don't think anyone had looked at her twice before that but puberty hit her like a brick wall and then like stacked dominos all the girls in my class grew out their boobs and, well, as you can see I didn't get my fair share in that department." She smiled ruefully.

"The thing is though that I only had these hormonal changes over the summer vacations that year which let me tell you by the way is the worst ever because suddenly you're a completely different person. No one recognized me at first. Like, I came back at least five or six inches taller and with my hair all grown out – you know I was the tallest girl in my entire grade of about two hundred kids. I mean forget about the guys, the shorties didn't even make eye contact with me if I was coming down the hallway, and the others I mean … I don't know. I guess they just found it easier to make fun of me than think about how insecure I made them, I used to run competitively back then you see. That paired with the girls literally poking my stomach had me perfectly messed up in school."

She looked at her interlaced ankles and smoked.

"Do you know how absolutely terrible kids can be? One day I had a bruise on my knee because I'd slipped and fallen while running on the field and they started a rumour that I got it from offering blowjobs to old guys in my apartment complex. Including like the watchmen and stuff. First it was just the people in my class, then it spread through the grade, and one day someone I'd never seen nor spoken to came up to me and asked me if I'd do it free."

The silence was deafening. Gayatri tossed her hair over the shoulder and puffed out a cloud of smoke. The light hit her in a way that threw every bony edge, every crevice in relief. She was a ghost of the girl she once was. If she sat upright you'd see the ribs through her white shirt.

"I mean, okay let's be real for a minute, no one grows up with the knowledge of what body dysmorphia even is really but I got the feeling that something wasn't right when one day my arts teacher pointed something out. I had fine arts as one of my subjects you see, and I was really close with my teacher. She pointed out that all my human figures were distorted. I remember stepping back and seeing that she was right, the torsos were fine but the legs stretched almost all the way down the sheet. It was hilarious but I did wonder what the hell was wrong with me, my proportions shouldn't have been *that* off considering we had exams coming up!" She gave a mirthless laugh. "I knew she was going to shout at me telling me I haven't practiced enough and I'm just wasting time between samosa breaks and running track so I lied saying it was a new style I was trying out. I don't know she bought it at the time so I just continued doing it, I really impressed myself with that one."

She leaned over and picked up her mug of coffee, the day's fourth.

"You know I think that's really the starting point of it all, of the ... oh I don't know what's the right word for it – desire? The Need? The *desperation* to be thin? Compulsively checking my weight? You get the idea, right? Anyway, I started trying out diet fads like they were jeans, like literally trying them out recreationally. You remember that time, I think it was the first time the GM diet became a real thing in India and everyone was like losing their shit over it. That was my first time.

"I started smoking even before I graduated from school because I read somewhere that it helped you lose weight. Don't get me wrong, that's not the reason I smoke now I just like to keep my hands busy – all the coffee and the Red Bull leave me jittery. So yeah, none of the diets ever really worked the way that I wanted them to, I don't know why but I'd just wake up every day and still find cellulite on my body. I remember I used to stand in front of the mirror in my underwear and just pinch and pull at it as if I could rip it off my body and I would tell myself every day that I was fine, I was going to be thin soon, everything would be okay. I wasn't going to stop till I was the thinnest girl in school. It didn't happen though and after the last round of exams I just stopped eating altogether.

"I would eat a little in front of my mother then not at all for the rest of the day. Soon I just started lying to her telling her I'd already eaten every time she'd ask me. Really, can you imagine how checked-out a parent has to be to believe their child just like that? It was just too easy. She worked at a PR firm then and I mean you can only imagine what her life was like. I shed thirteen kilos that month of May."

Gayatri reveled in the raised eyebrows. They were like putty in her hands now.

"It was amazing."

She could sense how awed they were.

Shashi leaned in and whispered in her ear.

"This is my favourite part."

"I was beautiful." she almost-whispered.

The camera zoomed into her face slowly, close enough till she could see her own pores blown up on the 20x50 foot screen. Her eyes were burrowing through the feed and then the video cut to black before Neil's monologue began.

Gayatri wasn't as impressed as Shashi though, her eyes were burning and goosebumps crawled all over her legs. The pads of her feet throbbed against her shoes and she could feel the exhaustion radiating in waves through her. She promised herself that the next time she'd walk a red carpet, there'd be a change of shoes at hand.

She wondered if this was possibly the longest February in the history of time. Her month had begun in New York from where they went to Rome, and now Berlin. She was measuring time through flights, red carpets and screenings, and what felt like an endless barrage of tittered conversation. The director had only given them one piece of advice – *walk like you're already among their ranks*. He wasn't taking them as newbies; they were to be seasoned stars. And stars they were when they walked through the salons and talked cinema with the crème de la crème.

She couldn't have heard it enough. How lucky they were, so lucky to have been selected from thousands of applicants and then to get the chance to showcase their film. The critics, the foreign press, the inevitable catapulting to fame. She'd heard it all and now she had the worst headache of her life.

By the third week, Gayatri had taught her mind to leave the physical realm and meditate. The glittering commotion belonged to another world then. The movie never changed, it didn't end differently. It was the same hollow stares, the same fights, pacing her apartment, reliving their total loss of control, picking up Neil off the street, and dying for the camera over and over and over again. It was the same. Staring at her dead face blown up into larger than life cinemascope, it was numbing her. Always followed by the same awed silence and the same fast banter later on. The same giggle and humbled dip of her head to misplaced commentary on the actors' finesse in speaking English despite not being native speakers.

She hugged her jacket tighter, Berlin was beautiful in February but if Kabir Baruacha didn't know her penchant for fur she might've frozen.

Neil eyed her jacket with jealousy.

"You sure you can't share?"

"No, help me up let's get a drink," she held onto his hand and stood up. Her feet were going to give up in those shoes.

"I'm so confused today, aren't you? I can't decide if I'm having the time of my life or so terribly homesick I could cry." She could see him fight the urge to check his hair.

Neil was shifty, hunting for the nearest reflective surface and she couldn't blame him. Were she as comfortably dressed in pants and a jacket she'd have taken a quick nap too.

"Your hair is perfect don't get the crazy eyes right now," they walked through the groups of men and women almost all smoking in the wet winter evening.

He turned back to her. "I know it sounds petulant but I just really fuckin' want my bed. But I know as soon as I'm back I'll miss the thrill of all this."

She threw her head back and laughed.

"You're such a cliché right now, you know that right? Pretty but dumb –"

"Yeah but that's irrelevant," he shrugged.

The words were familiar but the timing wasn't right and the setting wasn't right, and *he* wasn't right either. They belonged to someone else, a special set of eyes and lips that curved into a smile. She shrugged off the memory and wove her way through the barrage of tan overcoats and sparkling wine. Neil handed her a drink, charmingly unaware as always.

"Are you sure about the jacket? I'm freezing here."

She looked up.

"Wear a dress then we'll talk!"

In her first month living in Bombay, Gayatri had decided on a few things as absolutions; truths that helped her make sense of the world she now lived in. The first was that people who wore *kolhapuri chappals* rarely had anything interesting to say. That people who listened to Nucleya were smarter than others. And that she hated sunsets. She hated sunsets more than anything else now, because her house on Pali Hill had a stunning view of sunsets and she hated the end of another day. Hated that she was the same person at the end of it as when the day began. Then she would sit and wonder if it was worse to be stupid or rationalize her emotions.

Once they started filming, her life turned into a long panorama of call times, fittings, and cold readings, spending most of her free time stuck in traffic. She couldn't drink because she had to lose weight. She couldn't have sugar in her morning tea because she had to lose weight; soon she stopped adding milk too. She gave up non-vegetarian food except on Sunday afternoon and she doubled her workouts. She had to lose weight. It was with these thoughts in mind that Gayatri sat to write her speech on the thirteen hour flight back home.

Neil snorted at the state of her notebook nearly bursting with stapled odd bits of paper of scribbled notes and post-its. She always pulled her mind away from them, her private torturers. He collapsed into the seat beside her and immediately settled into his favourite douchey pose.

"Come on" he nudged her side.

She leaned in and smiled for the selfie.

"Why do you do that?" she pushed him to sit straighter.

He looked at the notebook, all signs of humour gone from his face.

"Why do you do *that*?"

"I'm fine" she squared her shoulders. "I'm just going through them as a thing you know, like a chef reading the recipe or something. It's supposed to be therapeutic."

He cocked an eyebrow at her.

"I'm serious. I mean I think it's supposed to be, I don't know."

"I'm confiscating that as soon as we land. You have" he grimaced at the screen in front of him, "a million years to finish the speech, and then I'm hiding that piece of shit journal."

Gayatri didn't want to cry, it would've made things worse. He probably would've torn it up right then. So she smiled and nodded.

It wasn't love, not the way she'd once defined it and not the kinds you'd find on a Pinterest quote. Somewhere between playing lovers, spooning, and taking care of each other through the filming schedule, Neil and Gayatri had forged a bond of a different nature altogether. She had picked him off the floor when he was three sheets to the wind, driven him home when he was blinded from the bottle, she stopped him from choking on his own vomit. He made sure she didn't die of starvation. He'd force her out for walks, buy groceries and cook for her. They simply helped each other survive.

She wondered if in retrospect she regretted falling so deep into the rabbit hole when the whole audition was a joke and who in their right mind would walk into a casting call without preparing something?

While the elevator took them up to the office, Gayatri could feel her apathy fading. She'd been joking and laughing the whole day but in that moment she could understand how real it all was. It was just for laughs, they didn't even have legitimate headshots – it was a quick printout job. They picked up plain white t-shirts from the nearest Zara and ran over, heads swimming from the mid-morning beers at Doolally.

But when the doors opened and they saw what was an endless corridor of doppelgangers in that same white shirt and black pants, Gayatri could feel the blood drain from her face. *Tall*: most of them had legs streamlined by six inch heels and tight pants. *Fit*: shoulders so slender it was magical how they could've slung a bag on it. *Long hair*: it was an army of perfect hair, only a handful had it up in a bun.

Some of them had accessorized, most of them had over an hour's worth of makeup. Every single one of them had at least two acting jobs to their credit and over a thousand auditions. There was logically no chance for her. She balked, the beer rising higher up her throat.

Seven girls went in and out before they called her name.

When Gayatri stood she was worried she'd shit herself, not from fear but the beer. She decided then never to touch another pint.

"Are you coming or what?"

Under different circumstances, she would've slapped the tiny girl for taking that tone with her, but she just walked in silently.

"Please remove your shoes, bag, and any other accessories by the table", one of the guys at the desk burped between his tea. The tone of his voice made her yawn.

Someone read out the scribbled cv she'd tacked along with her photo, she nodded through most of it. They asked her questions, basic questions about her life and she sat straighter with every answer, fighting against the dull energy of the room. The director didn't even look up from his phone. They asked her to look into the camera and talk about herself. She asked them what she was supposed to talk about.

"Madam talk about whatever you like, there's no right answer here."

He left for a smoke break.

They asked her some more questions.

"No I used to crossfit for a while but it wasn't my thing. I run mostly, I used to take dance classes when I was in school."

They asked her why she stopped dancing.

"I got bored."

Would she be willing to lose weight for the movie? Would she do it if she got the part?

"Would it make you notice me better?"

Some of them huffed at her, some giggled, Gayatri told herself to keep walking. She'd vomited into the plants as soon as she made it outside.

Neil was lost in sleep beside her. He was of the particularly irritating variety of people who could sleep through any length of a flight – sometimes even before the plane left solid ground. He explained how it felt like being lulled to sleep but Gayatri couldn't afford to lose focus. Her fingers deftly danced over the keys, notebook splayed out on her lap, the same note scribbled over and over and over and over on aesthetically placed post-its.

YouAre Worthless YouAre Worthless YouAre Worthless YouAre Worthless YOUAREWORTHLESSYOUAREWORTHLESS YOUAREWORTHLESSYOUAREWORTHLESSWORTHLESS WORTHLESSWORTHLESS

It was a week into her first schedule when she'd written them, placing them all over her vanity. Anyone who saw them looked at her differently, to the point that she was convinced she didn't belong. Their awkward glances chafed her skin, even the interns who ran errands. Shashi an ever present bee checking in on her, took it upon herself to shoo away anyone who lingered. They were all over the dressing table, the mirror, the bathroom door, the mini fridge – constant reminders.

Just looking at the words brought back every bit of the hurt. Gayatri promised herself to get rid of that journal.

One.
Two.
Three.
Breathe.
One.
Two.
Three.
Smile.
One.
You are in control.
Two.
You are the creator and destroyer of your own world.
Three.
Savour the power.
One.
Two.
Three.
Push the knife deeper in his chest.
One. Two. Three.
Ruin him.
One. Two. Three.
One. Two. Three.
One. Two. Three.
One two three. One two three. One two three one two three one two three one two three one two three.

Kama woke up, not with a jolt but a sigh. Her hands ached from gripping the pillow so hard. The nightmare itself didn't seem as strange anymore, she'd been thinking about it more often over the past few days. What threw her off was that she'd ben straddling the pillow. Frequency notwithstanding her dreams had never manifested in physical reactions this way.

Her hair was a sweaty mess matted across her face, she scratched at it, dabbing away the thick beads of sweat. Her arms ached from the obvious physical strain but she said a prayer for patience, for peace and serenity in the sleep cycle or some such collection of words. She ended with a mental note to call her trusty hairdresser for a cut and pushed herself off the bed to light exactly five incense sticks even though it was the middle of the night.

She found her mind drifting to the argument with Ria that had put an abrupt end to dinner earlier. It had finally happened, that most dreaded moment of a mother's life. Her daughter had begun drifting away from her, no longer the mature confidante, the trustworthy companion she had thus far been. To worsen the situation, Ria's line of questioning had broadened to include her father. That was a bigger betrayal.

Kama shook her head and danced the incense sticks around her. Something about the smell of lavender incense really enlivened her chakras, she'd tell whoever bothered to listen, and it grounded her with the earth. In all honesty, she simply had nothing else to fill her mind anymore. It was as empty as her pages. She decided to take a stroll through the house and let the sweet smoke flow through the halls.

"Huh" he said as the car rolled to a stop.

"What's the matter?"

"Nothing." Something was obviously on his mind.

Gayatri massaged her forehead wearily. "I'll really hit you right now. I haven't slept you know..."

She turned to open the door.

The watchman came running out to help with her bloated suitcases. She breathed in the salty sea air, perfectly cool in the early morning while the sun crept up the other side of the building.

"It's just that it'll be, I don't know, weird."

She turned back to him, struck by the way he glowed in the morning light. Against better judgment she admitted to herself that Neil, just in the way he rested his chin on the hood of the car, was undeniably beautiful.

"Why? What'll be weird?"

He stared at the hood of the car like it was the most interesting thing in the world, pouting like a child.

"I don't know," he reached across to her, "I think I'm just too used to having you within reach."

Gayatri sighed, a breath hitched in her throat. They had yet to talk about the night when she slept over for the first time. He had knocked on her door till she woke up but her anger had vanished at the sight of his cadaverous face. She wasn't anybody's first choice for seeking comfort, in fact Gayatri was known to be the least helpful person during a crisis. The sight of him three sheets to the wind and barely standing up had disarmed the usual sarcasm, she pulled him in more on instinct than common sense. That night she held him as he half moaned in sleep oblivious to her goodnight kisses on his damp forehead. Eventually sleep came for her too, she settled with an arm draped across his chest. They were almost done with the principle filming. He was sipping on gin and juice every hour. She hadn't eaten for two days.

Gayatri shook her head clear.

"No listen I'm still me and you're still you. Call me whenever you want." She shifted under his gaze. "Anyway now you know where to find me."

Pacified for the moment, he waved goodbye.

The elevator ride was spent in containing her thoughts, away from Neil and towards her bed. In her current frame of mind, somewhere past the landscape of utter exhaustion, Gayatri only had in mind the moment she'd walk barefoot and melt onto the bed. What she didn't expect was the sight of Ankit, cup of coffee in hand by the bay windows. The sunlight hit him fully like he was a mirage borne from sleeplessness but he was real.

"What ..." she didn't have it in her to deal with whatever was going on.

"I still had my key and the watchman recognized me."

"Well I'm definitely having him fired first thing tomorrow ..." she let her backpack fall next to the suitcases.

"Look, can we just talk?"

"You talk, I'll listen. Start by what the fuck you're doing here when I told you the last time –"

"–Hey hey!! If you wanna let me talk, let me talk. Just sit down please you look like you're going to faint."

She glared at him. "Well can you blame me? I've been up for almost twenty four hours now. I was kinda hoping to have some peace and quiet when I got back home, to my apartment."

"Just sit please, I'll make you some tea."

"I don't want your fucking tea I want to know why the hell you're in my house Ankit!"

He paused somewhere between setting his cup down and racing to the kitchen. In the months they'd been apart it was clear he had lost weight, she could see the way his cheeks sagged, the hint of dark circles. He stared at her with the same imploring eyes till she sat down.

"Gayatri ..." she didn't meet his eyes. "Just-just hear me out okay."

She huffed.

"I was an idiot. I was an absolute asshole, especially to you and I've-I've really been thinking about it the last few weeks and I think I understand why. I think I know why I just completely checked out of the relationship or whatever you'd called it. It's because somewhere like on a subconscience level I knew –"

"*Subconscious,*" she rolled her eyes.

"Yeah that, I was aware that it wouldn't last between us. Like I was aware in my mind but not in my heart and then my heart sort of heard it and refused to accept it but then, I don't know, it just did."

"Bloody hell ya do you actually have a point to make here or what?"

He stalked behind her into the kitchen. "Listen, I knew we wouldn't survive a long-distance relationship."

"Uhh really? You didn't dump me because of the long-distance thing, you did it because you had to like go and make a fucking career and shit."

He opened his mouth to protest.

"And I get it, I get that it was the right move for you. I didn't back then but I get it now and I'm absolutely fine with it. I don't however understand what the fuck you want now!"

"Okay look so the firm has me in Bombay for two months for a project, I'm going home for Holi but otherwise I'm here, and I want to spend every waking moment with you Gayatri, I-I still love you."

"Oh you've got to be kidding me," they jumped at Neil's voice.

"Sorry, the door was open and you two weren't exactly keeping it down."

"Who the fuck is this?" Ankit jabbed a finger in the air.

"The fuck are you bro? I'm her friend."

"Well I'm her *boyfriend*."

"EX-boyfriend, shut up Ankit." She was dizzy and sick. The two men had sucked all the air out of the apartment.

"Neil, what's up?"

"How do you even know this dipshit?" Ankit furiously crossed his arms.

"I wanted to talk to you." Neil looked past him.

"Okay, can we do this some other time?" she gestured at Ankit, "I'm kind of in the middle of something here."

"Yeah but –" Neil was moving closer and Gayatri's skin crawled.

"Okay no *buts*, out!" she pushed him all the way out. "I will call you when I manage to wake up from this nightmare. I need sleep, many many hours of sleep."

She reached for the collar of his jacket, "But I promise I will call."

It was against his better judgment to leave just then, but Neil would never know how much she respected him for it.

Gayatri stood there in the hallway with a throbbing head in her hands, she clawed at her hair wishing she could just stay there forever. An eternity in limbo had to have been better than having to deal with whatever Ankit Kalra's pendulum heart, with Neil's unprecedented intensity, with the constant texts from her PR manager Shashi reminding her of schedule changes with all the grace of a woodpecker sharply rapping the back of her head. Was this adulthood, she mused, because so far everything was just a shitstorm. An ever growing shitstorm. Messier by the minute. Ankit cleared his throat from the living room behind her.

She wasn't sure what to do about him but went in anyway.

"I want to share the next two months and have every waking moment with you by my side, Gayatri, please."

They were words she once wanted desperately to hear, waited for them to come like a madwoman.

"Yeah, you already said that."

But that was five months ago.

"I really mean it, Gayatri."

She snorted a 'huh' at him and plopped back on the couch.

There was something immediately empowering about it, sitting on the couch with her legs wide apart, eyes burrowing holes into his thick skull. He looked like he was veering off the edge, like he'd be on his knees begging at any moment. He wanted to spend time with her, she should've been happy about it. It wasn't so long ago that she felt that way – but that was then and this was now and now she didn't have two months to spare. He would leave again, that she knew for sure, and once again she'd be the dirty whore. His job was the only thing Ankit could love, she was only a mistress.

"Get the fuck out."

Chapter NINE

No Remedy For Memory (*Interlude*)

Hi Daddy

It's been some time since I heard from you. Been a while since I wrote as well.

I don't have much to update you on, really everything is quite usual and ordinary here. Ordinary – strange word isn't it. It says everything's calm, almost droll, but also maybe pleasant. I don't know. Ria told me everything you said to her, I cannot believe you treated my daughter, your granddaughter so terribly daddy!! How could you? That poor girl has done nothing but look up to you, she listens to you like you are the smartest man in the world. You called her ordinary ... I will show you what an extraordinary girl she is.

You told her to talk to me about where she came from. You told her to ask me who her father was. You blamed me for the reason you hate her, why you can't stand to have her in front of you. And I did. I told her everything. And I'm

proud of it. I will never regret the decision to have her and don't you doubt it for a minute.

But I know you feel this way because all you have wanted for me is to have the best version of my life, but I want you to know dad that *she* is the best part of my life. I have no doubt about it. She has kept me sane, she has kept me whole. I hope you can see that some day too. Till then I think it is best if we don't see each other for some time at least.
With all my love,

Kama.

She was seventeen when it happened. She was supposed to be married in the next two years; her parents were already eyeing prospective matches. She was desperately in love with him, and how could she not be? Shailender was the grooviest boy in college. Older boys like him were hot property, with their thick mustaches, rakish smiles and easy sex appeal. He was the first person she ever shared her cola with, she was the first girl to ride his Pushpak.

They'd been dating for six months. She baked him a cake and made up a night-stay story at home. It was a well set up web of white lies because Shail and Kama wanted to spend the night together, it was the biggest night of her life. All day she'd been equally anxious and excited and her nerves hadn't settled even as she snuck into his borrowed car at dusk.

They giggled and talked till the drive to the guesthouse, nothing fancy because it was all he could afford from saving fractions of his pocket money. They hadn't planned on doing much, but the heat was palpable between them. He wanted their first time to be extra special, he said he wanted to make love to her like the starlet that she was. The room was clean with beige walls and a comfortable bed. An overall pleasant vibe finished with velveteen curtains. She kept her crocheted bag on the table, touching the beads with a soft smile thinking of the day her mother had taught her how to twist and loop the yarn to crochet. She thought of her mother and how happy she would be the day she could meet Shailender and they would announce their wishes to get married.

He had to run for an errand, there were no colas available at the hotel and there was a general store just down the road. "Don't open the door for anyone unless it is me," he said before leaving, "just keep it locked. Read something; take it light, keep it tight. I'll be back as soon as I can." She gave him a hug and kissed him, proud of her boldness at being the first one to kiss the other. Kama settled down on the bed and flipped through the Filmfare on the table. The bed was softer than anything she had sat on before.

But Shailender never came back.

The minutes turned to half an hour and her skin prickled with worry. The nervousness gave way to anger as the hour passed, how could he take so long to bring back two bottles of coca cola? What was the point – they would be warm by the time he returned anyway. She planned her tantrum, how she'd hit him: tight fisted but not hard enough to actually hurt him too much.

The second hour passed and she wept bitterly because she didn't know what was going on, she couldn't breathe. She couldn't think. She could only feel her heart breaking piece by piece. Everything ached. She went to the bathroom and cleaned her face because all her makeup was ruined. She thought of her mother, how she had trusted Kama on her word that she would be safe at her friend's house. How disappointed she would be when she found out her daughter had lied. That crumpled face of disappointment in her mind only brought more tears more pain. She broke a glass and cried. She broke another one and stopped. She was exhausted. Shailender had been gone for almost three hours. Three. Hours.

She cleaned up the broken glass, wrapping the bigger shards in a hand towel and using damp pages of the magazine to pick up the smaller pieces. She wondered if it was better to just go home.

Or if she could find a way to call her friend, the guesthouse would definitely have had a phone she could call from.

But how would she have explained any of it?

What would she do with Shailender's things?

What would she say to her friend's mother? Or her father? What would she say to *her own father*? He was only back for a month after almost a year of being away at service. He would have her married off by the time he left. Or worse he too would stare at her with that scowl, ashamed at rising her to be a liar. She felt sick.

The four walls started closing in on her.

She called for a Saradon and some water. She ignored the leering man who came to give it. She took the medicine and slept.

It was another hour later when Shailender banged on the door. He was drunk, so drunk she felt her stomach turn at the faintest whiff of his breath. He leaned in and kissed her wetly. The hallway was dark behind him so she couldn't see just then that he wasn't alone. Shailender had seven other friends with him, his tongue had loosened with every drink, and he brought them all back to the guest room to meet her. She was a friendly girl after all, he just wanted them to meet his pretty, friendly girlfriend Kama.

Kama thought the night would never end.

Thought they would never stop.

Eight men.

Eight men were enough to subdue one woman.

Enough to silence her screams.

Eight men were enough to hold one woman down.

Eight men were enough to tear off her clothes.

Eight pairs of hands.

Sixteen hands on her body.

Their hands were everywhere.

Every where.

Kama thought they would never stop.

They didn't.

One. Two. Three.

There were too many of them.

One. Two. Three.

She couldn't breathe.

One. Two. Three.

Hands everywhere.

One. Two. Three.

A pain like she'd never felt before.

One. Two. Three.

They couldn't hear her.

One. Two. Three.

NO, she screamed.

One. Two. Three.

NO!

One. Two. Three.

They laughed. They grunted. They shifted off and on her.

One. Two. Three.

One by one.

One. Two. Three.

Even when they stopped, the hands never left her body. Pinching, caressing, slapping.

One.

Two.

Three.

It seemed the night would never end.

One.

Two.

Three.

"It was the worst thing that ever happened to me," she wiped away a tear. Despite herself it was funny that she cried. "Actually I think there may be too few things worse than that to happen to anybody."

Ria sat there stupefied. She reached a hand out and held her mother's warm hand. The same familiar hand she'd held for sixteen years, now just felt heavier.

The sun had come up sometime while they talked. She blinked her eyes and suddenly everything just seemed brighter. She told herself to switch the light off but couldn't bring herself to move. Her bones had fused at the joints, her muscles atrophied; she never wanted to leave her mother's sight. If she let go of her hand she thought she might die.

"So the Commander ..."

"He ..." she choked. "He couldn't understand why. None of us could. Why had something like that happened? In a way I think he took it the hardest in the family, it was – it just shook him up in a way that he could never recover from."

Ria swallowed the lump in her throat.

"He sees in you everything that I went through, which is completely unfair. I don't condone it at all. I think he just has a hard time, he doesn't have anyone to talk to, to share his words with."

"I mean I don't blame him!"

"Arey it's not that simple", Kama smiled sadly, "he sees you and he remembers *everything*. He sees what I went through yes but also what I gave up. What I could have been and never got to be; the future I sacrificed to have you."

"But don't get me wrong, I have never for a second of my life cared about that." She couldn't hold back the tears anymore. Her chest ached as if someone had knocked the air out of her. "I have loved you more than anything in this world beta, and I will love you for ever. If daddy can't find love for you in his heart that's his problem not ours."

Ria stood and hugged her mother, resolved to be as fearless as her mother. Every crippling habit now, too soon, made too much sense.

"Parents place a lot of trust in their kids, beta. Every day. We trust that we have raised good children. We trust that we have taught you right from wrong, we trust that you will make good choices and learn from your failures." She sniffed into the sleeve of her kurta. "I don't want to hold you back in any way. You're smarter than anyone your age, no doubt about it. I just want you to be cautious."

Ria caught the subtle flicker of her gaze to the room below where her boyfriend was sleeping but chose not to comment on it.

"Make your own choices so long as you can live with them, otherwise I'm here for any kind of help" she smiled. "I will kill you if you get pregnant though. I am not going to let you piss your life away because of some shitty boy."

Ria swallowed, unsure of how to discuss going on the pill.

Kama smiled then. "But this one seems like a decent one."

Chapter TEN

Milk And Toast

The wind shocked her as she walked down the steps, past the miniature parking space, to the backside of the inn. Sunaina had always heard people say that mountain air was crisp, but from the way it stung her smarting cheek she realized it was a lie. The cigarette clung to her dry lips, impatience getting the better of her the longer she fumbled with her lighter. Hot tears turned cold as they pooled under her eyes, equal parts furious and ashamed.

The man walked up from behind, ashen faced and apologetic. He offered to light her cigarette and she ceded. Neither met each other's eyes.

"I'm really truly sorry." He shoved his hands deep into his pockets. "We're leaving. We don't want to cause any more trouble than we already have."

She caught him staring down her shirt, stained with water and iced tea.

"What happened exactly? I don't know how –"

"My brother has autism but he's usually very well adjusted, I mean he works at an art studio and everything. It's probably the mountain air, I'm ... gosh I'm not sure what set him off. I'm just so terribly sorry."

She winced as the ice pack went back on her cheek.

"We've paid for the damages ... I'll be more than happy to compensate –"

"Wow," the hundred rupee note hit harder than his brother's back handed slap. "Please leave NOW."

Faisal cleared his throat from behind. She saw the man balk.

"Is there a problem here?" he asked gruffly.

"It's nothing, he was just leaving." She took a step away from the man.

"Listen buddy –" Faisal placed a heavy hand on his shoulder, fully aware of the condescending nature of his gesture. "You should get a move on."

He saw the way it made his teeth grind, it would've been too easy to take him down. The man was a prime specimen of the kind of guys whose fitness regime never strayed too far from pumping their chest and biceps. Hand to hand combat was not a priority. Faisal knew he'd be useless as putty in a chokehold, their difference in height notwithstanding.

"I think you've caused enough trouble here."

"Are you the fucking manager or what? I was just apologizing to her," he shot her one last lewd look.

They turned at the sound of a horn blowing from the street. Sunaina saw her assailant siting in the front with a childlike pout, made stark by the general stoicism of the others. He walked off muttering under his breath.

"Fucking bitch."

It was deliberate. Sunaina felt it in her bones.

She threw her cigarette and held Faisal back with both hands, digging her heels into the soft ground.

"Stop, stop it. He's just trying to rile you up."

He grit his teeth. "I don't fucking care I'll break his bones if I have to."

"Over my dead body! We're not having any more drama here, I'll lose my bloody job."

He turned with a withering glare. “No one’s firing you begum. It wasn’t your fault.”

She reached for him, their anger collectively softening even as adrenaline raged through them. But before she could say her thank you he strode out of reach.

“Whatever, I have work to get to.”

“Well fine!” she gasped at his retreating back. “It’s not like I don’t have better things to do.”

“Maybe you should do them then instead of slacking off here.”

“I wasn’t sla –”

“Oh save it for someone who cares begum.”

She stormed past him. “Well if you didn’t care then why’d you come save me?”

She saw the surprise in his honey eyes. “So you did need my help, didn’t you? Couldn’t just say thanks and get it over with.”

“I would have if you weren’t such a piece of shit.” He flung a middle finger through the air and disappeared into the street.

Sunaina stormed past the confused manager, having finally emerged from his office to address the commotion. In the two months she’d known him, Faisal had the art of grating against her skin down to perfection. They had first properly met at a bonfire by the riverside but really their paths had crossed much earlier. It had been her first solo trek and she’d been distracted by taking pictures along the way so the sun was high up by the time Sunaina had even made it halfway. The halfway mark itself was a half-eaten carcass and although she couldn’t look directly at it, she had a feeling it was a cow. From having fall off of a height the creature lay in a massive mess of disjointed bones and a fully exposed gut. It was the flies that hit her first, the sound of a thousand buzzing flies as though a beehive had been attacked. She choked as the smell of rotting flesh hit her with the force of a brick wall.

Faisal and the group of travelers he’d been guiding walked past her without sparing a glance. Sunaina had gasped and rinsed her mouth but the sight had coated her mouth like bitter oil. Toward the end of the trail the temperature had fallen so drastically that most of his winded companions had settled down for hot milky tea and maggi. Faisal had glared at the limber cliché of a girl who strode past them, head uncovered even though the air was heavy with moisture. He hoped she'd catch a cold and learn never to walk without a cap in her bag. Sunaina had stared at the bowls filled with hot soupy noodles and stifled a laugh, hoping none of them threw up on the trail back.

During her descent she'd scraped her hand against an unsteady rock, landing right into a puddle. Between fidgeting with her makeshift bandage and avoiding the mushiest parts of the trail, Sunaina had lost track of the time. As the afternoon had rolled into an early evening, the trees beside her that had thus far been sentient giants had come alive with a million different sounds. Something burped something chirped and her footsteps grew unsteady. They say a trail is one of the best places to lose yourself but not to get lost in. A thick mist had rolled down the side of the hill so swift and sure that her breath caught in her throat. She pulled out her phone, already knowing that there was no network on it. Sunaina turned around and spat behind her, a hundred old wives tales suddenly remembered, and continued forward – hoping the forward was the right forward and not to the wrong end. She'd had the worst nightmares that usually involved an angry tribal chieftain chasing her, brandishing a machete that could sever heads in one swoop. Faisal had watched her emerge from the trees pale as a ghost. Sunaina ignored the cheerful banter from the tea stall as she crossed them and at night cried herself to sleep in an unnecessarily uncomfortable tent.

The owner knew her friend, Jatin, who often lead camps to Leh from there and had allowed her to work at the café downstairs in exchange for a private room. Upon their introduction, Sunaina had found Faisal at first endearing, mostly for his low tolerance for Old Monk. From there on an unfortunate series of events had led them to share the room at the inn and she'd found him abrasive at best. Working all day in the fields he always came home stinking and short tempered, exhausted beyond reason unless they had a joint to split between them. There was no comfort in their shared space they were constantly arguing, racing to use the bathroom in the morning, shouting over the position of the toilet seat or his body hair in the shower drain. Sunaina had reached the conclusion that men were sick and although Faisal could beat up someone who was troubling her like the gentleman from the café, he was more trouble than he was worth.

Veeru winced at her bruise. “Aye maybe you should put some make up on that. Nobody wants to see it.”

Sunaina laughed at his grimace. “All my makeup dried up and died, wanna lend me yours?”

Veeru pointed at the store across the road and told her to help herself. The day went by rather easily from thereon, with a screechy show of *Karan Arjun* to fill up the lull before the dinnertime rush.

There was something about the late night air up in the mountains. The street outside was the darkest dark where the amber pools of light couldn’t reach. Most of the cafes had shut down for the night. They were only still open because of the group of five who had checked in just then, she’d agreed to stay back and serve them hot chocolate and let them smoke their hashish in peace. Veeru was reading *The Adventures of Huckleberry Finn* in rapture by the counter, not that there was much left to do. It was a battered old copy Sunaina had bought from a hole in the wall in Khrew. She eyed the spine, hoping he wasn’t putting too much pressure on it.

She untied her hair and massaged her temples while the laptop warmed up. Over the last few weeks she’d figured out how to work the ancient bulky thing, only to reply to her ghostwriter’s emails. Charu had spent half of it droning on about a new restaurant that was offering free membership and it was members only and they wanted her to come for the opening. Sunaina watched the words blur in and out of focus, the smell of burning hash made her head swim.

"Sunaina these people are going up to their room, are you almost done?" Veeru prodded her.

She threw him a loopy smile and shook her head.

"I can wait ... if you want?"

"Not at all, you please be on your way home I'll lock up."

He asked her if she was sure but looked ever grateful to be out of there. She put away the laptop and opened her notebook, filling out the pages with her musings, flights of fancy that Charu could turn into purposeful essays. Twenty minutes later she sighed and leaned back, admiring her work.

The street outside was desolate, no sign of energy living or otherwise. She was suddenly aware of how big the café was, empty chairs and curtained windows completing the look of a house long abandoned. The thing about the mountains on these nights was the absence of any noise. Except for footsteps, heavy and deliberate. She looked out the window and huffed at Faisal's silhouette drudging its way up the stairs.

He threw open the door without a knock.

"Are you some sort of caveman? What the hell is wrong –"

"Oh shut up Sunaina! Is there something to drink here?"

"Fuck off."

He stood there, face caked with dried sweat and dirt. He raised his eyebrows in a challenge, backpack sliding off his shoulder. She sighed loudly and pointed to the mini bottle of whiskey she'd left for him on the table. He grabbed at it and gave her a deep bow. Much to her own frustration, Sunaina felt bad about being rude to him. It was obvious that he was dead on his feet.

"There's um some hot water in the room."

Faisal didn't turn around. "You left the geyser on?"

"Yes" her voice came out mousey.

He just stood there, shoulders sagging under that ridiculously oversized sweater he insisted on wearing every day because it was the last thing his mother had knit. His hair was crusty with sweat, she could see it curling out from under his cap.

His nose came first as he half turned back, still not really looking at her. "Thanks", and he left her to her silence.

She pulled out the book he'd last given her, unlooping the thread bound necklace she used as a bookmark. It was a heavier subject than the other books he'd shared with her over the past two months, one that spoke of the beginnings of language, philosophy, and critical thinking. She unfolded the little paper on which she'd made her notes.

> **The word construct comes from conscience and structure. Where philosophers spoke of ideas, ideologies, and everything physical or otherwise as constructs. Of the mind, of society, everything. That's where you get a '*construction*' from. And a de-struction. A breaking down of a structure, whether by attacking the idea behind it, it's foundation, or the structure itself – as a whole.**
>
> ***I don't know where to go with this really but I want you to think of a way this can be applied into the feminist context. Keep it light and fairly simple to read I don't want something too flowery or whatever like do what you do best atm...**

She signed off and locked up the dollhouse double doors. Faisal wasn't yet done with his shower so she left her bag on the bed and stepped back out for a smoke. The night sky sprawled above, clear as an ocean with stars swimming in synchronized constellations. She stared at the smoke that looped up and out from her lips. There was no moon but the stars were out and in that moment they were hers to own so it was beautiful.

As always she sensed his presence before she heard him. "You know what's funny? I thought you'd come back smelling of apples – considering you work in an orchard – but two weeks later and I'm only getting fertilizer and sweat."

"Should I spray some *ittar* before seeing the begum?" he laughed.

"Your mom's a begum," she shoved him and ran inside.

He chased her, laughter booming through the quiet night. He stopped at the sight of her packed bag.

Their smiles faded.

"I meant to tell you about that."

"You know it's not safe."

"But it *is* Faisal", she threw her hands up in frustration, "it's completely safe which is why I need to start going back out there."

He sniffed disapprovingly.

"Look it's not like I'm leading the trek I'm only going as a 'tag-along guide' as per what Jatin said –"

"Does Jatin plan on paying you for this by any chance?" she could tell how hard he fought to keep his eyebrows from rising.

"Because you already have a job, downstairs. You work a single shift and they pay you more than needed, they've given us a place to stay practically rent free do you understand that."

"Oh of course I understand it man what is wrong with you. Listen it's just more ... I need more than to get up and serve coffee everyday. I want to walk out there."

"Well why can't you just wait for my workshops to get over?"

She snorted, "You? On a trek? Don't even ..."

"What's that supposed to mean? You don't even know me Sunaina, you think I haven't been on a stupid mountain trail before?"

"It's a trek across a frozen lake, you realize that's a whole different scenario, right?" And then it struck her. "Is this because it's Jatin?"

Faisal raked his hands through his hair, breathing in deeply before speaking again.

"It's not about him. I just ... I want to be there with you." she was surprised by how big his green eyes were. "Fuck the milquetoast, take me with you instead."

She broke into laughter. "What the fuck is a *milk toast*!"

He smiled at her indulgently. "Look it up later."

They turned down the bed and hurried to get under the blankets without freezing. He reached down and took off his socks because he could never sleep with them on, she reached out for them and put them on because of how warm he left them. She reached up and turned out the lights, he switched off his lamp and they lay with their backs to each other. Buried under her sweater sleeve, beneath the blankets, Sunaina replayed the past few minutes in her head.

She wanted to say something but he broke the silence first.

"How long are you going for?"

"It takes about nine days, I should be back by Thursday after next."

She held her breath.

"Hmm"

"I'll tell you what," she turned to face his back, "you finish your workshops at the orchard and I'll take you to this trail in the valley – about two, maybe three hours from here, it's absolutely beautiful."

"Where exactly is it?"

"It's too dark to draw you a map."

He could hear her smile.

She turned to face him, placing a hand between his shoulder blades. "I'll be back before you know it."

He sniggered into the darkness. "Could you have said anything more clichéd?"

She whacked him on the back and turned over to her side.

Sunaina was furious.

She took down the breakfast orders, almost everyone was dying to have scrambled eggs with bacon and pancakes, and served the steaming morning drinks. No one said a word when she put the empty tray on the counter with more force than necessary.

Faisal came in and sat at one of the last empty tables, taking her chance of a tip with it, and opened the menu as if he didn't have the same breakfast every day. Without a word she slammed the charred bread and milk in front of him.

He looked up with a cheerful twinkle in his eye.

"What is this madam I have a standing order of –"

"It's milk and toast. That's all you're getting today unless you're planning to pay for everything."

"Arey begum what is the matter?"

"Milquetoast really? That's a pathetic thing to call Jatin, I've known him for years you know. He's one of the nicest boys I know from school, like why even would you?"

"He's just annoying, begum why are you so riled up. It's such a beautiful morning."

She leaned in and he sank lower into his chair. "It's a perfect morning for milk and toast. Eat up."

"I'll be working in the field all day, you want me to die of starvation?"

She walked away from the table.

"Begum", he called after her.

"*Begum's dead!*"

Sunaina was staring at them, each a twisted doppelgänger of poker straight hair, overglossed lips, and jewel tone athleisure outfits.

"Well okay so like, what if we have to pee?" one of them half whispered – as if the concept of urination was meant for closed doors.

Jatin looked their way, apprehensive but amused. He'd been emailing with the group for a while, a total of nine specimens of Delhi's finest. Sunaina refocused, trying not to ask why they all wore matching chokers.

"Okay you can go behind a bush, with the location of where we'd be setting camp for the night, it's at a safe distance from any residential or commercial spot as such. There isn't a chance of being walked in on." She ignored their offensive eye rolls. "You walk about twelve steps in any direction, though I suggest you go in a group so you can call out for safety."

"Wait what –"

"Oh and if you're a loud one go another three steps away, there's usually enough ambient noise."

They squirmed, visibly shaken.

"Okay hold up, you just said it's like in the middle of nowhere, right? Why're we gonna need to like ask for help or whatever?"

"Listen you should help us because what if we get attacked?"

"Uh yeah! I heard there are leopards and all over here." She couldn't even look up from her phone while speaking.

"No, this isn't the time when they are likely to attack." Though Sunaina wondered for a moment if that were true, deciding to leave them pacified at the moment.

"Ska-weez me!! But what if there's a crazy inbred tribe –"

"There are no tribal communities here." She harrumphed.

"Arey but what if there's like an undiscovered one ya, like just jumping out and attacking us?"

"Yeah because they're all cannibals and like they don't believe in harming animals but we're basically like a buffet feast for them?"

"Do you really want the deaths of five young and beautiful innocent girls on your conscience?" The tallest one puffed out her chest, looking like she was about to cut her to size.

"Yeah like what the fuck man?"

They crossed their arms in unison like they'd never lost a war.

Sunaina swayed on her feet as the sinking feeling of déjà vu washed over her. "Look most of the times people don't die here from being attacked by an animal. It's because they behave like fools."

"Yeah but you can protect us right?"

"I'll tell you what, you try and not drink too much or fall into the river and anything else I've got your back." She felt the beginnings of a headache bloom.

Faisal announced his presence with a loud laugh. "Begum you should probably tell them about the piss spit while you're at it."

"Oh hell no, what the fuck is piss spit?"

Jatin walked over to intervene. "It's nothing, he's just kidding."

They looked at her with widened eyes.

"No really, just an old wives' tale. Way more fun to hear the story while you're actually *at* the camp." Her cheeks hurt from faking a smile.

Faisal threw his head back and roared with laughter as soon as Jatin had taken them away. He was such a private man in so many ways that seeing him laugh so openly was immediately and intensely endearing.

"You know you're *so* twisted," she couldn't help but laugh with him.

"That's one way to look at it." He shrugged.

"Wait," she pushed him into a seat, "why aren't you at the orchard today?"

"I'm going after lunch, we're prepping for a workshop on making yak cheese tomorrow so we're prepping for that."

"Yak cheese?" she scrunched her nose.

"Begum," he rolled his yes from behind the menu, "you've had it without knowing and you loved it."

"See, when you feed someone weird shit without telling them – that's twisted. When you leave the room in a fucking mess – that's twisted." She pursed her lips disapprovingly.

"I'm not making my own bed." He replied with a petulant pout.

She shook her head. "I'll tell you what, let's take a break from this side of town. My granddad lives in the valley, not too far from here; it's barely half a day's journey. I think it'll be therapeutic for the both of us to just disengage and," she exhaled sagely, "just be."

It was in that moment that Sunaina realized that something had permanently changed in her. She was thriving in her bucolic settings, adapting to the new landscape around her. Living off the grid had had its ups and downs so far, but it had saved her from veering off the wrong side of the edge of a blade ready at her wrist.

Faisal smiled and nodded, eager to have some time off the fields.

Chapter

ELEVEN

Second Star To The Right & Straight On 'Til Morning

-Hey wyd
-wyd?
-What're you doin? lol.. I thot u were supp 2 knw all of these
-Haha no I do just busy w sum stuff
-ohh ok
-talk later

--

-hey hey
-hi H.. what's happening
-nothin just hangin w my bros
-oh nice
-they're not my bros as such, like buddies
-Oh how fun! Guys nite?

-Totally.. u shud cum join
-Txt me when they're gone I'll let u kno

--

-hey gurl
-hii
-wha...

"Hassan! Come on man you've been at it for so long ya bugger, where's your beer?"

He pocketed his phone and returned to the grill where the fish sizzled dangerously. Hassan deftly flipped them and the smell of crushed ginger and lemongrass wafted through the room to appreciative nods. He picked up the corona and flipped it upside down, the warm dregs rolling down his tongue like vinegar. He raised it at Rajiv and asked for another one.

"Oh buddy that smells wonderful yaar!"

"Did you get this sorted all by yourself?" The grill twinkled in response.

Rajiv winked dramatically, "No no, he had some help from the maid."

Hassan roared with laughter. "Ay go to hell, you're just jealous or what..."

"Oh please, I could get anyone bhaisaab and I definitely wouldn't start with the help. I mean come on!"

"Try your luck and then we'll talk" he winked, ignoring the jab of guilt. "Anyway I had to let her go dude, she was starting to stir up trouble and shit."

Pranab studied him for a beat then stood up. "Well good riddance I say!"

They cheered and drank while Hassan plated up the fish.

"You're okay right?"

He turned around to face Pranab.

“I’m fine”, he handed over the plate. “Go pass this around we’ll talk later.”

“Just keep things low key for a while.” Pranab lowered his voice. “If I get another phone call in the middle of the night I’ll really have to step in then.”

“Just pass this fish out yaar, it’s crap if it gets cold. We’ll talk later.”

Monty Manchanda pointed a finger at the sign hanging above them. “Do I get to ask what this is even about?”

Pranab stared at the unlit neon lettering and raised a brow at his friend.

Hassan threw his hands up in resignation. “Arey bugger don’t ask me about that yaar. Sana did it while I was in Europe, fuckin’ looks like we’re sitting in a chawl instead of my living room.”

They weren’t the closest of friends, in fact if you were to ask Hassan to name his good friends Pranab Sahay’s name might not come up at all. Over the years of knowing each other the two men had become a part of each other’s daily life, forging a bond that didn’t need an outwardly acknowledgment.

-You there??

The downside was that Pranab had recently made a habit of involving himself in Hassan’s journey to reclaim lost youth. It had started out really simple: the idea was to get Hassan out of the house. He needed distraction from the fact that his wife and daughter had abandoned him, that his life was almost falling apart.

Distractions that had sprung in the form of Chanda, their maid. And then Kyra, the twenty something girl who met them at some pub in Gurgaon and told Hassan that he looked a little like Ben Affleck and soon they were, only casually, seeing each other. Distractions were now attracted to him like moths to a flame. He was working out every morning and night with the sort of determination that only belonged to people who made money off of their looks.

Pranab had warned him about signing up for Tinder before he had his separation legalized but Hassan was riding on the sort of high that didn't belong to his generation of people.

"Anyway, I made the chicken myself ya this fish I get it pre-marinated by this young fellow in East of Kailash. Bloody good chap, must try him out."

-Busy??

"It's too good ya bugger, you must give me his number."

-Do you wanna meet at our usual place?

"'Scuse me guys, I just need to make a quick phone call."

If Pranab shot him a look, he didn't turn to receive it. Hassan dashed up the stairs to call Priya and coordinate a time they could meet. Priya Sodhi – Rajiv's wife of almost twelve years who, upon discovering his crippling addiction to gambling due to an unfortunate incident involving a stuffed shark, a banana, and a single black hairpin, had started a longstanding series of affairs. A few years later when Rajiv had discovered the clandestine meetings his wife was conducting in their holiday villa in Goa, he had decided to negotiate a deal with her. The deal was simple, she was to continue loving and supporting him and he would limit his pastime to a bi-weekly game night while she could continue her pastimes so long as Rajiv knew about them. That was the story no one knew about the Sodhis' open marriage, until Hassan and Priya had found themselves at the last call of Townhall and needed another drink before calling it a night. She didn't shy away from letting her hands wander when he showed off his new tattoo and the thrill of keeping it a secret from Raj had brought about an overall joie de vivre.

His breath shuddered with every ring.

"Hey Priya ..."

"Hassan! Hey ya where have you been hiding I was texting you didn't reply back only."

It was great in the beginning, as all love affairs usually are. Priya was everything Chanda was not, mostly owing to her relatively extensive sexual experiences. Everything from the moment they met to the time they undressed each other was apathetic. She had the calculative ways of someone who knew what she was into and he preferred her silence. By their third time, when it was discussed finally, the idea of keeping their trysts a secret from his friend – her husband – a secret ignited between them a fire that only grew each time they met since. But as all things, their affair had an expiration date, at least in his mind.

"Okay let me explain this love, remember the last time we met and you forced yourself on me? Yeah that was super not cool and it's got me really bummed out."

"Huh? What're you saying you loved it ..." he could imagine how her face would crumple.

"No that's the opposite of what I'm saying. I am saying that I did in fact ... well did not. Love it that is."

"But –"

"Yeah okay so I was like super hard and stuff but any guy with blood flowing in his body will get hard if someone goes down on him. How do you think the gays were invented, they jus got sick of waiting for women to give good head –"

"Okay that's hideously bigoted. What kind of person even talks like that?!"

He rolled his eyes. "Look just because we were having super secret sex doesn't mean we can't stop."

"But I don't want to stop. You're the one –"

Hassan swiped at the sweat on his lip.

"Yeah I wanna stop. Because I feel like you're going a little cray-cray and I can't deal with it right now."

"How am I going crazy?"

"No, *I'm* the one who gets to be crazy for a while alright? I've just been adulting for too long."

"What's 'adulting'? What do you mean?" She was at her wit's end now.

"Ok adulting is a super young people's word, I guess I'll just have to explain that later – in a socially appropriate setting – but what I mean Priya is that I can't see you anymore and I think you're losing it."

"But we love each other!"

"No we don't."

"We literally said that last time ..."

"No. You said it while I gave you the best oh oh of your life and then I didn't say it back." He wiped the sweat off his brow, despite the cool post rain breeze.

"Of course you did."

"No I didn't." he eyed the spring of stubble along his jaw.

"That's why I wanna divorce Rajiv."

"Oh oh which brings me to the next phase of my beef with you. What possessed you to call Pranab – my best bud in the club – and ask him to help you file divorce papers to his friend, who is also my friend, Rajiv?!"

"But I'm doing it for us."

"You called him at three in the morning giggling and then when he said he'll call you the next day you called back crying. What the actual fuck is up?"

"Listen ..."

"You know what no actually. I don't think I wanna know. Let's just forget about this."

"But –"

"And let me and Rajiv be good buds."

"Hassan –"

"And please stay away from me."

"What the fu–"

He cut the call and blocked her number, temporarily only. Hassan swore to himself that he would unblock it within a few days when he'd need entry into the club. The Sodhis threw every important party of the season; they held fundraisers and organized auctions for charity. For all intents and purposes, they were the glittering jewels of South Delhi society.

Hassan undressed under the harsh light of the bathroom with an unfamiliar soundtrack for company. Eisha, his sort of girlfriend, had taken it upon herself to introduce him to the sounds of Kendrick Lamar and the Weeknd. He powdered a big white pill and felt every muscle come alive as it went up his nasal tract.

"Well boys it's been a great evening but I'll take your leave now. Feel free to order pizza and continue the game!" he padded down the stairs.

"Woah woah what the hell?"

"I gotta go."

"What's more important than Friday rituals?"

"Okay first of all Monty I think we established last time that we'd call it FRIYAY, I don't know why you're insisting on being a douchebag right now by not using our predecided awesome code."

Monty looked at him with a furrowed unibrow. "What's a douchebag?"

Pranab rolled his eyes.

"Second of all I have a date."

"A hot date is it? Don't be shy give us some details ..."

"Oh you met her don't you remember."

Rajiv looked impressed. "The one who called you uh ... who was it?"

"Ben Affleck," Pranab grunted.

"Yeah Ben fucking Affleck man!" He grinned.

"Isn't she what twenty years old or something?" Rajiv had abandoned his surreptitious tone.

"Twenty four actually."

"She's basically Sana's age what the fuck is wrong with you?" Monty guffawed.

"Yeah how'd you feel if oh I don't know one of us slept with your daughter?"

"Okay first of all," Hassan shrugged into his coat, "that's disgusting I would kill you, but it's totally not gonna happen. You know why?"

"Well, why?"

He bowed. "Because my daughter doesn't have daddy issues."

He left them rapt in impressed silence.

Hassan and Eisha had the kind of unapologetic sex that left them with bittersweet aches and a fine slick of sweat. They lay over each other in a post coital glow or perhaps it was just the way the string of lights reflected off the pale walls. He traced the curve of her back, sloping into a luxurious butt as she shifted and slid into a feline stretch over the sheets. Everything about the room had the dismal aura of cheapness that only specifically occurred at the cross junction of too much money and not enough love. She didn't want daddy's money, she'd tell you at a party, she wanted to make her life a work of art. The thing is she loved Leonard Cohen and Kurt Vonnegut and little else in between. And so Eisha had traded her Vasant Vihar bungalow for a nothing square foot apartment in Malviya Nagar where the paint was chipped and the balcony was shared with two tenants and a herb garden. She kissed with a reckless abandon and loved the graze of Hassan's nose pulling from the space between her thighs. He always asked her to get an airconditioner but she loved the sweat rolling off her skin, the way it matted her hair. She lay there naked as a baby, reading aloud from a worn out book of Pablo Neruda's poems when he interrupted.

"Babe, whose underwear is that?" he pointed to the corner of the room.

"Oh it's Gaurav's, he's sort of the neighbour's boyfriend but they had a fight and she like threw him out in the middle of the night so I just let him crash here."

"Wait, do you even know him?"

She pushed herself off the bed, no longer interested in the conversation or the poem. "We've talked a bit, while watering the plants mostly. Why?"

Nothing, he said. They dressed and made their way to the party. Before they'd made it all the way into Sainik Farms she'd pulled him into the backseat while whispering along to a love song.

"Oh shit, fuck I'm so sorry."

Eisha eyed the damp tshirt scrunched in his hands. "Dude what am I supposed to wear? That's going to stain."

She nudged him off her and pulled the kimono robe up her shoulders, trying to cover her bra up as far as possible. He tossed the funky tshirt to the floor and pulled up his jeans with a gruff. She leaned in and kissed him till the tension eased from his shoulders.

"I'm getting a divorce", he spoke into the nook of her shoulder.

"Why?" she bit his ear. "I don't want to be seeing a divorced man, that oh that makes you sound so old."

He ignored the stab of hurt and kissed her once on the forehead. "That doesn't matter. Don't you want to be with me, and I mean really be with me."

Eisha looked at him with her big sad eyes. "I'm scared I'll fall in love with you."

"What's there to be scared of, love? Okay but seriously, *do* you think I'm too old for you?" She shook her head. "Am I going to be the oldest person at this party?"

She tousled her wild hair. "Listen these people are artists and lovers of love, no one's going to care how old you are or where you come from."

He watched in wonderment as she wove her way through the party with unrehearsed ease. It seemed as though she was unfettered by every compliment and wink. The only trouble with Eisha was she didn't know when the party was over and there was too much liquor and cigarette smoke fuming out of her. She beckoned to Hassan from the couch, a stranger's heavy head resting on her lap.

"Babe I feel like we've barely spoken. Did you try the baked cheese oh my gawsh I just died and went to heaven." She threw her head back and laughed.

The boy reached for her glass and she let him sip from it as though he were a lost traveler and she a water nymph. Hassan watched the scene with jealousy and arousal poisoning his gut. He knelt at her feet and sneered at her.

"How much longer do you plan to drink for Eisha?"

She pointed to her chest. "Till it stops hurting."

The boy in her lap turned to the side and nuzzled deeper. Hassan grit his teeth to avoid snapping back. It was at this point that he found himself wondering how he chose his women so terribly. She was just a child, a sulking little girl begging for attention. In some ways, he realized with a rising panic, she was just a different version of Tina.

"I'll go out and get drunk whenever I feel sad and – oh where are my manners!" she plucked the cigarette from his mouth and arced her hand out grandly.

"Raghav Dewan, meet my lover mister Ben Affleck", she giggled. "Mr. Affleck meet Raghav Dewan, banker by day and painter by night."

Hassan felt the bottom of his gut give way as the older Dewan brother turned back to look at him. Instantly they recognized each other and Raghav watched in mild amusement as Hassan scrambled away from them and into the bushes outside to spill his guts.

It was well into the night by the time Hassan made his way home. He saw his ashen face reflected in the mirror and put on the practiced smile.

"I have had a revelation." He announced.

Pranab looked up from the bar, everyone else had left.

"Take a seat. I hope this has something to do with the problem you need to take care of *before anything else*." He shot a pointed stare.

"What, the Priya thing? Arey Pranab saheb don't worry, already taken care of that. I spoke to her before leaving and it's all good." Hassan popped a beer.

"So she isn't planning on divorcing Rajiv then?"

"Well she can do whatever she wants honestly, it just won't be on my conscience." He ignored the fizz of his churning bowels.

"You cannot just ignore something as big as this Hassan, sit the fuck down and talk to me bud."

He sighed. "You're right. I don't know what to do."

Pranab was ostensibly surprised. He had hoped for some way to approach the situation without word letting out. The weight of an impending divorce already hung heavy on his own house, Hassan did not need another complication.

"My dad called today" Hassan sighed.

"Woah," Pranab drank deeply. "That's ... damn, how long has it been since you last spoke?"

"Seven months. He sounded off; I don't know what to make of it. I hope he isn't sick because with the way winters are up in Himachal it could get very bad for him and you know ya buddy it's not the best place for expecting quick medical help."

Pranab offered his whiskey, which he took and then continued. "He wants me to come see him. Actually he wants all of us to go Kama, Geetu, and me. I know Geetika will have no problems but I don't know what to do about Kama. Yaar she doesn't leave her house at all, like ever. I don't know how many occasions she's missed, bloody hell she didn't even come for Geetu and Dev's wedding yaar! You were there did you see her?"

He sighed. "And I don't know why it's bothering me this much but he was talking to me in a way he hasn't for years. I don't remember the last time he actually sounded so *nice*. He wants to – I think he wants to discuss his will and shit."

Not knowing what else to say or do, Pranab clapped him on his shoulder.

"Would you like me to come with you?"

Hassan scoffed at him. "As a friend or a lawyer?"

"Whatever you need buddy. Whatever you need."

Chapter TWELVE

Ladies Who Lunch (*Interlude*)

"So that's it then, you've just decided not to come." Geetu tapped the ash off her cigarette, both fuming.

Kama tucked a stray lock of hair behind her ear. "Oh it isn't that, I mean what even is there to consider?"

She lit the joint between her fingers and grimaced delicately at the first toke. "I think it's rather ridiculous that daddy would expect me to come anyway."

Hassan sat at an equal distance apart from them, polar opposites of each other. Geetu had always had the deep thick voice that commanded immediate attention, even though she stood almost a foot shorter than her sister. Over the years she'd learnt the craft of words though, how to cut deep without leaving a mark. She'd mastered the art of piercing stares and dramatic hand gestures. Kama on the other hand, tall and dainty as always, had the sweet demeanour of one who never meant harm. But all the years of giving everyone a shoulder to cry and complain on meant that she had secrets that could well tear them apart.

"Oh really" Geetu stood with a loud stamp of the foot. "And why would that be? Are you some divine being that cannot leave her celestial throne?"

Kama chuckled at her indulgently. "Oh come on, don't be silly Geetika."

"No really," her earrings jangled threateningly, "are you a deity whose feet we need to bow down at, just so you could come with us to see your own damn father?"

Kama thrust the joint toward Hassan.

"Oh shut up." She said pointedly. "I don't get how either of you can say anything to me, I'm the only one who even knows what's going on in his life."

Hassan massaged his forehead, now annoyed. "What have I done? Don't drag me into this okay, I'd probably drive up to see him more if he wasn't such a dick to me all the time."

"True as that may be, it doesn't change the facts!" Kama regally pulled a shawl across her shoulders. "You know Geetu how badly he behaved with Ria, I know Surya told you all about it. Why should I now go all the way?"

"Because he's still your father! And look we're having dinner outside, which means you're obviously doing better. What's the harm ya, it'll barely be for a few days."

"Okay to be fair," Hassan pointed to the glass ceiling, "we're technically still inside the house."

"Shut up", they chimed.

"Look I'm choosing to no longer discuss the matter because you're really ruining this lunch right now."

"Oh cut the crap. As if you've prepared it." Geetu waved the smoke off her face. "You didn't even order it, you made your daughter-assistant do it."

Hassan puffed at the joint to avoid catching in the crossfire.

"That's irrelevant. I don't want to eat warm sushi."

"It's December, are you on crack?"

Kama spun around, all airs abandoned. “I’ll show you a crack if you say one more word.”

Hassan pushed up from the chair unsteadily. Though he couldn’t feel his face anymore, he pushed between them. “Yeah I’m putting the sushi to chill for a while, it’s not as cold as you think.”

“Oh fuck off Hassan”, Kama walked over to the antique table and poured wine for them. “What’s this really about ya Geetu?”

Geetika Shroff shook her head in resignation. Only her sister could’ve served merlot with sushi. Only her daughter would be characteristically ungrateful.

“It’s just this wedding, I haven’t heard from Surya or Dev since last week and we need to send out invitations soon because otherwise nobody will attend the ceremony in Jodhpur. Fucking Jodhpur of all places, do you remember my first marriage?” She huffed. “And then there’s papa who won’t answer my calls, I’m so stressed that he’s sick again.”

“It’s going to be okay.” Kama spoke in her saccharine voice.

She stood and put the jazz café channel on iRadio and drifted around with another glass in tow for Hassan.

Geetu’s head swooned dangerously. “What’s in this joint, I’m completely gone right now.”

She shrugged in response. “I have no clue, I confiscated it from Ria’s room.”

“That’s some stellar parenting,” Hassan said as Kama left them to fetch some munchies.

“As for you”, Geetu turned to Hassan so ferociously he had the urge to stand and click his heels in attention. “I need to talk to you.”

She leaned in. “It isn’t just this wedding and dad stuff, I heard some crap from the gossip grapevine and if it’s true I will fucking stab you.”

“Huh?” Hassan yelped as his sister smacked him on the head.

The scene of the crime, as it always was, had been the Delhi Social Club. A members-only affair with the best cocktails in town, it also served as the weekly meeting place for Priya Sodhi and her friends. When she had declared it the new venue, it had everyone who was anyone clamoring to sign up for fingerprint and retinal scans, cutting cheques without a thought.

The Delhi Social Club's menu claimed to be completely gluten-pesticide-dairy-free, and non-GMO of course, but the ladies went for the gin and discreet service. They were the daughters of the armed forces, each of them equipped with a sharp tongue and memories of boarding schools that had anointed them with inimitable grace and etiquette. And so among the chatter of a particularly warm Saturday afternoon, everyone had forgotten to compliment Priya's new ensemble.

"Can we order drinks ladies, or should I just go ahead and call for a round of whatever I want?"

Silence had descended on the table like a cold fog.

"Quick, someone exorcise her with coke before she kills us all," Parmeet leaned in and whispered to Geetu.

It was pitifully obvious that Priya hadn't slept well for many nights. Her blouse was sheer Chanel but it did nothing to the pallor that came from crying too much, the dryness around the mouth from guzzling vodka. Farida, who was sitting closest to her didn't point out the fact that her nail polish was chipped in exactly three different places. None of them addressed the signs because every woman at that table had known them all too well.

Things had taken a turn for the worse as Ritika tried to lighten the mood.

"So Priya, I wanted to ask you ya –"

"Is everyone finc with gin?" she flipped the menu so hard her hair fluttered with it.

"My daughter-in-law seems like she might enjoy some company and all –"

"I'm ordering gin and tonics for now ya, you guys decide whatever you want for after that."

"I mean I was thinking why don't we –"

"Ritika, when I need your suggestions I will ask for them. As of now you can bring whomever you like, pick a bitch off the street if you want, as long as they can afford to get in here."

She looked around the silent table. "If you're gloating about having a daughter-in-law or whatever I think it's just stupid. You realize that it actually makes you seem older than the rest of us right? Except for Farida I don't think anyone's child is married here. If you want to bring her, do it. I don't care."

Everyone shifted uncomfortably like birds in a menagerie but nobody had the gall to stand up in defense. Much to Geetika's chagrin that was the point Param had changed the topic to Hassan. She'd seen him working out shirtless in his backyard, she had a bee sting to prove it. And while everyone tittered, Priya looked as though she might vomit all over the table. There was a reason she couldn't meet anyone's eyes, a reason why she cleared her throat and spoke at Param's last season Michael Kors sunglasses.

"Serves you right for looking into someone else's home."

Geetu took her leave then, having bridged gaps she shouldn't have. They stared at her retreating back with mild humour, debating the importance of keeping up an appointment with a designer – no matter how exclusive an atelier. No sooner had she left the club, Geetu had called Pranab's office to validate her suspicions.

If anything, the look on Hassan's face had confirmed it all.

"Okay look" he raised his hands defensively "she came on to me."

"Of course she did. I knew she was trash from the moment I laid eyes on her." She smacked him on the head again. "And you, you must be out of your mind to drive the rebound train between her legs. She's in a bloody open marriage for god's sake."

"Hello? Who said I was on the rebound?"

She crossed her arms and stared at him with disgust dripping off her eyes. "So planning to settle down with the twelve year old who thinks you look like Clint Eastwood?"

"What – Clint Eastwood, really? That's not even close. First of all it's Ben Affleck and second she's not twelve what is wrong with you."

"What is wrong with you?" Kama placed the heavy plate of entrees on the table. "She's practically the same age as Sana."

Hassan pinched the bridge of his nose, unable to rehash that argument. "How do you even know about my girlfriend by the way?"

"How typical of you to forget," Geetu clapped loudly. "Pranab told me and I obviously told her. When have we ever had secrets, him and I? He helped me back when we played hide and seek, when the two of you'd gang up against me, and he helps me now too."

Kama drained her glass of wine too fast and refilled unsteadily.

"That doesn't change what she's trying to say, Hassan. You should know better than to get into bed with Priya Sodhi. That woman just spells trouble everywhere she nests."

"Okay she's not so bad you know –"

"She's mad as a fucking snake" Kama threw back the wine, already slurring. "Get your shit together."

As the sky faded to the lightest lilac and Kama swapped the merlot for an icy vodka, Geetu felt the seeds of an evil plan germinate.

Chapter THIRTEEN

Nobody's Business

As consciousness dawned on Kama, she became aware of three terrible things. She was no longer on the patio, in fact she didn't know where she was. That her dehydrated tongue had swollen stiff, so when she screamed it came out a garbled moan. That they were moving, in a car, uphill.

Inertia hit her with the force of a brick wall and she viciously vomited out the open window.

The fear of waking up in unfamiliar surroundings, with no memory of how you got there, it sends your soul into free fall. That weightlessness is usually followed by a burn of bile rising up your throat, while your heart echoes emptily inside you. Kama closed her eyes and tried to remember the last time she had been inside a moving car – fifteen years ago, for Geetu's birthday. She had spent a week locked in her room to recover from the shock, no food no water, and the betrayal was still fresh as if it were yesterday.

She opened her eyes when the hands groped her, ready to attack her molestor but it was Geetu. She looked around the cavernous vehicle and put names to faces – her brother, Geetu's new husband and Pranab Sahay who for some reason had his head out the window. The smell of bile hit her and she vomited again this time directly into Geetu's hands who then abandoned hope of cleaning her up. Pranab retched in reaction, now half outside the window himself. They stopped at the next restaurant-guest house and ordered tea while the ladies rushed to the bathroom.

The toilet was filthy but Kama thought nothing of it and sat down, head swirling and heavy in her hands. She had read countless experiences that described an out-of-body experience and the feeling of your soul drifting in the cosmic unknown as you sleep, it all seemed like hyperbolic trash compared to the cold sweat waterfalling down her face. The smell of drying vomit was intoxicating, sweet and sour at the same time considering she'd been drinking red wine for three days straight – three whole days from whatever words perforated the cloud between Geetu and her. Now it all felt like vinegar, like her insides had pickled. She stared at the tiled floor, once upon a time white but now crusty with dirt and other grime. Her insides were gravitationally unbound, revolving around a different point altogether, trying to push themselves out of her flesh prison. Once she had thrown up a third time, Kama stood despondently as Geetu scrubbed the stains off of her kurta.

The plain cotton shift was thin but fresh, it smelled of lavender detergent evoking the memory of home, of mixing store bought soap with her own ingenious mix. She remembered Ria and was overwhelmed with the need to sit and cry for an hour or so because in that completely foreign setting she could understand the depth of her devotion. Of her family, who sat around the table tense and ready to swoop in at the first sign of hysteria. She saw the pill bottles poking out of Geetu's handbag, the way Hassan monitored her tea, even offering to taste it for her to see if it was how she liked it. When she excused herself everyone asked if she needed help, she turned down an offer to be accompanied to the bathroom twice. She stood in front of the tiny basin shared by the men and women's toilets, though the dank smell only came if you stood at a specific angle. She washed her face and dabbed at it with the back of her hand. With the sky clear and the wind low, the sun was a warm cloak bathing the open meadow in bright light very unlike her idea of a winter afternoon. A body of water split the land in two, sometimes an odd ripple would catch and shatter the sunlight drawing her attention. In the distance the hills rolled into higher mountains. It should've been more overwhelming from what she knew of her agoraphobia, the technicolour assault on her senses would have sent her into a panic attack, she braced herself against it but it never came. Her knuckles whitened against the dirty railing when the wind picked up, she wondered how far it could lift and take her – whether it could take her back home.

She looked down at her tunic and felt naked in the plain sheath of cotton, her version of Victorian underclothes. The wind cooled so she walked back to the restaurant and finished her tea. Every passing car made her jump, she could feel the sweet milky tea roiling around in her gut. Pranab helped her pull out a cardigan from the back but the chill had already set in. She sat in the front seat of the car and rested her head on the dashboard.

They were deep in the valley chasing the last shred of daylight and still a few kilometers from the house while Kama sat sucking on lemons like candy trying to settle her insides. Geetu had abandoned her pollyanna notions of a truce; the tension was heavy even when they passed familiar landmarks from another era. If Sunaina had answered any of Hassan's calls they would've been surprised to find her camping with Faisal just a few hundred metres to their north, off the trail that lead to the reserve. He drove with reckless precision, swerving sharply around bends and driving over rubble as though they were in a monster truck than a humble Scuba Blue Q5. Their heads spun at every bend and swoop of the road but no one complained anymore.

At long last the familiar bridge gave way to the unkempt road leading up to the house, they thought of stopping for tea at the little café but once past the village it was only a few minutes away. Kama turned and stared at the little café door, wondering why it felt familiar but the excitable blabber broke her thoughts.

They drove past the gate and the watchman hurried to shut it behind them, the colonial style house rose up in front of them surrounded by deep blue mountains, the sky now a darkened canvas. With the last turn up the driveway the lawn chairs came into view and they realized that the Commander wasn't alone.

Kama felt the blood drain from her face. "Fuck."

Hassan leaned forward, eyes squinting.

"Who the fuck is that? Why is she sitting so close to papa?"

Geetu leapt forward and laughed once. "It looks like they're – are they drinking?"

Kama turned around and launched into a quick version of what she knew about Leela, how Asim had been helping her run the tea stall which had now obviously expanded into a full café and they had grown close. She'd been helping him to return the favour, but Kama didn't know too much about that.

Asim had walked up to the car by then; Hassan noted how ridiculous his uniform of polo shirts looked in that particular blood orange tone.

"What's the matter? Are you planning on spending the entire weekend in your car?" Hassan noted that the Commander still spoke with militant authority, like they were children up to no good.

"Why, are you embarrassed of us already?"

"Don't worry Hassan, with you there's nothing new about it."

He slammed both hands on the wheel. "See I told you this was a stupid fucking idea!"

"Arey Papa don't rile him up we've just arrived ya."

"Geetu please, it's not like he is going to listen to you right now."

"I'm just joking why does he have to take everything so seriously?" Asim let his arms drop in faux disappointment.

"Dad because you always do this – I'm not an idiot young boy dammit!"

"Watch your tone you –" He leaned in, wide eyed. "Kama is that you?!"

They'd never heard him make the sound before but it sounded like a mother bird cooing.

Pranab and Dev sat back and observed.

Kama ran out of the car and hugged Asim, while the others made their exit somberly.

"Arey Pranab my boy it's been ages since I've seen you", he poked his gut, "looks like the missus is keeping you well fed eh?"

He shook Dev's hand firmly, "Ahha Mr. Shroff, I'm glad you're here ya, finally good to have you on the estate."

They shared a quick hug, the kind that men reserved for each other. It ended with a firm pat on the back.

"Geetika my love", he pulled her in, "it's been too long. Next time I want to see the girls also. How's Vir? I haven't heard from him in ages."

"Oh he's good ya daddy, you know how he is." She pulled out a cigarette. "Keeps to himself no matter how brilliant he is, I'm lucky if I get an update here or there."

Hassan waited for his turn, the cursory greeting of a one armed hug and an 'All good beta?' which had been tradition ever since his marriage.

Once out of the car, the party stood awkwardly everyone aware of the young woman standing patiently by her wicker chair. She had a warm smile on but only Geetu noticed the tightness in her eyes, there were secrets waiting to be told. She closed her own eyes and sent out a prayer that her father would wait till breakfast the next day.

"Come come everyone, I have a very special lady to introduce you to." Asim gestured grandly towards the garden.

Hassan sighed. "Daddy we're all exhausted, wouldn't it be better if we could wash up and then do – you know... whatever this is."

Asim turned and shot daggers at him. Hassan was surprised the moustache didn't spontaneously combust.

"Just come and say hello, it won't bloody kill you."

When you're young it's a strange thing watching a parent interact with another person lovingly. As you grow older the relations between two people tend to become easier to discern, you can tell if someone genuinely cares about another person and their wellbeing, it's different from the person whose wellbeing and happiness is directly tied to your own. To have seen a father raise teenagers into adults, as fully functional as possible, was aggravating until they'd had to do it for themselves and still it wasn't half as easy as Asim had made it seem – even with a spouse around. To them he had always been a pillar of strength and doting commitment.

When they were younger it was easier to see him as a whole, as if there was never a need for another half to complete him. They had observed him at the parties he hosted and the ritual Sunday lunches in the garden, alternating between spicy pork curries and rajma-chawal he cooked himself. He had an unrelenting determination to make things work, to never allow a bubble of discontentment or loneliness into their family – even when they went through their second round of growing pains.

He introduced them to Leela with every word steeped in the syrupy joy of an altogether different nature, that much was obvious. Hassan and Geetika nodded and said hello, mirroring polite smiles that indicated they would talk about her at the first chance of being alone. Pranab and Dev were met with a warm handshake and a 'welcome to the house', which sounded odd from her lips because she was the stranger there, it was their house. The home of their childhood, of every high and lowest low. Kama gave her a hug simpering about how nice it was to finally meet her and then proceeded to ignore the dark looks that branded her as a traitor.

Hassan broke the spell of clinking cutlery in the otherwise silent dining hall.

"So how exactly do you two know each other?"

Pranab cleared his throat.

Leela looked downward.

"We met at her tea stall last year, it comes on my way to those yoga classes I take down by the river." He replied through pursed lips. "In exchange for her lovely tea I've been teaching her English."

"That doesn't explain what she's doing here daddy."

"I wanted her to meet my family, which I hope you're not giving me reason to reconsider." The threat undercutting his words was unmistakable.

"Not at all, I'm just curious as to who she really is –"

"Don't talk about her like she's not in the room, Hassan. Show some respect."

He glanced her way without apology. "My point is –"

"Your point is what exactly? You want to know how close we are or what?"

Geetu shifted loudly in her seat in the hopes that she could shut her brother up if only he'd look at her.

"Yes papa, please help us understand what exactly is going on here."

"What is going my son is that Leela keeps me company here while none of you idiots can be bothered to check up on your old man." He shot a furtive look at the rest of them as though to challenge a rebuff.

"Oh please I come and see you all the time," he scoffed.

"Twice a year is not all the time for god's sake this is exactly why I told you not to marry that fool from Bombay because I knew she'd turn you into a stupid man and not just lightly stupid I mean a truly blithering idiot."

"Oh", Hassan clapped loudly, "well congratulations daddy your predictions were all true."

"I know! I know all of it."

"Well if you know all of it why did you call us up here? To gloat? That you're happy?"

"Happy? You think I'm happy that my son's wife is holidaying in Europe with some random *younger* man?"

Hassan shot daggers at Kama.

"Oh don't look at her I'm the one talking to you. You think I'd bother at all if I wasn't worried about you lot."

"What are you even bothered about if you have *her* here to keep you company and drown you in all of her 'special tea'."

Asim slammed a fist on the table

"Don't you take that tone of voice about Leela. As long as you're under my roof you'll show some respect here."

"Arey but who even is she to you?"

"Oh fuck this," Geetu grumbled and pulled out a cigarette. Dev bit his cheeks beside her to maintain composure.

"She is living here with me!" he bellowed. "She's taking care of me so that I don't go mad living in this godforsaken useless fucking mansion all by myself."

"WHAT?!"

No one was eating anymore.

The chicken had roasted for four hours on a low flame, the cook had spent another hour perfecting the gravy and mashed potatoes. They'd even made fresh bread because Geetika had told Asim that Dev loved soaking his bread in gravy. Everything was now cold.

"SHE" he thrust a finger in her direction, "this random girl from the hills is living here in our house with you?"

Leela sat up straight. "Hey!"

"Sit your ass down Hassan," Asim was going to burst a vein. "Either sit down and talk like a grown up or get the hell out of this house."

No one said a word.

Kama strained her ears and was sure no one dared to breathe.

Geetu had spilled gravy on herself when she stood sometime during the conversation but her voice had fallen on deaf ears and the stain might never leave. She stared at the ruined kurta, it was limited edition Anita Dongre and completely wasted on the freakshow that was her family.

Dev discreetly slid his glass up for a huge gulp of wine, trying to smoothly place it back on the table.

He stared at the fresh roll of bread hardening in front of them asking to be slathered with herb butter, his stomach stirred in solace. Devendra Shroff came from a different world altogether – even with their extravagance his family always found a way back to each other. For Dev, home was where laughs and sorrows held equal footing, never these sort of vinegary displays of resentment.

"I don't understand what the hell is wrong with all of you," Asim showed no signs of calming down. "Instead of finding comfort or joy that I have some companionship, that I'm not dying alone here like some crazy old man, you're all sitting there on your failed marriages, out of control children, and whatever new problem your therapists cook up, and you're judging me!"

"Failed." He spat. "I have failed in raising you all because these spoilt brats in front of me aren't what I raised. You're all fucking imbeciles, it's a joke that you think you deserve any respect in life."

"Okay", Kama raised her hands defensively, "I think you're being a little unfair –"

"*Unfair?* When was the last time you left your fucking house, Kama? Your daughter is more independent than you, at least if something happens tomorrow she will be capable of defending herself."

Kama shrank back in horror. "What are you implying here, papa?"

"My dear I'm saying if tomorrow we are under attack or a natural disaster strikes, she has more chances of survival than anyone else at this table."

Dev raised a finger to interject. "You know –"

Geetu silenced him with a look.

Hassan rolled his eyes. "Fine, daddy, since we're all being so honest here let's get it all out. I think you're just the worst, I can't stand coming up here to see you."

Asim scoffed. "Do you even know where your daughter is? Do you know where your own life is headed? Are you legally separated from that snake or is she coming back some time to squeeze more money out of you? Of course you hate me because I'm the only one who's asking you these things."

Hassan looked around to a room of averting eyes.

"I just want everyone here to understand that I care for Leela a lot, she's been there for me when I had no one to turn to. She's kept me sane, saved me from talking to the walls in this ridiculous house."

Dev drained the remainder of his wine and reached for more, so long as he could choke back his laughs. Geetu scratched at the drying gravy spot with disdain. Since no one had offered her an ash tray, she'd taken to the little plastic bowl where bits of hummus crusted at the bottom.

"As a matter of fact Leela helped me in more ways than one; I've made a decision and that's really the reason I've called you all here. I'm turning the house into an exclusive Bed & Breakfast."

"Wait, what?"

"Yes, I'm turning both rooms on the ground and two of the upper floor rooms into guest bedrooms and suites. We'll have breakfast served on the big table in the verandah and Leela knows someone who can help us organize treks and nature walks nearby."

"Oh really now," Hassan sneered, "and does Leela have any other special powers."

"Shut up and listen for once Hassan."

"No really papa tell me, is she a gypsy who can predict whether this will even work? Have you seen the state of the economy?"

The Commander walked over and poured himself a whiskey from the small bar in the corner.

"Have you applied for a license even? You can't just flip a residential property into a commercial thing you know."

Geetu felt the beginnings of a headache. Kama simpered into a polka hankie, sipping lovingly from her large rum and coke.

Leela opened her mouth but he intervened. "We've actually already taken care of all those things thanks for your concern boy."

"I know a few people in the village because of my father so they were very agreeable." It was admirable that Leela still spoke with dignity.

"Oh I get it, you two are like business partners now right ... and where do you plan on getting initial investments, love? By selling tea?"

"Shut up," someone muttered.

"You see this is why you're an absolutely useless person to talk to, Hassan. This is probably why Tina left you in the first place."

"Oh daddy, don't get into that right now." Geetu swallowed her bitter gin and lit another cigarette. Between her father and brother, she wondered when she'd start greying.

"No really beta, someone has to tell him because he can't keep living in this dream world where everyone is tripping over to give Mr. Hassan Kochhar's boots a lick. It's ridiculous!"

"You think *you* can understand what went wrong with my marriage, papa? Are you on crack?"

"Leela's moved into the house and she's going to help me run the B&B, you either get on board or get out."

"What is with this constant threat of throwing us out papa?" Anger radiated in waves from where Geetu sat. "If you've called us here only to throw this crap in our face and tell us to get out over and over again then we can leave. It's fine!"

Asim's mask softened. "That's not what I meant."

"This is the fifth time you've said it ya what the hell."

"Maybe I should just go upstairs for a bit." By then even Kama couldn't bear Leela's gratingly saccharine voice. She drew her chair back noisily; all three siblings winced at the sound.

"Leela, please."

"No really it's fine." She dabbed at the corner of her mouth with the deep red napkin. "I didn't want anyone to be so upset about it."

She turned to the rest of the dinner party. “I’m really sorry about all this, please don’t ruin dinner.”

“He’s the one who ruined it!”

Asim glared at his son’s outstretched finger and watched it wilt.

“I don’t care, I’m not hungry anymore.” Geetu grumbled.

Dev raised his hand, “I could eat actually.”

Pranab meanwhile had opened a window and stood next to it smoking.

“Absolutely not. Now that you’ve fed us so much trash I’m not hungry either.”

Asim smiled, a smile that Geetika always dreaded. The one that gave way to his evil alter ego.

“Well stay for dessert then boy, I’ve added her to the will.”

Glass shattered against the wall. It slipped from numb fingers and fell to the floor. Dev ducked under his arm to protect himself against the shards ricocheting from both sides.

“What. The. FUCK.” Hassan bellowed.

“Papa what’s this new story now?”

“What do you mean ... you never said anything about that!” Kama was on the verge of hysterics.

“Wait, did you know about the other stuff?” Geetu loomed over her.

“No, well not all of it.”

“And you didn’t tell anyone?” Dev spoke from behind his hand.

“Daddy have you gone mad? I was supposed to inherit the house.”

“Uh no, I thought we all were getting an equal share?”

Asim cleared his throat.

“No. First of all, I’m thoroughly disappointed. You all already have a share of my assets, Geetu and Kama you sat and selected all of your mother’s possessions like it was an auction; the estate technically was going to all of your children.”

"Wait, that makes no sense. How would you divide one house between five children?"

Asim turned to Dev, "The whole point is to not divide the property kiddo."

"Well that's a pretty good deal I think ..."

"Oh shut up Dev," Hassan spewed, "you're not even legit family here nobody wants your opinion."

"How dare you talk to him like that you blithering cunt." Geetu stomped her foot, which only widened Dev's grin.

"I'll talk to him however I wa–"

"And let me tell you we already have offshore accounts with trust funds for our children. We have no need to run after property or assets." She turned to Kama. "I just wanted some things that belonged to ma so I could one day give them to my daughter."

Dev cleared his throat.

"Both my daughters."

Dev looked at her like she'd completely lost the plot. "Oh, really?"

"Yeah, isn't that what you were implying?"

"No I did that because my throat is closing up, I'm really thirsty. And hungry but I guess that's irrelevant now. Wait you know you don't have to give any real heirlooms to Gayatri and all, right?"

She giggled. "But I want to."

"Okay whatever that is I don't care ... my point is I'd rather have the estate stay in our family than some *pahadi* piece of trash."

Hassan's voice was cut off as fist connected to jaw and the chair toppled over. Asim was straddling him, roaring gutturally in a way that was both horrifying and amusing. Except no one was laughing anymore. In his state of shock Hassan could only protect his face, all thoughts of retaliation abandoned. He shouted at the Commander to get off, he shouted for help to get the madman off of him because he looked mildly like Ben Affleck and he couldn't lose that. Dev and Pranab tried to pull him off but were met with a fresh round of misfired blows. Dev clutched his nose, not yet aware of the blood that would soon come a-dripping. Kama stood as close as she could without getting hit herself, shouting at them to stop, stop, stop. Geetu just stood, hands covering her mouth uncertain of what to do. Pranab tried once again to pull Asim off but took a kick to the shin and doubled over, yowling in pain. Geetu yelled at Dev who tried to push past the flailing fists and position himself between the two men as they rolled over and pushed up against the wall but ended up being ejected from their roaring tornado, pushing Geetu straight into the bowl of gravy. Kama was now screaming at them to stop. Geetu turned around and saw the back of her dress which now looked like she'd had a bad case of explosive diarrhea. The shit stain ran the length and breadth of her butt. Her limited edition Anita Dongre was ruined. She turned to the cockfight that had now engulfed both Dev and Pranab so it looked like all four of them were locked in a strange semi-erotic wrestling stronghold. She walked over to the giant bowl of custard awaiting dessert time and upturned it on their heads with a warrior's scream.

Kama was a blubbering mess of tears and phlegm. The smell of vanilla custard was intoxicating.

Dev's face was a bloody mess, the blood now gushing out of his nose staining his shirt and whatever bits of custard still clung to him. His left eye was swollen.

Hassan and Asim were gasping for breath, having received the worst of the custard of vengeance; it fell in thick goops off their head, past their necks and down their backs.

Hassan touched his cheek and winced, a bruise blossomed in front of their eyes.

Asim had a single cut above his eyebrow most likely from Pranab's watch but he missed the glare shot at him because he was swiping madly at his face, trying to keep vanilla pudding out of his eyes. It had gone all the way up his nose and he couldn't breathe properly. Geetu looked at him when he took in a choked breath and burst into laughter.

They stared at her as she doubled over.

Kama wasn't feeling well, the smell was too heady and Geetu's cackling only worsened her nausea.

Asim looked at the motley pudding-covered crew and smiled, Hassan smiled back and laughed softly.

Soon they were all sighs and chuckles.

Kama didn't feel well. She doubled over and threw up, and everyone burst into laughter.

"What's the matter with her?"

"It's her thing now, let it be."

"She's been puking all day now," Hassan laughed, "it's all that psychotic energy coming out of her."

Dev looked up with his eye half shut. "You're all fucking mad."

Everyone laughed.

Asim turned around. "Where's Leela?"

The room grew silent again.

One.

Two.

Three.

Breathe.

One.

Two.

Three.

Wait.

One.

You are in control.

Wait.

It was the same dream.

Two.

You are the creator and destroyer of your own world.

Three.

But she was aware... she was aware that it was just a dream.

Savour the power.

One.

Two.

Three.

Push the knife deeper in his chest.

That wasn't normal.

One. Two. Three.

Ruin him.

Kama felt the warmth of his blood, the resistance of the blade pushing down through a ribcage.

One. Two. Three.

This was only a dream.

One. Two. Three.

The same dream.

One. Two. Three.

This wasn't like a dream.

One. Two. Three.

What was that on her?

She was dreaming, most likely...

One. Two. Three.

Did she soil herself?

One. Two. Three.

She looked down at Shailender's face.

One. Two. Three.

Anger flooded through her like poison and she brought her hands down with more force this time.

One two three. One two three. One two three one two three one two threc onc two three one two three.

First she hit the belly button, next as her assailant turned she hit the thigh, and with the third jab Kama drove the knife right through Leela's hand.

The scream ripped through the hallway and had Asim not drank from his private scotch reserve before bed, he would've heard it too. But the stress of the evening had driven him to drink and he would only know in the morning. Geetu was the first in through the door, she saw Kama and Leela wailing and clutching at each other. She saw the blood, steadily flowing from Leela's left hand down their gowns and the look in her sister's eyes that told her Kama wasn't all the way present in the room. In her mind she held on to Shail's paisley shirt but the shirt felt wrong because it was too loose on Leela's small frame.

Hassan walked into the room and immediately backed up hitting his head against the jamb. For all his machismo, he was read to faint at the sight of the carnage.

"WHAT THE FUCK!" he shrieked.

He threw open the bedside window and gulped in the cold air. It wasn't enough to clear his head but Geetu's voice helped.

"Hassan you asshole go and get Dev!"

Kama looked down at her icy fingers, locked so tightly her joints screamed in pain. Her knees ached from the pressure of standing up. And when she looked at Leela her mind caved in.

Geetu cursed. "Wait don't remove the knife", she grabbed Leela's hand, "it's kept you from bleeding out, let Dev come he has a kit with him. He'll stitch you up. You'll be fine, you'll be fine." She couldn't say it enough, more to reassure herself.

"Holy shit." Dev gasped. "How did this happen?"

Hassan remained in the corridor while Geetu ripped the bedsheet for a tourniquet. She threw a look of pure disgust as he gagged at the sight of the blood. Kama was now all but dead to the world, out cold from the shock of her nightmares' untimely manifestation

"How did this happen?"

Leela bit her lip so hard it bled but explained that she couldn't bear it. "I'm not like you people, this... you're monsters you're all fucking crazy and it's because of me... I'm sorry, I'm so sorry."

Dev wiped his brow and helped her to the bed. The wounds were mostly superficial except for the ten-inch blade through her palm.

"I can't do much about that without proper equipment ... we're risking infection here," he looked to his wife for support.

Geetu was on her last reserve of willpower. She threw her hands up and pulled out a cigarette from the bedside vanity. "Do whatever you can for now she can't keep sitting with that thing here."

The idea came to him as she lit her cigarette. They'd cauterize the cut and drop her to a hospital in the next town. Yes, they'd have to give her some money and tell her to leave their family alone because it was simply unacceptable to have the Kochhar family name associated with some common *pahadi* girl who –

"Dev! Shut up and fix her hand and get her out of here."

"I'm going to be sick," Hassan was turning grey in his crouch by the door. "No way in hell am I driving her."

"Hassan you really are good for nothing," she hissed.

"Can someone tell me why Kama sleeps with a fucking knife under her pillow?" It seemed like a fairly obvious question to ask but the look in Geetu's eyes told Hassan that he needed to sit in silence. He wasn't the best in dealing with blood, he'd fainted twice in the delivery room when Sana was born and they ultimately had to escort him to the other suit with a glucose drip. And now with his sister's eyes burning a hole into his skull, he sank to the floor and hung his head between his knees.

"Hassan buddy stay with us, you're not gonna black out are you?"

"No the ... the smell it's fucking me up." He took in a ragged breath through his mouth.

"I'm going to be so pissed with you if you puke right now Hassan!" Geetu was on the verge of losing it and everyone in the room, Leela included, knew there was no time left. "Go to the store room downstairs and get a pair of sheets. Can you do that you useless shit?"

The room grew warmer even with the open window. Geetu felt the heat rising hard and fast up the back of her neck, out through her ears. Kama was all but dead to the world. As for Leela, the minute Dev had withdrawn from her began threatening them with the police. In any other place there would be no panic because Geetu knew how easy it was to turn situations in her favour with the right amount of money. But they were no longer in Delhi and this was the occasion to panic. Leela cried and stammered her accusations that they'd tried to kill her and she'd make them pay for it.

"How much?" Dev muttered darkly. The calm smiling man they knew him to be was gone.

Hassan chuckled once from the bed where he had changed the sheets and helped put Kama to rest. "That's what it comes down to after all na? Fucking peasant just wants money. That's why you were sweet on dad, trying to swindle him from his fucking money." He walked over to her. "Women like you disgust me."

Leela remained impassive. "Just pay me enough to start over and you won't hear from me again."

Or we could just kill her and be done with it. It was a thought never voiced out but they all felt it for a flash. The lights had been turned off but the moon was full and bright outside, the night prime and electric for the mischief of fate.

Geetu – fist and teeth clenched in anger and embarrassment– finally escorted Leela with a shawl over her head. Dev met them by the foyer, his comfy slippers replaced with the brown loafers she particularly hated. He had never known his wife to be one for overt gestures but Geetu threw her arms around him and told him that she loved him. "Come back safe, I'm waiting."

He kissed the top of her head. "I'll be back before you know it, just don't be too hard on Hassan."

She rolled her eyes and left them to the night. Leela was never seen again.

The next morning brought a cold mist that even the sunshine couldn't drive away. Kama slithered into the bathroom and gasped at her reflection. Dried blood was smeared across her with the finesse of a paintbrush, arcing high and proud around her brow on one side, curving around her cheekbone on the other side and trailing down past the jaw to where the traditional Kochhar chin folded into her neck. In the refracted morning light she looked like a monster. She grabbed at the cold stone basin and ground her teeth because a monster scared of her own shadow didn't make for a good villain. And if she had to be a murderess she would do so with dignity.

Hassan was carefully regarding the room when she walked back in and she watched the dullness of disturbed sleep drain from his face. He looked at her like she was a rabid dog: unpredictable.

"Where's Leela?"

He gulped. "She's gone."

"I killed her didn't I?" Kama told herself she wouldn't cry.

"She's no longer a concern of this family Kama." He poured himself a glass of water and lit a cigarette. She hated the smell of a cigarette that early in the morning. "Just forget about her."

"Arey how can I just –"

"I said just forget about her!" he snapped. "Forget she ever existed, forget we came here, just fucking drive it out of your mind."

"You're such an asshole Hassan", she threw him a withering look and left the room.

They sat in the verandah by the bougainvillea wall, no more than a barren web of hardy vines in that late February chill. The morning dew sparkled even in the dim light, Geetu was lost in the tiny spider webs woven through the bushes. She found herself wondering if there was a way to save memories into webs such as those. Rid herself of the previous night. Dev reached out for her under the table and squeezed her hand in quiet reassurance. Hassan cleared his throat and fluttered the newspaper he'd been reading, directing everyone's attention to the house.

Asim came to the verandah, appropriately dressed in a classic black polo shirt and khaki chinos, mulling over the rather distasteful morning he'd just had. Geetika and Dev had prepared to break the news of Surya's wedding before Asim would enquire about Leela. Kama would find a way to divert conversation to her writing and Hassan would sit quietly and try – as Geetu had iterated thrice already – try hard not to catch any attention.

Asim however spoke first. "So, well, I guess you all were right to behave as you did toward Leela, she's gone."

Their jaws collectively dropped. Geetu felt as though her heart was going to burst in her chest. "What do you mean she's gone?"

"She – well firstly I would just like to say that regardless of that woman, your behaviour last night was inexcusable. Hassan, I am astounded at how old you've grown with the brain still of a fucking toddler. I'm disgusted!"

"Well that's great dad!" Hassan tossed his paper to the ground and sunk lower in his chair. "A good fucking morning to you too. We can't go even one day without –"

"Hassan just shut it for a second ya" Geetu spat at him. "Daddy what happened with Leela?"

The Commander stroked his moustache halfway lost in thought. "Right oh Leela yes right, well, you see beta she left me a note saying she's leaving town. No real explanation but with that circus show you idiots put up I don't think we need to really wonder why she left – nobody wants to be a part of this carnival of crazies."

Geetu rolled her eyes at the hyperbole; Kama filed it away for future reference.

"She just left? What about her tea place or whatever?" Dev asked. Asim pretended he simply wasn't there.

"That's not all. There was – now you need to just listen and not lose your heads at this – but I'd set up a small account for her," he shut his eyes at the commotion breaking out all the way down the table. "It's my money and I will do what I want with it! But I guess she found a way to access that money because it's been emptied out as of this morning."

"She could be anywhere by now," Pranab spoke from the back patio, "it's been hours since she left I'm assuming since nobody saw her leave. Let's just put this whole matter behind us shan't we?"

A dead silence descended on them as he joined the breakfast table with a glass of orange juice. Geetu glared at it as if it were personally mocking her.

Asim walked back to the house with mechanical steps.

"Daddy", Hassan leapt up, "what happened? Are you feeling okay?"

He had his arm around Asim's shoulders, an unfamiliar but welcomed gesture. He made no move to push it off. The breakfast party watched as the Commander shook his head in defeat, it seemed as though he was slowly shutting down. Dev sighed and pinched the bridge of his nose. In his mind the gesture was uncannily similar to Amitabh Bachchan's hyperbolic acting in the last movie they'd seen – he hated having to wait to share the joke with his wife at a more appropriate time. He hated being stuck in these social situations; the entire weekend getaway had thus far been one stressful event after another. He shook his head almost in sync with Asim, he decided they were all truly crazy and he'd simply have to make peace with it for the sake of his own sanity.

"Just," Asim muttered "I want to go sleep for a while."

"Arey baba just eat something first? We're all making a move back to the city by the evening." Geetu rolled her eyes and sighed. Hassan couldn't have chosen a worse way to make the situation better. "Just have some breakfast with us na?"

But Asim no longer looked as if he was listening, listening or aware of what was going on.

"Dad how much money did she take?" Hassan asked in a low voice.

"Nothing much really, it was just fifty grand, but the... but how could she just leave?"

Hassan looked back at the table where Geetika looked ready to set the garden on fire. "Some people dad, you just never know who they are till they show their true colours. Forget her."

Kama sat sipping her dark tea, lost in space. She had murdered Leela and this was all an elaborate ruse. But whether Leela had actually stolen from her father or not, Kama realized there was a potential story to be told. And so she stood and excused herself from the steadily cooling breakfast spread. Dev followed his wife as she stormed off from the table. Pranab had long given up hopes of keeping up with them and resigned himself to the scotch eggs in their nest of lettuce and slaw. It wasn't his business, he nodded to himself.

Geetu, Hassan, and Dev now stood in the shadow under the staircase fidgeting. Through the dumbwaiter – the singular functioning apex of Asim's pride and glory – the Commander could be heard barking instructions at some delivery company, apparently the linens were early and he didn't have enough storage space ready because the movers hadn't yet arrived to shift the furniture out of the room. Geetu slid the wooden panel shut to allow them some privacy.

"*That fucking snake!*" she whispered. "It's almost like she planned the whole thing."

"How much did you give her?" Hassan enquired.

"Twenty five thousand, and with the money she took off of daddy that's almost a fucking lakh just gone down the drain. This is just disastrous, it's an embarrassment ya."

Hassan bit back a comment on how left to their devices Gayatri and Surya could blow up the same on a shopping spree. "So now what do we do?"

Dev had had enough. "I swear to god I cannot deal with this shit show anymore," he hissed. "We listen to our own fucking advice on this and move the fuck on, just forget she even existed."

Geetu opened her mouth to protest but he cut her off. "No. NO! Not another word on the subject. I come here for a bloody holiday and this ... this little private party of madness is going to turn my hair white." He glared at them as if scolding a pair of miscreants. "You two need a therapist and someone needs to tell Kama what happened before she convinces herself she's some murderous *chudail*!"

He stormed off muttering to himself. "Crazy ... absolutely crazy."

Chapter

FOURTEEN

Jusqu'ici Tout Va Bien

There are few things in life more annoying than the sound of an unanswered FaceTime call. Surya sat crosslegged on the couch in their apartment shell. Beyond the French windows she could see the beginnings of a traffic jam. The gathering clouds had sent the post-office rush into madness. She wiped away the lint off her keyboard and dialed Vir again.

"Hey hey sis, what's happening?"

"Why do you always take so long to answer my damn call?" she glared at him.

"Get some chill in your grill, we're on our way out. I was in the lift when you called, and how you always manage such bad timing is beyond me." Her exasperation only made him laugh harder. "Why're you so salty today? Moving in with the husband not the dreamboat lovesong you'd imagined?"

"How high are you?" she leaned in as he pulled on the vape pen and blew out a cloud on his phone screen. Vir and his friends were walking to the neighborhood bar, a Friday night tradition Surya no longer remembered. She stared at the dusting cloth by her feet in disgust.

"It's too much fucking work, I'm dying. Worse still I can't deal with this domestic fucking life man, when are you getting here? Why aren't you booking your flights – what the hell!"

With the sound of laughter and fast Japanese in the background, Vir apologized and picked up his phone from where it had fallen. Surya sighed heavily and he simmered down.

"It's not just the move ya, like, my mind it just feels like it's disconnected. Like the neuro impulses are all off, they're not fired up. I have two client orders and they both want like proper custom designed wedding outfits. Seven outfits between each of them and like all I've got to show for the past week are these empty sheets of paper."

He shook his head with an indulgent smile, she could tell from his glassy eyes that he wasn't all there. "You're being stupid. Just go back to what inspires you, inspire yourself man. If it doesn't happen today, fuck it. Start tomorrow."

"Sure, thanks bhai. And listen, please book your tickets?"

Vir gave her a mock salute and signed off.

Surya stared at the ceiling, the corner where the cabinet almost touched it, wondering how comfortable it might be to crawl into a space that tight with her back pressed against the wall. The gossamer cobweb waved back, fluttering in a breeze that didn't reach her. She wondered how long the spiders would take to fill up the corners of their new home, though she had to urgently consider Dhiraj's reluctance to leave them be.

Granted it was oddly amusing to watch him stalk their spindly trail with a rolled up newspaper, the left foot slipper, or whatever else was nearest. She looked down at her engagement ring and chuckled, nothing was funnier than that though – he'd had a friend design a platinum band looping up front into a delicate web that also resembled a daddy long legs with eight diamonds. It was a tad excessive to wear everyday but she was definitely wearing it till they exchanged rings in front of seven hundred and eighty – and counting – of their closest family and friends.

It was strange how oddly contrasted it was to move houses in real life than movies. There weren't any stolen moments of giggles and kisses and running around through the empty rooms, both Dhiraj and Surya were exhausted, almost constantly covered in a light layer of dust and sweat, and buried in work. His website was about to go live, the developers wanted to push it out before their wedding so he wouldn't have to work through his honeymoon. She on her part had to figure out how to make a pre-wedding gown in shades of pink without making the thirty two year old lady look like a giant vagina. The discarded sketches of a thousand *anarkalis* looked up at her from the trashcan beseeching a second chance.

She pouted at her ankles, going through the motions of another congratulatory call, wondering if she could get liposuction to make them look daintier. Their questions worsened with every call – whether they'd already moved in before their marriage, whether she was making her own clothes, whether they had a reason for rushing the marriage. Dhiraj walked in pleasantly amused to find her tittering at the mystery caller.

"Fuck," she fell back onto the couch.

He leaned over and kissed her deeply, pulling out a wine bottle from his bag. She pulled out two glasses and poured more than necessary. He slid the window shut and flipped on the smartbot air purifier.

"How come you're home already?"

"I left early," he did the jazz hands. "But I have a bunch of reports to finish up so I figured it's better to do them here sitting next to you than be stuck out there."

"I wonder how long this one will last," she stared outside where the rain had begun pouring.

"How's the work going? Did you umm…" he stopped short at the sight of the balled up sketches.

"I can't do this anymore," she threw her pencil against the wall. "I try and everything comes out like some form of that stupid dress." She drank deeply from her glass. "I think I genuinely hate

Gayatri now. That gown, you know the one I'm talking about, nude-ish with a black lace top gosh it looked so beautiful but fuck I can't copy it. I don't want this lady thinking I'm just some boutique running dud who can't create anything authentic."

He set his glass down and knelt by the couch. "How can I help? Tell me and I'll do it."

His eyes were a warm night, when the flowers hung low and hot. She dabbed at the bead of sweat by his brow and kissed him on the forehead. His hair still had the smell of minty shampoo, she rested her cheek on it and held him tighter to her chest.

"I love you" they murmured. He suggested they order in earlier than usual so with the traffic delay it could arrive in time. That was the first thing that pinched her. He switched on a brighter light and made his way to change out of his clothes.

"Oh hey thanks for doing the laundry babe," he laughed from the bedroom. His words set her teeth on edge, perhaps the next day she'd meet him at the door with a glass of whiskey and help him take his shoes off too. Maybe the week after she'd find herself cooking his favourite comfort food for dinner. Of course it'd end with him balls deep in a younger girl within a year. She poured herself a coffee to ease her racing mind, ignoring the memory of her honey-man. The fact that Surya could picture Dhiraj's movements to the precise moment when he'd unbuckle his trousers, when he'd slip the t-shirt over his head, and that was the push. In her blind rage she ripped off the paper in front of her and unwittingly slit the skin of her thumb. Surya watched as the blood oozed up in a singular bubble of red, her mind told her to stand and take care of it. She had to wash it and sanitize, she'd have to clean the spots of blood from the floor.

"SURYA!" he yelled from the other end of the apartment. "Pick up the phone ya, who's calling?"

She stared at Gayatri's name.

Even though she had her mouth open to speak, Surya's throat tightened uncomfortably like she'd swallowed sand. The radio silence over the past few weeks from both her sisters was as bitter as the after oil of coffee on her tongue. Their Save-The-Date mailers were opened but not RSVP-ed to, and Geetu's assurances were growing weary. She winced as water hit the cut, pushing the tiniest sliver of flesh in the wrong direction so for a moment the cut deepened. She watched the blood wash away with the water stream but everything inside was clenched tight like she could heal her wound with willpower. Looking up at the sight of her trembling lower lip opened the floodgates to all she'd been keeping to herself and Surya dissolved into hiccupped hysterics. She missed her. She missed Sana. She had nobody to fall back on. And yet, there were no tears, just a strange gargled noise like someone was strangling a monkey in their bathroom.

Dhiraj knocked roughly and asked if she was okay. She stared at his silhouette on the other side of the frosted glass, noting that it was inappropriate to have a glass door for a bathroom, and sniffed an 'I'm okay' back at him.

Cut mended and warm cheeks now cooling, Surya straightened up.

"Oh," she said aloud, surprising herself. "I guess I actually am upset."

Dhiraj was waiting on the other side of the door for her. She launched herself at him, unbothered by his surprise or the sound of seams ripping.

She pushed him onto his bare back and sat on his chest so their warm skin fused together. He smiled into the drapery of her locks, she slid down his abdomen till the familiar fuzz of his happy trail tickled the insides of her thighs. Now when they kissed it wasn't the welcome home honey peck of pastel people but the untamed passion of two lovers.

"No dinner for you till you're drunk," she reached into his boxers. "I'm taking baby boy out for drinks and then we're gonna fuck in the car like it's 2003."

He let out a gasp as she planted another firm kiss on his lips.

Neil regarded her with curiosity. "Why're you so jittery tonight? The speech was perfect. You were perfect."

"It'd help if you could maintain eye contact and not look at my boobs while saying that." She jabbed at her phone and tucked it back into the hardbox clutch. "I was trying to get in touch with my sister."

"Okay but how are you even fitting inside that? I didn't mean to stare," he chuckled, "but really what keeps you from spilling out of that dress?"

Gayatri stared down the scalloped lace that plummeted halfway down her torso. "Lots and lots of boob tape, it's magic. Can we get back to my problem please?"

"Wait, when did you have a sister?" he shifted away from her and she ignored the fact that he was also blatantly checking her out. "We've been working together for so long and now it's like I don't even know who you are."

"Don't be a dick, it's my step sister. She's getting married, apparently there was a full invite and box of trinkets they sent over to my house and Shashi literally like intentionally didn't tell me about it because she was worried that it'd distract me from the gala and the press tour and now we've got this fucking premiere and I-I can't wait for this to get over so I can just ..." She exhaled loudly. "She's lost her fucking marbles, Shashi has. You know how many edits she'd made in my notes? She added in random pop culture references like 13 Reasons Why and fucking people coming out of the mental illness closet like I'm up there giving an acceptance speech for Most Popular Crazy."

They eyed the champagne canister and shifted closer to each other.

"She was like 'omg think of all the coverage we'll get if you shout out to homegirl Mallika Dua and that AIB guy', it's mental. She's just talking trash in my ear the whole day."

Neil couldn't hold himself back anymore. He reached out and cradled her hand in his. She wove their fingers together moving with unmitigated magneticism. A long night of being aware of every mildly congratulatory nod and smile later they were on their way to an after party and sitting in the back of the private car with those tinted windows and her hand in his, Gayatri could settle down.

"Wait but didn't you take a photo with Tanmay Bhatt afterward?" Neil questioned.

"Yes but" she sighed, that's irrelevant now. "I just can't trust Shashi anymore ya. My whole family is ignoring my calls like dad has literally never cut my call and he was just so cold. It sucks."

Gayatri was aware of every micro graze of their palms against each other. Every second of friction sent shockwaves through her heart. She was on the verge of losing track of her thoughts.

"So, what now?" he offered.

The fact that Neil could sit there and still speak so coolly made her want to grab him by the shoulders and shake him up. Every offhanded shrug made her skin crawl, his casual stroke of her wrist made her teeth grind.

She shrugged simply, suddenly too disconnected from him.

"I don't know, I fire her I guess." A part of him waited for her to say more, although he knew there wasn't much to say after that. He stared at the planes of her face delineated by the weaving beams of the sea link, like the moment the sun breaks through from behind an eclipsing moon. All he wanted to do was lean in and kiss her lips, just so he could feel whole again.

He looked down at their entwined hand and ever so gently grazed her wrist with his thumb. Gayatri seemed to not have noticed at all. The stretching silence made his teeth grind, it made his skin crawl.

Her phone vibrated with an ugly drumming noise that broke the spell and she peeled her hand off.

"Relax it's not the end of the world dammit!" Neil retreated from her. She scowled at him, biting back the sharp words edging off her tongue.

"It could be Surya, what's wrong with you?"

"Jeez whatever," the car turned a corner and he vanished into the shadows.

Gayatri stared at the combination of numbers wondering if any part of them was familiar. She wondered if Surya's phone had run out of battery and she was returning the call from her fiancé's phone. It could also be an absolute psychopath trying to track her down.

"I need your phone," she reached for Neil who hoped against hope that they wouldn't touch again.

He fished it from the pocket and held it out to her. She fed in the number and waited for the swiveling search results to show up. Curiosity got the better of him and Neil leaned in close enough that Gayatri could smell the cigarette and mint on his breath.

"Faisal Bakr-what? Who the hell is Faisal and why's he calling you?"

Shoulders slumped; Gayatri cancelled the call and blocked the number. "I don't know. It doesn't matter now does it?"

She rested her head on his shoulder.

"Don't go sleepy on me, we're almost there now." His cool breath fanned her forehead. "Go back to bitching about Shashi, at least that keeps you energized."

She chuckled. "She's such a piece of trash, like actually genuine trash. She's been pushing me to sign up for this TV commercial for these random ass things like one is a fucking fairness cream like oh my god stop. How they still make those I don't even get."

"Well to be fair those offers are better than not having any work at all right?"

She pushed herself upright, visibly perturbed. "What does that mean?"

"I mean think about it logically, you say no to these things and soon the offers stop coming in altogether – what happens then? You leave things as a one-hit wonder person, an actress who failed to launch before she reached for the stars."

"What if I find out that they're testing their shit on animals? Should I be aligning myself with just about anyone simply because I should be seen everywhere? That's such a myopic view, Neil, what is the matter with you?"

"Look it's not like I haven't received shitty offers, it's just that mine are diff–"

She threw her hands up. "Oh *of course*, silly fucking me, who'd ever think to offer an advertisement for fairness creams and products to a man?! You're a serious actor after all, right? Can't do something which won't involve at least one dramatic monologue."

"Wait, that's not what I meant. Why're you taking all this the wrong way?"

"Because that's exactly the kind of B-grade shit someone once told me I'd do in life."

Gayatri huffed and walked out as soon as the car rolled to a stop.

Sunaina blinked away her tears with a bitter smile. "Honestly I knew she wouldn't pick up."

"And that's enough Old Monk I think," Faisal reached across the table to hold her hand and retrieved her glass with the other. He asked a passing server to bring their meal.

Sunaina dipped her head onto their hands and let the tears spill over. Faisal watched the warm salty tears soak into the skin of his hand and jerked it away from her. She straightened up as her hair came undone, falling softly around her. The bowl of dark mutton curry came over and she immediately drained half of it over her bowl of rice.

"Easy begum, you're gonna choke if you don't chew properly."

She wiped the corner of her mouth and blushed. "Sorry, I'm just feeling a little overwhelmed I guess. It's literally the first time I've seen my friend and like here of all places."

"She was really rude," he ignored her dismissive shrug, "I'm always surprised at how you can smile so politely and talk such crap to each other."

"You – as in us women? Oh bhaisaab come with me to Delhi I'll show you grown ass men who can put little bitches like that Varsha Kalra to shame with half the effort." She shook her head, "I mean she's not a friend as such but it's a pity because her brother is actually such a sweetheart. He was dating one of my closest friends for some time but I'm guessing they're not together anymore either."

He pulled the glass away from her outstretched hand and finished the remainder of the drink, immediately regretting the pungent rum on his curry coated palate.

She smiled without mirth. "I was so horrible to her the last time we spoke which obviously explains why she wants nothing to do with me."

Faisal burped through moist lips into the back of his hand, stomach steadily gurgling now. "Sunaina –"

"To be honest though I was horrible to most people. And there was just so much negativity just festering in me." She threw him a dirty look and paid for the meal. "Let's get moving –"

"Let's walk slow, I need to" Faisal dreaded the worst with every hiccup, "that curry's asking to settle down."

"You're such a little bitch boy, just walk slow and you'll be fine." She pulled down the arms of her oversized sweater. "I swear you're such a disgrace when it comes to drinking na, you're just like my sister Surya."

They began the walk uphill, the scenic route back to the old town as Sunaina blathered on about her family while Faisal fought the cold sweats. Somewhere between the circles of streetlights and rainwater, he collapsed onto his knees.

"I... I can't breathe." He heaved even as Sunaian rubbed his back.

"Just keep your eyes open and try to breathe through your nose, I'm calling for help." She took her phone out to dial Jatin but the incoming call drained the last reserves of battery. She screamed at the lifeless mobile and shrugged off her backpack.

"Begum," he reached out for her. "I think I'm going to black out."

She fished out the strange amber bottle and shoved it under his nose. "Breathe through your nose, just stay for now and focus on breathing."

One whiff and he emptied his belly on the wall of the Legom Himalayan Lodge at the mouth of the old town. Sunaina sighed in relief and helped him to his feet, grateful that she hadn't driven them to the Commander's house in that state.

"Hassan babe", Eisha stood at the bedroom door swaying in her heavily fringed sweater. "I need a little pick me up, gimme some sugar daddy!"

She threw her hands up in the air like a witch in ritual and that was the tipping point for Hassan. After having spent the whole evening sitting on their laps and pouring out champagne with giggles, reveling at being the center of attention no matter which room she was in, Eisha had returned to him when she needed her hit. His knuckles whitened around the phone where the monotone voice continued its song of the cancelled call.

"No." he growled.

She clutched at an invisible pearl necklace on her chest, "Oh what do you mean no? What's the matter with you?"

Her breathy gasps once recklessly arousing now cut across his skin because it was like Hassan could finally hear all their words of caution – his friends and sisters now made sense. Eisha was a fucked up version of his daughter.

"Just get the fuck out of my house, you're making me sick."

Her airs washed off. "Babe, really what's going on? Why're you being mean to me?"

"Are you fucking stupid, you've been behaving like such trash the whole night flirting with whoever calls out to you *in my house* no less, and you wanna know what the matter is? You're behaving like a fucking whore, I don't know what your scene is Eisha. I don't know why you're so damaged or pretend to be so damaged but I just don't have the patience to put up with this behaviour."

"Okay calm down firstly, if this is because I kissed Pranab on the cheek –"

He had to control the part of himself that itched to jettison the phone at her head. "That's really not the problem here."

"Then what is it?" she moved close enough to grind against him. "Tell me what you want."

His growing disdain was obvious in the way he regarded her feline caresses, when he pushed her away she seemed to enjoy it. "Get the fuck out of my house dammit!"

She turned unbothered by the way her t-shirt drooped down her bare shoulder, yet aware that it showed off her nakedness. "I thought you were different, Hassan. Turns out you're no better than the others."

She turned back to him at the entrance, ready to dole out one last feebly poetic line.

"Go home Eisha," he slammed the door and dialed Sunaina again.

Chapter

FIFTEEN

Rejection, Reflection, Redemption

It's an inevitable truth that in the month leading up to a wedding sees every self-important woman in attendance hit the spa, even more so the mother of the bride. A wedding tends to be the social event of every season, one that never goes out of style. It's worse when you have to plan one and manage a Shahpur Jat atelier. Geetu sat in her robe, fresh out of a Dead Sea salt scrub with a cigarette and scowl.

"Hullo?"

"Aye haye, why do you sound like that?" Geetu's raspy voice stabbed him through the phone.

"What do you want?"

"Listen I need a favour – wait, are you just waking up?"

Hassan rolled over to the warmer side of the bed. "Talk a little softly please I'm a mess right now..."

"How are you hungover on a Friday morning?"

"What are you calling for Geetika?"

"Well clearly there's no point having the conversation over the phone, in your current state I doubt you'll register a thing I have to say." He heard the crackle of a cigarette.

"You always have some shit or the other to say can I go back to sleep now..."

"No listen I called to ask you what time the Soods are getting in, Dev just got back from the train station and he can drive you to the airport if it's in the next hour."

"Who?"

"Are you serious right now?! I'll come there and break both your legs!"

"Can you stop shouting and tell me what you're talking about you mad cow."

"Arey yaar, Sid and Sunita Sood, are you on crack? They're flying in today and you were meeting them up at the airport."

Hassan jerked upright and immediately regretted it.

"I know I know" he groaned, "I only offered to pick them up. I'm a fucking idiot."

"Oh there's no doubt about that." She drawled.

He held his head even as it continued spinning like a spaceship. "I even made them cancel their hotel booking because I thought it'd be a good idea to have them stay here and the guest bedrooms haven't been fixed up yet."

"Ay it's okay. This is Siddie we're talking about. You know daddy would've killed you if he went to a hotel." Her voice softened.

Through the onslaught of filtered sunlight and headache Hassan began to remember as well the many mornings spent racing over hilltops together, traversing the narrow roads as if they were explorers in a new world. Siddhant Sood had spent every summer vacation at their house till he and Geetika passed the tenth grade. Even from across the world, and US only seemed further away in those days, he'd always come to meet them before his own family. He would post a letter or two to the Commander though nowhere as regularly as Kama – it was in his opinion the most permanent way to be remembered by someone.

Even through the toughest of times he never let go of them, although he was heartbroken when only Geetu and Hassan showed up to his father's funeral. Sid Sood always maintained that Kama's phobias were curable; he had seen what a crippled life was, what it took to care after someone who'd been physically impaired – and he told them that she wasn't. Of course Kama didn't take it too well at the time but it was all forgotten with the first bite of her signature roast chicken. Geetu joked that it was the only way to get his attention when he was visiting, sharing those meals that always ended in heartbreak because they'd never know when they'd meet again.

"Wait but what am I supposed to do with Sunita?"

"What do you mean –oh oh shit they separated na ... but I'm sure they don't want to advertise that to these socialite bitches."

"Oh lord is this something to do with me and Tina now? Are you passing some passive aggressive comment here?"

"No." She held the phone away. "*Oh hi Farida, hawaryouu – good good ya, just getting this stuff done quickly then I've to get back to work.*"

"Good god stop it, I'm already nauseous."

"Then maybe you should watch how much you drink." She hissed.

"Definitely. I'll just stick to casual drug abuse like you ah."

"Oh fuck off Hassan." She slammed the phone.

He groped the table for a cigarette but only found sticky stains of the night before. Every muscle ached as he realigned the joints of his spine, suddenly aware that he was naked except for a pair of H&M boxer briefs. The only good thing Eisha ever gave him. He walked through the cardboard box of a house with unfocused eyes. Around him the tabletops gathered the same layer of dust, wiped by the same tired hands as the servants followed the same path of cleaning up. There was no sound. Hassan fished through the bottom drawer behind the shoe boxes where Sana once kept her prized possessions and a backup box of cigarettes. The only sounds heard inside were Vikram's footsteps down the stairs and the pipes settling in his bathroom. He held his breath and waited for anything else to disturb the peace. Somewhere a bird might have squeaked but it was barely audible in her room. Outside the seasons had changed and inside Hassan Kochhar had turned into the shadow of his former self, Crossfit and binge drinking notwithstanding. Sunglasses indoors to hide his worn soul, shifting weight from bare foot to bare foot in that Sisyphean bungalow.

His phone vibrated with a text from Dev.

-Gayatri's flight delayed so Ram is picking her up. Shud
-I tell him to get Sid and all too?
-No I should go. C u in the eve!

The sun was high, he lit his cigarette and pulled a chair by the pool immediately vomiting as the smoke hit his nose. As if on cue Pranab appeared, clapping at the noontime show. Hassan turned to look at his face dripping with disgust, wiping his own as he did.

"I thought you had hit rock bottom already but buddy you're proving me wrong every day. My faith is restored that the worst is yet to come."

"Fuck you," he grunted.

Pranab called out to Vikram and headed for the living room where he fixed up a cocktail of egg, Tabasco, and gin for his friend's hangover.

"It's a fight on the way down," he patted his back as Hassan retched, "but you'll be good as new in a bit."

Hassan shook his head in disgust and gulped his way through a glass of cold water. Then he began cutting himself a line, impervious to Pranab's nervous presence.

"I have some news for you ... uh you should sit."

"Can't. I need to sort myself out before daddy gets here, he's already hit Rohini." He picked up a throw pillow and placed it back. "And a gin and tonic, yes that's what we need a good G&T."

They heard the car pull in and Hassan's stomach lurched. Vikram came running in to tell him that saheb had arrived but waited to be told to help with his bags.

Pranab fixed two gins as Asim's boisterous greeting echoed in.

The sight of wild hair and a rucksack took his breath away. Hassan stood at the other end of the foyer, staring at Leela in horror. If there was anything left in his belly, he'd have vomited once more. And then she moved closer and he saw her shift, Sunaina walked up to her father looking as out of place as she felt.

"Sana? Is that you?" he ran forward and picked her up into a hug. "Where have you been my baccha I..." he exhaled into her hair to keep from crying.

"I've missed you papa." She wondered if there was a word for the kind of hug that should feel warm but didn't.

"You don't know how good it is to see you my love." She felt the warm teardrops on her shoulder.

She pushed him away. "What have I missed? Tell me everything."

Hassan opened his mouth to speak but didn't know where to begin. He was losing control of his life. He was slowly descending into alcoholism. Ending a messy affair with his friend's wife. Lying to everyone about his coke stash at work, and at home, and a spare gram in the car. So he went with a smile and noncommittal wave of the hands.

Sunaina stared grimly at the space between them.

"Nothing's changed. I can smell the alcohol on your breath. And nobody calls me Sana anymore."

Asim entered the house looking happier than anyone had ever seen him. His smile faltered at the sight of their looks, the frigidity of the room. The next few moments ruined all his hopes for bringing the family together. Sunaina excused herself, though not before she could pointedly ask if the maid still worked there. Hassan cussed and stalked off to his gin. Pranab excused himself. The Commander looked around with his heart sinking, wondering why he'd left an empty house to come to another one.

On his way out, Pranab caught the tail end of a gooey conversation. He walked into the group of ladies in tasteful dark athleisure, vultures who walked one way then another feeding on carcasses of their friends' social lives.

"Someone should really do a pooja in that house ya," Param clucked her tongue. "They need a proper *havan* to cure that curse left by you-know-who."

"Who you-know-who?"

"Minal are you fucking kidding me right now."

"Arey Tina ya, she's just messed those two up I'm telling you. That Sonakshi is there na, the gym girl, she was telling me he asked her out on a date and she was telling him 'no ya I have a boyfriend' and all and apparently he said 'I don't mind.' Both father-daughter are just a mess."

"Babe I toh think maybe it's like a family thing. Look at Geetu's daughter, not even married and already staying with that fellow... what's his name ya, the Gurgaon chap."

"Dhiraj something. I think he's a *jaat*."

A symphony of gasps ensued.

"Good evening ladies," he spoke icily.

"Oh hi Pranab, hawaryooou." They harmonized. "We were just on our way to play bridge."

He bowed mockingly. "Indeed. Don't stop on my account."

For someone who'd spent so much of her year trekking, Sunaina was pitifully tired by the time she reached the landing. With every stair her bag weighed heavier and now her forearms pulsed in protest. She dragged the rucksack into her room, once alive with her energy but now silent. It resonated with the cheerlessness that often bleached the brick and mortar of a room no one lived in any more. Even the corner of the wall where Gayatri had once spilled her drink had faded, the stain barely visible. Nothing about coming home was what she'd expected, what she needed.

The week had gone by in calming her nerves, controlling her thoughts from wondering about her dad, how the moment they'd finally see each other might be. Now all she could do was swallow the bile on the back of her throat, walk past the bed that was too soft, over the carpet that was too clean, and into the bathroom. The bathroom where she'd lost the final shreds of her dignity. It was the week after Gayatri had left the city. She'd called the only one who could've helped, but her lifeline was out with her new boyfriend. Surya had told her to lighten up, to get out of bed and go have fun. At the end of the night Ankit had fucked her on the bathroom counter.

The next morning was the first time she'd picked up the blade and put it to her wrist. Who was it that had told her of the incomparable rush of cutting wrists? It didn't matter anymore because what she'd done was worse; she'd talked herself out of it because she couldn't bear the thought of the pain. That was who she was, the weak girl with a bad heart. No matter how much she drank, how horribly she spoke to everyone, she couldn't swallow it. That was the season Sunaina Kochhar stopped looking into the mirror to see if she was still there.

Now, back in the same room that had seen every heartache and heartbreak, she braced herself for the overwhelming flood of emotions but all she felt was the same apathy as her plastic-covered clothes. She remembered everything, she felt them too, but what did any of it matter now? She smiled ruefully.

The sweat and dust had formed a crust and she could feel her skin turning adhesive. Sunaina let the water beat down on her, suddenly too tired to move a muscle. Only upon stepping out did she realize her towel was still in the bag by the door, the door that was open and anyone could walk in. She stood there dripping and debating, completely unaware of the full rack of towels to her right. Lying next to them was her pink satin robe, a reminder of the person she once was that now seemed as daunting as meeting the rest of the family. Answering their questions. Where had she been? What had she been doing? Who was she now that she didn't belong among them or was she pretending to be someone else for effect? Sunaina massaged her forehead, driving the voices away. Nobody would ask her that outright – or so she hoped.

The towels were too soft to the touch, worsened by the realization that she was too severe in her judgments. Maybe the heady smell of honey-lily shower gel just needed more time to get used to. Sunaina was surprised at how much her tastes had changed.

The sun was high but the wind still had the bite of a lasting winter, she threw on a pair of shorts and the same oversize sweater Faisal loved to hate on. She made her way downstairs to the already familiar sound of bickering.

The Commander sat fiddling with his teacup, obviously eyeing the glass of gin her father was refilling.

"It's my summer drink," he explained from behind the bar. "It's just perfect daddy leave your tea and switch to the good stuff."

"Is it summer already?" Sunaina asked, eyeing his leather jacket. The ridiculously perfect fit across his shoulders made her cringe, he looked younger than half the men he was friends with. Suddenly all the stories she'd heard from her grandfather made sense.

Her words cut through the tension, Hassan shifted uncomfortably and removed his sunglasses. "You can have some no matter how hot or cold it is outside, it was just a phrase."

He looked like he wanted to say more but didn't. She refused his offer to share a drink.

"Why don't you go easy on those if you're driving to the airport?" Asim adjusted the collar of his shirt.

"Don't rile him up, he'll only end up driving rashly and it'll just become a thing."

Hassan smiled sourly. "You sound just like her." He shook his head.

"Anyway how's everything back at the house? Are you still dreaming up your B&B scenes?"

Asim nodded "I'm surprised you remember."

"So I guess there's no way to talk you out of it then."

She shot him a warning look.

"Not a chance Hassan don't be an idiot, in fact I want Sunaina to help me with the business since literally nobody else seems to be capable of it."

"What do you mean?" he slammed his glass on the bar.

"I can't manage the whole operation myself–"

"That's not what I meant", he turned to her "are you not staying back? I thought you were ready to come home for good Sunaina."

She balked under his red-eyed gaze, everything about his appearance seemed to be imploring her to stay back. It was nothing if not a call for attention, his styled hair and ripped jeans channeling every anybody's Instagram feed and it only added to the aura of despondency that hung like a rancid smell in their house. Sunaina felt the familiar weight on her chest, the one a child feels when they need to be an adult for their parents. It was nothing as tragic as what her mother had put her through, but too often the behaviours of aging women are deemed worse than their male counterparts.

In trying to speak her white lies, mostly to ease the situation, her throat closed up and she wondered if it was irony or divine intervention. Hassan however didn't take it as lightly, gin addled brain assuming the worst.

"This wedding is still weeks away beta, you have plenty of time to think about this." Asim pushed the now cold tea away. "Why do we need to be so melodramatic all the time?"

"No of course, I haven't put a timeline on moving back to Delhi just yet ... I don't know." Sunaina realized there wasn't much left to save the conversation anymore. She turned to Hassan and smiled "For now it's just good to be home."

He pulled her into a tight hug and whispered an 'I love you' and for the moment that was all they had to give each other.

"Take it easy na papa," she pulled him away from the bar. "Let's do a little detox for some days, I'll even do it with you."

"No no that's not necessary, the only real trouble will be keeping Sid entertained. He can outdrink us both without blinking, really you remember don't you?"

Asim chuckled. "I once thrashed him for stealing my rum."

Hassan turned back to her, "Only because it was cheap rum."

"How's his boy now, better I hope?"

"Oh dad don't bring up his wife under any circumstances okay? Last time was embarrassing enough, Kama got sozzled and just didn't shut up about it."

Sunaina frowned in confusion.

"His son's wife died in a hit and run, some drunk fellow..." he stopped short. "I'll take the driver with me, Vikram's cleaning out the guest room. Both the rooms on the ground floor are still being painted – it's a mess. Beta are you okay to take the fouton in the basement for a few days?"

She put on a smile and nodded, ignoring the pitfall in her stomach.

Sunaina was fifteen when she had realized that the best spot to smoke without being detected was the ledge between her room and the terrace. It was nothing short of a precarious climb but over the years she had it down to a minute and three seconds. She sat with her legs crossed, cigarette in contorted mouth, raking her fingers through the mess of wind dried hair. Pulling her fingers free, she took the cigarette and watched the ash flow with the breeze down.

"Hey."

The sun was beating its retreat and although the wind was still warm, there was a nip in the air. She stood to watch the last slivers of orange in a lilac sky, the only view in Delhi uninterrupted by trees or high rise buildings. She followed the streets lined with neatly trimmed trees to the house at the end of the lane where–

"HEY!"

She turned around.

"Down here!"

The first thing she saw were the tattoos curling up his arms in a helix, poking out the neck of his T-shirt on one side.

"What?" she shouted back.

He squinted at her like he was dealing with an invalid.

"What 'what', what're you doing up there? Don't kill yourself, you're too beautiful."

She threw him her worst scowl, only to have it shrugged off with a side smile she knew was the byproduct of manipulative consideration. Sunaina wanted to slap him just for that smile.

"Who the hell are you?"

"Get down from there please you could really hurt yourself."

She was immediately aware of the things that made him a douchebad. The 70's style pornstache. The buzzcut. The tattoos – each of which no doubt came with a preemptively prepared story.

Eyebrows drawn against the late evening sun, Sohrab Sood beamed at her until the corner of her lips quirked up.

"Alright wait a minute," he set down the carton from his hands and spread them up to the skies. "Okay now jump, I'll catch you."

She laughed incredulously. "Seriously, does that line ever work for you?"

"I'll tell you if you come down here."

"Come come beta", she heard her father calling from inside the house, "it's too hot outside."

Sunaina flicked the cigarette in his direction and made her way back to the balcony of her room where the entourage had arrived. Hassan looked at her making no efforts to hide his surprise.

"Bacche, what's up with your hair?"

"Whatever, papa who's the weirdo in our driveway?"

"Sunaina don't be rude they're our guests." He grit his teeth.

"Yes Sunaina," she whipped around to see him standing there smirking at her from the bathroom door. She averted her eyes from the Calvin Klein model physique, made worse by the way he crossed his arms. "Don't be rude."

She was resolved to not give him the satisfaction of seeing her blush.

"Sorry if we got off on the wrong foot," he held out his hand, "I'm Sohrab Sood."

"How charming," she gave a firm handshake and made to leave.

"Sunaina!" Hassan chided. "Why don't you be nice and help Sohrab find his way through the room."

It took every fibre of her being to not ask her father to shove it. She closed her eyes and reminded herself of the invincible summer of patience and kindness she'd discovered within over the past year. Yet, all she wanted was to knock that self-assured smirk off of Sohrab's face. An itch gnawed at the inside of her belly, polluting her conscious mind with a brassy need to push him away from her, into a wall. To at once hit him and crash into him.

"He's already here isn't he?" she deadpanned.

"Oh but I'm terribly lost," he stared at her with innocent eyes. "Can't find my way through anything."

She pointed behind him. "Bathroom and spa facilities, extra towels in the rack above the mirror. Bed, TV, you can use the cupboard for your crap, whatever you need to clear out you can just shove it under the bed."

He snorted. "Are you usually this salty or is it because I got your room?"

She rolled her eyes. "Call Vikram if you need anything."

"Why can't you help him Sunaina?" Hassan demanded.

"Just because I'm a girl doesn't mean I'm gonna wait on him for every little need papa." She left fuming.

"Wha… that doesn't even make sense." Sohrab called out to her.

She thudded down the stairs, letting her anger fuel every beat, and found her grandfather in the guest bedroom lounging on the wicker chair. The garden stretched out in front of them, darkening in the dusk where time slowed down and the crickets came to life.

"He's quite a handful isn't he?"

Sunaina settled down by the warm stone steps. "Papa's always been this neurotic, hasn't he? I guess over the years I barely saw him for long enough to realize it."

He smiled. "Or maybe he just paled in front of your mother."

"I can tell we're all savage with our jokes," she giggled. "So that explains where I get my dose of the crazies from."

"Oh don't be so sure just yet. Your father didn't even believe me when I told him I was having trouble taking stairs – he went on this tirade about how I don't have any trouble navigating the walk down to the river every day and working in the garden ..." he shook his head. "How would he even know better? He only stays long enough to fulfill his own need for a break and then it's back to the city life and those hyenas he calls his friends."

She withered under his gaze. "Always be careful about who you trust, Sunaina, they'd throw you to the wolves sooner than save you. They're not your friends."

He shook his head and stared into nothingness. "Not your friends."

"I think maybe we should go easy on him he's stressed out, you know what I mean? He's constantly got this wide smile – fake as shit of course – and it's just permanently plastered on."

The Commander guffawed. "Oh just you wait beta, if you think he's got it bad you should see your Geetu bua. That's been her defense mechanism since she was your age. Any crisis comes up and she has that veiny look on her neck, like she can't breathe, and the smile comes up."

It was then that Asim remembered when he'd last seen it, the smile on Geetu's face that weekend when they met at the same table for brunch. The morning after Leela had abandoned him like the rats that leave a sinking ship.

Sunaina left him to his musings and found herself facing a coffee machine that looked more like a spaceship. From the hall she heard them.

"Arey I'm sure it's the new style, us oldies won't get it."

"Nonsense!" Siddhant saw her in the kitchen. "My god Sana beta you've grown so much since I last saw you. How've you been bacche?"

He smiled and nodded in that specific way when someone pays no attention to what you're saying. It didn't necessarily make him a bad person, he was fresh off a long flight, but it was a terribly typical reaction. She noted his lack of interest and trailed off, coffee couldn't make itself no matter how fancy the machine.

"Arey bud listen I hope it's okay that you're bunking with me yaar, dad's just not doing too well with his knees and the mattress in the other room is a fuckin mess." Hassan punched in a secret code and the inky coffee poured out.

"Abbe don't be petty ya now. Just let me know if you're bringing someone home I'll figure something out, or watch TV for a few hours. Remember college days ..." he looked at Sunaina and stopped short.

"Oh my lord uncle you're toh just as bad as he is" she cringed. "And please don't give him any more ideas, the house is at full capacity right now anyway."

It had been a while since Hassan laughed that openly. "Arey what you guys don't know shit. Remember in hostel how we were packed into those dorms?"

"Ohh lord don't remind me ya with that bell the caretaker would ring for a full hour, and then Juggy would take his socks off."

They dissolved into howls of laughter.

"I swear, Sana after that summer your dad and I did everything we could to never go back to school. Oh gosh he could put out an elephant with that toe jam, and they made him practice football till the end ah."

She chuckled. "Well then why did you go back?"

"Yeh bhaisaab found a girl to run after, abandoned the plot midway and turned on me. Believe it or not but Hassan wasn't always so down in luck with women ah," he clapped him on the back, "he was worse. One look and bas Tina Sodhi was all we ever heard from him."

"Oh not like you were of any help," Hassan shoved him in jest, "this idiot pushed me into the riverstream once because –"

"Because you took her to our spot. I mean come on ya, we – your buas included – had played there by the river for years. Every day of every summer. You just broke that sanctity."

"Yeah and you broke my tooth." Hassan replied wistfully.

"Hey hey what'd I miss?" Sohrab had stationed himself by the counter before she knew it. Now, when she saw him, he'd sucked all the air of the room out.

Sohrab Sood had the presence of the person who shoves himself between the occupants of a small bench and then makes himself at home. Every breath he drew in chafed against her spirit. And so, just as the kitchen was warming up to her, just when she was beginning to feel like home was home and she might not leave it again, he came into the room.

"Dad if you don't mind I'm gonna take a shower."

She grit her teeth. It was his accent, among the other things immediately offensive about him was his American Boy accent.

"Super Sid you also get recharged. Take a nap if you want then we can get some dinner."

"Arey Hassan what're you saying let's unpack the whiskey buddy! If I sleep I'll be dead for the next twenty four hours."

"Sunaina why don't you make dinner reservations for us."

She swallowed her betrayal with the coffee and wondered who she could call for a recommendation. Sohrab smiling like nothing made him happier than to watch her squirm, leaned over to bump his shoulder against hers.

"Yes Sunaina," he was distorting her name on purpose, "find us a good restaurant na beta." She grit her teeth. "*Please*."

She put on a smile and excused herself.

Chapter SIXTEEN

To The Moon And Back (*BadluckSoulmate#9*)

The air was trilling with tension since the Thursday of 15th when the email came in, not in the least because it disrupted their ritual screening of a Studio Ghibli film that Usui insisted was a part of the cultural zeitgeist and thus imperative for them all. Sentences were cut short and nerves drawn tight. The atmosphere at work was no less stressful that at home.

Vir stared at the sinew stretching across his neck as Usui straightened up, the final artwork now staring back at them in quiet anticipation. On his other side Lyra had her head on his shoulder completing the diorama. She squinted at the screen, he waited till her eyes softened before swinging his head in the finalizing nod though it wasn't enough to validate the weeks' worth of hard work on the part of the design team.

"We're good to go then?" Usui asked gruffly.

"It's stunning," Lyra leaned over and hugged his waist. "But I think there is some tension here and we need to have an open dialogue."

Both Vir and Usui rolled their eyes.

"Now don't behave like children, I'm heating some miso soup and we'll talk about it – we can do it here or we can go get hammered downstairs and then talk."

"I fuckin' hate miso soup," Vir said but no one believed him so he continued sulking. Lyra made him swallow every last spoonful with a promise of cold soba noodles after.

With her camera wrapped firmly around her fist, she led them downstairs and pushed them right to the same hole in the wall bar at the tail end of the business district where university kids and businessmen drank side by side and the night always ended with a free round of sake for the worst karaoke singer. Usui had a standing record for selecting one song and singing another so even though he did the most unusual mashups they turned out well and nobody wanted to give them free sake no matter how much honey they spewed. As luck would have it, Usui ran into a *gaijin* group who were on their way to a party.

"What party?" Vir balked. "We should get to the office early if you want to –"

"Oh fuck off, it's an anything-goes party," he threw back a sakëbomb and handed one to the both of them. "You're leaving us anyway right?"

Vir fiddled with his ear gauge, trying to think of how to reply while also calculate how long it had been since his last drink. "So that's the deal then, you think I'm abandoning you guys?"

Lyra pushed her way between them. "What's an anything-goes party?"

The queen in Grace Jones drag brushing past them at the entrance was answer enough. Usui allowed himself to be carried into the thick of it, he had a way with charming out of towners into buying him drinks. Lyra held her bag close to her chest and Vir by her side; they pushed their way to the bar. One drink with a shot of alcohol and some anywater soda every hour alternating with a full glass of water and then a long drawn cigarette break every forty minutes – Vir's sobriety plans were flawless. He never factored in the possibility of a party pill dropped in by the bespectacled bartender with his stiff collar like antennae he'd use to feel them up. The room was a mess of sweating strangers of every size and shape rendered into that same rhythm of yellow, then blue, then pink. With his sweat breaking through, in tandem with the first set of shirt buttons coming loose, Vir staggered away from his spot where Lyra had her shitbox camera pointed at the Grace Jones madame.

He awoke to the angry bark of the cabbie who cursed him and his *gaijin* trash for singlehandedly buttfucking the country. He scrubbed his bristly buzzcut with cool sweat-numbed fingers and with his weaving stagger managed to find his way back to the apartment. Usui was still sulking, he could feel it in the marrow of his bones, so with a quivering helpless lip he pulled out the futon and fell asleep before he could undress.

Back home waking up was one of the hardest things Vir had to do in his day. He would set alarms at fifteen minute intervals and keep hitting snooze till he couldn't sleep anymore. All in all from the first ring it took him a full hour to roll out of bed. He was the boy who could sleep all morning and start his day with a beer and two hour workout, only otherwise leaving the house to go to a bar. *Clubbing-shubbing*, as the folks back home called it, was his thing. It was everybody's thing those days; the party literally never stopped. No one stopped him from ordering another round of tequila, from driving his nose down another line of coke in the bathroom, or the hood of a car, or his girlfriend's navel. No one stopped him from smoking too much, or driving too fast, no one told him NO because Vir Pratap Singh had lost his father and was simply mourning in his own way and it wasn't anybody's business to judge, but then at Sameer and Vrinda's wedding their best friend died of an overdose. It wasn't the first wedding in Delhi where something like that had happened, it wouldn't be the last, and no one said anything. It was Vir's stash. He could've gone to jail, or so he was told, and from the moment he saw the body carried into the ambulance and the way they tossed the bag with the bag of skin and bones like it was nothing more than daily trash – nothing was ever the same.

Sweat dribbled off of him like rain so he made a mental note to wipe down the machine properly. High intensity interval training was supposed to be this miraculous makeover for his body but so far the late nights and skipped meals had largely nullified his efforts. Some mornings the sun was too strong, some days he just needed an extra hour of sleep.

He missed the freedom of running in a proper park, the kinds that had a stone path lined on both sides by Ashoka trees, fresh morning air filling his lungs. But from everything he'd read about the condition of the Delhi air, it didn't seem like the safest option anymore. With a flush he recalled the mask Usui had bought for him.

There is a certain freedom that comes with shedding your older self, sadly it's one of those very specifically indescribable things about life that exists in the no man's land of feeling and the absence of it. It is the weight lifting off your chest that leaves you light headed, like the soul residing in your body has begun healing itself. Looking back at who he had been once was more than just a way for Vir to feel better about himself, it was the deep lungful of air while sprinting the last mile on the treadmill that faced the sprawling city below. As the sun rose higher Vir unfurled from the lotus position and went back downstairs to wake up the others and begin to make amends for having to go home.

Back at the apartment Usui was still sulking, Vir stared at the wide set of his shoulders as Lyra leaned over from behind and hugged him, her hair veiling them in platinum blond silk. She spotted him by the door and called him over, kissing him on the head when he curled up against them, ignoring the obvious discomfort it caused Usui. He filled his lungs with her smell, the thought of his flight home looming ominously closer. She muttered a reassurance in his ear and walked over to the kitchen to heat a pot of miso soup.

Usui grumbled something about how he hated miso soup, which she immediately dismissed and as the warmth wafted through the house everyone settled down.

"Don't go." They now sat facing each other both too tall to fit in the couch without their knees and legs brushing against each other.

"I have to" Vir tried not to sound too sad, "my sister's getting married."

He took a foot and began massaging in the hope that the touch of skin against skin would convey what words couldn't.

"Then let's move up the launch, we'll talk to Miya and get it all sorted but you can't not be here. Why don't you get it?"

Vir stared back patiently. "Lyra a little help here?"

"You should stay back till we're live Viro!" She called out. "How can you forget how long you've been at that stupid 3d printer?"

"I already rescheduled my flight twice to keep up with these changes and now I can't afford any more delays. It's my sister's wedding."

Lyra walked over. "So we have a soft launch, what's the problem?"

She kissed the top of their heads and pulled them over to the glass dining table where the broth sat simmering in a fat porcelain pot.

It was a familiar feeling, being stared at. Some folks tried to be discreet while others looked at him like a raging flamingo on the loose. Vir stood at least six inches taller than everyone no matter where he was, only the mixed crowd of an airport brought him the comfort of anonymity. There his short crop of hair wasn't odd, his ear gauges weren't an eyesore, his uncomfortable smile wasn't catered to – everyone had that too wide smile that usually accompanied the anxiety of having to encounter large crowds or the general flatulence bubbled out between connecting flights.

His lips still lingered with the sweet kiss of goodbye, he'd promised Lyra and Usui that he'd call as soon as he landed – but for now all he wanted was to wear their touch on him like a stamp of love, an impenetrable bubble of warmth that couldn't be broken by the others. He walked past the raised eyebrows and the discreet exchange of looks – he was an immediate scandal dressed for comfort not street style – and took his seat at the rear end of the business class cabin.

Everyone Vir ever knew claimed a certain reaction to airports and flights, usually polar views depending on where they were and who they were with. Some absolutely loved airports, the thronging travelers each with a distinct personality coming together to create the sort of scene found in Renaissance paintings. Like a reality show playing out for your eyes only. Some people spoke of their utter disdain of waiting in queues, having to navigate stray bags, feet, sometimes the smell of sweaty backs. Worse still was sitting next to a child of any age younger than fifteen – which may have been the only acceptable age for a person to be seen outside and be tolerable. They mourned of sitting next to a *fatty-pattie* or someone who pushed their elbows off the armrest, worsened only by solo travelers who enjoyed striking up conversation like it was their god-given right.

Vir found that airports didn't bother him and given a comfortable seat with enough leg room, neither did the flight. Because he only felt the stares, an acknowledgment of his otherness more often than not blatantly tossed at him. It wasn't always negative given the volume of American and European tourists that flew in and out of the city, he only sparked interest when the words flew out of his mouth with the practiced precision of a native. He was the undisputed brown-boy Jane Goodall though not always received as warmly – in fact he'd had to change his grocer-cum-launderer twice as a student.

As they pushed through the grey-brown haze the seatbelt sign dinged all across and he moved to fetch the mask from his backpack, only to have a stewardess rush him to his seat with a garble of Japanese and English. He opened his mouth to argue but the eyes directed his way pushed him down to his seat. The stewardess resumed her innocent face and walked back to the front galley. When she looked back at the cabin to draw the curtain she nearly fainted – Vir had a long arm snaking upwards to the overhead compartment. He picked up his bag and brought it to his lap barely breaking a sweat, he removed the mask and restored the backpack to the bin, locking it in place without even unbuckling his seat belt. He deliberately flashed the girl a smile and thumbs up as the aircraft began its descent into the sepia city.

The difference was immediate, and it had nothing to do with the blaring sunlight burning up the tarmac outside or the mix of odors that puffed up every time a shoe hit the carpeted floor inside. Once again he found himself thinking about the kind of people who claimed to be intrigued by airports – at the transient quality of them, the constant flow of people of all shapes and colours. As for him Vir wove his way between flatulent uncles and aunties in hoodies over silk suits, bickering over how many trolleys to take. He brushed past the instagrammers, the pajama travelers, the businessmen who'd wither as soon as they'd hit the hotel bed.

The baggage carousel was another shitshow altogether, a tableaux of people already edgy from the flight with elbows brushing against each other to somehow take their bags before anybody else, with the mustachioed dads standing wide legged to hog up all the space and with the ladies who wore sunglasses indoors. They were the worst, easiest to recognize with the belt that looked more like a runway for Nappa Dori's latest, clutching their Louis Vuitton bags and brows risen so high they'd cut you down with a look. He felt their eyes follow him past the trunks and suitcases and the oddball rucksack pulled up by a smiling dreadlocked hippie who hadn't bothered showering the India off of them.

He stopped himself short.

It was the hunger, not the fact that Benaras was suddenly hot tourist property again, that drove his thoughts to acid. He pulled his bags one by one and found that the tightening in his gut had lesser to do with the anxiety of the crowd than a need for food. He called Surya but she didn't answer, so he set out to book an Uber where the signal seemed strong enough.

Devendra's call interrupted him and he debated whether to answer or not. Like his opinion on the people vomiting out of the gates, Vir was largely unbothered by his stepfather. It was a game of facts, really – Dev's inclusion had healed his mother in ways you couldn't put to words. He'd been the one to push for Vir's design course, Geetu still worried he'd fall off the wagon. He'd shown patience and kindness when both Vir and Surya were hard on him; with his strange sense of humor he'd made his own space in their hearts.

Heaving a sigh Vir answered the call.

"Thanks for picking me up, Dev." He slipped the mask off once the air purifier lit up a pleasant blue.

"Arey what thanks, I didn't want you to have to sit through a taxi in this heat."

He smiled back politely.

"It's the car isn't it? It's too much ..."

"Definitely the car, let's burn it down." Vir reclined his seat backward, smirking. "How's everything? Has mum driven everyone mad yet?"

"Nonsense, I'm as sane as I ever was though not for lack of trying on her part." Dev sniggered. "No really, everything is super stress free. Look at me, do I look tired at all?"

"You could use a vacation."

"If only vacations could last a year," he chuckled. "In all seriousness though Vir if you decide to get married anytime soon I will kill myself. No, first I think your mother will kill me to just exorcise herself; I'll be brought back to life and then I'll kill myself."

"I'm not getting married anytime before I turn thirty. Even then there's the whole matter of my –"

"Oh I'd really wait to tell your mother about that buddy!"

Vir wondered if there was a correct way to string words together so he could tell them his truths and not be hated for it. His smile withered as the sun beat down on the collecting traffic, it was one of those unacknowledged facts of life that everyone had an open mind and liberal heart until the tragedy struck at home. So he'd do as Dev decreed and wait but would it ever be worthwhile in the end?

With each passing hour it was harder to find a moment's peace in which to call home, the local sim wasn't activating on his phone and he had no way of getting to a laptop without Geetu peering over his shoulder. She was breathing down the necks of the boys draping flowers all over the living room till it resembled a garden, heady with the scent of marigold and roses. She insisted on referring to his ear gauges as buttplugs till he removed them. Everyone's outfits were steam ironed and placed on hangers, while Gayatri and Surya had the special privilege of sleeping in.

The kurta cut into his throat, cut too snugly around his shoulders, and Dev's bemused consolation was of no help. He felt like a clown, not only because the last time he'd worn a traditional kurta was at his father's funeral but also because the shade of purple gave him the appearance of a peacock. An uncomfortable peacock who was introduced to a thousand different aunties none of whom made any efforts to hide their scrutiny of how suitable a suitor he was.

"So beta what are you up to these days?"

"Arrey I've heard you're starting your own company and all in Osaka."

"Roppongi –err it's in Tokyo actually, but Osaka is a beautiful –"

"Yeah I went there for a holiday last year."

"So bacche you didn't tell us what you do."

"Oh ho don't hound him like that he's just shy."

"No no aunty I assure you it's nothing like that. I –"

"I didn't tell you guys?" Geetu had popped over to recommend they try the coconut water cocktail. "He's started his own line of high-end bags."

"Luxe backpacks, ma, don't make it sound like a boutique store for clutch bags."

"Wait like backpacks, like the stuff kids take to school and all?"

"Mmhmm exactly," Vir sipped his drink to calm his nerves. "Except these are made of beautiful cowhide and studded with 3D printed embellishments. Not really suitable for children."

"Wow beta that's really ... impressive." Paramjeet smirked.

"Yeah, look at what all jobs are coming up now!"

"Arey Minal it's about taking control ya, he's following his passion. In our days toh you could either be a doctor, lawyer, or teacher."

And yet you chose to be none of those. He bit back his words.

"So if not kids then what's your ideal market bacche?"

"Look at you Priya, straightaway in business mode and all ah! Let the poor boy wet his whistle first."

"I don't drink actually."

Looks were exchanged.

"Also, they're unsuitable for children because of choking hazards and I'm sure they wouldn't be able to afford them." He said quietly.

"*Afford* them." Priya Sodhi lifted her glass of champagne to salute him. "Well *inshallah* beta, I hope you find the best clients. And really Geetu you *must* show me these bags sometime."

He pulled at the collar of his kurta and excused himself.

Param raised an eyebrow at his retreating back. "He's quite distracted today ah Geetu, is everything okay?"

"Nonsense he's just landed a few hours back ya, he's exhausted that's all."

"Not too tired to be on the phone," Priya tittered, "he must be talking to his girlfriend."

"He's not single?" Minal deflated, matchmaking dreams deflating.

"He is."

“Chalo that’s nice, even if he is dating I mean it can’t be serious otherwise he’d tell you right? These days if they don’t come up to us and say, ‘hey mummy this is so and so’ every relationship can be broken up ya.” Priya high-fived Farida.

“Well, he’s not dating anyone right now. And I would know if he had a girlfriend,” Geetu willed her cheeks to cool down. “We don’t have any secrets.”

“No girlfriend then… maybe a boyfriend?” Farida laughed the loudest as always at her own joke, unbothered by the champagne spilling over her glass. Geetu excused herself and made the rounds looking for her husband. She adjusted her sunglasses, tossed out a smile to whoever looked her way, the picture of ease.

The sun wasn’t as harsh anymore, signaling that cocktails were now free for the taking and the Shroff sundowner went off into full swing.

Surya met her mother in the hallway and told her she was on her way out.

“Beta for one day can’t you two just sit at home?”

“Mumma please don’t stress me out, Gayatri and I can’t miss Lara’s roka function it’s so cheap ya. We can’t expect her to show up at our functions if we don’t go to hers.”

“Fine,” she made her way to the kitchen. “Oh listen, why don’t you take Sunaina also? She must be on her way.”

“Mom puh-lease! She wasn’t invited to begin with and if she can’t make it in time to our house why should I take her there? It’s just embarrassing. I’m embarrassed for you for suggesting it.”

Geetu rolled her eyes and entered the kitchen to have the blood drain from her face so fast she thought she’d faint. Were she not still holding the door she might’ve. The meat kebabs were plated and heading out the door – she peeked out at the garden where the guests were drinking and eating. The unmistakable orange of chicken tikka pierced through her heart and set her soul on fire; even Dev’s calming hand on her arm couldn’t help her unsee the horror.

"WHO SERVES MEAT AT A POOJA? DO WE LOOK LIKE FUCKING MUSLIMS TO YOU?!"

"Okay Geetu, you're being very loud right now." The door clicked shut behind them.

"Madam you only placed an order for shammi kebabs and tikkas for starters –"

"I wanted VEGETARIAN SHAMMI KEBABS and PANEER TIKKA. What nonsense is this?"

"Madam we're serving what we were told, you'll have to talk to the manager about this."

"I definitely will but bhaisaab what do we do about right now? You've completely embarrassed us, our reputation is *ruined*. Not one person out there is going to forget that we don't even know how to cater a small pooja-party."

"Ma'am –"

"Are you aware that my daughter is getting married, I have so many functions to host after this. Do you understand what a disaster this is?! I have nowhere to hide my face!"

"Geetu ..."

"No Dev this is *disastrous*, I'm going to be sick!"

"You're not going to fall sick, please hydrate. We'll speak to the caterer today evening."

"We're not paying for this. And I want to cancel him for everything he's booked." She turned back to the nervous kid. "Just try and get another job in this city, you piece of garbage."

Dev opened his mouth to protest, advance payments had been made but she was irredeemably deaf to reason.

"Geetu, please just have some water." He pushed a glass into the dispenser.

"Oh fuck off Dev don't patronize me. Do I look like a child to you?" she glared at him over her hands, lighting another cigarette.

He bit back a laugh. "No baby –"

"Ma, what's going on?" Vir stared between the two of them as another tray of kebabs was carried out.

She whipped around. "And you! Where have you been?"

"I was on a call."

"With who?"

"*Whom*," Dev muttered.

"My business partners – ma firstly I already told you that I'm going to be very busy we've just barely launched our website and I'm having to coordinate everything from what is a literal black hole of network connectivity. I have to stay updated on a lot."

"No, you were smoking weren't you? I can smell it."

He stared pointedly at the lit cigarette in her left hand.

"Nonsense, it's on you I can smell it. Tell me, if it's not cigarettes it has to be pot. Beta are you back to using drugs?"

"Mumma are you crazy? Need I remind you that *you* wanted proof that I've been putting your 'investment' in my business to use." He snarled. "Also no one gives a fuck whether you're serving kebabs of palak or beef they will be judgmental either way. They're your friends after all."

"What is that supposed to mean?"

"And please, *please* don't talk to everyone you meet about my company because I'm really not ready for that kind of extraneous publicity."

"Why don't we get you a drink?"

"No thank you," Vir huffed on his way out.

"Disaster," Geetu muttered even as she was ushered out.

Another typically atypical Delhi bar, a reunion of old friends and it is always the same dance. A routine of matador and bull treading in careful choreography around the same things they always talk about with the same put-on airs of nostalgia for a different time. It's the same talk, the same mouths, with a shift in setting between bars that cling to their forced aesthetic with the same desperation that people meet with – that hunger for a connection. And if it doesn't happen in the first few moments, there's a chance it wouldn't at all. You can see it in their shifty eyes, the one-too-many nods, their mindless hummed ascent – they ask you how you are but they only wait for the hole in your answer to hook their own story into. And then the tables have turned. And now you're the matador and they're the bull. The same dance, the same dance as always.

They compare dick measurements in vacation spots and paychecks, happiness with the ring of platinum and diamonds, a completion of life's basics. On their own they can't stand to talk to each other long enough to last a full meal, and so they drink. They drink and the same fucking dance ensues.

They drink their drinks and talk of who's dating whom, who has talks of an upcoming wedding in the mix, who's screwing who on the side and how much, and all of it is okay because then they go home and lie next to their version of a happy sort of everafter. They feverishly stare into their phones because it saves them from having an authentic thought. They talked of the same people they did the last time he met them and so Vir found himself tuning out their words as the banter swelled into the late evening. They were grown up versions of the same, tired high school clichés that once trolled around the canteen during lunchtime to ceaselessly judge and bully.

They were mere shadows of their former selves – smart, successful, and shamelessly rich of course and they seemed content being just that. Maybe it was because they got what they always wanted, became exactly who they set out to be from the day they had discussed career goals in fifth grade. That's what happened to the ghosts that peaked in high school, Vir realized solemnly. He handed them their wedding invites and left, paying his share of the bill no matter how much they insisted he didn't.

"Au revoir, Vir!" Rubina Raman waved at him from the car.

He smiled and waved back, regretting the moment he told her about wanting to learn French.

Vir walked out of the mall passing self-important groups of sharply dressed people on their way to binge-drink the night away. He might've been the only guy that evening not wearing super skinny H&M jeans but the weather was kind to his denim jacket, he hugged it closer allowing the synth and bass from his headphones to drown out the usual Saturday night babble. He stood outside in the balmy breeze, a lone shadow against the bright window displays, perfectly content till a sharp jab disturbed him.

"Hey you!" Gayatri panted, weighed down by a few dozen garment bags each emblazoned with a designer's initials. "What are you doing here?"

"I was just meeting some old friends. Don't you have an assistant to help with all this?"

"She's on a whole other set of errands, don't ask. Here take some of these won't you *big brother*." He clicked his tongue disapprovingly but helped her ease the bags into the back of the awaiting car.

"So what is all of this for, dare I ask?"

"The wedding of course, some designer-friends sent in options for me to try on and I'll wear something if I like it." She turned to the backseat. "I'm not sure yet."

"What if you don't like any of them?"

"I guess my assistant sends it back, I don't know."

"Just like that?" he didn't see it working out in her favour. "Why do you get freebies though?"

"It's a thing, just get with the program." She pulled her hair into a knot. "Anyway, how was your day? Is Geetu ma's bickering finally getting to you?"

"Mumma's never been good with stress," he smiled indulgently. "What I don't understand is why you and Surya were so rude to Sunaina today."

"Okay well I'm absolutely fine, I called her a while back to ask her if she's coming for the cards party tonight and she just like 'yeah I'll-let-you-know'ed' me so I'm just giving her space now. But okay she did have a point that Surya knew when she came back and she didn't go over and say hey and didn't tell her about the wedding and Dhiraj but then Sunaina herself made no efforts either right?"

He barged in to the room where Surya sat smoking, the skirts of her *anarkali* pulled up to cool her thighs.

"Shut the door it's like a furnace outside!"

"Can you stop being immature and just call Sunaina?"

Gayatri appeared behind him ashen faced. "I'm not even getting into this, I've to get ready and all."

Surya shot daggers at the pair of them. "Could you find the lock to the closet so this time there's no one barging in to look at my wedding outfits?"

"Can you answer my question – why can't you two put your egos aside and just talk?"

"What's it to you? If she wants to talk to me she can very well come over here and get it out, she's just being a prissy bitch and avoiding confrontation."

"Funny because that's exactly what she said and now I'm convinced that you're both bat shit crazy." He glared at her even as she straightened up, knocking the glass with ash and water all over the carpet. "This is ridiculous , I'm going over there and I'll drag her here if I have to."

"Vir I want no part in this –" he slammed the door behind him.

Sunaina tested the volume swiveling the dial left to right so it was just loud enough to cut through the sound of the evening wind, cooling against the trickle of sweat that formed down her throat. The wine sanguineous and swirling over the tip of her glass down her open lips was just cool enough to mask the bitter aftertaste of tannins. She plucked a java plum and crushed it between her lips on her way to the bar for a refill. The wine had her walking on clouds. Her thoughts were like overexposed photographs. She lit a cigarette and swung her hips to Savage Garden, throwing open the doors dramatically belting out the high notes like she was the star of her own show.

"Wow, so this is where the real party is!"

"What the fuck," she wrapped the robe tighter around her waist. "I thought you were at bua's house."

Sohrab sighed. "Yeah hate to disappoint you but I'm not into poker."

"Oh that's terrible," she threw her head back and laughed. "You'll never survive this side of town then."

"I don't mind sitting out, but these guys just take the game way too seriously."

He pointed an accusatory finger at her. "Wait a minute, you cut your hair? *That's* how you got to skip out on that pooja today?"

She shrugged. "What can I say, I really needed a haircut."

He tried to be cross but couldn't help himself. "You know that pooja nearly choked me to death. And your dad got into a nasty argument just now so I just took a walk."

"What happened?" she poured him a glass of wine.

"Uhh I don't know how to say this – I figured he'd have told you already." She braced herself for the worst. "Your mum sent in the divorce papers."

"Oh."

"Sorry I know it's not my place to tell you but I think you have a right to know."

"No, I'm actually not that surprised. Maybe this way he can just start to move on from this mess."

He looked at her with piercing dark eyes.

"Divorce isn't messy Sunaina, death is." Sohrab drained his wine and reached for the lit cigarette between her fingers.

She felt the pull of guilt in her stomach. "I'm sorry I didn't –"

He waved a dismissive hand. "No, don't please. I'm just tired otherwise I wouldn't have said it that way."

"No but it's true though."

He hummed in consent and poured himself another glass, walking out to the patio.

"Hey can I change the song? You should hear something from this century really."

She pouted. "I try okay. Sometimes one is simply in the mood for a little retro –"

"Jesus Sunaina, don't embarrass yourself."

"Okay firstly it's just wrong to swear on Jesus, because you're still Indian you know, it's culturally inappropriate."

"As is running away from your home and becoming some weird hippie drifter," he wiggled his eyebrows at her.

"Ick, I can't believe that's what my father told you. Out of everything... whatever. I have nothing to be embarrassed about because bad music choice is nothing in front of bad facial hair."

He drew away from her aghast.

"I fuckin' love my moustache." He took a hand to the chest.

She looked away from the peek of dark chest hair.

"You look like a bad pornstar from the seventies," she giggled into her wine glass.

"Okay sure, that's rich coming from the girl who was singing along to a hundred year old song."

She shoved him, skillfully enough to not spill any wine from either glass. He shoved her back and wine dripped from the lip of both glasses.

"Now, mountain girl," he plugged his phone into the dock, "let's educate you."

"*Mountain Girl*, really?" she flicked at his shoulder. "You make me sound like a cavewoman."

"No proof on the contrary yet, now shut up and listen will ya?"

They settled on the patio chairs and against his better judgment Sohrab mentioned the overheard conversation where someone had joked about Sunaina's failed attempt at hitching Daksh Dhiman – the erstwhile most-eligible of the lot – for good.

"I'm sorry. If there was any way I could've changed the topic I would've," he held up a hand solemnly.

"That's sweet of you, but none of it matters now. Don't believe everything you hear about me, you'd think I'm mad as a snake."

He looked down at her hand wrapped around his and she snatched it away too soon. Sohrab cleared his throat and picked at the bowl of cheese shavings but the gruyere melting on his tongue did nothing to ease the tension.

"I actually love this song."

"Ya see why I love it?"

They fell into silence while the song painfully throbbed on.

"I can change it if you want, tell me if you don't like it."

"But I just told you that I do."

He nodded politely.

"Okay just ask already. About the guy. You're ruining wine hour."

She cooled at the sound of his laughter. "What the hell is wine hour all about?"

"Wine Hour is something to keep my mind off things such as my parents' divorce," she shrugged. "Maybe our family's cursed with bad luck in soulmates."

He smiled at her, hyperaware of the way his heartbeat had shifted tempo to match her bare feet stroking the naked blades of grass. "Soul mates, really? Maybe you are crazy."

"Wait a minute," she leaned in so close he could smell her honeysuckle shampoo. "You don't believe in soul mates?"

"No," he drank from his glass and leaned in to her, "because I'm an actual grownup."

"Oh get over yourself."

He laughed mirthlessly. "I had a soulmate, Sunaina, and then she got cancer and died on me, taking a piece of me with her every passing day."

Sohrab saw the moisture in her eyes and it irritated him, she was ruining the moment. Or perhaps he was. He considered what 'the moment' even was, he was an old widower and she was a kid trying to find herself. He looked back and wanted to slap the pitiful look right off her face. The fist clenched tighter, his nails digging into the palm of his hand.

"Well," she clinked her glass to his, "you're alive and sitting here, that's gotta count for something right?"

In the split second the song changed he heard the trilling orchestra of crickets all around them. He followed her glass of wine to the lips that enclosed it and the head that threw back to drain the last of her drink. His body moved of its own will. Sunaina felt the force of his gaze, the solidity of his body pushing her backwards onto the marble island. Her fingers slid over the damp crop of his hair as she pulled him close enough that their lips were a hair's breadth away and they knew that they were about to cross a line they couldn't look back from but she was catching fire with every breath. Their kiss was laced with the salt of sweat and wine oiled need, the summer night was weighing down heavily around them. In that moment Sohrab Sood only knew one thing for sure, that he'd never kissed anyone like that before.

Chapter SEVENTEEN

A Study In Sabyasachi (*Interlude*)

"So that's a no for the app idea?"

Gayatri nestled deeper into the couch. "Definite no. Everybody has an app now, it's done to death."

Zoya, Gayatri's de facto assistant frowned into her notes. "Born a lobster, boiled to death. What about a website? You're fresh off a movie and viral speech about mental health, these days everyone's using depression or whatever-you-may for launching themselves."

"Are you serious right now?"

"Deadly so. It's the new foolproof marketing tool. We could work it into a design collaboration, you could look into setting up a blog or – oooh how about a website that works as a blog but then you can put in whatever you like. Like a travelogue, we could shoot some quick fun videos of you whenever you're on the move."

She massaged her head. "I don't know, this is all a bit much no?"

They stared at the silent screen, waiting for it to crackle. "It's not a bad idea."

Gayatri could picture her agent on the other end of the line, pensively poking her chin with the back of a pen.

"It's definitely a smart way to show that you're actually not a dumbass – wait Gayatri don't you write as well? I think Neil said something about a poetry journal?"

The sound of his name was enough to bring her down.

"I don't know about that." She sank lower into herself. "I think this whole thing is too excessive. I'd like to keep some air of privacy please."

Gayatri was losing herself in the cheap hotel room where she held him in cold shivers and sweat until he could sleep, hearing the thud of his heart reverberate through her bones even with a whole camera crew hovering around them. And the heat couldn't melt them, the cold couldn't invade them.

Zoya leaned in. "I thought we wanted to keep her relevant in the public eye for as long as possible, no?"

The sharp slope of his nose grazing the side of her face, Neil's reassuring hand on the small of her back when she was ready to shit herself on the red carpet.

"No but she has a point, this is a bit much. We don't want people to think she has all the time in the world it could potentially be detrimental."

Gayatri was back in the backseat of the car and she was so mad she wanted to cry. And then he was pulling away from her and that was worse than being homesick.

Neil barging into her room to make sure she'd thrown her book away, the one she abused herself in.

"Well if your writing is good we could look into a book deal?"

"No," Gayatri sat upright with more force than necessary. "That's a commitment I don't have time for right now."

"Alright alright, how about a guest editor spot? I'll make some calls."

Neil didn't talk to her anymore. He'd shut her out and Gayatri wondered if she was caught up in the bond that developed through working in such close quarters, one that naturally diluted over time. Or maybe she was unable to separate herself from the fiction of it all.

"Okay I don't see this going anywhere, I have a wedding to attend in the evening. Get back to me when we have something definitive to go on." She said her goodbyes and left.

In the time it took her car to find its way to the front, Sunaina called.

"Where you at bish?"

"The Lalit – don't ask." she heaved a sigh, "what's up?"

"We're headed to the Sabyasachi showroom. Come along?"

"Yeah I'll see you there. Who's with you?"

"Just take Aurobindo Marg and you can skip the worst of traffic. I'm with Vir and Sohrab, the boys need to be fitted for their *achkans* and bhai's in a bad mood because he got into a fight with his girlfriend–"

Vir shouted incoherently from the back.

"Oh wow, tell him we'll go for cocktails once we're done from there."

"Oh my god, perf!"

Unavoidable as it was, Gayatri found herself sitting in chockablock traffic because the omnipresent blue boards and tape cordoned off half the road. It was a theory shared by many that the people that drove Wagon Rs were generally the worst drivers. She glared at the man poised to cut her off at the diversion and the jerky swerve left him gawking and skidmarks on the road. Stuck in more traffic, Gayatri sat fiddling with the magnets for seven and a half minutes, phone positioned to the right angle so she could find the right hook at her septum. Following a brief period where she'd considered permanently piercing she'd been gifted the set of magnetic studs that passed off as almost real. So she found herself working the faux stud with sweaty fingers, stuck at the Outer Ring Road junction. She took five sets of photos with and without sunglasses and a separate close up for the live feed. Even as the commentary poured in, she switched off her notifications and walked in.

If Jane Austen ever wrote of the Bennet sisters living in Delhi, they'd surely mortgage the estate for an outfit that came in a signature red trunk.Tthat Sabyasachi and Delhi weddings are meant for each other is a universal truth.

That Sunaina and the others entered without pausing to fully take in the grandeur of Delhi's mecca did not go unnoticed by the staff's eyes. None of them could've seen her for the mess of nerves that she was, perturbed even by the whiff of his cologne as Sohrab passed her by to the fitting room.

Gayatri crept up from behind her. "What's a good but noncommittal caption?"

"Woah is that a real piercing?" Sunaina pointed at her septum.

"No I thought it might be a bit much to get one just for an insta post," she pouted in deepest contemplation. "How about a simple 'Yaas'? Can't go wrong with a yaas."

"Mmm yaas queen." Sunaina brushed her hair off her shoulder. "Seriously though what is up with this Instagram story shit, you know it took me like forever to figure out how this works now, so many updates I've missed out on."

Gayatri pulled her in for a selfie. "Sorry I just had to do a post for this new pendant, some brand Lara's mother or something has started."

Sunaina rolled her eyes for effect, not yet willing to acknowledge how hurt she was that Lara Varma who once was a her closest friend, hadn't invited her for the engagement yet both Gayatri and Surya had been present for everything. She didn't care to admit that she'd been following the wedding hashtag like a manic stalker one step shy of frothing at the mouth in disbelief and embarrassment.

"Sorry, was that shady? I didn't mean to bring that up."

They passed the displays, idly picking at outfits simply on how bright they shone.

“No forget about that, listen I kinda need to talk to you about something.” Sunaina pulled out a delicate sari. “Just before Vir came over yesterday, in the evening I mean, something err… something that shouldn’t have happened sort of happened.”

Gayatri pulled her into a different wing while picking out a floor length embroidered dress. An assistant came up behind them to handle the garments and directed them to the trial room. As the haphazard selection of clothes were brought in for their perusal, Sunaina narrated the story of how she’d almost slept with Sohrab and they’d only just managed to pull themselves together before Vir had barged in and declared that they come to the party.

“So you and Sohrab Sood, really?” her eyes bulged for effect.

“Shit dude, it’s like a little out of control.” Sunaina fanned herself. “I feel like I’m going to burst into flames if we’re in the same room for a long time.”

“Isn’t he like … *old*?”

“Not as such, yeah he’s old*er* if you’re getting into semantics.”

“Semantics?” she laughed, “Big words for little Sunaina.”

“Shut up. I don’t know what to do about him.”

“I don’t see if you have to do anything really. If it’s a crush you let it be and it’ll go away. Or you tell him and …” she shrugged.

“I don’t know if it’s that simple G, I think … I don’t know what to think.”

“HO-LY-FUCK, are you like falling for him? I mean he’s hot in the like daddy way.”

Sunaina pulled out a deep blue ensemble. “Shush, one doesn’t sit in the house of god and talk that way about love.”

“That and the fact that you’ve not had the best luck in *love*. Chill the fuck out.”

“Exactly. So now I just need to clear my head and I figured this was a good place as any to do that.” She lost herself under the weight of the skirt.

"I don't know," Gayatri found her thoughts a mess. She stared at the incoming call and wondered why Ankit was ringing her. "Come out and show me the *lehenga* na."

"Dude it's way too much."

"Too much what?"

She walked out in the double layered sari with painted flowers and sequins. "Just much *much*."

Gayatri gasped. "Oh my god you *have* to wear this or I'll die! It's perfect for the wedding."

"It's weighing me down, like chainmail."

"Okay I don't even know what you're talking about it's stunning."

"Fine, let's find you something as well."

Gayatri chose a deep maroon *anarkali* – sequined all over so with every step she glittered from head to toe. And while she silently mourned the white hand painted sari she'd left behind, she was unaware that it would arrive in a week with a personalized letter.

Gayatri gestured grandly to the clothes that lay around them. "Still think it was a good idea to have retail therapy here of all places?"

"Papa's going to kill me." She turned to the sales lady, "Oh I'm also supposed to pick up an order for alterations, the name is Hassan Kochhar."

"Jeez he also is wearing a Sabyasachi outfit?"

She turned back to look at Gayatri. "Yeah why?"

For a moment she lost track of everything, they'd made their way back down the stairs and the full force of Sohrab dressed in head to toe black knocked her senseless. It was the way the coat hugged his shoulders, the infinitude of the black fabric broken only by the starry buttons. Vir who was struggling with the collar of his *bandhgala* beckoned for help but she could've been hit by a meteor and not noticed.

"What do you think?" he twisted his lips into a rakish grin.

She nodded appreciatively, unsure of her words in the moment.

"So basically at this point I think everyone at the wedding will be wearing a Sabyasachi except the bride."

Gayatri shook her head sagely. "No babe, we're not wearing these to the actual wedding that's done to fucking death. These are for the youngsters/Diwali party on Friday."

Chapter EIGHTEEN

I Always Thought It Would Be Your Hand (*Holding Mine*)

The book did not belong to Sunaina, she was sure of that because she couldn't stand Pablo Neruda's hyperbolic verse, because any book she had on her person belonged to Faisal and thus had his name scrawled on the last page. More than that, she knew she could never leave a mess of dried flowers in the pages of a book because it wasn't the 90's and she didn't live in a movie – that didn't stop her from posting a picture of it though. The book belonged to someone else because the halfwritten lovenote started with Hassan's name, but now the sun was vanishing and she had other places to be. It was the night of Surya's youngsters/Diwali party and they were also celebrating Dhiraj's birthday. The farmhouse had been pimped out and as ever the risks of tempers short-circuiting were high – not in the least because of the low neckline of her *choli*. Next to the delicately draped double-layered Sabyasachi sari was the dress

Geetu had made for her. On any other night, the choice would've been obvious, but Sunaina couldn't fight the feeling that she'd be stealing the spotlight with the sari. She wanted it to be all about Surya and as many eyes off her as possible.

With Gayatri's promise of helping her make a decision, she'd done her make up and hair to effortless perfection as time took turns slowing down and then speeding up so it felt like even though she'd been waiting for forever, it had only been an hour, but they were also running late. She primed her brows and double checked her teeth for any stains. Her lipstick was even, hair perfectly tousled, and the knock knocked at the perfect time.

"Gayatri?"

Another knock.

"Did you die on the way here?"

Sunaina ran into Sohrab's chest. Their eyes met for a moment and then slid down to her loosely tied robe, both of them slowly realizing that his hands were still around her arms.

"Oh."

She pulled the robe tight but not before he had a peek at her nude underwear.

"*Jesus* I'm sorry, I thought you were ready to go."

Sohrab didn't know whether to rush forward or back off and stood there stupidly trying to look anywhere except directly at her and failing miserably in his attempts. She slammed the door mid-apology.

"Just leave me here to die please," Sunaina pressed herself against the door. Her stomach coiled in on itself.

His breath shuddered through the door like it was more air than wood, she wondered if he might force himself in and kiss her right then, maybe a part of her did want him to, but there were other things to consider. He was a friend of the family. He'd been married once. He was older. He was also still muttering some apology but she couldn't find it in her to speak, worried that were she to open her mouth her heart might jump right out of it.

She was playing with fire.

There was a certain self destruction that came with falling for Sohrab Neruda would gladly approve of – but this was not the night to be caught up in the poetry of bad decisions.

But wasn't that why the nights were made? To make all the bad decisions. He was just a winter fling, he was just a winter fling and she-

A deep sigh echoed both inside and out.

The door vibrated as a fist rapped twice.

"Yes?" she called out meekly.

"It's me ya, why's you door locked?" Gayatri demanded from the other side.

She grabbed her by the arm and yanked her in. "Fuck my fucking life. Did you see Sohrab?"

"Yeah, he's downstairs with your dad. Listen what is it about men in a black kurta ... like oof!" she laughed. "Okay let's get you sorted I don't wanna be late."

"Dude it's not even about the kurta it's just him ..." Sunaina sighed. "I can't stop thinking about him."

Gayatri considered the mood before speaking. "Well the point is does he think about you?" she walked over to the bed. "Also there's no question here you should just fuckin wear the sari and stop being so sombre."

Sunaina shrugged. "I mean I already threw myself at him in my fucking underwear so I don't see how this night can get any worse. I'm kinda bloated though, I just wanna stay home and be comfy in my fluffy ass pajamas, chin-fucking-deep in ice cream. Why does no one eat ice cream in this weather?"

"Comfy my ass, you're not ditching. Look, I know you've got this whole bougie children of the mother earth vibe going on and, okay, it was great at first but you really need to get your shit together and get dressed."

"You're right. Fuck this." Sunaina ripped the robe off her skin and walked over to the pleat her sari.

Gayatri helped her accessorise and an hour later they shared a cigarette outside Surya's house both silently acknowledging the end of an era. Separated by the perimeter wall and a row of primed shrubbery was Vir speaking in that perverse mix of Japanese and English they'd come to associate with conversations not to be overheard. From running a quick errand, shopping for clothes, while reading a book to dinnertime, the calls grew conspiratorial and frequent as the days went by. And while Geetu looked at him with murder in her eyes, the others learnt to tune them out.

They watched him pace and blather on, unperturbed by his audience as tone changed from sarcastic to loving. Both Sunaina and Gayatri knew that the pressure of finding a wife and settling down was the worst for him. Sunaina thought of the elbow jabs and wiggled brows as aunties asked her if she'd jump the gun and announce her marriage plans before anyone else. Gayatri wondered how to talk about Ankit and Neil and everything that came in between because she needed something that had nothing to do with work to make sense.

Sunaina broke the silence first.

"What ever happened to the Dewans?"

"Who?"

"You know, Lakshman Dewan and his family ...?"

"Oh," she tried not to let the surprise show on her face. "Well actually I don't know the full story myself but basically his dad was caught up in some embezzlement scene."

"I thought he pulled strings and kept that from public records?"

"I don't know about that but since then things were shit for them, especially for that older son – what was his name?"

Sunaina remembered but shrugged anyway.

"That guy just spelled trouble from the start, he had it coming sooner or later. Anyway after that I guess things were still relatively okay but Lakshman just vanished. Now obviously everyone and their mother has a theory about where he went but who knows for sure, right?"

"So then?"

Gayatri shrugged. "That's all I know. Promise me, if I get caught up in controversy – promise me you won't just abandon me."

"Oh you better not," Gayatri's publicist-assistant walked up the driveway. "Sorry we're late but OMG the traffic was insane."

Sunaina smiled politely and looked over to where Vir was finishing his phone call.

"It's mad in there," he walked over to where they stood.

"This outfit is div-vine honey!" The tiny publicist – whose name might've been Zoya except Sunaina had forgotten it as soon as they'd met – walked around Gayatri checking for any creases or snags. "Fabulous. Now, we're gonna take some amazing but tasteful photos and put them up. I want this night to be about what you're wearing and your flawless hair and who you talk to, everything."

"Let's not get carried away, tonight's about Dhiraj and Surya."

"Oh of course of course we'll get her a little shoutout or something too. But sweetie you should see yourself right now, you're ready to launch a thousand ships."

Sunaina rolled her eyes and turned back to Vir. "What's going on inside?"

Her answer came in the sound of glass crashing against a wall. They rushed into the house to find the usual congregation of relatives tinted red with rage. Geetu, Hassan, and Kama were possibly the source of the resounding crash, Sunaina looked around and saw the erstwhile vase of fresh flowers not too far from where they stood. The wallpaper was soaked through with water but no one seemed to notice it as they continued their row. Asim had taken to a wing-backed armchair as his throne, the perfect spot to bellow his disappointments at the family with the intensity of a bookie at a wrestling match.

"Who told you that you have the right to make this into a fucking marketing campaign?"

Kama turned around agahast and teary eyed. "This has absolutely nothing to do with marketing, how can you be so cruel?"

"I don't see what's so wrong about it," Dev muttered. Kama simpered at him.

"Dev do not even think about getting involved in this." Geetu turned back. "For a change Hassan's absolutely right you have no idea of the mess you're making."

"That is so not fair Geetu ya how can you say that. It's my first foray into fiction and you two are just *ruining it for everyone*." She held up the crushed handkerchief to her nose.

Hassan clapped theatrically, forehead vein ready to pop. "Oh really! And out of everything, every possibility under the sun you could have written about, you chose to write about a murder?"

"WHY DO YOU CARE NOW, YOU USELESS PIG!" Asim sputtered.

"It's a murder mystery set in Doon valley," she squealed, "and it's obviously not a real story how stupid do you think I am dammit?"

"What I can't understand is why you chose tonight of all nights to talk about it, a night that's not even yours to ruin."

As Kama dove face-first into a meltdown, Sid Sood's voice stole the show.

"You think just because we're separated you're allowed to go out and sign up for speed dating or something?"

Gayatri tried to control her laughter but the out of place American accent was too much for her.

"I'm not!" Sunita screamed back at him. "Should I remind you that *you'rc* thc reason we separated–"

He theatrically clapped in her face. "Wow! I knew you were self-centered but I had no idea you were so delusional. You think *I'm* the reason our marriage ended and not the twenty-something barista across your office?"

"Okay he was thirty two and you know that."

"He was a fucking chaiwallah!"

"Fuck you Siddie, how convenient for you to forget your bartender from last year?"

"She's getting married to Greg! I'm going for their wedding, you stupid cow –"

He spluttered the end of his sentence as Sunita Sood splashed all the wine from her glass into his face.

Sunaina watched the merlot soak its way through the ikat print of his white kurta. Asim craned his neck to watch as Siddhant threw his own glass at his ex-wife's feet who stumbled right into the side table. On her way down she made the unfortunate decision to grab at the runner, pulling with it the serving dish of Geetika's famous seven layer dip.

In the middle of this tableau of chaos Sohrab sat nursing a stiff drink like a lone ranger at the end of the world.

"Oh-kay," Zoya whistled. "I'll wait outside."

"Jesus Sunaina how long does it take you to get ready?" Sohrab walked over, standing too close for comfort.

"I'm sorry," she looked behind him as Hassan wheeled around from Geetu and Kama to land a punch right into Dev's chin. "I-I couldn't find the right earrings."

"Get me out of here, please." He looked at her with tortured eyes and she fought the urge to hug him because behind them, Vir was pulling Dev and Hassan apart while Geetu screamed at her weeping sister and Sunita locked herself up in the nearest bedroom. Gayatri was shaking the Commander by the shoulders, who seemed to have had a heart attack while no one was looking. She stood over him, one leg on each side so that the slit in her *anarkali* opened all the way up her thigh.

"Water, Sunaina get me a glass of water!"

She lunged instead for the jug and emptied it straight on Asim's head, waking him up not from cardiac arrest but a nap. He roared like a beast and everyone finally stopped.

"You're all fucking crazy!"

Vir hugged his mother tightly, who still shook with anger and muttered about the night being an utter disaster. His phone rang and she looked like she might throw up in disgust.

Hassan leaned down and gave Devendra an ice pack, apologizing for his behaviour. Kama sniffed in response but chose not to say anything. Unfortunately, she would never get to finish the manuscript she'd been drafting because tragedy waits for no one. She wouldn't find the time to write again for many years to come.

Geetu straightened the sleeve of her brocade blouse and pulled herself together. Vir's phone buzzed again and she'd had enough of it. He stared in horror as she flung it in a graceful arc to the far end of the living room and the following silence was like a black hole.

"Go ahead and answer your phone calls now."

Sunaina buried her laugh in Sohrab's shoulder.

Surya and Dhiraj descended the stairs with arms entwined to the sound of cheers and tasteful fratboy whoops. And for the first time in as long as she could remember, all eyes were on *her* – not Sunaina, or Gayatri, not even Lara who had a talent for seeking attention. In a sari of gold lamé she was the goddess of love blessing the event. She smirked at the squeals of joy as they walked to the center of the room and Dhiraj leaned down to kiss her cheek in a picture perfect moment fed straight into the multiverse via live video feed.

Walking past the cameras and the row of champagne bottles lined and primed to pop, in the reverent looks of their closest friends, Surya understood the glory of being the center of attention. For one night she could stand on the pedestal that her sisters had spent their whole lives on and yet, standing next to Dhiraj dulled the shine. The charm wore off as quickly as it had taken hold of her and now all that attention felt unnecessary. She turned to him and understood in the warmth of his smile that the custom made three-tier birthday cake could've been swapped by something they'd baked together. At home. Just the two of them. Dhiraj did not need these things. They could've celebrated with family than pump expensive liquor into these hyenas with their counterfeit compliments. The night was long and full of errors, her new shoes cut into her skin from every side, Dhiraj stood with watery eyes from the constant smoke of cigarettes because everyone wanted to get a word in and he was too polite to say no.

As the cocktails were poured the party begun the customary division, some seated themselves around the professional blackjack dealer, some around the deluxe roulette setup, a full team of pros in maroon vests setting the mood. *Teen Patti* is often regarded with the same diligence as Russian roulette, and players often drink themselves into a stupor by the end of the night. Yet there were some whose jovial anecdotes and enquiries about outfits and honeymoon destinations could not be deterred. For Surya, it was only a matter of keeping a lid on the clashing egos between families till the last round of the *phéras* – it was common knowledge that the Jodhpur ceremony was just a designated party. However her mood took a nosedive as Gayatri and Sunaina walked in.

There is nothing worse than walking into a room and seeing every head turn your way. Not when the talk dies down, not when the smiles falter, not when the glittering assholes retreat behind their manicured hands and talk with the stinging sweetness of a young girl with a spider in her hands about to play a mean trick on you. There were a few who seemed genuinely happy to see them, but the overall contempt dribbled down every chin. Their onyx eyes gave away the sourness behind their smiles. They said 'it is not fair that you moved on', 'that you became better than us'. Sunaina and Gayatri held each other's hands for sanity.

Vir squared his shoulders and met their awed hostility with the brightest smile. "Well I know it's been a while but come on, I'm no celebrity guys!"

Even though the ice broke, the cold vibes didn't completely go away.

Sunaina walked up to Surya and hugged her, whispering an apology for being late.

"Oh my god don't even, bhai told me what was happening at home," she rolled her eyes, "I told mumma not to wear double layered spanx dude she can't handle it and shit just gets ugly. As for you... missy... don't be tryna steal my thunder and all now, kay?"

"Excuse me?"

"You heard me." Surya waved off the cameraman who was veering dangerously close. "You just up and left and didn't even bother to let me know if you were alive or ... I don't know"

"I went because I had nothing left here Surya."

"Seriously? What about me?"

She paused for a beat. "It looks like you've managed to find your happiness just fine without me Surya, why does that still make you feel like I would try to steal your thunder?"

"Because that's just who you are."

Gayatri cleared a throat from behind and spoke through a grit-toothed smile. "You bitches need to get your shit together, we have cameras everywhere."

Surya looked around at the discreet photographers moving around the foyer, lounge, and the outer deck while the guests had returned to their gilded tokens and glasses. She decided that that would be the only moment of regret for having spent a fortune on the wedding film.

Sunaina leaned in and placed a hand on her sister's arm. "Look I'm only here for you, the both of you. I don't want to upset you so just tell me what I can do."

"Hug it out!" Gayatri wrapped her long arms around the three of them.

"You're right. Oh my god guys, like, good vibes only." Surya flipped her sleek curtain of hair and pecked Dhiraj.

Sohrab had been lost to a conversation on Trump's America and with every passing minute turning into an hour, Sunaina remembered the reason she'd wanted to leave the city in the first place. After having been swallowed up in a gushing chat about the movie, Gayatri wove her way back to the mezzanine where they stood with Sam Manchanda at the center gearing up to school a cocky plus-one about public health awareness.

"Look don't get riled up, all I'm saying is that in my humble opinion there's like nothing to teach really. You just need to like go through a certain age to know this shit. India is just backward AF." He reveled in the few nods.

Samaira adjusted her oxidized silver *maang-tika*. "Excuse me sir, but your privilege is showing. How can you just sit in this like glass house or whatever and assume that everyone in this country has access to the same information that you do? There are villages where it's still considered a matter of shame to get your period."

"That's exactly my point," he stood straighter like a peacock preparing to dance. "Backward. As Eff."

Varsha Kalra hid her embarrassment in a loud show of being bored at the seriousness of the conversation even as the others rolled their eyes and dispersed.

"And that waste of space is Varsha's fiancé," Karishma nudged her way between them.

"Wait, I thought she called it off with him?"

She shook her head. "That was last month. This month they're back together. Oh and speaking of together, there's Lara and her fiancé."

"Lara's *engaged*?" Sunaian gasped. "When did this happen? Who's the guy?"

"Gaawsh Sana you really have been living under a rock. She got hitched to Daksh's cousin brother – remember Adarsh Arora? You used to like make fun of him and stuff back in the day?"

"Wait but that was forever ago, why is that a valid reason to exclude us?" Gayatri demanded.

"Oh my god, you guys have like a clue in life do you? He had like serious problems growing up, like he went to therapy for a long time to get over the bullying and shit. And well there's also the fact that Daksh was there and he's sort of ..." she lit a cigarette knowing fully that she had them hooked onto her every word, "well he's like living with that guy now, the older dude."

"Oh okay." Sunaina wondered if there was anything else she could say. "Well, as long as he's happy I guess it's all good."

Gayatri pulled her downstairs to the bar before Karishma could reply. "What does she know, her boyfriend only drinks rosé. Bitch."

"Hey guys," Surya walked over to where they stood, leading a tall leggy girl behind her. "This is Elina, she's Farida aunty's daughter. She's literally the person you wanna call if you're buying art."

They turned to the newcomer who may as well have been a runway model for her overall gazelle-like appearance. Sunaina groaned on the inside.

"So, Gayatri is in the movie biz she's like just gotten herself a place in Khar."

"Hill Road," she interjected but Surya carried on. "And Sunaina is like the Little Miss Wanderlust these days. When she's not fabulously flaunting her Gucci shoes," she giggled. Elina clinked her glass to Sunaina's appreciatively.

"Have either of you seen Sohrab? I've been meaning to introduce him to everyone as well."

"Oh I think he's with Dhiraj smoking outside." Sunaina tried to keep her voice even.

"Perfect, do you mind if I just see you there, Surya? I just gotta hit the bathroom real quick to powder my nose." Elina beamed.

As soon as Surya left though her regal smile twisted into something darker. "D'you want some Charlie girls, I swear cannot go through another intro sesh without a hit."

"Oh. Erm I'll uh catch you in the next round."

"Sure I'll find you." She turned to Sunaina expectantly. "And you?"

"Oh, right. Same. Next round."

Gayatri turned to her as soon as Elina was out of earshot. "Why the fuck would we want her coke? Do we look too poor to get our own stash? Bitch."

"She seems... nice-ish." Sunaina reasoned.

Surya hovered back to them for a refill. "Why were you looking for Sohrab by the way?"

"Oh okay so here's the goss. So she's basically recently divorced but she won like a ton of money because there was this tiny loophole in her prenup agreement and she's got like a summer home in the French fucking Riviera now and anyway mumma heard that Sohrab is single as well so that's basically why she invited him over. She like literally threatened Sid uncle if he didn't bring him he didn't need to come for my wedding."

"What?" Sunaina was sure she didn't hear it right.

"Yeah so you see why he's been stiff and all he's probably expecting some awkward arrangement to come up. And like how gorg would their kids be, amiright? Like, did you see her cheekbones you could cut glass off of them. Bitch."

Gayatri looked at Sunaina who held her glass with whitened knuckles, not in least because of the girl walking back with a thousand watt smile and the legs for days but because through curtain of tea lights and pink dusted roses appeared Lakshman Dewan.

There were three things Sunaina knew for certain – that Sohrab Sood had been imported to be married off to Elina Jones, they disappeared into the smokescreen of the pool deck without a glance her way, that Lakshman was at once exactly and nothing like he once was. His hair though pulled back was wildly outgrown matching a beard that was three shades lighter; his eyes still had that undiminished spark he used to cut through the bullshit. That the grip tightening around her wrist was Gayatri's whose own ghost had shown up behind Lakshman.

"Oh my god." Sunaina spoke with a shivered voice. They looked as Ankit Kalra walked over to Laksh and struck up a conversation followed by a back thumping hug the way men do to ease into social ways.

As if on cue or perhaps signaled by the brilliance of her dress, they turned to the granite top bar where the girls had somehow joined the tail end of a conversation dominated by the other Kalra sibling.

"Yeah so basically Freya no. 1 died because we like didn't know how sensitive huskies are to like weather or food I mean I didn't even know you gotta make their food like separately and carefully or whatever ya. Freya 2 died as a pup only poor soul, she had epileptic attacks. And we were only giving her like packet food cuz we were so stressed." There were consolatory headshakes as Varsha continued.

"Freya 3, well the maid's been fired but it's unforgivable ya she was locked out of the house for a few hours I mean that's just inhuman ya in 46 degrees of the summer! I swear I'd have a mental break if I think too much about it but dad's already bought home a new adorable puppy," she beamed. "We're calling her Freya 4. She's a purebred husky of course, and her insta already has 5k likes."

Sunaina leaned in and whispered, "I'm going to be sick."

"Let's hide in the bathroom for sometime." She steered them away just as Laksh and Ankit reached the dais.

"Hi Gayatri."

"Go choke on a bag of dicks, Ankit." She stormed off. He scrambled after her leaving them in their vacuum. Time stretched into nothingness with the inertia of a Dali painting and then he opened his mouth to speak.

"Hi Lakshman! Oh my god it's been forever," Elina glided over from behind and embraced him.

Sohrab looked between them in confusion. He turned to her, searching for something in her eyes but Sunaina was still reeling. She could feel his protective energy and it only worsened the situation, while Elina introduced everyone explained that she met Lakshman briefly in Nasik at the Sula Fest where he'd been doing something no one paid attention to. Her heart had swollen two sizes too much and ached in her chest. She turned down the drink refill and watched with horror as Sohrab and Elina shared private jokes and clinked their glasses. Lakshman stood beside her with all the charms of a scarecrow.

"So, how are you Dumpling Kochhar?" His voice strained with the effort it took to keep conversation light.

She huffed. "Super. Yeah. Everything's just *great*. My parents are getting divorced, pretty sure Surya doesn't want me here." She wanted to slap the pained look off his face.

"And you ... you've just made me so sad." The words were out before she knew it.

Sunaina wanted him to speak and for a moment it looked like he might – to say anything even as lame as 'I'm Sorry' – but he didn't and that was worse.

"Excuse me I need to go to the bathroom."

He followed her and people were beginning to look. "Where are you going?"

"Yeah I didn't eat much before that last drink, I just need to sit down for a minute."

"In the bathroom?"

"Why not?"

"No no, just asking" he raised his hands defensively. "I was gonna get you a chair but I guess that's not appropriate right now is it?"

She smiled against her better instincts. "When were you ever appropriate Laskhman?"

His eyes softened. When he spoke next he sounded like different, his voice thick and smooth. "I understand that there's not much I can say to make it better. There are times I really wish that that night never even happened. Like we woke up and found that it was the day after and I could find my way to you again."

She sipped her drink in silence, now impervious to the bitter aftertaste.

"Anyway, I want you to know that I'm sorry. I'm really sorry Sunaina, I never wanted to hurt you." The corner of his lips turned up in a rueful smile.

She wanted to tell him it was okay, that it hadn't hurt so much that he should still want to torture himself over it. But it had been worse for her. "Let's not talk about it anymore tonight."

This time his smirk had a tenderness to it, an acknowledgment of her mercy. She knew in a different time she might've raked him across the coals for a much longer time, the look in his eyes confirmed the same.

"How long does it take for you to walk out from under your own shadow, do you think? Like I stand here and I'm sure that nobody sees me as who I am but rather just the way they remember me, you know what I mean?"

"You're not the you I remember, are you?"

"You're not you and I'm not me, and nothing's what it seems to be."

His breath ran away from him. "Did you write that or is that the wine talking?"

She found no sign of sarcasm in his eyes and considered a moment before replying. "Just something stupid I was writing a while back," she shook her head.

"Don't do that."

"What?"

"Don't dismiss yourself. You're too brilliant for that, Sunaina."

Lakshman knew it was unfair to say those things, he saw it in her eyes and he couldn't break away from them. But he no longer knew how to behave around her, maybe she was right. He wasn't himself and whoever this new rendition was, it was beginning to feel alien to him. He knew he was saying the wrong things. He shouldn't have been there. He dragged a hand through his hair, certain that people considered him an indulgent asshole who couldn't even bother to clean up for a party that came with its own camera crew. He excused himself.

Ankit, who was by then mindlessly drunk, intercepted Gayatri's short walk back to the couch apologizing profusely with the same adages. He'd been an idiot. She was the best thing that had ever happened to him. Being apart was like having tiny holes drilled very slowly into his heart. She didn't need to listen to him for too long because had Vir not intervened just then, he would've left with a broken nose at least.

He wedged himself between them but not before Gayatri smacked Ankit on the side of his head with her bag. He volunteered to take him upstairs to the guest suite and the last anyone saw of them that night was Vir carrying Ankit, with his head nestled into his neck. Gayatri declared her need for a drink but there was no one to hear her. The families had entered the party and it was time for a cake to be cut and a birthday song slurred.

Sohrab appeared out of nowhere at her side and Sunaina considered ditching the party for a moment of peace. He allowed her to pull him out to the back lawn.

"I've been looking for you," he lit her cigarette.

"You were a little preoccupied."

"What's that supposed to mean?"

"Umm I mean what the fuck are you doing with Elina?"

"I could ask you the same about Mr. Man Bun ya know."

She massaged her forehead, needing a stiffer drink. When she reached for his whiskey he pulled it out of reach and raised his eyebrows demanding an answer.

"I don't think I should've come back I mean, I think it's actually possible that this place, that these people are worse than what I'd left behind. It's just complicated as fuck."

"Let me simplify things for you."

He pulled her in by the waist and kissed her with a force that tipped her backwards but his hand was already at her back. In her mind she knew how tacky it was to make out in the dark but it didn't matter then. His lips injected sunshine through her bones. The lawn was dimly lit even though it was a Diwali party so neither of them, even as they pulled apart to catch their breath, could have seen Hassan watching them from a dark corner.

Chapter NINETEEN

DREAMING IN A TECHNICOLOR BEAT

There was a nip in the morning air signaling a change in season. The sky had only just begun to lighten in the distance and the morning looked like it might be a clear one. The trees and hedges hummed with a thousand birdsongs as Sunaina snuggled into her coffee. A lot had changed in two weeks, largely for the better. Surya and Geetu had taken to hour long Buddhism prayers and hot yoga to manage their stress. Gayatri, Ria, and Sunaina were living at their house for the remainder of the wedding which now seemed to be on a fast track as they raced against days to learn choreographed dance moves and how to play the *dhol* and help pack up an ever expanding trousseau.

Sohrab had taken to nightly walks on account of indigestion but really it was an excuse to see Sunaina in the safety of the unlit back porch. They'd share a joint under the canopy swing hidden from view by the first floor balcony. He'd tell her that she was the best thing that ever happened to him. She'd cradle him to her chest till the danger of falling asleep would separate them and he'd have to go home – where Hassan was growing suspicious every day. For the past three nights he'd insisted on accompanying Sohrab on his walks, expertly pushing Geetu's agenda on the possibility of marriage to Elina. Elina who knew about his feelings for Sunaina because he'd told her the minute they were alone at the party but wouldn't mind marrying him anyway because it could put an end to her mother's impatience.

Unaware of these covert games, Sunaina smiled into her cup and watched the sun break through the clouds when a cough disturbed her.

"Hey kiddo, what's up?"

"Good morning." She replied groggily.

"Morning. Can't sleep?"

Ria walked over to the edge of the balcony and sighed heavily.

"Hey are you okay?"

"Yeah, I think so."

"You *think* so? You're either okay or you're not." Hypocritical as it was, the prospect of sounding that rational in front of her younger sister made Sunaina feel important, intelligent even.

"What's with these cameras man? I feel like we can't find one moment alone. Just," she scratched at the sleeves of her hoodie, "just to talk."

Sunaina straightened up. "Well we're talking now and I don't see no cameras around."

"That's a double negative," Ria muttered.

She smiled, remembering how Faisal had once corrected her on the same thing. "So tell me why you're so meh."

Dread washed over Sunaina in a cold wave as Ria turned around pale as a ghost, tears brimming in her eyes. "I" she took in a ragged breath, "I had an abortion last week."

Sunaina felt the blood drained from her face. "You what?"

"Had an abortion, yeah. Oh god didi it was just so *invasive* I had no idea. The other girls I know who've had one they never said anything about that and I've just been feeling like shit, you know what I mean. It's like something's died inside of me."

She pulled her into a fierce hug, still unsure of how to process it.

"I'm fine, I think I'm actually fine now, but I'm just worried about mumma. How do I tell mumma about this?"

"Wait a second, how did you pay for it?"

She went silent.

"How did you pay for the abortion Ria?"

"I used my credit card. The one I got for in case of an emergency."

"Emergency sounds about right. Wait, you paid for the whole thing by yourself? What about the asshole that did this to you?"

"'Kay he's not an asshole firstly, he was there with me every day, and obv he paid for half of it, what kind of guy wouldn't."

"Oh you'd be surprised!"

"Varun's not like that ya, he loves me."

"*Loves* you?" the skin prickled on her neck. "You're sixteen years old what do you know about love?"

"I'm almost seventeen Sunaina I'm not a child anymore. And Varun isn't either, he's been in love before."

"How old is he?"

"He's barely older than me."

"By how much?"

"Four stupid years," she ignored Sunaina's gasp.

"Just because you love somebody does not mean they have to love you back. You're drugged up on your first love Ria don't let it define who you are."

"Oh for fuck's sake save the monologue for one of your Instagram disciples, Dumpling. How do I get rid of the thing showing up on my bank account?"

"Your bank statement," she corrected. "And it's showing up no matter what. How do you even have the money for an abortion?"

"I have a credit card, are you stupid? I just told you."

"How will you pay for it?"

"What do you mean 'how' – with the credit card obviously."

"*Who's putting the money in your credit card*" Sunaina couldn't believe it.

"FUCK" she spat.

Ria stood to leave and ran right into Dev who'd chosen the worst time to leave his bed for a glass of water. The collision loosened his grip and for a second no one moved as it bounced on the carpeted floor. Sunaina leaned over to check the source of the noise and considered how the situation could possibly have worsened – the answer was that it couldn't've. Her stomach contracted and the coffee threatened to do a double take.

"I err ... I was just getting water."

"How much did you hear?"

"You think he just happened to cross by at the exact moment you were leaving?" Sunaina stormed past them.

"Wait, where are you going?" Ria called out.

"I need a fucking cigarette!"

Not breaking from tradition, the entire party was dressed before the bride-to-be and helping themselves to pre-party tipples and gossip behind French manicures and tastefully styled beards. Geetu busied herself with perfecting sari pleats to avoid sinking into the well of emotions because although it wasn't the first time Surya had dressed up that much, it was overwhelming just the same. The wedding Geetu had always dreamed about was finally happening. The hair dresser gave one final cry to evacuate the room of everyone who was unnecessary and in single file with pocketed phones they left. Wreath of gold hairpins crowning her hair, Surya swallowed the dry ball of bile a final time and sipped her water through a straw. Gayatri swatted away the offer to have more bronzer smeared across her chest, regretting the low cut of her dusty rose jumpsuit, offering it instead to Ria who was whiter than her embroidered dress. Surya who'd offered to design the dress asked about the fit but she only responded in clipped words.

Surya spoke with a detached patience. "But sweetie didn't you want the cape over the dress when you came to me?"

"I know what I said but capes are stupid. No one wears them anymore except tacky girls from Bombay." Ria snapped.

"Watch it," Gayatri remarked.

"You know it's true."

There was a soft knock on the door.

"Ria is your mum okay with you going out in a strapless dress?" Gayatri bent low to check Surya's pleats.

Dev peeked his head in and beamed.

"Is your mom okay with you going out looking like a slut, Gayatri?"

"What the fuck Ria?"

"I'll come back later," Dev remarked with the same smile.

"Shit, that's not what I meant."

"You meant my dead mother or Geetu-ma? Tell me. Since you're such a grown up you should be able to tell the difference right away. What the hell did you mean by that you insolent bitch!"

Geetu burst through the door and grabbed Ria's wrist. "Out. Come with me. NOW."

The hairdresser handed a tissue to Gayatri who tipped her head back and dabbed at the corner of her eyes. Surya reached a hand out behind her and squeezed her palm when they met.

"I have a joint in my bag if you want, Lara's getting more for later. I was supposed to have it as soon as I woke up but mumma didn't give me a second to myself."

Sunaina entered with a glass of whiskey disguised in cola and stopped short at the sight of the golden halo of pins – an idea she'd shared with her friends back when she'd been planning her own wedding. Catching her faltered smile, she decided that Surya must have found the same inspiration on Pinterest and it was all a coincidence.

"You guys I can't believe it after today Surya's officially going to be the bride, it's like the end of an era." She handed the drink over to adjust her dhoti pants.

"Just an hour to go," Gayatri giggled.

"I swear these are giving me the worst wedgie. Gayatri, if you see the shalwar sticking to my butt stop me immediately."

"Why the hell am I on wedgie patrol?" she grimaced.

"Because I love you." She swirled her pleated kurta. "Also now I'm wondering if I look like a Gujju folk singer."

"You look great," Gayatri swallowed her laugh.

They stepped out for a cigarette at the exact time when the flower arrangements were being shifted onto the gently sloping garden; enormous marble vats were piled up to seven feet high with white bougainvillea and fairylight bushels. Sunaina balked at the resemblance to a haphazard sketch from her notebook. The golden sashes hanging down faux marble columns, the wreaths of grapes and crystal goblets perpendicularly placed on the tables, even the violently colorful centerpieces were directly lifted from her notebook, her Pinterest board. Surya was having the engagement party Sunaina had planned for herself. She poked her head out to ask for a quick drag.

"Oh listen Sunaina before I forget, I wanted to let you know that Lakshman is coming. After our last talk I know you told me it doesn't matter and all and obvi Sohrab is there but I just wanted to give you a heads-up. We're serving his wine today."

"*His* wine? What do you mean?" Gayatri made no efforts to blow the smoke away from her.

"The wine from his vineyard. Were you guys not listening to my story at all? Yeah he owns and runs his own vineyard down in Nasik, when mumma found out she rang him up and arranged like a tasting and shit and before I knew it they'd ordered like a few hundred cases or something. Yeah he even got our wedding crest monogrammed on these little cards hanging around the bottle neck."

Sunaina was still taking in the decor as guests started arriving. She turned around with a withering smile. "Did you steal all my ideas or is something your own too?"

She pushed her way out, deaf to the muttered disbelief Surya feigned at her retreating back. On the other side of the hall Kama locked the double doors softly and sat Ria down on the windowside loveseat.

Knowing fully well what was about to happen Ria felt the childish need to break into tears and hug her mother, because there was a time when that would've been enough to fix any mistake. But there were things that couldn't be overlooked as easily and when Kama finally spoke there was not a tremble or pause in her speech.

"You know the reason why I told you about what had happened to me? It wasn't because I saw that boy coming out of your room, or what ever happened with your grandfather. It was because I knew in my heart that it was the right time to tell you – that you were mature enough to understand it. To know what to do with it."

"And I failed you." She bit her lip so hard it bled.

"No, don't take this as failing me, Ria. You only failed yourself. You say it day in and day out that you're not a child anymore, that you're a grown up. So I'm talking to you like a grown up because you've assured me of your ability to handle yourself. I just wish you'd trusted me enough to talk to me before doing anything like this."

"It's not about trust mumma," she blubbered.

"Whatever it may be about then, I just think I could've been of some help when you went to the clinic."

"I know you're hurt but ... I didn't want to hurt you by seeing me in that state."

"That sounds awfully selfish Ria. I know I raised you better than that," she smiled sardonically from the butt of her cigarette.

There was nothing she could do but nod, head shamefully drooping. "So what now?"

"Well for starters you can forget about summer school in New York. The rest you figure out, you're a smart girl." Kama stood up and straightened her sari.

"Mumma that is so unfair! How dare you?" She ignored Ria's impatient grunt.

"Oh and if that boy show's up, tell him he won't live to see the sunset." She turned back, her voice lowered. "I won't lose sleep over it, either. I'll kill him."

Sunaina was half-hiding – not too hard considering the guest list of five hundred – and somewhat considering the idea of tipping over the small cottage sized vat of flowers. She eyed the guests cooing at the borrowed aesthetics, right down to the individual mini-succulents placed at every table setting as party favours. The final distraction was Kabir's grip on her right earpiece. He'd taken a day away from his design studio just for them but navigating traffic while screaming into his phone wasn't as fun as he'd hoped to have. As he maneuvered the small lanes leading up to the venue Sunaina made her way to the elaborate table settings.

Another cursory glance confirmed that handmade artisanal chocolates had added a tasteful finishing touch and if her suspicions were correct they came from *her* secret chocolatier in Lower Parel. She considered the effort in crushing someone under the mammoth bougainvillea dome looming over her and it proved to be too much. She closed her eyes and breathed deeply, invoking every zen spirit she could recall.

"Admiring the flowers eh, beta?" she jumped at the sound of his voice.

"Oh papa! I was just looking for you. Listen I ... what?"

He pointed at the phone and she cancelled the call without another wasted second.

"Do you remember this fat notebook, the one bound in acid green satin. It had all those business cards, menus, and private landlines on it."

He squinted over her shoulder trying to jog his memory. "Yeah? Oh yeah of course I do. Geetu and all were over for dinner a couple of months back and Surya had it in her hands when she came back from the loo."

She felt a chill even as the sun climbed higher and sunglasses came on in a Mexican Wave.

"Is something wrong? She told me it was just for wedding research and all."

"It's nothing." She pushed the sunglasses up her nose. "Do you think we're a messed up family?"

"Well yeah but whose family isn't bat shit crazy these days," he turned to her, "right?"

She sighed. "I don't know, I think we're winning this round."

Surya walked into view in her grey and gold ensemble as a collective sigh shivered through the party. "And what about you? How're you holding up?"

He shrugged his shoulders. "I'm indestructible, don't you know that?"

Hassan flashed a side-smile and put a reassuring arm around her.

"Yeah but you don't have to be like the super-dad all the time you know." She pulled him into a signature brief hug.

"I think I've been off duty long enough, so far it's only made a mess of things." He kissed the top of her head. "Someone should look after you too you know. You're like your mum in so many ways – all the best ones. It's both amazing and scary.

She was just as passionate and headstrong, walked into a room and had everyone's attention without having to demand it."

"I don't command attention at all." They followed the slow procession headed toward the marquee.

"You do, you do so without even trying my love. Never let go of that."

She cast him a worried glance. "How do you want me to hold on to a habit I didn't even know I had?"

He considered it for a moment. "Just do what you're doing anyway, I know you know the difference between who's right and who's wrong."

He picked up a chocolate from the table to their right and popped it into his mouth. She ignored his impressed hum – already aware of how delicious the treats were. "Wait you mean what's right and wrong, right?"

He looked at her with deliberation in his eyes. "I think you know what I mean. Now go up there, the ring ceremony's about to begin."

She called Kabir on her way as chairs swiveled to face the glowing couple, the hum of chinwag died as a round of champagne flutes were served. She called him again while Vir helped her climb up. She rang him a third time while swatting at a deviant bee before she realized it was after the flowers behind her. She flicked it off expertly and bent lower to avoid being seen with her phone in hand. There was a brief well-meaning but funny speech that ended too soon, and even as Kabir raced through the lawns and past the guests the rings were exchanged and she let her phone drop next to Gayatri's clutch.

She looked at her gaping neckline and nudged, Gayatri immediately twisted sideways to adjust the fabric of her jumpsuit. Surya Shroff and Dhiraj Sahdev flashed a dazzling smile to the congregation of friends and family as matching bands of platinum were slid into each other's finger and the glasses rose in toast to the sound of cheers and camera phones. Sunaina saw Kabir manoeuvre his way to her side before Surya had time to notice his absence.

He leaned in to her ear. "Did I miss it?"

"Literally by half a minute." She whispered back. "It was beautiful, you almost cried. We're all very happy."

"Good", he huffed, "because I'd kill for a drink right now."

She guided him to the bar by way of honey glazed prawns-on-a-stick laid out in a row over a napkin bed while Kabir ordered his large vodka-tonic.

"So what else did I miss?"

"Oh nothing major. There's a chance my family's insane and this might literally be the engagement party I was supposed to have with Daksh Dhiman."

"Ooh la la. Cheers babe." He gulped deeply. "So, who's killed whom?"

She kept her focus on aligning the prawns just right. "My parents are getting divorced, it's about to get super ugly like they're going into litigation or whatev."

"What else?"

"About a thousand other things."

"Are you even going to eat all of those?"

She popped a whole giant prawn in her mouth and then struggled to chow it down.

"No it's to keep you from getting sloppy drunk."

"I've never been sloppy in the drinking history of the universe."

As a group hovered over to them she changed the subject. "So, when are you showing up for dance practice? We're still at an odd number."

"Omg Kabir you should totes come ya it's so fun."

"Ya bro," Adarsh clapped his back oblivious to the sour vibes. "If not for the dance, come for the drinks."

Lara smiled widely behind her bee-glasses. "I hope you're doing better now, Baruacha. So sorry to hear about aunty ya."

A quick sympathetic nod ensued from all present.

"Thank you. But well cancer is cancer, can't do anything about it. We've been considering how to move on from it because it's just a lot to deal with sometimes you know?"

Samaira squeezed his arm solemnly. "You should allow yourself to begin the healing process. I say go on a sabbatical, like a spa-cation. Just disengage for some time ya."

"We're actually considering that. But anyway with the money that came in afterward I've just been thinking of what to do with it and we're getting a yacht –friend of the family runs a dealership and all so yeah I think it'll be great for all of us. And it's the perfect way to honour her memory you know, it'll be like having her there with us. We're obviously naming it after her."

"That's beautiful," Lara sniffed. "Oh on that note, guess who broke her engagement! You didn't hear this from me but last night we were at a Diwali party and we took a break from cards for literally like half a sec and someone said oh let's do Never Have I Ever because why the fuck not. Anyway Varsha Kalra and fiancé got into this whole totally embarrassing fight because he had done one of those amateur DSLR photo shoots at HKV gardens I mean can you even *imagine*!"

"Wait so that's reason enough to call off her wedding?"

"Well apparently some of it, was like erotic and shit ..." Lara looked back with an ostensibly souring look. "And seriously, you were so much more fun when you were a bitch."

Sunaina looked over her shoulder and excused herself. Lakshman looked different in a way that had nothing to do with the clarity of daylight. His hair was much shorter, slicked back to red carpet perfection.

"Hi," he gave her a surprised grin.

"You're not you and I'm not me, and nothing's what it seems to be

So tonight put the lights out, sing me to the moon

It may not be there tomorrow, so where'd we be, so where'd we go."

She had wanted her words to be soft but they'd soured on the way out. Like a raindrop falling on cotton candy the moment wilted away and Lakshman shifted weight awkwardly.

"See I told you it was a stupid poem."

He chuckled. "It's hardly stupid, Sunaina!"

"Whatever." She tried not to blush.

"So where's your friend today? The guy with the tattoos." His voice had a clear edge to it.

"Oh Sohrab! He couldn't make it, Sunita aunty's very sick she has some stomach bug and she's got a raging fever. So he's just taking care of her but he said he'd try and make it here by lunch time." She looked down at her phone glumly, "I haven't heard from him yet."

Lakshman didn't wish aloud that he never showed up.

"Yeah why's the cell reception always so bad at these places?"

"Maybe that way people might actually talk to each other," he wiggled his brows.

She rolled her eyes. A server drifted their way with wine and she'd almost refused before catching herself. She took a goblet of the red and turned to Laksh with narrowed eyes, "So when do I get to hear about how you ended up a winemaker out of everything?"

He flashed her a proud smile. "Well first you have to tell me, do you like it?"

She nodded like it was the most obvious thing in the world.

"Well basically things weren't working out here for a long time. In the end it was just me and dad living at our place and after a while he too sort of just packed his bags and left. It didn't take the cops too long to seize the house but I was gone too by then."

"Where'd you go? And when did this happen?"

"Some time after Diwali last year. I went to this yoga ashram Samaira had told me about and I worked there for a bit."

Of all the things she'd imagined, Laksh working at an ashram was the most improbable.

Satisfied with the reaction, he continued. "I took the bus from Rishikesh with some friends I made to this NGO in Leh and we stayed for a few months, you wouldn't believe how cold it gets there. But oh man I was so happy!" he smiled from ear to ear. "And then some shit happened so I caught a flight back here and then to Bombay from where I made my way to Nasik – I was mostly at the end of my money by then. When I got there I went to meet the lawyer who'd called me because my chachu had passed away."

"Who? Sachin uncle?"

"Yeah, I can't believe you remember him. Anyway he owned a vineyard there and it wasn't in good shape but he'd left it to me and I- I mean I obviously couldn't just let it rot it's ten bloody acres of prime untapped land at this point."

"What did you do then?"

"I wrote to a whole bunch of vineyards in Europe through this website for volunteering on organic farms. I called up dad's lawyers and had some money transferred to my account and by then I'd heard back from this establishment in Burgundy. I stayed on the farm and studied how to make wine and stuff."

"Does this story get any crazier or can I start believing it?"

He let out a booming laugh. "You're not the first person to tell me it sounds like a load of shit but yeah that's how it happened."

"And now you make wine at your Nasik vineyard."

He nodded. "And you, what ever happened to baby Kochhar?"

She smiled indulgently. "Nothing as adventurous as that I can assure you, but I do know how cold Leh gets. I did the trek over Chadar Lake last year."

They fell into an uncomfortable silence at the prospect of having been in the same town at the same time and two hearts broke a little more as the music swelled and the cocktails stiffened.

Chapter TWENTY

I Won't Listen To Your Dogma

Geetu zipped her way through the tipsy throng, giggling over their gimlets and beers cursing her daughter inwardly for demanding the largest group of dancers at a sangeet performance – worsened by having already tipped off Buzzfeed and the likes for a feature. Twenty seven reasonably attractive couples coordinated to perfection on a single stage meant a lot of tension, rivalry, and downright chaos. With each passing dance practice the attendees had multiplied till the upper basement looked more like a social event than rehearsal while the choreographer and a strongarmed minion of Surya's clapped and screamed the dancers into form. She walked past the vegan homemade paté and cracker platter and swooped out of the way of a one armed hug to grab the choreographer's elbow and jerk him out of earshot.

"Listen bubba we gotta talk about something." She pulled up her most convincing voice (a domineering tone perfected over the years). "I think we need to switch up the pairing a little bit, keep Gayatri and Vir front and centre but let's swap Lakshman with Sohrab – I think it's throwing the aesthetic off balance ya completely shoddy job I must say."

He looked at her like she'd force-fed him sour milk.

"So, Sohrab and Elina on one side and Lakshman can go with Sunaina, put Kabir at the other side with Karishma, he's far too short to be that much in the middle."

Before he could say anything she thwacked him on the back and quit the scene.

Everyone followed the directions with grit teeth, Sunaina cast a dark look at Surya's back who at that moment was deflecting the most tedious forms of small talk and Priya's pressing comments on how being gay was totally normal. She prayed Geetu wouldn't hear any of it.

As Sohrab brushed past Lakshman with good natured whoops from the back to which Elina bowed deeply, Sunaina willed her soul to leave its fleshy prison. She vowed never to return the next time she could leave the city. The unnecessarily long medley of Bollywood's finest songs – selected after a week's worth of discussion on a whatsapp group everybody subsequently quit – blared from the speakers and they stepped in formation. With the every hip thrust it grew easier to enjoy the dance and by the time she ended up with her arms entwined around Lakshman's spinning in sync with the others, Sunaina was actually enjoying herself. Sohrab swallowed the stab in his chest at the sight of them, the ease with which they fit together, the way he made her laugh.

The fourteen minute performance left them winded but there was enough applause to consider the efforts worthwhile. She fanned herself with the edge of her satsuma coloured kurta and pressed the icy glass of gin and juice to her neck.

"Wait how do you plan to manage all that on the day of the *mehendi* function?" Kabir demanded.

Karishma tied her hair up with a smug scoff. "I'll figure something out I mean come on ya it's a Penn Masala set like how can you miss something like that?"

Kabir pressed his lips together, at a complete loss for words.

"Look I mean at least RSVP on Facebok for the sake of keeping up with civilized society. It's just, I mean how can you consider yourself cultured if you can't even go see a Penn Masala performance?" she stared at him aghast. "That's like saying you don't like Prateek Kuhad."

He turned to Sunaina for help. "I just ... I don't even know ..."

She shook her head to his tune, biting back a smile. "It's okay. Just say you know him–"

"Guys what the fack! You don't know *Prateek Kuhad*?"

Five pairs of eyes turned to them, bulging at the disgraceful news.

Kabir buried his face into Sunaina's shoulder. "I can't. I can't with this."

"No I mean I've heard *of* him," Sunaina gasped from the effort of keeping a straight face. "I just ... I don't think I've heard his music."

"Stahp what the hell, please educate yourselves guys it's not funny." Karishma genuinely looked offended as the pair of them shook with silent laughter. "You guys are sick."

Elina smiled as she forced herself into the conversation. It was the kind of smile girls reserved for easy access to have their way. And Elina had learnt early on that bad girls knew where to find the party. "I'm so bummed, anyone up for doing a line?"

She had company quicker than she could blink.

Meanwhile, Lara had unwittingly drifted over. "Seriously, I just had to ask. What do you guys even do if you don't go to Piano Man to hear these guys play?"

Kabir straightened up with his steely best. "We've moved on from Piano Man sweetie."

Unfortunately the rest of his comeback was drowned in the bellowed argument making its way up the stairs as Vir chased his mother who, having caught him on the phone for the last time, had confiscated the borrowed iPhone and stormed to a private room to unleash her rage. Gayatri found her way to Sunaina and pulled her from the increasingly dissonant gathering – an after-party had broken out and nobody else had been close enough to hear the argument break out.

The door slammed shut behind her and Geetu wasted no time in pulling out the big gay gun.

"Priya gave me an interesting piece of information, she saw you and Ankit Kalra kissing on the night of the youngsters."

"WHAT?" Gayatri froze at the door but Geetu was not to be interrupted.

"On top of the fact that your so-called brand is fake. There's no company is there? You've just been lying to us this entire time!"

Surya brushed past her mother. "Wait bhai what's going on? What is mumma talking about?"

"Minal and Fari wanted to see the catalog of your brother's collection –"

"Mumma I told you not to talk about the bags –"

"And it turns out that there are no bags! And just now when you claimed to have been on a *work call* I caught him talking to someone in French. When did you even learn French, Vir?"

"Mumma don't be ridiculous I was actually taking a work call."

"Oh my god beta, don't even think of talking such crap. I may be old and irrelevant in your mind but even I know how to say 'I love you' in French!"

He swallowed the lump in his throat, no longer sure what to say.

"Why don't you fucking start with who you were talking to? What are you hiding from me?"

Dev and Asim closed the door behind them.

"Beta are you involved in some trouble again?"

He pulled the neck of his ratty t-shirt away to swallow but the cotton ball was lodged in his throat.

"Why don't you say something!"

“It’s not what you think mumma, I don’t know why you insist on making such a fucking big deal about this!”

“Don’t you fuck with me Vir! A mother knows when her son is hiding something from her, no matter how big bad the secret is just tell me. What is going on with you.”

“Geetu please, let’s calm down for a second before we go making any accusations here.” Nobody had heard Dev speak so gravely. “If this is about what Priya saw...”

“Wait mumma what she saw has no merit she’s probs just making this shit up.” Surya crossed her hands defensively.

Geetu lit her cigarette and whispered throatily. “Are you ... beta are you a gay?”

He knew perfectly that his mother had gay friends in her life so it would’ve been impossible for her not to know the incorrectness of prefixing the word gay with an ‘a’. He saw the double standard in her fierce stare, she was fine with being friendly to somebody else’s gay son but the thought of her own following suit was like being disemboweled with a blunt knife.

“Geetu-ma I think that’s a bit harsh –”

“How’s it even relevant?” Sunaina threw her hands up in disbelief.

Asim overlooked the swelling scene in shock.

“Okay before anyone else says anything else I need to get this off my chest.”

“Oh god” Geetu clutched her chest dramatically, “Haye Raam I knew it!”

“Knew what?”

“He’s gay.” She reported in their general direction.

“Mumma just fucking stop for a second!” Vir’s face flamed in anger. “Look I know you all think I’m hiding something from you, I know my being on the phone is irritating and Surya I’m sorry if I haven’t been there enough for you.”

“Chill bhai I know you have important shit going on in your life.”

Gayatri scoffed and whispered to Sunaina, "Bitch couldn't've been this understanding with us."

"Yeah but my behaviour's been shit I know. Look it's because the company needs me right now."

Geetu's head shot up. "What fucking company beta? You've just been lying to us, making a fool of us all."

"Mumma I don't make backpacks. I gave up on that two years ago."

"What do you mean you gave up on it?" She laughed once. "You made bags for Surya and Dhiraj ... didn't you?"

Vir raked his fingers through his hair, trying not to rip them off. "Yes but that's not what the company does."

The room fell silent. He shot a fleeting glance at his grandfather and decided he couldn't lie anymore.

"We ..." he took in a deep breath. "We make novelty collector's items for umm for adult pleasures."

He rolled his eyes at the room of confused faces.

"We make eco-friendly sex toys, specifically for fetish purposes. Costumes for role-play are something we're looking into. It's still very high end because of the engineering and raw materials we use so it's not like I work in a stall on the street in Bangkok, but that's what I do. I also customize nightlife travel programmes for people who want to experience the sex clubs of the Shinjuku district."

Geetu collapsed onto the couch.

Sunaina felt her jaw drop. "Wait, there's a market for sex tours?"

Vir laughed nervously. "Like you'd never imagine!"

"Wait, so you're not gay?" Gayatri asked meekly.

"What?"

"You're not gay then? Because I think that's what Geetu-ma was most afraid of really. Well, before this."

"I'm not gay."

Geetika barely choked out a sigh before he continued.

"I'm in a bisexual threeway relationship."

Gayatri covered her smile, lest she be stabbed for it. Sunaina nodded, clearly impressed. Surya tried her best to share in his relief. Dev reached out and squeezed his wife's shoulder to make sure she was still alive, wondering if her heart sputtered the same arrhythmic song.

The Commander clapped loud enough to make them jump not only as it ripped through the hush but also in reminder of his presence.

"Is this what you were sent him out of the country for?" he seethed, voice rising dangerously. "To burn your money, to sully our name in society, to do this bullshit?!"

"You think I knew about this?" she choked back her tears.

"Geetika, your son is a *randibaaz*!" he bellowed. "Do you have nothing better to say?"

Gayatri whipped out her phone. "And once more for the camera please!"

Sunaina held onto her shoulder, convulsing with laughter.

"I don't care who you are, you don't talk to her like that!" Dev roared, redfaced and unbothered by the flash of the camera.

"Abbey you fuck off, bloody wimp."

"He's right," Geetu whispered. "You've left us with no way to face society Vir."

"Are you kidding right now mumma?" Surya screamed. "You can't control who you love any more than you control gossip. You should maybe reevaluate your friends if you're so afraid of their judgment."

"And what about his *living conditions*?!"

Gayatri closed her eyes and took a deep breath before answering. "Are you saying you'd be okay if he was with a guy?"

"No."

"Then?"

"He should be with a girl."

"Why? Who decides that?"

"What do you mean 'why', because it's not ***normal!***"

"There's no normal where love is concerned, ma. If he loves two people he loves two people – that's that."

"But what even about grandchildren? How does that work in his condition?"

"In his *relationship*. And even then it's not about what you want. It's their decision. What if tomorrow Surya declares she never wants to have kids or whatever, would you hire a surrogate and pretend that it's hers?"

"Ugh I cannot deal with this crap anymore!" she threw her hands to the heavens.

"You shouldn't have to." Sunaina sighed. "Nobody has asked you to 'deal' with it because it isn't something you have to solve. It's three people who care about each other –"

"*Three people*" Asim snapped, "is a math problem not a healthy living situation."

"Just try and understand him instead!" Even as Gayatri raised her voice, Vir had left the building.

Surya sat on the bathroom floor with her knees drawn in; the tiles cooled her burning skin. She'd taken to aggressively fiddling her ring – as yet unfamiliar on her finger – while rereading the argument she'd just had with Dhiraj. It was becoming increasingly obvious that he saw irredeemable flaws in her family, every passing day brought out the ugly truth while the world was looking the other way. Outside, Gayatri hugged Vir till the shivers of anger and humiliation died down. Inside, Surya's fingers ached to call Dhiraj because to hear his voice would put an end to all the doubts and fears burrowing a hole through her belly.

Vir looked up from his clenched fist at the sound of the door.

"You know mom's lost it right?" Surya entered warily.

He beamed at her even through his red eyes. "We should alert the management at the asylum."

"Let's keep a guy on-call. Just sedate her any time she's about to speak." Her smile faltered. "I think she's really going off the rails."

"Sit" he patted the bed. "You know I only came here because of you right? If I hadn't I probably would've just left her to her version of the story."

"That wouldn't have stopped her from asking questions, Vir. About work or your plans for settling down."

He tilted his head. "I don't know if I ever really want to get married."

"Why, couldn't you have a hippy communal-type wedding?"

He stared at Surya like she'd lost it.

"That was meant to be a joke."

"You used to be funnier."

"Maybe that lack of good humour runs in the family." Gayatri muttered from the closet. She ripped the packaging from a forgotten welcome basket, pulling out the only medicine available – a bottle Patron.

"Oh, so you mean to imply that we're all insane and there's no hope for us?"

She nodded, dissolving into a fit of giggles.

He wagged a finger at them. "Oh I think there might still be hope for you two."

"I don't know about that." Surya scowled at her phone. "What if it's a family curse? Like what if that's what sets off the psychosis?"

"Well then I trust Dhiraj to keep you sane."

Gayatri poured out the tequila. "Shit, who'll keep him from going crazy then?"

He threw his head back and laughed. "Nah I wouldn't worry about him."

"I guess only time will tell," Surya shrugged.

The sky lit up outside with a far off bolt of lightning and Vir allowed the knot that'd tightened with each passing day to unwind.

Sunaina lay upside down in her bed, feet propped up against the wall, book of shorts cradled with her mind miles away. To her side was the phone no longer displaying an unanswered text to Sohrab, a whatsapp group still blowing up with last minute dance practice schedules, someone really needed a dealer's number in RK Puram. Her eyes flitted with every beep but none of it was what she wanted to read, so she lay there like a forgotten doll with a half formed scowl staring blankly into Balzac.

The city was like a dead zone, not enough wind to shuffle a fallen leaf even though the summer had breathed its last and the evenings were thick with cricketsong and steam. She threw the balcony open and leaned as far as she could, the rising fever of the ground burning her naked feet. That night she could light a fire just by rubbing her thighs, light a cigarette by snapping her kindling fingers. She pulled on the cigarette and arced it away to keep the smoke from her eyes, but it hung around her in a punishing cloud with no wind to give it direction. Sunaina stood and choked on the smoke for as long as she could and then when she'd had enough she resumed her upturned position on the bed.

An hour later, the door to the backyard slid open with ease. To let in the salty sweet breeze before a storm and to let her out. Stray leaves rustled along the path she jogged, thudding on the still warm concrete down the road that connected the rear gardens of every house on the street. She made her way toward the house where she hoped Sohrab was awake and waiting for her. There was a pinch in her throat that told her otherwise, that told her she should've known better – a woman's intuition as her mother had once put it – but Sunaina ignored it.

Lately it was as if the whole family had conspired against them, leaving no more than a few private sighs between him and her. They talked with the nondescript air of friendly banter where she'd ask about Sunita aunty or he'd pass a light comment on the red-faced choreographer who presided over dance practices with militant authority. She'd catch him staring but he'd look away too soon, and she spent her nights waiting till the seat of the swing hardened her back. Sunaina missed their conspiratorial smiles, the ease his closeness brought to her. To make matters worse forced between them was the ever alluring Elina, whose endgame was beginning to matter less and less every day.

A power cut knocked out every light on the street and took her breath away. Sunaina realized she'd walked too far ahead and now stood at the wrong end of the curb with shadows rising all around her. With only the purple sky and phone light, she felt her way to the other side, peering through overgrown vines into a marble engraving for the house number. Like a current sparking through her she shivered, staring back at the house where Devina Dewan, Lakshman's mother, had once thrown glittering soirees.

The iron gate swung freely under her hand, frail with years of rust. The sky above disappeared into a canopy of overlapping branches, heavy with leaves and critters. Sunaina walked with her heart in her throat, every muscle prepared to jettison herself from the swamp. A branch snapped and her hands flew up to protect herself, she gasped aloud and turned in every possible direction to find the source of the noise but the darkness just stretched to infinity. And then a pair of hands wrapped her wrist and Sunaina screamed like the girl who saw the old hag emerge from the shadows in a grainy black and white film right before she pushed her down the stairs to her doom and death. Lakshman, white as a sheet, screamed back half in surprise and half in anger.

"What the fuck are you doing here?"

She clutched her knees for support, not the least bothered by his grip because if he hadn't held her then she would've fainted. Between catching her breath she explained that she didn't expect to find someone at the house. The house, they turned back to see, was a shell of its former self. Thc walls had weathered and the colours had cracked.

"Holy shit I think I peed myself," she huffed.

He laughed and pulled her to his chest. The sound of his racing heart put her to ease and she didn't know or care how long they stood there.

The room was lit by an old fashioned handheld lamp that threw more shadows that actual light, he settled on the stool by the Steinway baby grand leaving her to find a seat for herself. In that particular proximity her thoughts turned to mush.

"You're not living here are you?"

He shrugged. "It's not like anyone comes here anymore."

The bluish glow of the lamp matched the morbidity of the room, the house as a hole. His eyes followed hers as Sunaina took in the rest of the space, the little parlour that lay beyond the door to the left – every conceivable object, big or small, blanketed under a heavy white sheet. She craned her neck to the high ceiling where once hung a chandelier skirted with seventeen blown glass seashells. *'An heirloom,'* his mother had remarked over her shoulder, throwing that magnetic smile to her audience as they moved to the next stop on the house tour.

And now it was just him and her surrounded by the spectral furniture set to the tunes of shuddering glass doors as a dust storm raged outside. The all-encompassing plastic that covered every surface only intensified the cold sterile atmosphere.

"I'm genuinely sorry. I didn't mean to scare you like that."

"It's okay. I was just ..." she turned to him, "I don't know I just needed to get out of the house."

"So you sneak in to other people's houses?" he looked at her like she was crazy.

"Not often enough" the ghost of a smile played on her lips.

He hummed in amusement, but the way he bit his lip told her there was more he wanted to say.

"I didn't know you could play the piano." Her tone mockingly accusatory.

"It never came up." He smiled at her sullen look. "It was just a way to keep me occupied, my dad was convinced I had ADD because that was the disability du jour. Not like I was ever any good at it."

"So why'd you hide it from me – umm, from everyone?"

"Does it matter?" He rolled his eyes.

"Shouldn't it?"

Lakshman sighed in exasperation with that same air of burden that left her feeling inferior. "I don't think anything really matters anymore, Sunaina. It's like every conversation I hear now just makes me so mad, I'm so mad all the fucking time. What kind of place is this? What am I here for?!"

His words echoed in her mind. "I know what you mean, that's why I left too."

"And yet, when you're here you fit right in," he sneered.

"Wow," she pushed herself off the too-small stool. "You are so delusional. You think nobody notices your Comme des Garçons t-shirt just because it's under a non-designer jacket? You think everybody's under the impression that you're living a bohemian backpacker's life while supplying enough wine to knock out an army. You're no better than any of them no matter how much you stare down your nose –"

He shut her up with a kiss too quick and awkward to have been something.

Outside the dust had settled but the storm was far from over and Sunaina looked as though she might need his windbreaker soon. Lakshman hated the idea of her walking home in the rain. He considered reaching for it, just at the foot of the piano and wrapping it around her but worried that she'd be gone before he stood up.

Sunaina was still seizing. "I should go."

He pushed himself in her way as thunder wailed outside. Lakshman slowly shook his head and the way his eyes darkened it told her that that was it – the moment he'd reveal the big truth. She waited for him to tell her why he'd left her, the burning question hung mid air eating up every last molecule.

"Don't look at me like that," he sagged.

"Don't you have anything to say for yourself?"

He shrugged in a way that said – that's that. "I don't owe any answers for breaking your heart, Sunaina."

What he really wanted to say was – I have never known the loss of trust, I don't know how to fill it up. He watched the pain turn to disdain in her eyes.

The spell had broken. Sunaina pushed past his pleading palms and her moist eyes. Neither the garden nor the thunderstorm scared her anymore, all she knew was she had to escape him. Because looking at Lakshman was like looking directly into the sun, even in the throes of melancholia, and she wasn't ready to burn again. The first drops of rain hit the road as she thudded her way back to the Ashoka tree-lined pavement.

Sohrab sat waiting for her at the back porch. He had the entire conversation planned in his head and the moment he saw her running through the little entrance he imagined that she would run right into his arms. Just as he began to raise his arms she arced around him and dashed inside. He pushed himself off and made a beeline through the glossy but empty kitchen and up the stairs where Geetika was on her way down, still seething. She regarded the pair in front of her, a paused chase sequence, and narrowed her eyes at the man behind her niece. Sunaina defiantly jutted her chin out, demanding another hateful word and she left them to their games.

Sohrab caught up with Sunaina easily and grasped her shoulders imploring her to give him a chance to explain.

"Mum's really sick, Sunaina." His breath hitched. "She has a severely perforated bowel and needs surgery. It's not looking good."

A part of her wished she'd never left her bed that night.

"Dad's lost his mind. He's booked their flights, he's just deaf to reason right now. Everyone's been telling him to get the surgery done here – Asim uncle even called up his friend at Fortis – but he's adamant about going home."

It took her a beat to recall that home meant the other side of the world.

"They're leaving tonight."

"Oh," was all she could muster.

"I want you to come with me," his grip tightened on her wrist. "I'll look after you and love you and god I don't know Sunaina, I'll never let you down."

"Okay stop, Sohrab please. Stop before this gets too much."

He settled halfway but the desperation in his eyes remained.

"My grandfather died because of a botched up surgery, it was nothing. A removal of the appendix. But he never made it back and dad never forgot. And on top of that, dad wants me to actively spend more time with Elina and seriously consider settling down with her."

She brushed his hands off her arms. "Jeez why is marriage such a life goal for everyone? Do you even want to? With her?"

"NO! Sunaina, I don't even look at her with those intentions," he stroked her hair. "And why would I?"

"I don't know, you two seemed friendly enough last I saw you." She didn't mean it. She understood his predicament. She was offering him a way out.

He closed his eyes and sagely shook his head. "Elina just needed someone to bitch her ex out to. That being said I won't deny that it is easier to talk to her on some level because she is closer to my age."

"Easier to talk to – than *me*?"

"Snap out of it" he reprimanded her. "Wherever you're about to go right now, just stop. I'd give up talking to everyone if it meant I got to have you with me everyday."

"But I don't know if I can marry you."

"And I haven't asked you to." He replied.

"Then why did you just ask me to run away with you?" she scowled.

"Because this is what I'm afraid of," he gestured to the space between them. "I'm afraid if I lose it, I don't think it's something I'll ever recover from. *You're* something I'll never recover from."

"And what if I asked you to leave everything behind and run away with me? Would you be able to do that? Leave your home, your parents, and come to me?"

He deliberated in silence. There was no hint of sarcasm to her words. He allowed the dream to replay in his head, the one where he began and ended his day holding her in his arms. He waited to see if the backdrop might change.

Sunaina held her breath without knowing it.

Sohrab dropped his eyes to their entwined fingers and her heart plummeted. With a ragged breath she felt the force of an unmitigated heartbreak, now fully convinced that she should never have left the safety of the inn.

"It doesn't matter," he half-smiled. "I'll go anywhere you take me."

"Wait, what?" she shook her head clear.

"Look I'll be honest I never planned for any of this to happen, and I mean *any* of it – for Christ's sake I came here thinking it'll be a holiday and so far it's been a rollercoaster not always the good kind and I don't think I got a seatbelt." She chuckled. "I didn't know you'd be you. You've been unexpected. The best kind of surprise. But," he paused, "there are loose ends that need tying up."

She clocked an eyebrow in question.

"Ma's in a critical condition, that's just what we need to focus on right now."

She smiled a brief sad smile. "So where does that leave us?"

"I'll come back for you, if you'll wait for me," her heart soared at his words.

He kissed her hand and in the morbidity of the moment it was so absurdly valiant, Sunaina would never forget it.

"It'll take me some time but I will come back."

"That doesn't answer my question though."

"I don't have all the answers just yet," he shrugged plainly.

Sunaina shook her head. "We're going in circles."

"Can you wait for me or not?"

She nodded without giving herself time to think about it. He stood up to leave but found a hand pulling at his wrist.

"Don't go."

The table was too quiet.

Hassan glared at his sister as the steaming bowl of *sambhar* was placed on the table. Geetika on her part appraised the over-the-top brunch spread and told the maid to fry more *papad*. She met his eyes for a second before returning to the newspaper where she was halfway between solving the crossword and sudoku puzzles.

He turned to look at Asim and wondered how long the peace would last. The Commander lazily sipped at his third cup of tea and admired the crisp edges of the plate of *vadai*. Hassan looked to Dev at the sound of a throat clearing. He meaningfully shook his head once and that was enough to pacify him for the moment.

It had taken one phone call. One call that lasted seventeen minutes and fifty seconds and Tina had retracted all her demands. The divorce papers had been signed, any day a judge would approve it and that was that.

Hassan looked back at Dev and tried to discern if there was an improvement in the atmosphere since the night before, though Vir's terse presence at the table confirmed a cease-fire for the moment. Much to his relief Geetu playfully swatted her husband's offer for help and maybe even cracked a smile.

Vir on his part was disgusted with the way his parents were canoodling on the breakfast table. He was also wary of his grandfather's presence, which might've been a comfort at one point, a source of old stories. There was always a sense of completeness at having him present on the table but now all he felt was the cold hiss of dread in his stomach. Gayatri and Surya were stupefied into reverence, swiping through their Instagram feed comparing who looked better and where people were vacationing. Surya had been restrained from shoveling down the food because it was the day of the *mehendi* and she had four hours of sitting still ahead of her. Kama reached forward and aligned her fork and knife, darting nervous looks around as if, like Vir, she suspected the picture perfect peace to be disrupted too soon.

Geetu pushed her paper and pen to the side with finality, brunch was about to begin with or without Sunaina. She leaned forward and took her glasses off from their perch at the tip of her nose. Hassan shivered as if doused in an ice bath, she was about to broach the topic of her bloody book again. His eyes widened at her as if to persuade her into silence. He mouthed a 'no' at her and she shook her head to let him know she'd already made up her mind. He kicked Kama's foot from under the table but it didn't garner much response, not until it was too late and Geetu was already calling attention to herself with a strange hawk.

"Daddy," Hassan violently shook his head at her. "There's something I need to tell you."

Vir turned to Gayatri and Surya neither of whom had bothered to look up.

"What's happening?" Kama squinted at her.

"I think I owe everyone an apology for my behaviour, especially to you Vir. I promise from hereon it's just happy vibes only."

Kama slid her chair back noisily. "Well since it's a morning of announcements I might as well throw in my fair share too."

She walked over to the wine cooler and pulled out a prosecco.

"Kama, I think your story can wait," Hassan grit his teeth at her.

"Nonsense. Everyone, I'm done with the first draft of my next book," she threw out her arms grandly. "So far the editors have loved it, they're calling it the season's hottest horror. By god's grace it'll be out in a few months."

No one joined Surya in clapping.

"You know nothing about writing fiction."

"That's besides the point daddy. Just be happy for me won't you?" she shimmied over with the wine.

"What's it about?" Dev offered. Geetu elbowed him in the gut.

"Oooh it's a murder mystery like no other. It's set in Darjeeling where a family of four lives with their mother and stepfather. Now the kids don't like him because he's a total gold digger, the mother's like this super chic tea estate heiress. But then one day he turns up dead –"

"Or maybe they're just being delusional and nobody actually died," Geetu spoke through grit teeth.

"Nonsense! Anyway so what happens..."

A loud thump interrupted her speech. It was the very specific sort of noise – that of a knee bumping into a doorway. Everyone turned to see Sunaina standing red-faced at the entrance to the living room with her arms theatrically splayed.

"Morning everyone!" she sang.

"Beta it's almost twelve in the afternoon," Hassan looked at her with disdain.

Gayatri narrowed her eyes conspiratorially but Surya spoke up first.

"Oh it's okay, she just had a late night ya. Let her be."

"Late night?" Hassan looked confused.

"Late night?" Geetu echoed dangerously.

If possible Sunaina blushed a deeper red and rushed to take the empty chair next to Vir. Surya snaked a finger around the neck of her t-shirt and pulled to reveal a constellation of bruises that vanished lower into her collarbone.

"I see hickies!" she announced.

Sunaina slapped her hand away even as Gayatri offered a high-five.

"I feel so attacked right now, can you just not?"

Kama laughed once without humour. "Excuse me, what do you even know of being attacked?"

Dev bit his lip to remain stoic.

Hassan shot daggers at his daughter from across the table. "What's going on Sunaina?"

"That's what I'd like to know," Geetu sneered. "Was it that boy?"

"What boy?"

"The 'boy' boy, Hassan uncle!" Surya slapped the table, laughing uncontrollably.

"Fuckin' hell you're such a bitch!" Sunaina turned around and slapped her across the face hard enough to knock her down.

Asim banged a fist on the table. "Girls! Use your words not your hands. Honestly have you taught your children *nothing*?"

"Hey everybody! Good morning." Sohrab walked in from the living room looking not at all freshly showered in a t-shirt last seen in Vir's cupboard. Hassan let out a savage roar and ran toward him like a bull. On the other side of the table Surya had picked herself up and scratched out at Sunaina, knocking over the jug of water all across the mahogany table.

Sohrab didn't have time to react. He registered the man headed toward him and drew back a fist, only aiming for a protective shot. No one in that room had anticipated that Hassan would be knocked out by a single punch to the nose. Kama screamed in horror, the prosecco already a mess around her feet. Asim's disgusted face moved into view, unimpressed with Hassan's antics even upside down.

Sohrab looked at him with horror. "I'm sorry. I freaked out. Are you okay?"

He looked up at Sunaina who seemed to have frozen midway in her catfight.

"Sunaina, I didn't mean to hit him I swear."

"Help him up, you idiot!" Asim was flipping out.

Sohrab bent forward and offered his hand to Hassan who gripped it and then with both hands secured around both of his hands, pulled himself up. But he only made it halfway. Hassan deftly bent forward and head-butted Sohrab right out the double doors that led to the backyard. Geetu let out a bloodcurdling scream as the men fell into a pile of shattered glass and wood.

"*Oh hell no!*" Dev bellowed.

"What the fuck have you done," he ran out the now gaping hole in the wall and launched himself onto the struggling pair. One thick fisted punch later everyone was silent. Everyone was panting.

Surya stood whimpering into Kama's shoulder, hand pressed onto her cheek where Sunaina had slapped her so hard the skin had blistered. She waited for Sunaina to look at her but ultimately left when she didn't. Geetu stood conflicted between her husband and brother, and her daughter. She wondered silently if there was anyone who wanted to comfort her in that moment. The three men all bruised and bloodied in their own motley ways unfurled from each other and lay in a line like breathless planks. Hassan had landed on his right arm and could feel the broken bones swelling, though the adrenaline that still blipped through him dulled everything else.

"Oh. My. God." Everyone who was still indoors turned to Geetu. She wasn't still reeling from shock, or upset about the broken doors. Sunaina gasped and Gayatri stifled a laugh as Geetu held up inky hands to her face. Kama's eyes looked like they might pop out of her head and she lifted a finger to her mouth. When she checked her face on the selfie mode of her phone camera, Geetu realized the ink had leaked from her pen and now spread across the lower half of her face like an ocean. The phone slipped from her hands and fell. She no longer had air in her lungs to turn into a cry.

Asim picked up his sunglasses from the table and offered everyone a kind smile. He twiddled his moustache and brought his hands together in thunderous claps that hit everyone.

"Jolly good show. If you'll excuse me now I'm going for a nap. Leela might be expecting me."

Vir turned to Gayatri and whispered. "How about we let them sort this on their own?"

She picked up the keys and led the way out.

Chapter | TWENTY ONE

The Bougainvilleas Have Wilted (*Denouement*)

It was the morning of the wedding. Surya Shroff woke up with a knot in her stomach that only tightened as they donned their bridal crew robes and took pictures in front of the lightbulb-lined mirror for social media posting. It had been the quickest dinner party, with everyone halfway ready to sleep or drink in private and prepare for the full day ahead. Just like that she was going to be somebody else.

Sunaina stood at the entrance of the suite balcony, smoking a cigarette watching the marquees set up. In the dull pre-morning hour the peach fabric was as stark as the moon.

"It's going to rain." Surya remarked.

"It's not going to rain." She stared at the indigo sky – a terrible sign for dawn. It was going to rain.

"I know it will. It's my wedding day and of course it's going to rain. The sunrise photo I'd drafted to post is going to go to waste and," she sighed, "it's going to rain."

Sunaina fidgeted with the hair tie. Her skull dully protested the severe ponytail Surya had insisted for 'aesthetic purposes'.

"Don't open your hair it's going to fucking reek of smoke before we even get out."

"I'm not, I'm not touching it." She leaned forward, just out sight, to retie the string a little looser. The cigarette burnt relentlessly in her mouth and she held her breath and shut her eyes, grappling with the knot.

Sunaina leaned back and took in the form of her sister, seated in full bridal glow that had nothing to do with the enormous mirror setup. She had to admit though even with the crew documenting every move behind the scenes, Surya's vitriolic disposition hadn't worn out.

"You know that gold facial has done wonders. You almost can't even see the rash on your cheek anymore."

Surya snorted, still stung from the slap. "It burns every time I touch it."

Sunaina ducked her head back out. "I'm sorry."

"Listen but maybe we should do waterproof make up just in case it rains, you know what I mean." Surya couldn't move her head but the make up artist rushed over for a touch-up.

"Way ahead of you. I have this liquid foundation, see," she spread it on her hand and blew it dry. Then she spat on it and scrubbed with a finger to show that it wouldn't smudge.

Sunaina watched her bewildered and when six pairs of eyes turned to her for approval she nodded her head with gusto.

"Hey is that what you're doing with your hair?"

Surya whipped around to stare at her. "Why you don't like it?"

There were three stylists working out the folds and ends of hair extensions that draped across the back of Surya's chair and hung several feet behind like a train.

The head stylist glowered at Sunaina.

"No. Forget I said anything. It's like a shart, it just flew out of my mouth."

Surya flushed. "Is there anything you can keep to yourself?"

"It's nothing to be embarrassed about – okay this is ridiculous. Just forget I spoke in the last two minutes."

Ria entered, though still in her bridesmaid blush robe her hair was perfectly coiffed into a high ponytail. No one missed her towering fuck-me heels.

"Hey, woah I love the hair Su!"

"Thanks I was going for the whole Shakuntala meets Surya vibe."

"It looks super chic."

"Wait why is your hair like that? Ria, no, I told you that all sisters and bridesmaids need to have soft *undulating* curls. I don't see undulating."

"Oh that's totally fine, I'll curl the end of my ponytail and it can sit in the front."

Surya exhaled loudly and turned her head as much as possible to one of the stylists.

"Could you curl her fucking hair after you're done with me?"

He grunted in assent.

She turned back to Sunaina.

"Wait, honestly tell me what you think of the hair."

"It's fine, no really. I didn't know you were going to tie it up or something ..."

"Obvi, it'll be a perfect braid that flows over my shoulder to my knees."

Sunaina nodded vigorously. "Perfect."

She reached behind and opened her hair. As it fell around her like a curtain the stylist stood up.

"Wait, do you need extensions too?"

"No, I'm fine just like this."

"But you're going to get it styled right? Everyone has to follow the aesthetic of the wedding." Surya sipped her glass of wine.

"For sure." Sunaina tied her robe tighter. "I'm just gonna head to our room and help Gayatri pull out the outfits."

Surya had already turned back to the mirror.

"Seems like it's gonna rain." She said to Ria's reflection.

"Oh nuh-uh, I checked the forecast and iWeather's like never wrong. Also I cannot get my hair wet I'll die."

"Wait Sunaina, before you go I really need your help today. You cannot let things go out of control."

"Of course, what do you want me to do?"

"Just keep the vibe like super chill alright? You have to make sure everyone's being happy and positive because I can't deal right now."

"Sure thing, Su. Whatever you need."

She couldn't get out of there fast enough.

The air conditioning was brutal in the hallway, or perhaps the overcast had penetrated the hotel itself. The lights brightened as the windows turned sepia under the blanket of rain-heavy clouds. Sunaina hugged herself and walked quickly to the room she was sharing with Gayatri, who was being subjected to a final barrage of hairspray. She was drowning in enormous hair rollers but Sunaina bit her lips and headed straight to the bathroom.

Gayatri snatched her glass of wine and sipped vigorously, admiringher croquembouche of rollers.

The hair stylist cleaned her comb and remarked, "It's going to rain."

"It's not going to fucking rain, god can you keep the vibe happy here? My sister's getting married." She refilled her glass and settled onto the bed, unbothered by the fact that her robe had come undone.

A high pitched cry rang through the rooms like an alarm, everyone kept their glasses of wine aside as more squealing and commotion ensued, ricocheting down the upper level rooms. Gayatri stood up heart hammering in her chest, when Geetika burst through the door without knocking. Zoya, who'd been a thorn on everyone's side because she'd insisted on pre-approving all footage with Gayatri, followed ashen faced.

"You didn't tell me he was coming!" she was panting. "Nearly caused a bloody stampede downstairs, there was a panditji from somebody else's function who totally lost it at the entrance."

Gayatri gaped at her. "Dude, what are you talking about?"

"Gayatri are you on crack? I'm so mad I will ... I will spank you right now!" Geetu was livid beyond reason, they had a schedule to follow and a *gurudwaara* to get to.

Zoya was already dressed in an unnecessary bright silk dress. She made an impatient noise as if Gayatri were asking all the wrong questions.

"Neil is here! Neil fucking Kapoor is here!"

"What. The. Fuck."

They heard a toilet seat slam and a hurried flush from the bathroom.

"Where is he?"

"He's waiting in the spare room at the end of the corridor to your left, just follow down from the lift area. I swear if there are any more surprises I will shoot you down."

"Don't worry there's security everywhere, no one is coming up." Zoya quipped.

"Shit." Gayatri set her glass on the table and darted out the door.

"Good luck." Zoya called out, and then to herself, "I should go check on Hassan."

"What?" the door slammed behind Sunaina.

Geetu stared between them and grunted at her niece to handle the situation.

They watched as Zoya tried to compose her features but failed to recover and instead settled on cockiness. "Hassan. We've sort of been seeing each other."

The mornings of a wedding are generally known to be stressful, and with everyone on edge it is considered polite to take care of all personal problems with as little as possible distress or noise. All missing drawstrings and shortage of safety pins are sorted in rushed whispers. Everyone is responsible for dressing themselves and showing up on time. This was one of the worst moments for Sunaina to hear about her father's latest romance and as she pounded down the hall her '*OH HELL NO*'s echoed into every room so by the time Lakshman had intercepted her, half the family and their plus ones were watching.

If she could've seen him amongst the crowd of family members in various stages of dressing Sunaina would've avoided him entirely and made her way on to her father's room, but she didn't. They stood still for a moment; he'd caught her before she could knock him off with the force of her rage.

Zoya caught up with her but Sunaina shrugged her off, backing her up against the wall so hard her head bounced.

"Back off me you slut!"

Lakshman held on to her wrist with reverence, his eyes set her skin on fire. But she was already burning with her shame and her anger. She wanted to push him off but when she tried he just held on tighter.

"Wait, Sunaina listen to me. Listen, I don't know what's going on but I know if I don't tell you I think I might die."

"Can you let me go I have to speak to papa, *right now*!"

"Sun-Sunaina listen please, I'm trying to tell you," she wriggled her way out so he had to run after her. "Sunaina I love you!"

Someone in the crowd gasped.

Between squirming her way past his ocean-eyed grip and spewing acid at Zoya, she had nowhere to run. "Lakshman, don't do this. I can't –"

The sound of her name roared across the hall cut her short. Hassan had emerged with hair still wet from the shower.

With an audience of every family member watching Sunaina walked over to him, hands furiously fisted. Geetu felt she might faint. Asim regarded the scene with mild interest. Sunaina for her part didn't care anymore that her father had fractured his arm in two places and dislocated a thumb.

"Papa –"

"Hassan –"

"SHUT UP ZOYA."

"Sunaina what the hell is going on? You're making a bloody scene today of all days?!" His voice rang all the way down the hall.

"That's not even what you're worried about papa, and now I finally get it. I get why the Commander is always so pissed off with you – because you just can't help but disappoint, can you?"

Asim leaned in to Dev. "Who's the Commander?"

Dev buried his face in his hands, unable to control his laughter anymore.

"I get now why Geetu bua always is on edge when you're around, because you're a selfish reckless piece of garbage. You're garbage, papa. That's why Tina left too, right? That's why Pranab uncle's always running after you because he has to clean up your shit and you just keep churning out more and more like a man-child. The ink on your divorce papers hasn't dried and you're already piledriving into the first whore-hole that's willing –"

The slap that cut her off was one they'd talk about for years to come. Hassan didn't know it just then but he'd irrevocably severed ties with that blow. Half of the audience was too stunned to react the other knew it was a long time coming, Sunaina Kochhar was just a spoilt brat who needed to learn the ways of life.

They turned at the sound of a door and Surya emerged to remind them of the day. Her hair was a vision, tied into a thick braid that trailed almost to her feet. It was halfway decorated with pins of golden webbing. Sunaina swallowed thickly and blinked away her tears, pushing past everyone to her room. Lakshman made to follow but found himself with a locked door to face.

"Get. Your. Shit. Together." Surya clapped between every word, spat out at the army of relatives. "All of you. Get it together *now*!"

Eyes widened at the tone of her voice but no one made a move.

"You need to go downstairs for the breakfast in exactly twenty minutes. Whoever isn't there, will be fucking stabbed so hard."

She called out to Sunaina as the crowd hustled back to their rooms. "And you. Absolutely not the time for whatever episode of Revenge-of-the-Sana-Monster this is. Get dressed and come to my room."

Neil gaped at her.

"If you say anything about the hair I'll kill you."

He dissolved into laughter. As soon as their eyes had met Gayatri knew she'd never been happier to see him.

"It's not so bad."

She noticed how his eyes crinkled when he laughed.

"Please, I look like a snapchat filter." She grumbled.

"Oh yeah, you do! Wait, come here," he pulled her in and took a photo of them.

"You're disgusting." She reached into his pocket for the pack of cigarettes and immediately withdrew. "Is this you apologizing for ignoring me for the past few months?"

His eyes softened. "Whatever helps my case to be honest."

Suddenly aware of her exposed skin, she wrapped the robe tighter and lit the cigarette from the other end of the room.

"It looks like it'll rain today." He sighed.

"Don't say that to anyone you meet."

"So, she's really getting married huh?"

"What do you mean?" She didn't look directly at him.

He shrugged.

"I don't know, just feels like the sort of thing you'd say at a wedding."

"Is that how hopeless you are without a script telling you what to do?"

"Hey I'm here aren't I? No one told me to be here."

"Why are you here?" Her heart lodged itself in her throat.

He walked over and knelt at her feet. The weight of his chin resting on her knee was enough to drown her. "I came for you, it was instinct."

"Don't say that. No. You don't get to be total jerk and then pull this out of the bag."

"Why not?" he followed the trail of her billowing smoke.

"Because I have enough to deal with from my garbage-people family. They're all fucking crazy and I think if I'm here long enough I might lose my mind too."

"That's bullshit." He rested his cheek against her thigh.

"It's not. And fuck you."

Neil looked up at her with an indulgent smile. He stroked her hand with a tentative finger then dropped it to his side. Then he reached up and took her hands in his, weaving their fingers together.

"So, what? You're here to tell me you're madly in love with me now that you've had your share of finding yourself in the world?" she snapped.

"I never said 'I love you', and definitely not *madly*."

She shoved him off. "Then what're you doing here?"

"I don't know. It was so long since I saw you I was beginning to forget how you looked ... and I can't sleep." Neil went from cocky to vulnerable so fast she lost her breath. "I can't find anything to dream about. I don't know where to hide. I don't sleep anymore Gayatri."

"Oh really." She sneered over crossed arms. "So how long will you stay with me? Shall I prepare coffee, or prepare my life?"

"Coffee, yes. Your life, maybe not so soon," he sighed. "What do you want?"

"I don't have your answers Neil. I just think it's rude to inflict your life on someone before you've sorted it on your own."

"Fine," he sighed gruffly. In the next moment he pulled her into a kiss.

She pushed him off. "You don't get to do that Neil."

Gayatri looked into his eyes and kissed him.

He pulled back. "Are you sure about this?"

She drowned the end of his sentence in her kiss. Neil let out a moan and they lost themselves in gasped breaths even as the hallway screaming hit the other side of the door. He was everywhere, hands and lips and the smell of his skin – she couldn't have pulled herself away even if she wanted to. He pushed her up against the door and laid a trail of kissed along her neck down to her collarbone. At the lightest touch of her hands he stopped.

"You have to go," he breathed hotly against her.

"I have to go." She nodded.

She kissed the top of his head. "I don't love you, Neil."

"Good because I don't love you either."

"You will break my heart." She corrected her robe. "I know it."

He looked up at her, searched her eyes. She could tell he was lost, the moment growing colder as he searched for words. Neil stood and swooped her into a rib-crushing hug. "Never."

She willed her heart to settle down. "Find me after the wedding. I'll send my assistant to get you a suit."

He bowed deeply. "How kind of you Lady Snapchat."

A deep grumble rolled from the concrete clouds outside.

"Shit," she muttered on her way out.

Everyone gathered in the suite for one last picture in their matching Team Bride robes. Surya pushed Karishma to the edge of the huddle for sleeping in and missing most of the morning. They raised their palms out to show the varying shades of *mehendi* stained onto everyone's palms. The photographer aligned them in dispersal all over the room so that they looked like models on a magazine cover. Surya almost broke into tears at the mere sight of her brother but Lara interrupted her with the promise of a joint. As soon as their round of photos were over, whoever was ready hot-boxed the bride while the others changed.

Even as the skies continued to darken to blue ash, one by one the wedding party stepped into their cars and set off for the *gurudwaara*.

Neil was the last man standing. In his newly fitted suit walking out the doors he realized he'd forgotten to call a cab but Lakshman who was waiting downstairs smoking offered him a ride. Neil had to bite back his tongue, almost letting slip that he knew him as the ex, and accepted graciously.

Gayatri was having her make up finished when there was a knock on the door, a final visitor they didn't have time for.

Sunaina stepped out and pecked Sohrab, reminding him of their plan.

"Last kiss before the wedding."

"No more till it's over," he held up both hands. "I promise. It's your sister's wedding I know how big of a day this is for you."

"I don't know how much I'll be able to chill with you."

"Relax, I've been hanging with your friends for a while I'll be fine."

"Plus there's always Elina ..." she offered.

"She's no Sunaina."

"No" she held up a finger. "No emotional talk. It's been an insane morning as it is."

"Okay. No emotional talk." He smirked at her. "But I love you."

"No."

He chuckled.

"How's Sunita aunty?"

"She's still in recovery. I'll let you know more as soon as I do."

She gave him the briefest hug and kissed his ear before pushing him down the highway.

Back in the room she found Gayatri had already changed into her pants, her dazzling *anarkali* ready to be adorned. She raced into the bathroom and put on her blouse and heels. With Gayatri's help she climbed into the *lehenga*, the heavy blue Sabyasachi she'd fallen in love with at first sight. It billowed gently to the floor as she helped Gayatri set all the folds right on her suit. Neither of them acknowledged the trembling hands or labored breaths, the gravity of the morning had finally sunk in while no one was watching. A sharp rap on the door made them jump, the wedding planner called out five minutes to departure and they rushed to put on their jewelry.

Surya was fully transformed into a bride when they entered the suite. The energy had changed in the room from nervousness to excitement. Everyone was ready. Surya stared at herself in the mirror, grateful that everything considered she still looked like herself.

"This is the day," she said with a shuddered voice. "This is my wedding day."

They paled in comparison to her outfit, a stunning creation of brilliant gold and sunset orange. She had the million glass bangles on and the shower of golden *kaliras* delicately sloping down her sides as they began the slow walk to the elevator, led by Vir.

The bridal convoy departed from the hotel set to the tune of grumbling clouds. On the way to the *gurudwaara* no one spoke more than a few words, no one could believe how soon the weeks had passed. Surya made for a stunning bride – a fact reiterated by the gasps as she disembarked at the gate. Ria was upset that no one told her when it was time for the official bridal entrance, the fact that she missed the momentous procession from the entrance of the prayer hall to where Dhiraj sat – a prince in waiting – would be a permanent chip on her shoulder. She was the first one to cry at the wedding. Surya needed assistance every time she had to stand for a *parikrama*, her skirt was seven kilos on its own. Dhiraj on his part, dressed in the fine silk *achkan* of rose gold with white pants, was there to hold her every time with a dazzling smile. It set a good precursor to their marriage – the aunties whispered through the room – that he was there to help her since the very beginning. That she didn't look to anyone else for support. Sunaina and Gayatri rolled their eyes to near blindness.

From the moment she first sat down, Sunaina had a lump in her throat. With every breath it seemed as if Surya was going to dissolve into tears but it was just the shine of her embroidered blouse. It seemed that everyone in the hall was on the verge of tears watching them circumnavigate the prayer area. Too soon they were husband and wife and bittersweet tears took over. Dhiraj made an effort to keep the smile on his face; he hated the sight of Surya crying. He gave her the quickest hug before they were overwhelmed by relatives from both sides and then by friends. Almost no one cared for the unrelenting downpour outside. Thunderclaps couldn't penetrate the calm aura of the ceremony. Their legs were numb from sitting but Sunaina and Gayatri followed the couple right till they were ushered into the car under oversized umbrellas. They stood amidst the gushing aunties and the quietly proud uncles as one of their own bid them farewell. It was the end of an era.

Geetu's arms found them and embraced the girls with the quiet dignity of a woman holding herself together. That was the worst part of weddings, watching the parents of the bride let her go – a final signifier that lives were changing. They found Vir sitting on a bench on the other side, head buried in his hands. The three of them sat there while the party drove out in their cars. Whenever someone came over to rush them into a car and make way to the reception, Gayatri sombrely shook her head. They stayed there until the last car had driven away, which by a turn of fate turned out to be for the best because otherwise they might have missed the sight of their grandfather walking barefoot on the road into a random apartment complex. Brushing away their tears they ran, calling out to him with a stab of fear in their chests. He turned only at the sound of his name and jerked back, surprised that three strangers had just approached him breathless and far too well dressed for a regular Sunday pooja. They asked him questions that didn't make sense and he smiled apologetically, he was only looking for someone but couldn't seem to find them. The boy asked him whom he was trying to find and he took her name. Sunaina felt the ground give way beneath her at the sound of her grandmother's name, a wave of fresh tears overtaking her.

Asim wondered why the girl cried at the name, he asked if she knew her. Whether she might be able to direct him to her house. The other girl told him she didn't live there but that was nonsense, he recognized the water fountain that would be seen just at the next turn – the three of them knew there was no water fountain.

He explained that he was running late, he had to meet her father he had to ask for her hand in marriage, they'd promoted him to Lieutenant Colonel you see. Vir ground his teeth as pain shot through him, a dull ache arthritically ruining his bones. Gayatri bit her lip and reached for the old man's hand and offered to drive him to the house. He was standing at the wrong apartment complex really; when she pointed to the colour of the buildings he understood that they were all wrong. The Commander fell asleep almost as soon as he made it to the backseat of the car. The person from the wedding planner's team who had stayed back to wait for them had been silenced. He stared grimly as they escorted him to the car and drove off. Heaving a sigh of relief not big enough to release his tension, the boy spoke into his earpiece and announced their departure.

It took Gayatri, Vir, and Sunaina a very long time to be driven back to the hotel. Gayatri slammed her impatient hands on the dashboard and volunteered to drive as fast as she could. Vir sat at the back, staring at his grandfather's wilting moustache as the rain soaked city blurred outside the windows.

Surya made everyone call them. Sunaina answered every time. They'd had some trouble finding the Commander's shoes. They had to turn back because she'd lost an earring. They were having car trouble. There was a little traffic, nothing to worry about. They had to stop for fuel. They rode in silence till they reached; Devendra was waiting for them in the parking lot. His pallor betrayed none of the toll the day had taken on him, it wasn't over just yet. He escorted Asim to a bedroom on a wheelchair – that Gayatri couldn't bear to watch. The girls retouched their make up and Vir combed back his hair, taking turns to sip the gasoline from his hip flask.

The reception was set in a sprawling lawn of moist grass so green it stained the underside of their shoes. The sun had finally burst forth, bathing the trio of marquees in fairytale glow. Light jazz trilled through the air and Sunaina found herself looking for someone to comfort her. Until time could work its healing spell, Gayatri's hand holding hers was everything she needed.

The party was divided between hearty conversation by the bar and the quieter lot by the buffet who'd been hungry all morning. Surya almost leapt off the stage when they came into view but she made do with vigorously waving them over. They hugged her and Dhiraj in turns with equal love and fierceness, no one ready yet to divulge details of their delay. Geetu reminded them that they needed family photographs and so she arranged herself and Gayatri with Dev by her side around the couple. Then came Kama bua and Ria, a tighter frame. Then it was Hassan and Sunaina's turn and she couldn't smile even if she wanted to. Yet with a squeeze of his hand she confirmed that although they were hurting, each other was all they had. And as the rest of the family joined in, someone exclaimed that Asim was missing. Dev announced that he was sleeping off the exhaustion of the pooja, Geetu had never heard him speak in that tone of finality but the time wasn't right so she swallowed her words.

So there they stood, arms around each other to complete the family on their own. Everybody turned to look, everyone's head turned and drinks lowered. It was a moment of awe, of reverence at the handsome family of the Kochhars and the Shroffs. The sisters helped Surya change into a lighter outfit – lighter but by no means less dazzling so that no one could miss that she was the bride. They danced, losing themselves to the music the moment where nothing mattered – not the trying times that awaited them, nor the ones that they'd been through. They made the city's longest human train with the most success; no one broke the line as they danced till their stomachs grumbled for a proper meal. After a meal carefully designed to be the epitome of #foodporn, Sunaina and Gayatri gave a brief speech and cried through another heart wrenching farewell – the bride and groom walked out with the biggest smiles on their faces through a waterfall of white rose petals – until nothing remained but a gently setting sun and the swaying fabric tents.

"I hate weddings," Gayatri stood with Neil's arms wrapped around her.

Sunaina, her skirt splayed out expansively on both sides, nodded and drank her beer.

"We've got company," Vir remarked with a devilish smirk.

She turned and saw Lakshman walk over. The sun sinking lower behind him, casting him in a glow that was obvious and perfect and hit her like a ton of bricks. He paused as if waiting for permission, she only nodded at the sight of the bottles in his hand.

They sat in silence for a while.

"The song was good, I didn't know if you were going to play today."

He dipped his head. "That's why I was practicing that night."

"You didn't sing along that night though."

He took a beer for himself and drank. "I had other words on my mind."

"Could you play it again for me some time?"

He nodded.

"I spoke to your friend Sohrab by the way." His lips turned up at the corner. "He's a nice guy."

"Ugh please Lakshman, not now."

"Relax, not everything's about you Miss Kochhar."

She burned in a pyre of shame, only cooled by the beer in her hands.

Beside her Gayatri was nuzzled against Neil, unbothered by the company. They spotted Elina smoking in the corner and waved her over.

Sunaina exhaled, tired and blue.

"God I hate this city. I hate the people and I hate what it does to me. I think and this part's the most tragic, but I feel like I'm at my worst self here – here with my family and friends, I'm just toxic."

She shook her head in resignation.

"So what're you gonna do now?" Sohrab leaned over from behind.

"I ... I don't know. I had a lot of plans but I don't think the Commander is alright. Maybe the B&B will have to wait for some time."

"Why?" Lakshman asked.

"Because I'm not you. I can't run a whole thing by myself."

He nodded solemnly. "Lots to figure out then."

"Too much. I don't know how much I can handle right now honestly."

Sohrab and Lakshman exchanged a solemn nod and drank to the bitter taste of irony. If it came down to it, time would either heal the heartbreak or bring them together.

Gayatri sighed. "You're right though. This city is a mess, look at the side it brings out in each one of us. Kama masi's cutting off from the family. I heard her talking to Geetu ma, she's leaving the country. Maybe we all should."

Neil held her closer, eager to fly her back to the west coast.

"I guess it's true. But you should know it's okay to fully be every part of you though – the good and the bad." Vir regarded the lawn emptying out in front of them, the last drunkenly guests staggering off to sleep in the backseats of their cars. The staff timidly wrapping up the tables and chairs.

The sun had set. The flowers had wilted. A cool breeze shook them out of the reverie, with sighs and smiles they stood to walk back to their rooms.

Vir raised his beer in a toast as fireworks lit up the night sky. "No matter what you say about this place though, it is home."

The End

ACKNOWLEDGEMENTS

There are people without whom this book wouldn't be what it is today and in all honesty this was a book I never knew I had in me so seeing it come alive has been an interesting process. To start with, I am supremely indebted to my friends and family who've put up with all my neurosis in the time I've written this. I wouldn't be anywhere without people like them who have listened to me blather on about plots and characters over drinks and then helped me through every obstacle that came my way. A special shoutout goes to my editor Himanjali whose patience has been limitless and who believed in this book even when I had my doubts and insecurities about it. To the music of Arctic Monkeys who literally kept me going when I was feverishly writing this book day and night, and then some more when the ink was running dry.

ABOUT THE AUTHOR

Rohan Dahiya is currently living in Delhi NCR seeking to weed out the clichés of Indian writing and test the boundaries of fiction as it currently stands. Drawing inspiration from his misadventures in the city, *The Bitter Pill Social Club* is his second novel. On most days he can be found at Chapter 101, a quaint bookstore in Gurgaon.

www.ingramcontent.com/pod-product-compliance
Ingram Content Group UK Ltd.
Pitfield, Milton Keynes, MK11 3LW, UK
UKHW041436020826
14184UKWH00025B/136

9 789387 457898